In short, everyone wanted a piece of Anderson. And from his reputation, he evidently had a lot of pieces to go around.

Except for right now, when his entire attention seemed focused on me.

"You gonna make it, Red?" he whispered, so softly that only I could hear. His breath brushed against my earlobe as he spoke, sending shivers straight to my toes—and let's be honest, other places as well.

Oh God. Eligible, indeed.

I swallowed hard, trying to ignore the warmth spreading through my belly. To focus instead on the stupidity of the question. Was I going to make it? What the hell was that supposed to mean? Was this all some kind of big joke to him?

Annoyance churned in my gut. At him, for asking. At myself, for needing to be asked. Hell, at my freaking extremities for shivering over something as stupid as warm breath against cold ears.

I knew I should have been grateful for his impromptu rescue. His demand that the show go on. The alternative— breaking up the wedding and causing a scene in front of half of my coworkers and bosses—would have been utter humiliation, and career suicide to boot. But at the same time, I was still so embarrassed, it was hard to muster up the appropriate gratitude.

"I'm fine. You can let me go now," I muttered, even though his warm hands admittedly felt pretty good on my freezing skin. Or maybe because of that fact. Truth was, a large traitorous part of me wanted him to stay there, holding me up until the ceremony was over. Until I could retreat to higher ground.

But that would be weird.

Berkley Sensation Titles by Mari Madison

JUST THIS NIGHT
BREAK OF DAY

Break of Day

MARI MADISON

BERKLEY SENSATION, NEW YORK

BERKLEY SENSATION

An imprint of Penguin Random House LLC
375 Hudson Street, New York, New York 10014

BREAK OF DAY

A Berkley Sensation Book / published by arrangement with the author

ISBN: 9780425283141

PUBLISHING HISTORY
Berkley Sensation mass-market edition / August 2016

PRINTED IN THE UNITED STATES OF AMERICA

10 9 8 7 6 5 4 3 2 1

Cover photo CAUCASIAN COUPLE HUGGING ON BEACH © GS / Gallery Stock.
Cover design by Alana Colucci.
Interior text design by Kristin del Rosario.

Penguin
Random
House

To Diana "Louise" Peterfreund,
Here's to our next adventure—and all the ones after that!
May they always include laughter, sushi, and
at least one bottle of Nobilo.

Thank you to my awesome editor Kate Seaver who has edited and championed my books for over ten years now—we continue to make an awesome team! And to the rest of the team at Penguin Random House who work so hard to get the books onto store shelves and into the readers' hands—I couldn't do this without you! Special shout-outs to Ryanne Probst and Katherine Pelz who are both awesome and very patient!

A special shout-out to B&N romance buyer Jules Herbert who chose JUST THIS NIGHT as a March Bookseller Pick. I am SO honored to be chosen! And to all the booksellers out there who select and hand-sell my books to romance readers. You are the unsung heroes of a writer's world!

Thank you to Sarah Simpson-Weiss, my amazing assistant who keeps me organized and sane. Your tireless enthusiasm means the world to me and I'm lucky to have you in my life!

And to continue from the first book the list of amazing TV news colleagues I've had the pleasure to work with over the years—especially my fellow producers and reporters. From Ivanhoe Broadcast News: Alison Jordan, Susan Vernon-Devlin, and Elizabeth Buchanan McCarthy. (And, of course, Hector the cat, RIP.) At KFMB-TV: Pam Jessen, Jamie Nguyen, Denise Yamada, Gail Stewart, and Bob Hansen, just to name a few. And, of course, my dear WHDH-TV friends: Mary Schwager, Hank Phillippi-Ryan, Deanna Lites, Michelle Weber, Jennifer Savio Dial, Joe Abouzeid, Mike Boudo, Stacy Neale, Tiffany Middleton, Ben Thompson, Kelly Henry, Eddie Felker, Rin-rin Yu, and Kate Kahn—and so many more! And last, but not least, Better Show alums: Juli Auclair, Audra Lowe, Ashley Diamond-Hirsch, Sarah Sweeney, Rebecca Millman, Tracy Langer Chevrier, Seth Feldman, Mark Berrhill, and the rest.

Lastly, thank you to my dear husband Jacob who keeps everything running when I'm on deadline and never once complains. And to my dearest daughter Avalon for being the best little girl in the world. I love you more than anything and can't imagine life without you!

one

_____

PIPER

I , Elizabeth White, take this man . . ."

Hold it together, Piper. Just hold it together.

I clutched the bouquet of roses with white-knuckled fingers, pressing my lips together so hard they hurt as my heart thumped wildly in my chest and my veins raced with ice water. I tried to focus on my roommate, Beth, standing on the beach in front of me, looking ridiculously radiant in her simple white dress with its empire waist, baby blue flowers woven into her long blond hair. Tried to focus on the look in her eyes as she gazed adoringly at her soon-to-be-husband, Jake "Mac" MacDonald. A look that was truly breathtaking.

Or would have been, anyway, had I had any breath left in my lungs.

"To be my lawfully wedded husband."

It's almost over. It'll be over in a second.

I stole a glance at the ocean behind me, then immediately wished I hadn't. The vast blue-black waters seemed to throb and undulate menacingly, taunting me as they stretched out to meet the distant horizon.

Some people thought the ocean was beautiful. Peaceful.

Some people were fucking crazy.

"To have and to hold from this day forward . . ."

The nausea rose to my throat again and I struggled to breathe, turning back to the bride and groom, trying to focus on them—to ignore the icy horror licking at my feet. When Beth had first asked me to be her maid of honor I'd been over the moon. And I'd accepted the job before she told me the rest of her plans. That it would be a simple ceremony.

On the beach.

By the water.

"For better, for worse. For richer, for poorer."

In other words, my worst nightmare come true.

Just keep your eyes on Beth and Mac. Pretend you're in a church.

But a church didn't have crashing waves, thundering in your ears. The sting of salt stabbing at your nose. Your skin—oh God, why had Beth insisted on bare feet?—crawling with sticky, prickly sand. The wind gusted, whipping my copper curls in my face. I reached up to swipe them away . . .

"In sickness and in health . . ."

"Shit!"

I shrieked—practically jumping out of my skin—as a sudden wave rose up and splashed me from behind, soaking the back of my dress. I staggered, nearly falling over backward as panic rioted through me.

And everyone in the audience burst out laughing.

My face burned as I desperately tried to pull myself back together. To brush it off. To not run away screaming in the other direction. To not ruin my best friend's big day.

It was just a wave, I scolded myself. *Everything's fine. No big deal.*

But then . . . Michael had probably thought that once, too.

My mother definitely had when she'd left him in my care.

Piper! Wake up!

Where's your brother?

Darkness. Black water. Desperate splashing.

Where the HELL is your brother?

"Till death do us part."

My stomach heaved, black spots swimming before my eyes. My knees buckled out from under me, my pulse racing out of control, my heart practically bursting through my rib cage.

I had to get out of here. I had to get to higher ground.

Where it was safe.

Where I could breathe.

Where I could—

"Easy, Red."

A deep, velvety voice jerked me back to the present, strong hands gripping my arms from behind. I whirled around, to find none other than Mac's best man, News 9 meteorologist Asher Anderson, standing behind me.

Literally the only thing, at that moment, keeping me standing.

Shit, shit, shit.

I glanced around, realizing, horrifyingly, that the beach had fallen silent. The minister had stopped the ceremony. Everyone was staring at me. I bit my lower lip, my heart still burning hot in my chest. From the corner of my eye I could see Beth turn, concern clouding her face. She took a step toward me . . .

"Hey, don't stop now, Preach. You're almost to the good part."

What?

Asher's voice crashed over the beach, like another errant wave, and everyone laughed again, though thankfully this time at him and not me. As I stared at him, dumbfounded, he winked then turned to Beth.

"And you, runaway bride," he added in a scolding voice, "get back over there with your man. He's not done with you yet."

More laughter, followed by a smattering of applause. Beth shot me a doubtful look, but I managed to give her a weak smile and a shaky thumbs-up. She shook her head, as if she didn't quite believe I was okay, but thankfully returned to Mac's side.

And the wedding resumed where it had left off.

Thank God. I nearly collapsed in relief. I probably would

have, in fact, if it hadn't meant falling like a rag doll into the arms of Asher Anderson.

Asher Anderson of all people. Ughhhh.

You gotta understand. Asher wasn't your typical local news weatherman. The guy was practically SoCal royalty. His mother's family had owned News 9—my employer—since its very first broadcast and his father was beloved legendary meteorologist Stormy Anderson, whose early prediction of the 1980 Mission Valley flooding had saved countless lives. Dad had retired three years ago after an auto accident had put him in a wheelchair and his son had taken on the Doppler 9000 in his stead, becoming the golden boy of not only News 9 but pretty much the entire San Diego community.

In other words, when Asher Anderson did something, people usually noticed. And I really didn't need them noticing me now. Not at this particular moment—far from my finest hour.

In front of half of the suits at News 9.

I stifled a groan. It was ironic, really: Here I'd been, trying to get the attention of the News 9 bosses for months now, the invisible worker bee in the giant newsroom hive. Now I'd finally managed to make an impression. Unfortunately, not that of a girl who had been working tirelessly in the trenches for more than a year, trying to prove herself worthy of a promotion. But rather a total freak who had the nerve to disrupt their star reporter's big day by flipping the fuck out over a teeny, tiny wave.

By needing Golden Boy to save the day.

Ugh. Ugh. UGH.

I realized suddenly that Asher was still standing there, still holding me, still watching me closely, those infamous emerald eyes of his still locked on my face. This close up I couldn't help but notice that the deep green of those eyes—the green that had launched a hundred fan girl Tumblrs—was actually flecked with blues and yellows, giving them the look of a storm-tossed sea. A ridiculous detail, to be sure. But at the moment something to focus on that wasn't the churning water behind me.

People around the newsroom liked to say Asher was the trifecta. As in rich, powerful, and hot as hell. He was often compared to a young Matthew McConaughey with sandy brown hair that hung slightly too long and curled up at the ends and a devilish, carefree smile always playing on his lips—as if he found life itself amusing.

And then there was his body. Even now, encased in a tux, you couldn't help but appreciate his physique—tall, well built. Broad shoulders tapering to a narrow waist. It was a body honed by hours of surfing the Baja California coastline, which, according to the Most Eligible Bachelor in San Diego issues of all the magazines, was his favorite pastime.

In short, everyone wanted a piece of Anderson. And from his reputation, he evidently had a lot of pieces to go around.

Except for right now, when his entire attention seemed focused on me.

"You gonna make it, Red?" he whispered, so softly that only I could hear. His breath brushed against my earlobe as he spoke, sending shivers straight to my toes—and let's be honest, other places as well.

Oh God. Eligible, indeed.

I swallowed hard, trying to ignore the warmth spreading through my belly. To focus instead on the stupidity of the question. Was I going to make it? What the hell was that supposed to mean? Was this all some kind of big joke to him?

Annoyance churned in my gut. At him, for asking. At myself, for needing to be asked. Hell, at my freaking extremities for shivering over something as stupid as warm breath against cold ears.

I knew I should have been grateful for his impromptu rescue. His demand that the show go on. The alternative—breaking up the wedding and causing a scene in front of half of my coworkers and bosses—would have been utter humiliation, and career suicide to boot. But at the same time, I was still so embarrassed, it was hard to muster up the appropriate gratitude.

"I'm fine. You can let me go now," I muttered, even though his warm hands admittedly felt pretty good on my freezing skin. Or maybe because of that fact. Truth was, a large trai-torous part of me wanted him to stay there, holding me up until the ceremony was over. Until I could retreat to higher ground.

But that would be weird. And I'd already proven myself weird enough for one afternoon.

Turned out, it didn't matter anyway because Asher didn't seem interested in letting go of my arms, despite my sugges-tion. And I couldn't exactly force him to do so without caus-ing another scene. And so I stood there, his hands still snug on my arms, his breath tickling the back of my neck. Trying to keep it together as the minister droned on and on. At least now I had something else to focus on instead of the ocean. Though I wasn't entirely sure this particular focus served to make me feel any calmer. In fact my heart was beating fast as a racehorse, and I only hoped he couldn't tell.

Finally, after what seemed an eternity, the minister got to the so-called "good part." Mac was instructed to kiss his bride. And I dropped my shoulders in relief.

Thank freaking God.

I stepped forward, now managing to shrug out of Asher's grip, trying to shore up my sanity so I could finish the job. I had only a few more minutes to keep it together before I could head to the stairs, up to the La Jolla mansion on the cliff where the reception was being held. Out of the reach of the ocean's icy grip.

I could do this. I could totally do this.

Beth turned from her first married kiss to look at me, grinning from ear to ear. I forced a smile to my own lips, then handed her back her bouquet. "Nice work," I said, forcing my voice to sound light and unaffected. "And just think—you didn't trip once, despite all your worries." Beth had been having nightmares of falling on her face during the walk down the aisle for weeks now. But in real life she looked as if she were walking on water.

"Hey! Don't jinx me!" she protested now, gesturing to the makeshift path between the guests. "I still have to walk back down the aisle, you know."

"Don't worry, baby," Mac interjected, slipping an arm around her waist. "I won't let you fall."

The love in his eyes made tears spring to my own. And for a moment, I forgot to be afraid—I was too happy for them to worry about myself. It was nice to see two people who deserved each other fully get their happily ever.

Beth smiled at him, her face practically glowing with adoration. Then she turned back to me. "Are you okay?" she asked in a soft voice. "Earlier I thought—"

I waved her off, my cheeks heating all over again, both appreciating and hating her concern. At this point I just wanted to move forward. Forget it ever happened.

Not to mention get off this freaking beach, ASAP.

"I'm fine," I assured her. "Now go! Finish this thing!"

Beth laughed and hugged me, then took Mac's arm, starting down the aisle as friends, family, and coworkers whooped and cheered. The couple stopped for only a moment, to kiss the flower girl, Mac's daughter, Ashley, who was jumping up and down wildly from her place beside his sister. The five-year-old took that as her invitation and chased after them as they continued down the aisle, prompting laughter from the other guests.

"Hey, Red. We're up."

I nearly jumped out of my skin at the sound of Asher's voice, rippling across my ears again. I'd been so wrapped up in Beth and Mac I hadn't realized he'd returned to my side. As I glanced over at him now, he gave me a roguish smile, then held out his arm. As if he were some gallant knight in shining armor and I was the pathetic damsel in distress, needing rescue from the big bad waves.

Sadly it wasn't far from the truth.

Reluctantly, I took his arm, feeling my traitorous skin flush all over again at the warmth that came from our interlocking elbows. God, what was it about this guy that had me zero to sixty with just a simple touch? I sucked in a breath, pasted a smile on my face, and tried to calm my racing heart as I forced myself to focus on the job at hand, rather than on the hotness on my arm.

Easier said than done, especially given all the stares I was getting from the audience. Well, the stares Asher was getting, anyway, from all the women. I fleetingly wondered which one (or two?) he would end up bedding later that night. Hell, with his looks and money and celebrity he probably had the pick of the party. Even now the girls were slobbering like Saint Bernards as we walked by.

Must be good to be the king.

When we reached the top of the stairs, Asher stopped. I jerked my arm away from his, with a little more force than I'd meant to. He chuckled, his green eyes flashing merrily.

"That anxious to be rid of me, huh?" he teased. "Or just angling to be first in line for the buffet?"

I groaned. "More like the deep dark hole I'll be crawling into so I can die of humiliation in private, thank you very much."

He laughed. But to my surprise it was a nice laugh. A laugh that said, "I'm laughing with you not at you." Even though, at the moment, I was still having a hard time finding any of this funny.

"Don't worry, Red. It happens to the best of us," he assured me. "I mean hell, if I had a buck for every wave that snuck up from behind and scared the bejesus out of me? I'd be a rich man."

I raised my eyebrows. He laughed again.

"Okay, fine. A richer man," he corrected. "And," he added, waving a finger, his voice overly serious, "I would donate every penny of that newfound wealth to splash research. So someday scientists could figure out a way to stop those bad waves from happening to good people."

He shot me a teasing grin and I couldn't help a small smile in return. Now that I had distance between the ocean and myself I was able to relax a bit. The former sharp terror dulled to a lingering ache.

"Well, thank you," I said sheepishly. "For the rescue, I mean. Now the News 9 powers-that-be can assume I'm only a tiny bit crazy. Instead of a full-on candidate for strait-jacketdom."

"Please." Asher waved me off. "Have you ever been to a TV newsroom wedding? By the end of the night they'll be so blind drunk they won't remember their own names, never mind your little surf-and-turf snafu."

I snorted. "Maybe I need to start spiking drinks just in case . . ."

"That's my girl!" He held up his fist and I reluctantly bumped it with my own, my face flashing fire all over again. It was tough to be a redhead on the best of days. But this guy seemed to have "making me blush" as his superpower.

"Just do me a solid and skip my drink, okay?" he teased. "I have to give the best man toast later on and will need to keep my ability to speak in complete sentences if I'm some-how going to muddle through it."

"That's right! The toasts!" I exclaimed. With all that had happened during the ceremony I'd almost forgotten I still had a few maid of honor duties left. Reaching into my dress's pocket I pulled out the paper I'd been working on the night before, studying it with critical eyes.

Asher gave a low whistle. "Wow, you came prepared," he noted, looking impressed. "And here I was just thinking of winging mine."

Before I could stop him, he reached out and plucked the paper from my hands, unfolding it and scanning the words I'd written. Once again I felt my cheeks heat as I stood there, awkwardly, not sure what to say.

"It's just a stupid little thing I whipped up . . ." I stammered.

He looked over at me. "This is really good," he exclaimed, as if he were surprised. I didn't know whether to be pleased or insulted by that. He handed the paper back to me. "I'm going to sound like a total tool in comparison."

I rolled my eyes. "I'm sure you'll do fine. It's not rocket science, you know."

"Well, obviously not for you," he muttered. "I, on the other hand . . ."

"Asher Anderson! There you are!"

I looked up, just in time to see a vivacious blonde, wearing a dress cut far too low to be considered proper wedding attire, practically throw herself on top of Asher. As one did, I supposed, if you were a hot blonde in a low-cut dress. As she kissed him soundly on both cheeks, he simultaneously tried to peel her off his body. I stifled an unexpected grin at the annoyed look on his face.

Maybe it wasn't so good to be the king all the time.

"Hey, Jess," he said, his voice measured. "I didn't realize you were on the guest list."

"Of course!" the girl—Jess—cried, almost indignantly. Then she giggled. "Okay, fine. I'm totally crashing. But how could I just leave you here, all by your lonesome, with all these bridesmaids wandering around, looking to hook up?" She gave me a derisive look, obviously lumping me into the aforementioned category. "Just consider me your plus one," she cooed. "Now come on, let's go raid the buffet. Those lobster tails are not going to just eat themselves, you know."

"Okay, okay!" Asher said holding up his hands in surrender. He gave me an impish shrug, then mouthed *sorry* before turning back to his little girlfriend. "Just hands off the tux, okay?"

She grinned. "You saying that only makes me want to rough it up more."

And with that, she practically dragged him across the lawn, toward the main house. I watched the two of them go, surprised at the shimmer of disappointment I suddenly felt flutter through my stomach. Which was completely stupid, of course. I mean, it wasn't as if I had wanted him to stick around or anything. Sure, he was funny and nice. And he'd made me feel better about everything that had happened with his silly jokes. And yes, he was incredibly easy on the eyes and my body was still humming a little from his touch.

But that was where it ended. Where it had to end.

Because he was Asher Anderson. And I was . . . well, me. We may have been paired for the wedding, but in real life? We might as well have come from different planets. No matter what happened tonight, tomorrow I would cease to exist in his world. That was just reality.

Besides, if he had known what had truly freaked me out back on that beach? The real reason I was so scared of those waves? He wouldn't be interested in talking to me anymore anyway. In fact, he'd probably be the one to run away screaming.

I sighed, my mood sobering again as I turned back to the ocean, forcing myself to stare out into the water, watching the waves beat up the shore. I bit my lower lip, feeling my pulse kick up in my veins all over again.

Piper! Where's your brother?
Where the HELL is your brother?

Some people thought the ocean was beautiful. Peaceful. But to me, it was nothing more than a graveyard.

two

ASHER

"Dude! What was that all about?" I demanded as Jess dragged me toward the main house where the wedding reception was taking place. "I was in the middle of a conversation there."

Jess turned to me, raising an eyebrow. "Hey, you're the one who asked me to play wing girl, remember?" she reminded me, tossing her bleach blond locks over her shoulder. "Save you from all those Stage Five clingers? In fact, if I remember right you even offered a cash reward for a job well done."

I groaned. "I asked you for protection from clingers, yes. That was Beth's maid of honor, for Christ's sake."

"Beth's maid of honor who was totally clinging to you during the ceremony," Jess pointed out. "Like, literally, I'm pretty sure you were the only thing keeping her standing upright at one point. And if that's not Asher Anderson DEF-CON One, you need to refresh me on the definition."

She had a point. Under any other circumstances I would have been entirely grateful for her quick and effective extraction. Why, I could think of some weddings where I was stuck talking to some obnoxious gold digger or another for painful hours, unable to drag myself away. Which was why I'd suggested Jess "pop in" immediately after the ceremony in the first place. More often than not I found myself in need of her services at these sorts of things. A girl who wanted nothing more from me than friendship and maybe a ride to the beach every once in a while.

Which in my world was a very rare unicorn indeed.

But in this case . . . I stole a glance behind me, back to where Piper was still standing, still staring out into the sea. I'd actually kind of wanted a few more minutes to talk. Which was so unlike me, but there it was.

I'd met the girl briefly at the rehearsal dinner the night before. Mac told me she worked at News 9, but I was pretty sure I'd never seen her there. After all, she was nothing if not memorable with those crazy corkscrew curls and big, doelike brown eyes, framed by sooty lashes. Pair that with the generous dusting of golden freckles on her skin and her cute button nose and it had been all I could do not to break out into a full-on rendition of "Tomorrow," Orphan Annie–style, in hopes of watching her pale skin flush bright red. I had always dug redheads for this reason. They usually wore their emotions on their sleeves. Nice for guys like me who were terrible at picking up the passive-aggressive cues most women liked to throw down in droves.

But during the ceremony? Her skin hadn't turned red—it had turned stark white. Like so white that for a moment I thought she was going to go all iZombie on me and start eating people's brains. Or at least pass out right where she stood. I'd never seen anyone get so freaked out over a simple wave before. I mean, sure, she was probably embarrassed more than anything—yelling *shit* in the middle of a wedding ceremony would do that to the best of us. But the thing was, she didn't seem embarrassed—at least not at first.

She seemed scared to death. As if she'd seen a ghost or something, rising from the water.

I realized Jess was still staring at me, an amused expression dancing on her face. "Look, I was just being a gentleman," I told her. "No big deal."

She snorted at this. I couldn't blame her either. While I was a lot of things, *gentleman* didn't exactly top the list. Nor did *superhero* or *knight in shining armor saving damsels in distress* for that matter. Hell, in most cases I was probably more likely to be voted the asshole that the damsels in distress needed to be saved from.

I found my gaze flickering back to Piper. What was it about her that had suddenly made me go all caveman down there? I mean, sure, she was cute. She was hot, too. Especially in that dress she was wearing. Which by the way was so not fair. I mean, bridesmaids dresses were supposed to be hideous, right? Obnoxious colors, too many frills? They certainly weren't supposed to cling to every curve, accentuate a perfect ass. God, there was one point during the ceremony where she'd asked me to let her go and I literally couldn't step away. Not unless I wanted the entire guest list to know just how much I liked her in that dress. Or at least how much a certain part of me did.

Which was totally obnoxious, I know. I did mention caveman, right? I mean there she was, scared to death, ready to bolt, and I was thinking about what it'd be like to pull her into the water and strip her bare. Grab that supple ass and pull her to me, grinding up against her, those luscious breasts of hers squashed against my chest. I imagined licking her, tasting the salt on her skin as the water splashed against us.

"Wow." Jess let out a low whistle, effectively interrupting my fantasy. "I have to say, you're suddenly looking a little stalkery there yourself, bro. Maybe I need to go offer *her* my services instead."

"Don't even," I warned, flashing her a scolding look, mostly to hide my blush. Since when did I get so carried away by some chick? "You work for me and don't you forget it."

I reached into my pocket and pulled out a wad of bills, pushing it in her direction without bothering to count it. She raised her eyebrows, looking down at the money.

"I'm pretty sure we agreed on twenty bucks," she reminded me.

"Consider it a tip," I said, pushing the money at her again. "After all, I know how big an acting job it is for you to pretend you find me attractive."

"While it is, indeed, true I find the cock between your legs a huge turnoff," she said with a smile, "I'm not your charity case anymore. Greta is making bank down at the bar these days. And I'm finally living the life I should have always been accustomed to."

I turned to her, frowning. "So what, that's it? You're content to be a kept woman from here on out?"

"Certainly not," she declared. "I'm aiming for full-on trophy wife." She gave me a maddening grin and I couldn't help but laugh. Girl was too much.

"Well then," I said, "it's good to know at least one of us has their priorities in order. But just keep the cash, okay? Hell, even a trophy wife needs a little pocket money from time to time. The kind that doesn't come with strings attached."

After all, I knew all too well about strings.

Jess caught my expression. "Uh-oh," she said, giving me a knowing look. "Let me guess. Mommie Dearest has been on your jock again."

I snorted. "I'm pretty sure she's set up permanent residence at this point."

"You do know you could just walk away, right?" she reminded me, throwing me a pitying smile. "I mean, you don't have to live under her thumb. You don't have to play her games . . ."

I frowned, scrubbing the back of my neck with my hand. I hated when she said things like this. When she made it seem so black-and-white. So easy. And to her it was, I guess. Because to her it was just a matter of money. She had no idea the true strings attached. No one did.

And as far as I was concerned? No one ever would.

And so instead, I forced a laugh. "Walk away?" I repeated, making my voice sound incredulous. "And what? Miss out on the mansions, the money, the Maserati?" I shook my head. "Yeah, that would be a definite no-go, captain."

She rolled her eyes. "Man, I can only pray that someday I

have first world problems like yours, Anderson." She punched me lightly on the arm. "Now what do you say we get the hell out of here? River texted me just before I got here and said there's a killer swell going on right now, just off of Black's."

I paused, tempted. Surfing sounded pretty damn good right about now. The feel of fiberglass beneath my feet, the roar of the waves in my ears. The chance to push all these troubling thoughts aside and become one with the water. I was pretty sure I could get away with it, too; just give some stupid excuse and take off—no one would really care. In fact, they probably expected it of me.

But then I found myself glancing over at Piper, who was now talking to Beth. She had had every reason to take off herself—after what had happened on the beach no one would have blamed her. Unlike me, she'd actually had a real excuse to bail.

But instead, she'd stayed.

And suddenly I wanted to stay, too. I wanted to talk to her more. Maybe find out what had really freaked her out. Make sure she was really okay.

I turned to Jess. "Sorry," I said. "I've got to give a toast."

Jess laughed, glancing over at Piper. "A toast, huh?" she teased. "Is that what the kids are calling it these days? Hey, baby, you want to toast and chill?"

"Har, har. I'm the best man, remember? I have duties!"

She giggled. "He said *duties*."

"Oh my God, are you five?" I laughed. "Seriously, just get the hell out of here. I will find you later, I promise."

"Sure you will. At five AM when you call me looking for a ride home to avoid the walk of shame."

"You don't have to pick up the phone."

She held up her hands. "What can I say? I've always had a soft spot for billionaire breeders." She reached over and gave me a hug. "Have fun," she told me. "And call me if you need me. I'm serious."

"I know you are," I assured her. "And I appreciate that. More than you know. But I'm pretty sure I'll just be giving a toast tonight. And then I'll be heading home."

"If you say so, bro."

And with that, Jess took off toward the parking lot. I watched her go, a smile playing on my lips. She was something, my friend. I loved the hell out of her. Even if she was completely off her rocker half the time.

Even if she had no idea what my so-called "first world problems" were really like.

I rose to my feet, ready to head back to the ceremonies. Maybe I could find a quiet corner and work on my speech. I had planned to just wing it—like I did most everything else in life. But Piper's speech had been really good. I mean, really heartfelt and sweet. I was going to look like a total douche, following her. At the very least I needed to scribble something down. Something—

A golf cart cut me off, then stopped in front of me. I looked up, my face sagging as I saw who was inside.

Speak of the devil. Mommie Dearest in the flesh.

I had been hoping all her charity duties would have forced her to miss this little shindig. But luck was clearly not my lady tonight.

"Hi, Mom," I said reluctantly, watching her climb out of the cart. She was dressed in full-on wedding finery, as if she were the mother of the bride herself. My mother did not, as she'd said on many occasions, "do garden party casual." If there was a party—garden or otherwise—she'd attend dripping in diamonds or she wouldn't be attending at all.

We should all be so lucky . . .

"Baby!" she cooed, as if she were surprised to see me. I watched as she made her way toward me, her high heels immediately sinking into the soft lawn. She looked down disdainfully, as if the grass itself were to blame for her own inappropriate choice in beach wedding footwear. Then she clomped over to me, holding out her arms. I reluctantly gave her a hug.

"Hey, Mom," I said. "I didn't know you were going to be here today."

"Why, of course I was!" she exclaimed, looking offended

that I would even suggest otherwise. "How could I miss the wedding of two of our finest employees?"

By *finest employees* she meant cash cows. And she wasn't wrong in that respect. Beth had practically put the station on the map the year before, breaking a huge story about an Internet hacker who had released confidential CIA documents online. Overnight News 9 had gone from number three to a solid number one in the ratings and Mom had been leveraging the advantage ever since.

That was her superpower, after all.

"You looked very handsome up there," she said, reaching up to fix my bow tie, which didn't need fixing, thank you very much. "And very sweet of you to come to the rescue of that poor girl. What was her problem, anyway? She practically ruined the wedding with those theatrics." She huffed.

"She just got startled, that's all," I said with a frown. "I hardly think it ruined the wedding."

My mother sniffed, letting me know she disagreed, but thankfully couldn't be bothered to get into a full-blown debate. After all, why pick on a stranger when she could go after her own son?

"So," she said, giving me a pointed look, proving me right, "will you be making an appearance at the station this week?"

And here we went.

"Sure," I said. "Seems likely. It is where I work, after all."

"Is it? Sometimes I wonder." She gave me a pointed look. "Especially after hearing from Richard that you taped your forecast three times last week so you could skip out before the show and go surfing."

I scowled. *And . . . thank you, Richard.*

"It was an accurate forecast, wasn't it?" I protested. "I mean, it's not exactly like the weather changes here much." Hell, I could have probably taped a week's worth of broadcasts and no one would have been the wiser.

Mom gave an exasperated sigh. "For the thousandth time, Asher, if you don't want to do the job, let me hire a producer to do it for you. They can do all the research and forecasting. All you'd have to do is show your handsome face on TV."

I shook my head. We'd had this discussion a hundred times. But there was no way I was going to give in. Let her cut off my balls and put me on a leash.

"Or I could just quit?" I suggested, waggling my eyebrows at her. "Maybe you'd like that?"

Her face clouded. "Do not even say that. You know what that would do to your father. Not to mention the community. They've depended on the Anderson family to forecast their weather for the last thirty-five years. This is your legacy, Asher. What your father worked his whole life to give you. It's time you start acting like you care about that. That you care about him."

I swallowed hard, my stomach churning as I waited for her to finish her lecture. It was one I'd heard a thousand times before. And one I would probably hear a thousand times again. The one argument I could never walk away from. The one argument I could never win.

I looked up, catching the small smirk on my mother's face as she watched, waiting for my reaction. But she didn't really need to wait. She already knew what I'd say. What I had no choice but to say.

"I'll see you Monday," I muttered.

She beamed. "Wonderful. I'll be counting the hours."

And with that, she flounced back to the golf cart, climbing in and instructing the driver to head away. I watched them go, the anger burning in my gut again.

First world problems. And maybe they were.

But that didn't make them suck any less.

three

Piper! There you are!"

I looked up to see Beth on approach, looking radiant in her flowing white wedding dress and her bouncy long golden curls. Her stomach was only slightly rounded and if I didn't know better I would have assumed she'd just had too much of the wedding buffet. But I did know better. In a few months, Mac's daughter would become a big sister. And their little triangle family would become square.

"Sorry, did you need me for pictures?" I asked. "I'll be there in a second."

Beth waved me off. "No rush," she assured me. "I just wanted to make sure you were okay."

"Uh, I think I'm supposed to be the one looking out for you," I protested. "Clearly I'm doing a terrible job."

"You are doing an amazing job. Best maid of honor ever," Beth insisted. Then she laughed. "God, I still can't believe we actually pulled this off." She glanced back at the wedding tents, where her new husband was chasing his daughter around the lawn, the little girl squealing in mock terror.

"I didn't have a single doubt," I assured her. "You deserve all of this. And so much more."

Beth grinned. "I do, don't I? And it's not like I didn't put in the work."

I nodded, thinking back to all she'd been put through—with Mac's earlier commitment phobia and crazy ex-wife. But somehow Beth had hung in. She'd known Mac was worth it. And, in the end, she had come out on top.

It was nice to know that happy endings still existed—at least for some people.

"Though," I added, "don't think I'm not depressed as hell about losing my awesome roommate. Do you know how hard it's going to be to find someone who likes eighties movies as much as you?"

"Hey, I'm married, not dead," Beth protested with a laugh. "I can totally bail on wife-and-mother duty for the sake of John Hughes romance from time to time."

"I'll hold you to that."

"Speaking of holding . . ." Beth's eyes sparkled mischievously. "What was up with you and Asher at the wedding? I turn around and he's, like, all over you, whispering in your ear and groping you and stuff."

I laughed. "That was not groping, I promise you. That was simply him assisting me in not dying of embarrassment for interrupting your wedding."

"Are you sure? We are talking about Asher Anderson, right? The biggest flirt this side of the Pacific?"

"Who is probably knee-deep in wannabe bridesmaids at this point," I reminded her. "Trust me, I am so not his type."

"Have you even looked in the mirror today?" Beth demanded. "Seriously, you are so hot in that dress I half feel I should be pissed off at you—for upstaging the poor preggo bride."

I rolled my eyes. "As if that were even possible. You are glowing, Beth. Glowing like a freaking glow stick at Halloween."

"Or, you know, one of those pumpkin inflatables," Beth shot back, holding her stomach in her hands. But she looked pleased all the same. "In any case, don't change the subject. If not Asher, there must be someone here worthy of my beautiful maid of honor." She scanned the lawn. "We just need to find him."

"The only thing I want to find is a bowl of that lobster bisque you were raving about earlier," I assured her. "And maybe Richard."

"Richard?" Beth's eyes widened. "Like, news director Richard?" Her nose wrinkled with distaste.

"Ew! Not like that!" I protested, shaking my head. The news director was a great guy, but maybe not, let's say Asher Anderson caliber when it came to the looks department. Not to mention he was probably old enough to be my father. "I just wanted to see if Heather's really leaving the morning shift once she gives birth and whether they'll be posting the job opening when she does."

Beth shook her head. "That's my Piper. Always working, even when she's not getting paid."

I felt the blush creep to my cheeks again and wished I'd kept my mouth shut. I didn't want my best friend to think I was using my position as maid of honor as a chance to network.

But still, it *was* a chance to network. A really good one, too. My one chance to mingle with the bosses as an equal. Sure, it was probably tacky to bring up work over wine, but I'd been waiting for an opportunity like this since the day I'd arrived at News 9. I needed to make absolutely sure that Richard knew I wanted this job—that it wouldn't be right for him to give it to anyone else.

After all, while Beth and Asher and the others might have seen News 9 as just a job, to me it was my one chance to escape my past. To rise above the life I'd been born into and actually make something of myself. I'd clawed tooth and nail to get this far. And I wasn't about to stop—until I got where I wanted to be.

I found the lobster bisque and it was indeed delicious. Then I sat at my assigned table and made small talk with the other guests. From time to time my eyes wandered the tent, checking in on Richard. He was sitting at a far table with the other prestigious News 9 brass and hadn't gotten up once, as far as I'd noticed, even to go to the bathroom. Maybe I should have asked Beth to seat me next to him, but that might have been going too far, even for me. It was okay, though. He was bound to get up and wander around once everyone started dancing. I'd make my move then.

"So. About these toasts."

I looked up from my soup, surprised to see Asher had approached the table. He stood above me now, looking down. From behind me I could hear a few excited titters from the other girls sitting with me. But Asher ignored them all, his attention completely on me.

"You're back," I observed.

"I suppose I am." His lips curled and I felt my face heat. What was it about this guy that made me blush at the drop of a hat? I mean, yes, he was hot. There was no denying that. But totally not my type. If I even had a type, that was. It'd been a long time since I'd gone on a date. Working two jobs made it almost impossible to have a relationship. Not that I wanted one in the first place. I was married to my job, thank you very much. And work and I were very happy together.

I realized Asher was still looking at me. "What about the toasts?" I asked.

He grabbed a chair from a nearby table, not bothering to ask if anyone had been using it. He pulled it over and sat on it backward, next to me. He leaned in, and my stomach flip-flopped a little as his eyes locked on my face. "Want to help me write mine?"

I raised an eyebrow. "What happened to winging it?"

"Well, yes, that was the original plan," he agreed. "Until I read yours. Your Emmy Award–worthy wedding toast. Gotta admit, it got me a little nervous."

"I'm pretty sure they don't give out Emmys for wedding toasts," I said, a smile ghosting on my lips. "So you'll probably be okay."

He shook his head. "Can't take that risk. I mean, what if your toast brings everyone to tears? Or makes them laugh hysterically? And then I go up there, blabbing like an idiot . . ." He rubbed the back of his neck with his hand. "I clearly need to up my game."

I laughed. I couldn't help it. "It's not a competition!"

"It could be."

"What?"

I watched as Asher nodded his head thoughtfully. "Yes," he said, almost as if he were talking to himself. Then he turned back to me. "We could totally make it a competition. Like, who gets the most applause. Or the most tears or laughter. Or maybe a combination of all of the above?"

"Mmhm. And what would the winner get?"

"I don't know. What do you want?"

I opened my mouth to answer then fell silent as my eyes locked on Richard, rising from his seat and heading out of the tent. I sighed. Was he leaving already? Had I missed my chance? I considered running over to him now, but that would probably seem rude. And I didn't want to piss him off, at least until he heard what I had to say.

"For a certain someone to know I exist?" I muttered, half to myself.

Asher followed my gaze then raised his eyebrows. "Richard?" he asked, his voice not hiding his incredulity. "Really?"

"No!" I groaned, shoving him playfully. I couldn't believe I'd had to clarify that I did not have a crush on my boss twice in one day. "I just want him to give me a job."

"Don't you have a job? You already work at News 9, right? In the newsroom?" Now Asher sounded confused.

"Yes," I said, sinking back into my chair. I was surprised he even knew that much. Mac or Beth must have told him. After all, people at his level did not usually acknowledge the existence of little peons like me. "But I want a new one. I want to be a news writer and there's this position that might be opening up on the overnight shift . . ."

I trailed off, realizing Asher was wrinkling his nose in distaste. I frowned. "What?"

"Overnight shift?" he repeated. "What hours would that be?"

"One AM to seven AM."

He made a face. "That sounds like a terrible job."

I stared at him, anger rising up inside of me. Terrible job? What the hell was that supposed to mean? I mean, sure, the hours sucked. But I'd be a real writer for the newscast, not some glorified errand runner like I was currently. The scripts I wrote would be read on TV, which would make me quasi-famous, even if no one in the world actually knew I existed. This was what I'd been slaving away for. This would be a dream come true.

For me anyway. Evidently not for Golden Boy.

"Sorry," I growled before I could stop myself. "Not all of us get to have awesome prime time gigs handed to us at birth."

He stared at me, his eyes wide with surprise. I felt my face go tomato red as I realized what I'd just blurted out. Blurted out to the only son of my employer, I might add. The one guy here who could literally make or break me ever getting this so-called terrible job. Or any job in TV news for that matter.

"I'm so sorry," I cried, my stomach twisting in knots. It was all I could do not to puke right then and there. "I didn't mean—I mean, I totally shouldn't have—"

Asher reached out, pressing a finger to my lips to stop me from speaking. Which was probably for the best, as I had no idea what I was about to say. At most it probably would have been stupid. At worst—even more insulting.

I was such a fool. What if he went to his mom and told her what I'd said? What if she not only fired me, but black-listed me from TV in San Diego entirely? Everything I'd worked so hard for my entire life, gone in the blink of an eye.

Because of my stupid mouth.

I looked at Asher. He was looking back at me. The laughter had fled from his face, replaced by an ultra-serious look. A look that, if I didn't know any better, almost seemed . . . sad.

"You're right," he said in a quiet voice.

I shook my head. "No," I protested. "I'm so not right. I . . . it was a ridiculous thing to say and . . ." I somehow managed to stumble to my feet. "I should go."

He grabbed my hand, holding it tightly in his own. "Wait," he said.

I looked down, sure my face held a mess of mortification mixed with exasperation. "What?"

For a moment, he didn't answer. And the silence stretched out between us, long and insufferable. My heart pounded in my chest as I waited for him to say something—anything to relieve the torture of the moment. At the same time, my traitorous body was practically vibrating from the heat that radiated from his hand on mine.

Seriously, Piper, how can you think of sex at a time like this?

Finally, his mouth quirked. "I haven't told you what I want yet."

"Wh-what?" I stared at him, confused as hell. Then I remembered. The speech contest. The stupid speech contest.

I watched as he rose slowly from his seat, not letting go of my hand. My pulse was now racing, and I was pretty sure I was sweating, too. As I stood there, paralyzed, Asher reached his other hand up, cupping my chin and tilting my face upward to force me to meet his eyes. His piercing emerald eyes shining in the sunset. As he dragged those fingers along my jawline, I bit my lower lip so hard I was almost positive I would draw blood.

"So," he drawled, "if you win, you want the morning show writing position."

My face flamed. "I was just joking about that," I protested. But he shook his head, cutting me off.

"If I win," he said, "I want a date."

A what? I stared at him. Speechless. Seriously, at that moment I couldn't have been more surprised if a full-on tsunami had suddenly crested over the cliff and headed our way.

A date? Was this some kind of joke?

I stared up at him, trembling, his hand searing my chin. Half of me wanted to shove him backward to break this odd connection between us. The other half—well, that half wanted something else entirely. Something I should have entirely not wanted.

Suddenly, my phone broke out into song.

Saved by the bell. Literally.

I stumbled backward, managing to break away and put distance between us as I fumbled for my phone in my purse. My heart was beating so fast and hard I could barely breathe and I nearly dropped the phone onto the ground. All the while I could feel Asher's eyes, still on me, watching, waiting.

"Excuse me," I mumbled, glancing at the caller ID.

Shit. It was Mom.

Under any other circumstance I would have ignored the call. But at that very moment it was my only Get Out of Jail Free card and I couldn't pass it up. I held up a hand to Asher before cowardly retreating to the other side of the tent and answering the call.

Before I even said hello, I knew it was a bad idea.

"Sweetie!" my mother's voice cried from the other end. The connection was crackly. There wasn't great cell service out in the desert where she lived.

"What do you want, Mom?" I asked, gripping the phone tightly.

"What do I want? Can't a mother call her daughter just to say hello?"

I closed my eyes for a moment. Even through the static I could hear the squeakiness in her voice. The slight slur of her words. I so should have let this go to voice mail.

"Mom, I'm at Beth's wedding, remember? I was going to call you when I got to the Holloway House?"

"Oh yes. You and your fancy wedding. I bet there's a lot of food there, huh? Fancy food? And maybe some fancy wine? Lucky you, hobnobbing with the jet set while your poor mother sits in her trailer with an empty fridge."

I tightened my grip on the phone, my stomach now

churning. *Don't let her get to you*, I tried to scold myself. But, of course, that was impossible.

I glanced around the wedding tent. At all the happy people, talking and laughing. Enjoying the day without a care in the world. What must it be like to live like that? Where your only true worries were where you were going to eat that night, rather than whether you'd eat at all.

I reluctantly turned back to the phone.

"What do you want, Mom?" I asked in a tight voice. "Do you need me to pick up some groceries for you?" I glanced at my watch, biting my lower lip in frustration. I had timed everything perfectly to give my toast, then head to the Holloway House where I was working the night shift. There was no way I'd be able to do both and deliver groceries in time.

But the alternative . . .

"Oh, sweetie. You don't have to go grocery shopping for me," my mother cooed into the phone sweetly. Too sweetly. Alarm bells began to go off in my head. "I know how busy you are and I have nothing to do. So if you could just wire some money maybe, then I could go shopping myself. No big deal."

I sank into a nearby chair. "Mom, what's going on?"

"What do you mean?" Her voice got defensive. "Like I said, I just need some money for food."

"Is David there? Is he out of jail again?"

The questions left my mouth before I could stop them and I froze, suddenly looking up, my eyes darting around the reception tent, praying no one had been close enough to overhear the *J* word. Thankfully everyone appeared to be occupied, drinking the aforementioned fancy wine and eating the fancy food.

"Mom?" I repeated, my annoyance rising again.

Just one night, I wanted to scream at her. *I just wanted one night at the ball. But you couldn't even give me that, could you?*

There was a pause. I could practically hear the lies rolling around her empty head. "Well, yes, he is, actually. But I don't see how that has anything to do with . . ."

"Mom, I'll bring you some food. But I'm not wiring you any more money."

"You ungrateful girl," my mom snapped. "Your brother would have never done this to me. You brother would have—"

It took all my effort to hang up the phone and stuff it in my purse. I didn't need to hear anymore. I knew exactly what she was going to say anyway. What she would always say when she wanted to cut me deep.

"Everything okay?"

I whirled around to see Asher had come up behind me. My face burned. God, why wouldn't he just go away? Why couldn't he see that I was not the girl he wanted to flirt with? That he belonged with that blonde earlier. Or one of the other people who fit into his world.

Not me. Definitely not me.

I squeezed my eyes shut. Then opened them again.

"I have to go," I said. "It's an emergency with my mom. Please tell Beth I'm sorry? That I'll make it up to her later?" Ugh. I really hated bailing on my best friend on her big day. But Beth knew my mom. I hoped she'd understand.

He looked surprised, but to his credit, he nodded. "Can I help?" he asked. "Do you need me to get you a cab? Or drive you somewhere?"

I shook my head. Then I remembered my speech. I reached into my pocket, shoving the paper in his direction.

"Can you give the toast for me?" I asked.

He took the paper, looking down at it. His eyes danced a little as he looked back up at me. "Does this mean I win?" he teased.

I sighed. Of course it did. Because people like Asher Anderson always won.

And people like me were destined to lose.

four

PIPER

Michael! Where's Michael?"
    I grunt as rough hands shake me awake, nails like daggers digging into my bare flesh. Waving my arms I try to shoo them away.
    I'm so tired.
    I just want to sleep.
    "Five more minutes, Mom," I beg.
    "Where's your brother? You were supposed to be watching your brother!"
    My eyes shoot open. I sit up. Looking around, my heart beating fast in my chest as my foggy brain tries to comprehend what she's screaming about.
    Michael.
    Something about Michael.
    My eyes lock on to the dark water. The waves crashing to shore.
    Oh God. Michael.
    Little Michael . . .
    "WHERE'S YOUR FUCKING BROTHER?" my mother screams.

* * *

I jerked up in bed, my body drenched in sweat, my heart pounding, my breath coming in short gasps. I pulled my knees to my chest, burying my head against them.

"It's just a dream," I told myself, trying to steady my breath as the therapists had taught me to do long ago. "Just a bad dream."

But, of course, it wasn't.

It wasn't even close.

"Shit," I muttered under my breath as I glanced at the clock on my nightstand. I'd gotten the stupid thing at a garage sale a year ago and it had never worked right. Now I'd evidently slept through my phone's backup alarm as well.

Not surprising, I supposed. After leaving the wedding to hit the grocery store and then bring the groceries to Mom, I'd been almost an hour late for my shift at the Holloway House. I'd told them I'd stay an extra hour at the end to make up for it. Which meant not getting home until well after two AM.

And then the dreams had come. The horrible, horrible dreams. I hadn't had dreams like these in years—I'd thought they were gone forever. But evidently being on the beach yesterday had brought everything back with a vengeance.

God, I was going to be a zombie at work today.

Groaning, I swung my feet around, stepping down onto the cold tile floor. For a city with such a temperate climate like San Diego, mornings could still be pretty cold. Not quite cold enough to justify wasting money on heat, mind you, especially now that I had no roommate to split the bill with, but just cold enough to make me cringe as I made my way to the coffee pot.

After pouring myself a cup, I headed to the bathroom then stared at myself in the mirror for a moment. My hair was a hot mess, curls all askew, but there was no time to shower. People without curly hair had no idea what pain and suffering we curly girls went through on a daily basis. All they had to do was brush their hair out and go on their merry way. If I brushed mine out, I'd be guest starring at work as Bozo the Clown.

Sighing, I grabbed a bottle of leave-in conditioner spray and attempted my best patching job. In the end, I resigned myself to putting my hair up in what I hoped looked like an artfully messy ponytail, versus one constructed out of desperation and broken dreams. Then I spackled my face with a small amount of foundation and applied some mascara and lip gloss. I wasn't normally much of a makeup girl, but at News 9 all the on-air people walked around looking like models just off the runway. Which could be ego crushing to the rest of us mere mortals, to say the least.

Of course, that won't be a problem once I get the overnight writing job, I reminded myself. *Hardly anyone will be there to see me at that godforsaken hour. And the ones that are? They'll be too bleary-eyed to notice.*

If I got the job, I corrected myself. After all, it wasn't a done deal by any means. Especially since I had had to bail on the wedding early and never did get a chance to talk to Richard about it. But my immediate boss, the executive producer, Gary, had to know I was interested. He had to know how much I wanted to move up. And there was no one there more senior than I was. Meaning I was the obvious choice.

The thought got my motor running and I stepped out of the bathroom to change into my best suit. Which was also, admittedly, my only suit. Normally I didn't dress up too much—News 9 was pretty casual if you weren't on air. But today could be a very special day.

A thrill of anticipation wound up my spine as I slid my pencil skirt over my hips. A writing job. A real writing job. It would be a dream come true. Maybe not a glamorous dream—as Asher had so sweetly pointed out yesterday, the hours kind of sucked. And it wasn't as if I was suddenly going to be some on-air superstar like Beth.

But I'd be a journalist. An actual TV journalist. Contributing to an actual TV show. That alone was worth the crazy wake-up time. In fact, it was pretty much worth everything.

And that didn't even take into account the new salary I'd

be getting. My current position paid only a little over min-
imum wage and was only for thirty hours a week—hence
the second job at the Holloway House. This job, if I really
did get it, paid fifteen dollars an hour and could turn into
full-time work someday. Which would mean amazing,
hard-to-imagine things like 401(k)s and actual health benefits. Not to mention a chance to get my mother out of her
current living situation—and away from people like David.

Sure, I still had to get the job first. But I'd done everything
possible to make it happen and that had to mean something,
right? Over the past year I'd stayed late, I'd studied scripts
written by other writers. I'd written my own and uploaded
them to the server. Even left printouts on Gary's desk to read.
Sure, I had no idea if he actually ever did anything with them
except use them as coasters for his coffee. But surely his eyes
must have swept over one at some point, right? To see the
words I'd written? To realize I was the best candidate for
the job?

It was time to find out for sure.

I got to work with ten minutes to spare—a record, even for
me. The morning newscast had just finished and all the
morning writers were gathering up their things, ready to
head home. Some of them would go to a nearby deli and
order steak-and-cheese subs or fish tacos—not caring that
it was eight in the morning: For them it was dinnertime. I
wasn't sure how I was going to adjust to that kind of thing
if I got the job, but I was willing to make it work.

I was willing to make anything work for this.

Today, I realized, they were cleaning up from a good-bye
party for Heather. Which meant she was definitely leaving,
I realized excitedly, my eyes taking in the last crumbs of
the cake. The position was definitely open.

This could really happen for me at last.

Heart pounding, I headed over to Heather's desk. She
was busy packing her things into a cardboard box.

"Hey!" I said. "Congrats on the new gig." I motioned to

her bulging stomach. There was definitely a baby boom going on at News 9. I wondered if Beth would stay after she gave birth to her baby.

Heather gave me a smile that looked both weary and happy. "Thanks," she said. "At least I won't have any issues with late-night feeding after working these crazy hours."

I laughed. "Good point." Then I paused, shuffling from foot to foot.

Just ask, Piper. You'll never know unless you ask.

"So do you know . . . when they're filling your position?" I blurted out, feeling totally awkward for asking. But I couldn't wait another minute to know.

Heather frowned. "I think it's already filled," she said. "I heard they asked Anna."

Wait, what?

I stared at her, my heart thudding in my chest. "Anna?" I repeated slowly. "You mean Anna Jenkins?"

But no. That couldn't be. Anna had only come to News 9 two months ago. She'd worked as a production assistant like me, but hadn't done anything—as far as I knew anyway—to audition for a writer's position. In fact, Anna Jenkins barely did anything at all that didn't involve Facebook or texting her boyfriend.

Anna Jenkins could not possibly get my job.

I could feel Hannah's eyes on me. Her face was now full of concern. "Are you okay?" she asked. Then she gasped. "Oh God, you didn't want it, did you?"

I tried to swallow the huge lump that had suddenly formed in my throat. "No," I said quickly, waving her off. "I mean, it's fine. No big deal. Congrats again."

Her face twisted; she looked anguished. Which made me wonder what I looked like to her. "Piper, it's a crappy job," she tried. "You really didn't want it anyway."

"Sure," I said with a forced barking laugh. "After all, I do love sleeping at night."

But of course I didn't. I mean, I did, but I didn't want to. I wanted that job. Yes, it was a crappy job. But it was *my* crappy job. Or it was supposed to be anyway.

Until they'd given it to Anna Jenkins.

Half in a daze, I wandered over to the printers, where my fellow production assistants hung out, waiting for scripts to print. There were a couple of them already at work, collating the morning newsbreak. Anna Jenkins was among them, gabbing happily and accepting congratulations on her new gig.

My heart sank. So it was true.

"It's going to be *so* awful!" she was saying with a giggle. "Oh my God I can't even imagine waking up at midnight to go to work! It's like a nightmare!"

I watched, devastated as everyone tried to comfort her. To tell her it would be fine. That it was a big step and that now she was a real journalist and wasn't that totally exciting?

I dutifully said all those things, too. Even as my heart broke. Even as I realized that I would never be a "real journalist"—that I would be stuck in production assistant hell forever until I was forced to quit in exchange for a "real job" that paid more and offered health benefits. And then, that would be it. My dreams of a real broadcasting career would be over forever.

"Hey, Red!"

I looked up, just in time to see none other than Asher Anderson himself sauntering through the newsroom. He was dressed in a crisp linen shirt and a pair of dark-rinse Diesel jeans slung low on his narrow hips. His hair was slicked back with gel, but a few strands had escaped, falling into his green eyes. In short, he looked like a *GQ* model right off the page.

The cocky smile on his face, the confidence in his step caused anger to rise inside of me. I knew it wasn't justified; he had nothing to do with my not getting my promotion. But I couldn't help being furious at him all the same. It was just so easy for him, wasn't it? He never had to worry about being passed up for a promotion. His job had been passed down to him from birth. He didn't have to worry about working his way up the ladder. It was his ladder to begin with. He could just waltz into the newsroom like he owned the place.

Because he does *own the place*, something inside me snapped. *And you'd best remember that.*

I realized he'd approached the printers. The other production assistants—including Anna—were staring at him with wide eyes. Not surprising, I supposed. After all, someone like him should barely know of our existence on the planet, never mind deem us worthy of talking to.

He reached into his pocket and pulled out my speech. "I thought you might want it back," he told me. "You know, for memory's sake and all." He grinned. "I have to admit, it was an amazing toast. Got a lot of laughs. And I definitely saw some tears." He paused, then added, "You're a good writer, Red."

The words hit me hard and before I knew it, tears had sprung to my eyes. I turned away, not wanting him to see.

"What's wrong?" I heard him ask.

"Nothing," I snapped. "I'm fine."

But he was having none of that. And a moment later his hand was on my arm and he was dragging me into a nearby empty office. I let him—what else could I do?—knowing everyone was watching. Once he closed the door, he turned to me.

"What's wrong?" he asked, the joking lilt in his voice replaced by seriousness. "Are you okay? Is your mom okay?"

I looked up, surprised he had remembered why I had left the wedding. Then I sighed. "I'm fine," I said. "It's just . . ." I shook my head. "That job. That stupid job I told you about yesterday. They gave it to someone else."

"I know."

I looked up, confused. My eyes still blurry with tears. "You know?"

"Yeah." He shrugged. "Some girl named Anna or something? But whatever." He waved his hand dismissively. "Like I said, it was a terrible job." He winked at me and grinned.

Rage erupted inside me like a volcano. It was all I could do not to punch him in the face. "Do you think this is a joke?" I demanded, my voice cracking with fury. "Do you have any clue what we go through down here—just to catch a break?"

"Piper—"

"Yes, it was a crappy job. It was shitty hours and shittier

pay. But it was mine. I deserved it. And I'm not going to just stand here and let you make fun of me for wanting it."

I stopped, unable to continue. He was looking at me with the strangest eyes. I wanted to turn and run. But at the same time I didn't think I could go out there—to let everyone see how upset I was. I couldn't let them witness my defeat.

I swiped my eyes with my sleeve then reached for a tissue to blow my nose. "I've got to go," I muttered. "I have scripts to deliver."

"No," Asher said quietly, "you don't."

I turned back to him, a bitter taste in my mouth. "What?" I spit out. "Are you firing me, too?" Why not, right? At this point I wasn't even sure I cared.

"No," he said. "I'm promoting you." A smile played at the corner of his mouth.

I scowled. "Please don't. It's not funny."

"Good. Because it's not a joke."

"But Anna Jenkins . . ."

"Anna Jenkins got a terrible job. You're getting a better one."

Something thudded hard in my chest. "What is it?" I finally managed to say. "Is it . . . a daytime writing job?" My heart picked up its beat. Oh God, if he had really gotten me a daytime writing job . . .

Asher's eyes locked on to mine. Those beautiful emerald eyes—blasting full force on my face. "Actually, it's a producer job," he said. "From here on out, you'll be working with me."

five

PIPER

I stared at him, my mind racing with what he'd just said. What I thought he'd just said, anyway. The words had clearly been English, but I had to have been misinterpreting them somehow. 'Cause there was no way . . .

A producer job?

Working with him?

"I don't understand," I blurted out at last, feeling hot and stupid and flustered. "You want me to work with you? As your producer?"

He gave me a sheepish grin. "Sorry, I probably should have asked you if you were interested before I went to Richard."

I swallowed hard, my heart thumping in my chest. He'd asked for me? Asher Anderson had asked for me to be his producer?

"I don't have any experience," I protested. "I know nothing about weather."

He waved me off. "You don't have to. I'm the meteorologist. I just need someone to write scripts for me. To set up shoots. To do all the behind-the-scenes things so I can concentrate on the forecasts themselves. It's really not rocket science, trust me."

I closed my eyes, my head spinning. I didn't know what to say—what to do.

"What's wrong?" Asher asked, looking concerned. "I thought you'd be pleased."

I exhaled. I was pleased. I was so pleased. Thrilled, in fact. This was an opportunity of a lifetime. A big FU to everyone in the newsroom.

But did I deserve it? Or was this just Asher taking pity on me? Feeling sorry for me and my pathetic life? Or . . . Suddenly his words from the wedding came raging back to me.

If I win, I want a date.

Oh God. Was this all just one big joke? An elaborate scheme to get in my pants? One big game by a guy who didn't have anything to lose?

And had it cost me the job I really did deserve?

Rage flooded through me all over again as my mind treated me to a play-by-play of how it must have gone down. Asher cornering Richard at the wedding after I had left, asking about the job I'd told him I'd wanted. Telling Richard to give it to someone else—because he had other plans for me.

That bastard. That total fucking bastard.

"That was my job!" I screamed at Asher, not caring if anyone outside in the newsroom could hear. "Mine! You had no right to—"

"Uh, Piper? Richard wanted me to find you?"

I whirled around, shocked to see none other than Anna Jenkins herself, hovering in the office doorway. She gave me a worried look. "Sorry, I didn't mean to interrupt."

I closed my eyes, then opened them again, a vain attempt to restore my sanity. "It's fine. Thank you. Tell him I'll be right there."

Anna nodded and shut the door behind her. I could feel Asher's eyes on me, watching, waiting. I turned to look at him, sucking in a breath.

"Piper . . ." he started, but I held up my hand.

"No," I said. "Just no."

And with that, I headed out of the room, my legs feeling wooden as I crossed the newsroom to Richard's office. When I reached it, I slumped down in the chair across from his desk, feeling completely defeated. It was funny how a day that had started so well—with so much potential and excitement—had gone downhill so fast. Story of my life, I supposed.

"What's wrong?" Richard asked, eyeing me up and down from his seat behind his desk. "You look like someone ran over your pet puppy."

I sucked in a breath, trying to calm my voice. Whatever happened, I couldn't cry. I couldn't let him know my upset. I had to be professional, even if Asher refused to be.

"The morning writer job," I managed to say. "I had hoped . . ." I bit my lower lip. "I had hoped that Gary would give it to me. It usually goes to the most senior production assistant and I've been here months longer than Anna. And I've been writing a lot of scripts in practice." I trailed off, knowing I was protesting too much. But what else could I say? *I know you gave it to Anna because Asher asked you to. And you can't exactly go against the wishes of the station's golden son.* That wouldn't exactly go over too well.

"Piper, no one doubts your qualifications," Richard said in a comforting voice. "You've been a great employee since you've been here. Gary says you're professional, you come in on time, you do your work without complaining, and you put in overtime whenever we ask. But a far better opportunity has come up."

"Yeah, I know. The weather producer job. It's funny I never saw that one posted on the job boards," I said, not able to help the sarcastic note in my voice.

Richard studied me for a moment, then he sighed. "Piper, close the door, please," he said.

I reluctantly got to my feet and walked over to the door, shutting it behind me like a scolded child. I didn't know exactly what he was going to say next, but I was pretty sure it wouldn't be good.

When I returned to my seat, Richard leveled his eyes on me. "Look, I'm going to give it to you straight. Asher is very important to our station. In addition to his mom owning the place, his father was a legend and Asher needs to continue to follow in his footsteps. He's a legacy. A golden boy. And he's very good for the ratings," Richard added with a small snort. "Especially amongst the female demo, if you know what I mean."

Oh, I knew what he meant all right. Unfortunately all too well.

I sighed. "Yeah, but—"

But Richard wasn't finished. "Problem is, Asher isn't exactly the kind of guy who appreciates the good old nine-to-five. He tends to . . . wander. Or show up late. Or some days not at all. And that's been proving difficult when it comes to putting on a newscast." He made a face. "Anyone else? We would have fired them a year ago. But we can't fire Asher."

I rolled my eyes. "Must be nice to have that kind of job security."

Richard held up a hand. "Don't get me wrong. Asher's a great guy. And he's a really talented meteorologist like his father. If he put his mind to his work, I know he would be amazing. But getting him to focus . . ." He gave me a know-ing look. "Anyway, that's where you come in."

"As his producer," I concluded.

"Yes."

"And this was his idea?"

"*You* were his idea. I've been trying to give him a pro-ducer for two years now. His mother has, too. She's at her wits' end with him. But up until today he's refused everyone we've offered him—even really top candidates," Richard continued. "So imagine my surprise when I'm sitting in my office, offering Anna Jenkins a writing position, and he bursts in and asks for you."

Wait, what? I stared at him, jaw practically on the floor

as I digested what he'd just said. Not the part about Asher asking for me to be his producer. But the part where Richard was already giving Anna my job before Asher even came in.

No. Not my job. I sank back into my chair. *Her* job. It had never been mine to begin with. And if Asher hadn't stepped in . . .

Shit. Shit, shit, shit.

Richard's eyes zeroed in on me. "Look, Piper, I'm not going to lie. You'd be employed as a producer. You'd get paid as a producer. But in reality, you take this job and you're going to be doing a lot of babysitting. Asher's not easy to work with and it'll be a thankless job. And probably frustrating as hell." He shuddered a little, as if thinking about his own encounters with the guy. "Asher is going to do what he wants, when he wants to do it. And most times you'll just be playing catch-up."

I swallowed hard. "And if he changes his mind? If he decides he doesn't want me after all?"

Richard didn't answer at first, staring down at the papers on his desk. "Let's just hope we never need to discuss that," he said at last.

My heart sank a little in my chest. Not that I hadn't figured that to be his answer. Asher could get rid of me as easily as he had brought me on. No skin off his back. No big deal.

"I don't know . . ." I hedged. "Doesn't sound like much in the way of job security . . ."

"Maybe not," Richard agreed. "But it pays forty a year."

I stared at him, trying to keep my jaw off the floor. Forty thousand a year? Holy crap. Was he serious?

For forty a year I could keep my apartment. I wouldn't even need a roommate anymore. I could get my mom out of that crime scene of a trailer park and move her somewhere safe. Heck, I might even get to see a dentist once a year.

Forty thousand a year. To be someone's babysitter and pad my resume in the process? Yes, freaking please.

"I'll take it," I blurted out. Because really, what choice did I have?

Richard smiled. He held out his hand. "All right then," he said. "Guess Asher has himself a producer." We shook and he rose to his feet, escorting me out the door. "Congratulations," he said as I stepped across the threshold. "And good luck."

And as I walked away I could hear him mutter, just before he shut the door, "You're going to need it."

six

ASHER

We need to talk."

I looked up to see Piper enter the weather center, a frown pasted on her freckled face. I stifled a groan.

Here we go again.

Seriously, I was already regretting sticking out my nose to help her. Once again stepping in and playing knight in shining armor to an unwilling damsel in distress. A role that we'd already established was totally not me.

Also, it was one thing to come to her rescue at a wedding. Quite another to tether myself to her long term. After all, I'd spent the last two years trying to convince Richard and my mother that I didn't need a producer. And then here I was, going and actually offering them the perfect candidate on a silver platter. Hell, I might as well have walked into the news director's office and slapped my balls down on his desk, asking to be snipped like some horny dog. Stuck my neck out, begging for a leash and a collar.

"Hey, Red," I said, trying to keep my voice light and casual as, at the same time, I attempted to keep my eyes from raking over her body from head to toe. I had to admit, she may have been a leash, but goddamn was she a good-looking one. Even without the slinky bridesmaid's dress that I couldn't get out of my head all last night.

Truth be told, Piper was a far cry from my normal "type"— which usually consisted of waifish California blondes with daddy issues and big fake boobs. At the same time, she was also a convincing argument that my normal type was vastly overrated.

Case in point, today she was wearing a boxy suit that seemed to be working overtime to hide those soft curves of hers. But damn if my memory didn't fill in the blanks just the same. After all, a visual like yesterday's dress didn't just fade away overnight.

And then there were those windblown copper curls of hers, now constrained with an elastic band on top of her head. It was all I could do not to cross the room and tug on that band, freeing them to tumble down her back in the soft waves I remembered from the wedding.

But the expression on her face stopped me from making that mistake. Her brown eyes, flashing fire, her luscious pink mouth set in a distinct frown.

"Don't call me Red," she snapped at me. "My name is Piper and if we're going to be coworkers we need to start acting professional around one another."

A smile crept to my lips. Her ferocity was adorable to say the least. "So does that mean you took the job?" I asked, unable to keep the teasing lilt out of my voice this time.

"Of course I did," she growled, giving me an annoyed scowl. As if she were having a hard time admitting defeat. "What choice did I have?" she added, turning away and biting her lower lip in a way that was way too sexy to be work appropriate. "And . . . thank you," she muttered.

"I'm sorry?" I raised an eyebrow. "I didn't catch that last part."

She glared at me and I had to stifle a laugh. "Thank you," she repeated louder. She closed her eyes for a moment, then sighed heavily. "And I'm sorry about before. I just thought . . . I mean, I assumed . . ." She trailed off, looking miserable.

"You thought I sabotaged your chance to get the other job so I could have you all to myself," I concluded. "Aw, Red. That's so sweet. But sadly not true."

She nodded stiffly, scrubbing her face with her hands. "I know. I gathered that," she said in a quiet, almost defeated voice. "God, I feel like such an idiot."

The smirk slid from my face. I walked over and sat down next to her, putting an arm around her shoulder. The gesture was instinctual and was only meant to be friendly, but she stiffened under my touch all the same. I held up my hands in apology and scooted the chair backward to give her space.

"You're not an idiot," I told her in a firm voice. "They are. I don't know you very well, but you're clearly a hard, dedicated worker. And a good writer, too. They should have been begging you to take that crappy overnight job."

She looked up at me, her eyes a bit red. "How do you know I'm a good writer?" she spit out, still sounding angry. "Just from that stupid speech?"

"The speech was good," I assured her with a small smile. "But your scripts are much better."

She stared at me. I grinned, enjoying her shocked expression. "What? They were all on the server. Those dummy scripts you wrote for Gary? I logged in last night after the wedding and read through them."

"You . . . did?" she said, her eyes wide and astounded. "You read my scripts?"

"What did you think? I made you a producer out of pity? Not a chance. I had to make sure you'd make me look good on air before I took you on. I have a reputation to uphold, you know." I waggled my eyebrows at her, smiling.

The look on her face, the relief in her eyes, tore at something inside of me. I swallowed hard, forcing myself to continue. "The truth is, Richard has been after me about a producer for a long time now. My mom, too. And if I'm going to be forced to have one anyway, I want it to be someone I picked, not them. And so I picked you. Not because I felt sorry for you—trust me, I am way too much of a selfish bastard for that—ask anyone here.

"I picked you because, well, to be completely frank, I think you want it more than anyone else here. I saw the look in your eyes when you talked about that promotion back at the wedding. That passion, that hunger." I trailed off, my eyes drifting to the framed photo of my father hanging on the wall above my desk. My mind flashed back to the days when I had felt that passion, too. That pride of following in his footsteps.

Until I'd learned the truth.

I could feel Piper watching me with curious eyes. I shook my head, pushing the memories away before turning to face her again. "Look, I don't want you to feel as if you have no choice but to work with me. If you want, I'll go down to Richard right now and tell him I've changed my mind. I'll take Anna Jenkins as my producer and you can have the job you originally wanted."

She froze, staring up at me, an astonished look on her face. "You'd . . . do that?" she asked, her voice barely more than a whisper.

I nodded. "I wouldn't want to, though," I added, quickly. "I mean, no offense, but this Anna chick seems like a bit of a ditz. But I would. If it was what you wanted." I met her eyes with my own. "You've worked hard, Piper. You deserve to get what you want."

She dropped her gaze to her lap, staring down at her hands. She wrung them together and I could practically see the gears in her head whirring. I held my breath, waiting for her reply as the silence stretched out between us.

Finally she looked up. She met my eyes with her own— large and endless pools of dark chocolate, full of gratitude, excitement, and a bit of fear. I bit my lower lip, forcing myself to keep her gaze.

"I guess the real question is," I said slowly, "how do you feel about fish tacos at seven AM?"

Piper laughed, screwing up her face, and the tension broke between us. "Um, yeah. That would be a definite ew."

"Well, then." I shrugged. "I think you have your answer."

She groaned, holding out her hands in defeat. "I guess I

do." Then she shook her head. "Do you always get your way, Asher Anderson?" she asked, but I caught a twinkle in her eye as she asked. And it sent a flurry of excitement straight through me. Excitement I admittedly hadn't felt for a very long time.

I winked at her. "Only on days that end in *Y*."

seven

PIPER

Y ou know, honey, for a girl who got almost no sleep last
night, you're looking awfully bright-eyed and bushy-
tailed this afternoon."

I flashed Toby, the night manager at the Holloway House,
an excited smile as I walked into the front office and reached
to grab my time card from the stack on the wall. I punched
the clock, then put the time card back with the others before
walking over to sit down next to her. She observed me for
a moment.

"Does this mean what I think it means?" she asked
cautiously.

"Well, not exactly," I hedged. "I didn't get the writer's
job I was after."

"Oh, honey—"

"But!" I interrupted, holding up a hand, "I did get something else. Something . . . a lot better actually. A producer
position. For the weather center." I grinned. "It's full time,
too. And has health benefits and 401(k), vacation days—the
works!"

"Wow." Toby gave a low whistle. "Sounds pretty fancy.

Not that you won't be up to the challenge, I know." She gave me a toothy grin. "It's about time the people at that place recognized your brilliance, sweetie. It won't be long now until I can brag that I knew you when."

I felt a blush creep to my cheeks. Toby did, indeed, know me when. In fact, she'd known me from the very beginning and had been like a second mother to me after social services had dumped me here as a child. She'd been the one to take me under her wing when I'd first arrived at the Holloway House, skinny and scarred and scared of my own shadow. She'd even worked it out that I could have my own room for the first two months, until I got settled in. And she'd always sneak me special treats from the kitchen after hours, informing me she'd made it her life's work to "fatten me up."

Toby had also been the one to encourage me to pursue my interest in journalism. To take summer classes in high school, to apply for the school newspaper editor job in college. Without her influence I had no idea where I would have landed. Wherever it was, I was guessing "You want fries with that?" would have been part of my daily vocabulary.

"I'm pretty psyched," I admitted, happy to be able to show my true enthusiasm at last. I hadn't wanted to say too much in front of Asher. I still didn't like the idea of him swooping in and saving my career and I wished I could have gotten the job completely on my own. The randomness of the opportunity bothered me, too; what if Beth had chosen someone else as her maid of honor instead? Would she have been Asher's producer now? Would I still be stuck in production assistant hell, sick about being passed over for promotion yet again?

But I knew better than to say any of that in front of Toby. The woman had no tolerance for that kind of "woe is me" bullshit. Things happened for a reason, she always liked to say. And one didn't look a gift horse in the mouth. Or bite off your nose to spite your face, for that matter—which I had almost managed to do earlier that day. In Toby's world, if something good happens? You celebrate it. You appreciate the crap out of it. No matter how it came to pass. After all, life didn't hand people like us many gifts. And we weren't rich enough to refuse the ones it did out of some sense of stupid pride.

Besides, at the end of the day, I did deserve the job. Okay, maybe not this particular job—but a good job nonetheless. As Asher had reminded me, I worked hard. I stayed focused. I did everything right. Why shouldn't I reap the rewards? Someone had to—it might as well be me.

"So, superstar," Toby teased, "does this mean we're losing you for good?"

I smiled at her. I knew if I said yes, she would have been completely supportive of my decision. But I also knew how much she needed me to stay. The Holloway House had a shoestring budget, mostly funded by private grants, and they couldn't afford to hire enough qualified candidates to support the amount of kids that came through the doors. So many helpless kids. Kids just like I had been, back in the day.

"Nah," I said, waving her off. "I may have to switch around some of my hours, but you're not getting rid of me that easy."

Her face shone with relief, but her mouth stayed grave. "Are you sure, honey?" she asked. "I mean, a new job like this is going to have a lot of pressures attached. And you're going to want to be able to give it your all. I don't want you to feel conflicted. Like you're being pulled in two different directions. You've worked so hard to get here—you need to give yourself a chance to succeed."

I gave her a rueful smile. I knew she wasn't wrong. And with my new salary I no longer had to work two jobs to make ends meet. But at the same time there was no way I was just going to walk out on her and the kids now.

"I'm sure," I told her. "Now, tell me what needs to be done."

As usual she didn't hesitate with an answer. There was always something that needed to be done here and never enough hands to do it. "You can go check on Jayden," she told me. "He's having a rough day. Shut himself up in his room again."

"What happened?" I asked worriedly.

Toby gave a small shrug. "I think his mother called him. You know how he gets after hearing from her. He refuses to talk to anyone. Wouldn't come down for lunch either."

I sighed. Ten-year-old Jayden had been at the Holloway House for three years now and he was one of my favorites, even if most of the other staff couldn't stomach him. I didn't blame them—not really. Even when he was in a good mood he could be standoffish. When he was pissed off he could be downright violent. But it wasn't his fault. His records showed he'd been born to a heroin-addicted mother who had used drugs during her pregnancy. At one day old, the kid was already going through withdrawal and at one week Mom had been sent back to prison. His father's parents took him in for a bit and when they couldn't take him anymore, he bounced around from relative to relative for a few years. Finally, at age seven, he'd been dumped here. Where he would likely remain until he became legal. If he lasted that long.

"Can I take him some cake?" I asked, remembering the leftovers in the fridge from Toby's birthday celebration earlier in the week.

Toby snorted. "You spoil him," she scolded. But she smiled when she said it and I knew that was a yes. After all, she'd been the first to spoil me back in the day, and she knew she didn't have much of a leg to stand on.

After raiding the refrigerator, I headed upstairs, taking a left at the landing and stopping in front of his door. Balancing the cake in my left hand, I knocked with my right. There were no locks on the doors at Holloway, but I liked to give the kids some semblance of privacy anyway. I remembered, after all, how it had felt to live here, surrounded by so many people all the time, never having that feeling of personal space.

"Go away," came the voice from the other side of the door.

"Jayden, it's me," I called to him. "And I've got something I'm pretty sure you want."

The resounding silence spread out so long that I started

wondering if I'd need to come back later. I didn't want to force him to socialize if he wasn't ready, though I was pretty sure it would help if he did. But just as I was about to walk away, the door opened—just a sliver.

"What do you have?" Jayden demanded, sounding both suspicious and curious at the same time.

"Let me in and I'll show you."

He sighed loudly, but, to my relief, opened the door. I stepped inside his room, frowning as I did. It was trashed. Chairs knocked over, clothes ripped from the dresser, a shattered photo on the floor. My brow furrowed. Where did he even get a photo like that? Glass picture frames were contraband here—for obvious reasons.

He looked around the room, his cheeks coloring. Obviously embarrassed at the aftereffects of his tantrum. Then he turned back to me, giving me a defiant look, as if daring me to say something about it. To scold him. To tell him he was no good. Just as people had been telling him his entire life.

Just as people had once told me.

And so, instead, I ignored the mess. I held out the slice of cake. I watched as his eyes widened a little before he turned away.

"I'm not hungry," he growled.

"I was hoping you'd say that," I replied, not missing a beat. I reached down to right a chair so I could sit. "I'm starving myself." I set the cake on the nightstand and stabbed it with my fork. "Have you had any of this?" I asked. "It's, like, the best cake ever."

He shrugged, but I could see his eyes traveling back to the cake in question. He shuffled from foot to foot. I ignored him, taking a big bite, groaning in pleasure as the sugar hit my taste buds. I wasn't exaggerating to get him to eat—not entirely anyway. This cake was truly fabulous.

"I was so glad when I came in and saw there was some left," I continued, my mouth full of icing. "I missed the cake at the wedding I went to yesterday, since I had to leave early."

He slumped down on the bed. "Why'd you have to leave

early?" he asked, sounding curious despite his best intentions to stay aloof. Which was what I'd been counting on when I'd sat down. Jayden was a naturally inquisitive kid—something I loved about him. Even if he'd been told to shut up too many times in his young life.

"My mother," I told him, rolling my eyes for effect. "She needed me to go buy her some groceries."

Jayden looked offended on my behalf. "What, she got a broken leg or somethin'?"

I shrugged. "Or something."

He let out a puff of disgust. "Your mom sounds like mine."

I stopped eating, setting down my fork. *And here we go.*

"I heard she called," I said quietly.

He stared down at his hands, his face twisting. For a moment I thought I might have pushed too far too fast and he wasn't going to answer me. But at last he spoke.

"Yeah. She called this morning." He paused then added, "Told me she was moving."

"Moving?"

"I don't know. I guess she's got some new boyfriend. And she's pregnant. They're going to move to Vegas. His brother has a place there or something."

My heart squeezed at the anguish I saw on his face. Anguish he was clearly trying to hide. "Let me guess," I said, keeping my voice soft and nonjudgmental, "she wouldn't take you with them."

"No . . . yeah . . . I mean, I didn't want to go anyway," Jayden protested, rising back to his feet. "Her new boyfriend's stupid. And I bet the place they're going to sucks."

I gave him a rueful smile. "I know. But she's your mom. It's understandable that you want to be with her."

He shook his head, pacing the room like a caged tiger, his steps eating up the distance between the walls. "I just thought she might need my help, you know? With the new baby," he added, now seeming unable to stop the words from tumbling from his mouth. "I know how to change diapers from being here. And I could, like, watch him while she was at work or whatever. I don't know. He's my brother, right? My baby brother."

His voice broke and he trailed off. I rose from my seat and walked over to him. I held out my arms and he fell into them, burying his face in my chest.

"She said I couldn't come," he said mournfully. "She said there's no room. That his brother's place is small. Just one room for the two of them. The three of them once my brother comes. But no room for me."

"I'm so sorry, Jayden," I whispered, stroking his hair. "I know how much that must hurt."

"It doesn't hurt," he cried, jerking away. "Like I said, I didn't want to go anyway."

"I know," I assured him, giving him his space. "Trust me, I understand."

He shot me a scowl, as if saying that couldn't possibly be true. But it was true. Truer than he could ever imagine.

I stared down at my hands. I didn't like talking about my past. It still hurt, even so many years later. But Jayden was hurting, too. And he needed to understand he wasn't alone.

"One day, when I was about your age, my mom came to me," I began, feeling the all-too-familiar ache rise to my throat at the memory. "She'd just been released from prison a few months before and we had finally been reunited. I was so happy, let me tell you, to be a family again."

I looked up to make sure Jayden was listening. He was watching me with a cautious expression on his face. I drew in a breath and continued.

"Anyway, she says, 'Piper, we're going to your grand-mother's house for the weekend.' Told me to pack a bag, bring a couple of toys," I told him. "But," I added, "I didn't pack any toys. I packed my best pajamas. The ones Grandma had given me two years before, the last time I had seen her." I paused, then added, "They didn't really fit so well anymore. But I wanted Grandma to see how well I'd taken care of them. I thought maybe if she saw that she'd buy me a new pair."

"Did she?"

I shook my head. "We never got to Grandma's," I told him. "I don't know if plans changed or that was just my mom's story to get me packed and in the car. In any case, she drove me straight here and dropped me off at the front door. She had some story—like she was going to go pick up her boyfriend and that she'd be right back. But I knew. Somehow, as I watched her drive away, I knew she wasn't coming back this time. That she'd dumped me here yet again." I gave him a rueful look. "And man, did I wish then I'd packed some freaking toys."

My voice cracked. I stared down at my feet, the memories coming hard and fast. The disappointment I'd felt. The hopelessness. The knowledge that my own mother didn't want me around.

And why would she? Because of me, she'd lost her precious Michael. And even today I wondered, when she looked at me, if she still saw his face. If she didn't need me so much—or at least need my paychecks—would she even want me to come around? Or would she have banished me from her life long ago?

Lost in my troubled thoughts I almost didn't feel the hand on my arm. I looked up to see that Jayden had come to stand next to me, a concerned look on his face. It was funny—here I'd been trying to comfort him. And now he was turning the tables on me. "But she did come back, right?" he asked. "I mean, you just brought her groceries yesterday."

"Yeah," I said. "She did. Years later. But it was never the same. From that point on I felt like I couldn't trust her anymore. That I couldn't trust anyone at all."

"Except me!" Jayden broke in. "Miss Piper, you can totally count on me!"

I looked up at him through eyes veiled with tears. He looked so fierce. So protective. So affronted on my behalf. I smiled at him.

"Thank you, Jayden," I said. "I hope that you feel the same way about me."

He threw his arms around me and I hugged him tight. For a moment we just stayed like that, holding one another, both lost in our own memories. His raw and fresh, mine old and scarred, but no less painful. Finally Jayden broke away.

"Thanks," he said, looking a little sheepish. "And I'm sorry I trashed my room."

"Meh," I said, waving a dismissive hand. "If we work together we can clean it up quick. And then I'm going to finish that cake!"

"Wait!" he protested. "What about me?"

I gave him a skeptical look. "I thought you said you weren't hungry."

"Well . . ." He shrugged. "Maybe a little."

I pushed the cake in his direction. "Eat it," I told him. "And then start picking up. I'll go forage for a second slice. I think we both deserve our own, don't you?"

He grinned. "Absolutely."

eight

PIPER

'd love to say the little heart-to-heart with Jayden turned out to be therapeutic for me as well as him. But that would be a lie. That night I tossed and turned, the nightmares tormenting me without mercy. Nightmares of me, splashing through dark waters, desperately scanning the sea. Of frantically searching, but never finding. Of the icy waves, smacking against my skin, soaking my clothes. Of my mother's voice, screeching in my ears.

You horrible girl.

This is your fault.

You were supposed to be watching him.

I trusted you to watch him.

Where's your brother, Piper?

Where's your fucking brother?

I jerked up in bed, bathed in sweat. Sucking in a breath, I reached for the light, trying to still my pounding heart. Screw it. I'd rather be exhausted at work tomorrow than tortured in my sleep tonight.

After doing a few breathing exercises, trying to catch my breath, I grabbed my laptop off my nightstand and, after checking my email, loaded it up to the National Weather Service website. Why not, right? After all, I was going to need this stuff once I started my new job tomorrow.

I read through some of their forecasts and climate predictions. Then I clicked over to the NOAA website—the home of the National Oceanic and Atmospheric Administration—and I kept going from there.

Some of it was easy to understand. Other parts felt like Greek, which made me feel a little nervous about my upcoming assignment. Was I really going to be able to do this? To just become a weather producer with no experience at all? Asher said it wasn't rocket science, but then he'd been born into the job. He'd probably learned half of it before he could even walk, listening to his father. I, on the other hand, would be starting at ground zero.

But you can do this, I told myself. *You've faced challenges before. And you've always met them head-on. Why should this be any different?*

I glanced over at the motivational sign I'd placed to the side of my bed. *What would you attempt to do,* it read, *if you knew you could not fail?*

I closed my laptop. I settled back in bed. I forced myself to close my eyes and think about my new job. But surprisingly, instead of radars and weather charts, my mind kept wandering to something else.

Namely the guy who reported on them.

The really, really hot guy who was basically now my new boss.

Or should I say new partner? After all, normally a producer would be considered more of a partner than a subordinate to her reporter. But clearly Asher held all the strings in this particular scenario. I thought back to our encounter in the newsroom office when he'd first told me about the job. Where I had basically accused him of sabotaging the position I thought I was supposed to get. I was lucky he hadn't changed his mind right then and there and said forget it.

Still, the question lingered. Had he really promoted me because he thought I could do the job better than anyone else there? Or was it just a pity play he'd made on impulse after seeing my desperation at the wedding? Or, a more troubling thought: Could this just be an elaborate ploy for him to get me into bed?

Don't flatter yourself, Piper. This guy has women lining up for him. He doesn't need a casting couch.

But he *did* need a producer. A good one, according to Richard. Someone to keep him in line. Someone who was responsible and dedicated and good with details.

Someone like me.

I may not have known anything about weather. But I did know something about making irresponsible people accountable for their actions. After all, hadn't I done that for years with my own mother? Not that she wasn't still a frustrating work in progress. But she had a job now. A home. And it was all thanks to me.

Asher said he had chosen me because I wanted it more than anyone else. He hadn't been wrong about that. However it had happened, this was a chance of a lifetime and I was planning on taking full advantage.

One way or another I would prove to them all that even if I hadn't deserved to be given the job in the first place, I deserved to keep it. And no one—not even Asher himself—would be able to stop me.

nine

ASHER

Bang, bang, bang!

I groaned, pulling my pillow over my head as the incessant rapping bore into my brain. What was that? Was someone at my door? I peeked out from under the pillow, squinting at the early morning sunlight peering through my window from the gap in my blackout blinds. What the hell time was it anyway?

I'd admittedly stayed up way too late the night before, hanging with Jess and her bartender girlfriend at their new place in Mission Beach, watching them do tequila shots until nearly sunrise. I hadn't set my alarm on purpose, wanting to sleep it off before heading into work. Sure, I was technically supposed to be at work at nine, but I had done most of the prep the night before and figured I could just update last minute before going on air. Wouldn't be the first time. Wouldn't be the last.

Bang, bang, bang.

I scowled. Who the hell was at my door? And why weren't they taking the hint and going away? I mean, sure, Jess sometimes stopped by to use my house as her changing room before heading out into the surf (usually bringing donuts and coffee as payment) but the two of us had a deal: She would never try to wake me, even if she wanted me to come with her. She'd just leave a note as to where she'd be and I'd find her later.

Besides that, there was no way she'd be awake right now after the amount of tequila she'd poured down her gullet the night before.

"Asher? Are you in there?"

The voice sounded vaguely familiar, though I couldn't quite place it in my half-asleep state. Definitely female. Slightly irritated, but kind of cute all the same. Maybe some chick I'd hooked up with and then never called, returning to boil my bunny? But no, I usually talked them into going to their houses or booked a hotel in order to preemptively sidestep that type of fatal attraction.

Eventually curiosity won out over exhaustion and I swung my legs over the side of the bed and planted my feet on the tile. I grabbed a pair of boxer briefs from off the floor and slipped them over my hips before heading to the door, yanking it open to see who could possibly be on the other side.

I couldn't have been more surprised at who it turned out to be.

"Piper?" I said, now more confused than ever. I scrubbed my face, trying desperately to clear the fog in my head. "What are you doing here?"

She frowned. "I think the better question would be, what are *you* doing here?"

"Um, I live here?"

My gaze involuntarily raked over her, taking her in. She was dressed casually this morning in a simple button-down shirt and a pair of dark-rinse jeans that nicely showcased the swell of her hips. Even better, her hair had been set free from yesterday's constraints, copper curls bouncing off her shoulders. And while she didn't seem to be wearing any makeup, her face looked freshly scrubbed and clean.

In other words, total girl-next-door hotness. And though usually the girl-next-door look was not my type at all, I was suddenly quite willing to make an exception. In fact, it was all I could do not to toss her over my shoulder like a sack of potatoes and drag her back to bed with me, caveman-style.

Now *that* would be something worth waking up for.

I realized she was frowning at me. "What?" I asked.

"Do you have any idea what time it is?"

I glanced behind her, squinting at the sunlight. It was a trick my dad had taught me when I was a kid. How to tell time by the position of the sun in the sky, compared to the month of the year.

"Ten thirty," I guessed.

"Try eleven."

I shrugged. It had never been an exact science. "Okay. And that's relevant because?"

"It's a workday. And you didn't show up to work. Nor did you answer your phone." Her eyes locked on to mine. "I just wanted to make sure you were okay."

"Aw, Red," I said, giving her a smirk. "That's so sweet! You came all the way out here just to check up on me?" I wondered briefly how she'd figured out where I lived, but then remembered the employee directory. She was a resourceful one, my little producer.

Also, an angry one, it appeared.

Sure enough, a scowl slashed across her face. "I came here," she corrected in a hard voice, "to drag your ass to work. Where you are supposed to be. Now"—her gaze roved over my body—"if you could just go and get dressed?"

I grinned lazily, leaning against the doorframe, pretty happy now I hadn't bothered with a shirt. "You know, Red, you might be the very first girl in history to demand I put my clothes back *on*."

As I could have predicted, her face turned bright red. God, I loved redheads. I watched as she turned away, concentrating on staring at the flowers in my front garden. "I'll wait here until you're ready," she said.

"But I haven't even eaten my breakfast yet!"

"I'll swing you through a drive-through."

I shook my head. "Asher Anderson does not do drive-throughs, sweetheart."

I watched her bite her lower lip in frustration. God, the girl had kissable lips. I involuntarily licked my own lower lip, imagining what she must taste like.

"Look," I said, deciding to throw her a bone, "I'm sorry. You caught me off guard. Late night, you know? How about I make you a deal? You come in and let me make both of us some breakfast. Then, once we're done eating, we can head out to the station together. I'll even let you drive me, to ensure I don't try to make a run for the border."

She frowned, but I could see her hedging. "We're supposed to be there now."

"Please. We're not on the air till six. That gives us hours to eat and still make the broadcast." I shrugged. "Besides, if we're going to be working together, we should definitely spend time getting to know one another, right? And there's no better way to make friends than over a mountain of scrambled eggs. Which," I added with a wink, "just happen to be my specialty."

Piper let out a resigned sigh. "Fine," she muttered. "But only if you get dressed first."

"Spoilsport," I mock pouted. She shot me a dirty look.

"Okay, okay." I held up my hands in surrender. "Your wish is my command." I stepped out of the doorway and gestured grandly for her to enter. "Welcome to my sea palace, m'lady."

Piper gave me a skeptical look. "If you're about to say *where all the magic happens* I'm going to wait in the car."

I burst out laughing—I couldn't help it. "No magic, I promise!" I said with a grin. "Just scrambled eggs. Magically delicious scrambled eggs."

She rolled her eyes. "I can't wait."

And suddenly, neither could I.

ten

PIPER

Okay, Piper. What the hell do you think you're doing?
    I paced Asher's living room, getting more and more stressed out with every step. What was I doing here? What had possessed me to come here in the first place? And why the hell had I agreed to stay for breakfast, for goodness's sake?

I knew I should have just waited for him at the station. Hung out until he rolled in with his usual happy-go-lucky style. But when he hadn't shown up—on our very first official day of working together—I'd been a little pissed, to say the least. Especially when the six o'clock show producer stopped by and asked where he was, then looked at me as if I were to blame when I said I didn't know.

Richard had warned me that it would be like a glorified babysitting job. But I guess I hadn't truly believed it. Not when Asher had been so enthusiastic yesterday about the whole thing. I guess I thought maybe this was a step for him—to start taking his job more seriously. Or that he would at the very least shepherd me through the first couple weeks, until I got my feet wet and could do my part of the job in his absence. He knew I knew nothing about weather producing. The very least he could do was show me the ropes before throwing me in the deep end.

I scowled. I hadn't asked for this job. But since I had it, I was going to make the best of it. I had one chance to prove myself. To make the powers-that-be see I belonged there. And I wasn't about to let some spoiled, irresponsible little rich boy ruin it for me. If I was to be Asher's producer, Asher was going to get in line, if it killed me.

And if I had to witness him wearing nothing but a pair of boxer briefs again, it just might.

I groaned, plopping down on the couch, scrubbing my face with my hands as my mind treated me to a detailed flashback of him answering the door. Of his legendary washboard abs that I'd always heard about, but had never seen up close and personal. It was as if he had been sculpted out of marble—like one of those statues you see in museums. Perfect pecs with golden nipples, a solid six-pack, probably honed by all the surfing. A trail of light brown hair, disappearing into those boxer briefs.

Sweet baby Jesus. Those boxer briefs.

Get your mind out of the gutter, Piper, I scolded myself. *This is your boss, not your boyfriend.*

My boss—who had just somehow managed to convince me to come into his house and let him make me breakfast. This slope was getting slippery—fast. And I wasn't sure what to do about it.

At least he hadn't kicked me to the curb. I knew that was a risk when I'd shown up to his house to begin with. I mean, the guy was obviously not used to anyone giving him orders. He did what he wanted, when he wanted, and there was never any consequence to any of it. He could have told me to get off his front porch. He could have called the station and gotten me fired on the spot for overstepping my bounds. Instead, he'd invited me in. He'd suggested we get to know one another. That wasn't a bad thing, right? Baby steps, for both of us.

"Wow. I feel almost human again," Asher announced as

he stepped back into the living room. He'd showered and changed and was now wearing a tight white T-shirt that sadly did a very poor job of hiding those aforementioned abs, and a pair of board shorts that only managed to better showcase his tanned, rugged legs. His hair was still wet from the shower and drops of water glistened on his forehead.

Almost human, my ass. Effortlessly Greek God–like might be a better descriptor.

I rose to my feet. "Glad to hear it," I said, trying to sound casual, even though my heart was pounding in my chest. What was I doing here again? I should have just told him I'd meet him back at work. I was being paid, after all, to be at work. And instead I was hanging out at a beach cottage. I was following my new boss to the kitchen. I was walking over to the breakfast bar, trying not to check out his butt as he leaned down to pull a pan out from a drawer.

Okay, this had to stop. This was my new boss. My job depended on me staying professional. On getting him to take this whole thing seriously—take *me* seriously. If I allowed myself to go all girly girl on him, to succumb to his charms like the rest of the SoCal female population, I might as well just write my own pink slip now.

I watched, curious, as Asher opened the fridge and peered inside. I was surprised to see how full it was. For some reason I had imagined him as more of a takeout kind of guy. Instead it looked as if he had just returned from a farmer's market, with colorful, fresh produce on every shelf. Maybe he had a personal shopper to keep him stocked. Surely he could afford one.

He turned to me, a carton of eggs and a package of bacon in each hand. "Sit," he commanded.

I bit my lower lip. "I'm happy to help."

He smiled and shook his head, pointing again to the bar-stool. I sighed and walked over, scooting up onto it. Asher set the ingredients on the granite countertop and walked over to his coffee pot. He looked over at me and I nodded. He poured me a cup and set it in front of me.

"Cream and sugar?" he asked.

I shook my head. "This is perfect."

And it was kind of perfect, I had to admit, as I sipped my coffee and Asher got to work on the breakfast. I mean, by all rights it should have felt weird to be here—and pretty awkward to boot. To be in this man's kitchen, sipping coffee, while he worked on what was starting to look like quite the feast.

And yet, somehow, it felt good. Really chill. The coffee warming my insides, the faint strains of a Jack Johnson tune floating through the air. The smell of the eggs and the crackle of the bacon, making my mouth water.

I didn't usually eat breakfast; a habit I'd developed as a kid when we couldn't afford three meals a day. Even now it still seemed like a bit of a waste, an unnecessary indulgence. But obviously Asher could afford an indulgence or two and I might as well enjoy his hospitality. Especially since I was pretty sure he would allow nothing less.

"Bon appetit," he pronounced about ten minutes later, setting a steaming plate piled high with food in front of me. He placed his own plate on the counter across from me, leaning in on the granite. "Let me know what you think."

I nodded, scooping a large forkful of eggs into my mouth. Then I paused as the taste hit me full-on. *Oh my God, this is good.* A small moan of pleasure escaped my lips and Asher grinned like a schoolboy.

"You like?" he asked.

"I love," I corrected, staring down at the eggs. They looked completely normal. Like any other eggs on the planet. But that taste . . . "Seriously, what did you put in these? Crack?"

He waved me off. "I find crack a terrible seasoning. Not to mention a bit tricky to acquire. I usually substitute with pickled jalapeños instead."

I nodded, taking another bite, relishing the kick to my taste buds. Toby would love the hell out of these; I needed to convince Asher to give me the recipe next time it was my night to cook at the Holloway House.

I glanced up at him, marveling a little. Hot as hell, rich as anything, and a great cook, too. How was that even fair?

"So tell me, Piper," Asher said, after swallowing. Evidently it was time for the "getting acquainted" portion of the morning. "How did a nice girl like you who clearly has stellar taste when it comes to breakfast foods end up in a shitshow like News 9 San Diego?"

"What are you talking about? We're the number one news station," I protested.

"Sorry. A number one shitshow then."

I frowned, feeling a little insulted, though I wasn't exactly sure why. After all, it wasn't as if I took some kind of personal pride in News 9 as a station. And it wasn't even as if anyone had ever treated me particularly well since I'd started working there. But still! "Why do *you* work there?" I asked. "If it's so awful."

He raised an eyebrow, as if it were obvious. "I'm legacy, baby. Straight out of News 9 for life!" He twisted his arms in some kind of exaggerated made-up gang symbols. I snorted.

"I see . . ."

"Anyway, let me rephrase my question. How'd a nice girl like you end up at the lovely and popular grand institution that is known as News 9?"

I shrugged. "I don't know. I've always wanted to be a journalist, I guess."

Of course there was more to it than that. But he didn't need to know my whole white trash past, thank you very much. Someone like him would never understand.

"Let me guess," he said, tapping his finger to his chin. "You grew up watching Joy Justice at the anchor desk and said that's the glamorous life for me."

"Actually, I wanted to be an investigative producer. I mean, I still do."

"A producer? Not a reporter?"

"Let's just say I'm more of a behind-the-scenes kind of girl."

Asher laughed. "I don't blame you," he said. "Trust me, the on-air life is not all it's cracked up to be. All those hot girls, throwing themselves at you, begging for you to spend the night." He shook his head in mock horror.

"Aw, poor baby. It must be so tough for you."

He nodded grimly. "You don't know the half of it." Then he grinned. "Anyway, that sounds really cool. The investigative producer thing, I mean. From what I hear it's not an easy job. But I bet it's really interesting. I mean, you're basically solving crime, right? Like a superhero or something?"

I laughed. "I don't know about that!"

"Seriously," he insisted. "You're basically Batman at that point."

"Does that make you Robin?"

"Ouch!" Asher made a stabbing gesture to his heart, as if I had wounded him. "And here I thought you were going to say someone cool. Like the Joker."

"You're definitely a joker. There's no doubt about that."

He grinned wickedly. "Fair enough." Then he glanced at his watch. "Holy Bat Time, Batman. We'd better get to work!"

I looked up, surprised. "You're actually ready?"

"I might be." His eyes danced. "On one condition."

Uh-oh. "What's that?"

"You agree to go out with me after work. So we can continue this new coworker meet-and-greet."

I stared at him, not sure what to say. Did I want to continue this? And what was "this" really anyway? I mean, yes, I was having a good time. Good food, good company, friendly banter. But where did Asher see this going? Was he really only interested in getting to know his new coworker? Or was this all a front for him to make a move on me later on? After all, I knew all too well of his reputation. And I really didn't want to be that girl. My career depended on it.

"I don't know," I hedged.

"Come on," he cajoled. "I'm heading to work at Oh God Thirty for you. The least you can do is let me cook you dinner."

"But you already cooked me breakfast."

"And you enjoyed it, right?"

"I did but . . ."

"Trust me. These eggs have nothing on my carne guisada tacos."

This was clearly a losing battle. "If I say yes, you'll come to work now?"

"With bells on."

"And we'll work all day? No distractions?"

"Scout's honor."

I gave him a skeptical look. He laughed. "Okay, fine. I got kicked out of Scouts. Never did understand the point of the merit badges. But we will work our asses off, I promise."

I sighed. "Okay then. I guess you've got yourself a dinner guest."

And with that, the slippery slope I mentioned earlier? It was approaching full-on mudslide.

eleven

PIPER

Asher hadn't lied; we did work our asses off. Or at least I did as he showed me around the weather center and gave me a crash course in Weather 101. And while there was no way I was suddenly going to get my meteorology degree overnight, I did end the day with a better understanding of what went into a forecast and how that information got compiled. Turned out, a lot of it was just data mining from weather bureaus, satellites, and radars. Stuff I could gather myself then pass off to Asher, who could then turn it into a forecast to deliver on TV.

"A lot of stations don't even use actual meteorologists," he explained at one point. "Just weathermen."

"What's the difference?"

"Meteorologists are scientists. We study the atmosphere and examine its effects on the environment. We can predict weather and uncover larger climate trends," he explained. "Weathermen, on the other hand, simply read someone else's predictions on air. Pretty much anyone could do that with a few weeks' training. They just have to be good entertainers."

I nodded slowly, watching the Doppler radar swirl on the

monitor above us. "So you're, like, a real scientist. That's pretty cool."

"Trust me, it's not as impressive as it sounds. And I'm pretty sure I'm wrong in my predictions fifty percent of the time. If we weren't in San Diego, the land of sunshine and no rain, I'd probably have been out on my ass three years ago." He paused, then added, "Now my father on the other hand . . ."

He trailed off. I turned to him, curious. "He was good?" I asked.

"He was the best. He could predict a storm no one else saw coming. It was incredible. He could have worked for the National Weather Service if he had wanted to." Asher frowned, and I suddenly got the impression he disagreed with his dad's decision to stay local.

"Why did he stay here then?" I asked.

"For us, I guess," he replied. "My mom obviously couldn't move, not without selling the station, and that was not going to happen. So my dad was left with the choice. Either he could have left us and done the long distance thing or he could have stayed." He shrugged. "He chose to stay."

I watched his face closely. "You don't seem to approve."

He turned away from me. But not before I caught his eyes flashing something uncomfortable. "It's not my place to say. Everyone should make their own decisions about their careers, right?"

I raised an eyebrow. "Sure," I said. "Absolutely." But then I remembered what he had said earlier that day. About being a legacy. About being born to do his job. Had he been able to make his own decision? Or had he been forced into the family business, too?

Suddenly his reluctance to take his job seriously was making a little more sense.

"Well, your dad sounds like a great guy," I said. "And I know everyone loves him. I remember when he got into that car accident. It was like all of San Diego came together to support him through the tragedy."

Asher didn't reply, just nodded absently, and the

uncomfortable look on his face grew more intense. I cocked my head, puzzled. Was it just a tough memory for him? I mean, it had to be, right? The day he almost lost his father? But I thought there was something else, too, deep in his eyes. Something . . . angry. And . . . maybe a little hurt?

I decided not to press him, curious as I was. It wasn't my place to pry, after all. He was my coworker, nothing more. And if this was going to work, we had to keep our relationship professional. I didn't need to know his deep, dark family secrets. And he certainly would not be getting access to mine.

"So what does this thing do?" I asked, pointing to a monitor at the far end of the weather center.

He was all too happy to explain.

The day went by quickly and before I knew it, Asher was on the air, delivering his forecast for the six PM news. It was a typical San Diego forecast for this time of year. Temperatures in the mid seventies. Cooler at night. Residents liked to joke that people called it a heat wave when it went over seventy-five degrees—and a cold snap if it dropped under. As if blue skies and sunshine were considered a basic human right here in SoCal. And maybe they were.

By the end of the day, I was exhausted. Physically—from all my time pulling double-duty shifts at the station and the Holloway House—and mentally—from all the new work knowledge I'd crammed into my brain. I was sort of hoping Asher would let me off the hook for dinner—the idea of just crawling into my bed and watching eighties movies on Netflix while eating pizza delivery sounded pretty damn good right about now.

But, of course, that was just a fantasy. The second Asher got off set, he headed straight for me.

"You ready for that dinner, Batgirl?" he asked.

I groaned. "What if I begged for a bat check?"

"No way. We made a bat deal. I got to work early—"

"Um, you were still, like, three hours late."

"—and, in return, you agreed to let me take you to dinner."

"But I'm tired!"

He gave me a pointed look. "So was I when you woke me up."

Touché. I sighed, realizing I was once again going to lose.

"Besides," he added, "I made you look good today. Just look at Richard's face." He jerked his head to the side and I glanced over. Sure enough, the news director was standing there, across the newsroom, a big smile on his face. He caught my eye and gave me an enthusiastic thumbs-up.

"See?" Asher said. "He credits my presence here in the newsroom entirely to your awesomeness. That oughta be good for at least a three-course meal. Maybe four. After all, I've been pretty absent of late."

"Okay, okay." I held up my hands in defeat. "Dinner it is. But we have to do it now. I'm pretty sure by nine PM this Cinderella will turn back into a pumpkin. And trust me, it won't be pretty. Like drool in the corner of my mouth not pretty."

Asher's eyes danced with victory. "Fair enough," he agreed. "Do you want to meet me at my car in five?"

"I'll drive myself," I replied. "Then I can just leave your house when we're done eating and go home."

"Oh, we're not going to my house."

I cocked my head. "We aren't? But you said . . . ?"

"That I was a master cook with a carne guisada recipe to die for?"

I nodded.

"Yeah. That was a lie. Truth is, that jalapeño scramble is pretty much the only trick in my wheelhouse. Other than that, I can't boil water." He leaned down to the desk in front of him and scribbled something on a piece of paper, then pressed it into my hand. I looked down. It was an address for a place in Del Mar, a ritzy northern suburb on the beach.

"I'll see you there," he said, waggling his eyebrows at me before making a quick exit. Probably so I wouldn't have time to protest.

I sighed, then stuffed the piece of paper into my bag and

worked to gather the rest of my things before heading to my car.

Once I had gotten my stuff together, I stopped for a moment to look around the weather center. It was funny: When I'd walked in that morning, everything had seemed as if it belonged on some kind of alien spaceship. But now I could already identify a few of the radars and other monitors surrounding me. I also knew how to pull a forecast off the National Weather Center website and where I could gather information on incoming and outgoing tides.

I wasn't a meteorologist—not by a long shot. Hell, I wasn't even weathergirl caliber just yet. But it was a start. And a realization, too. That just like everything else in life that seemed out of reach, it was learnable, if you took it one step at a time. If you had a patient teacher.

Sure, I probably wasn't the most qualified person in the building to be given this job. But I was determined to prove that it hadn't been a mistake to give it to me. I would get Asher in line if it was the last thing I did. And I would become a great weather producer in the process. Then, if the worst were to happen, and he got sick of me and let me go, I would be able to parlay my new skills into a similar job at another station.

I would survive. As I always managed to do.

I got in my car and plugged the address he'd given me into my phone, then followed the GPS to the location listed. Del Mar was a little trek from where News 9 was located downtown and, as I sat in traffic, I wished I had asked Asher if we could have gone somewhere more local. But it was too late now.

As I grew closer to the destination, I felt a strange anticipation winding up inside of me. As tired as I was, I realized, I was also a little excited. Which was ridiculous, I knew. After all, this was just a meeting with my coworker. It certainly wasn't a date. Meaning there was no earthly reason I should have had butterflies dancing in my stomach at that moment. And my skin should certainly not have been humming with eagerness.

But all the logic in the world was lost on stomach and skin and no matter what I tried to do, I couldn't get either to chill the fuck out. To make matters worse, they eventually convinced my brain to join the party—by flashing me a visual of Asher this morning, clad in those damn boxer briefs of his.

Really, brain? Really? Aren't you supposed to be on my side here?

Finally, the GPS announced I had reached my destination. I looked up at the sign to see where it had taken me. My stomach sank.

The Del Mar Yacht Club.

Shit.

Of course Asher would take me here. This was exactly the kind of place a person like Asher would go. It was also exactly the opposite of the type of place that welcomed people like me. Especially people dressed like me. Let's just say I'd seen *Pretty Woman* in real life and trust me, it wasn't pretty.

I looked down at my outfit and cringed. What had possessed me to wear this today? It wasn't even thrift store chic. There was no way a place like this was going to let me in looking like I did. And it was going to be humiliation city when they publically shamed me and turned me away.

This was exactly why I needed to stay away from Asher to begin with. Like I'd said at the wedding. Different worlds. Hell, different solar systems.

I glanced out the window, wondering if I could just pull out now and flee for home. Tell Asher I got lost and didn't have his number to call to let him know. But the valet had already caught my eye and was waving me forward. I was trapped.

And so, against my better judgment, I pulled my beater of a Ford up alongside all the BMWs and Audis and Porsches. Then I killed the ignition. For a moment, I just remained in the car, not sure what to do, my heart throbbing in my chest. But then the driver's side door opened.

I turned, expecting to see the valet. But it was Asher,

grinning from ear to ear. "M'lady," he quipped, offering me a hand.

I took it—what else could I do?—and allowed him to pull me out of the car. As my stomach launched into a full-on rave party—it was having a field day with all of this—I looked around bleakly at all the soft, pretty lights in the trees, all the thick, plush grass blanketing the lawn. The nicely dressed, perfectly coiffed people, walking into the nearby restaurant.

"I'm not sure I'm actually dressed to go in there," I protested weakly.

"Please," Asher replied, not missing a beat. "You should have seen some of the stuff I wore back when I was a teen and my parents would drag me here. There was one time I had these sliced-up, acid-wash jeans. I thought my mom was going to have a heart attack." He laughed. "Yet they still let me in."

"Yeah," I protested. "But you were a kid. And a member."

"And *you* are gorgeous," he shot back. "Whatever you're wearing."

My face burned. He had to stop saying things like that. We were coworkers. Coworkers!

"In any case," he added. "We're not going in the restaurant."

I let out a breath of relief. "We're not?"

"Of course not. I would never subject you to that disgusting display of opulence and excess. We, my dear, are going out there."

Oh no. My body froze as my eyes followed his gesture, down the hill, toward the docks. My stomach wrenched as realization hit me with all the force of a ten-ton truck.

He didn't mean . . . He couldn't mean . . .

But of course he did.

"Sorry," Asher said, not sounding anything close to apologetic. "Didn't I mention? We're having supper on the water. I reserved a boat this morning."

I staggered backward, nearly managing to get myself run over by an approaching Porsche in the process. Asher grabbed my hand just in time, jerking me back to safety. Suddenly, I was flush against him, breasts pressed against his chest. My heart pounded. He looked down at me with sparkling eyes, his hand still hooked at my hips.

"Watch it, Red," he teased. "I'm told Chef Michaels has whipped up a delicious feast. It would be a shame if you got yourself run over before you had a chance to taste it."

I stared up at him, not sure what to say. My mind was racing, my stomach twisting into knots—and not in a good way this time. I struggled to pull away from his grip. "I'm sorry," I stammered. "I can't. I just—can't."

He frowned, releasing me. I stumbled backward, this time taking care to avoid the incoming cars. "What do you mean you can't?"

I could feel my face flaming now. This was so embarrassing. So, so embarrassing. "Look," I said. "The truth is, I'm not a very good swimmer."

"Good thing we're not going swimming then."

"But . . ." I glanced out over the dark water, my whole body vibrating with fear. "If it were to capsize . . ."

He laughed. "This isn't the *Titanic*, Red. I promise there are more than enough lifeboats on board. Besides, glacier season isn't for a couple months now."

Something snapped within me. Anger, mixed with embarrassment, mixed with horrifying fear.

"That's not funny," I shot back at him. "Not fucking funny at all."

Piper! Where's your brother?
Where the hell is your brother?

My eyes darted around for the valet, adrenaline racing like ice water through my veins. I had to get out of here. Before I embarrassed myself further. Before he realized how pathetic I really was. What was I thinking, coming here with him in the first place? I should have kept my distance, stayed professional. Not put myself in situations where I'd end up acting like a crazy girl.

"I've got to go," I choked out, tears pricking at my eyes. Before he could reply, I pivoted on my heel to head back to the valet. Needing to find my car, needing to get out of there as quickly as possible. But, I soon realized, the valet had already taken my car away, probably to avoid the ugly, beat-up thing offending the other guests.

"Piper . . ."

I could hear the concern in Asher's voice, but I ignored it, running over to the attendant at the podium, grabbing at his sleeve. "Excuse me? Excuse me?" I cried, the tears now splashing down my cheeks. Great. Now I looked like a psycho as well as a charity case. I could only hope they didn't speed-dial the cops. "I need my car back."

"Piper! Get back here!"

Rough hands grabbed me, jerking me backward. Only then did I realize I'd almost gotten myself run over by a second car. I tried to squirm away from my rescuer but Asher held me tight, my back pressed at his chest, his hands locked around my waist. I could feel his heartbeat pounding against my back. His hot breath at my neck.

"Let me go," I whispered.

"No. Not until you calm down and tell me what the hell is wrong."

I shut my eyes, sucking in a breath. "Please," I whimpered. "I just want to go home."

"Okay. I'll drive you."

"No. My car—"

"I'll have someone bring it to you. You are clearly in no shape to get behind the wheel."

I could feel my resolve slipping. My body, desperate to absorb his strength, even as my mind wanted to pull away.

"Piper." His voice was in my ear now, raspy and pleading. "Please let me take care of you."

Somehow I managed to nod, the fight going out of me, my shoulders collapsing. Asher led me over to a nearby bench then sat me down. Once I was settled, he ran over to the attendant and whispered something in his ear, before returning to me. Then, he sat down beside me, peering at me with those beautiful emerald eyes of his. And a face filled with concern.

"They're going to get my car," he informed me. "And when they do, I'll take you home." He paused for a moment, drawing in a breath. "But, Piper, please. Can you at least tell me what I did wrong?"

I stared down at my hands. They were clenched into fists. White knuckles stretched over bone. I didn't want to tell him. I really didn't want to tell him. But what choice did I have?

"I'm afraid of the ocean," I blurted out at last.

"Okay . . ."

I looked up, surprised, my eyes blurry with tears. "Okay?" I said doubtfully.

He shrugged. "Okay," he repeated. "You're afraid of the ocean. That's all you had to say."

I stared at him, relief washing over me in waves, and I allowed myself to take a shaky breath as I absorbed his words. Okay. It was going to be okay. I was going to be okay. Suddenly *okay* felt like the most magical word in the English language and I almost laughed out loud in relief.

I didn't know what I had expected from him. More jokes, maybe. A little incredulity? Perhaps disappointment, probably disgust. But now, as I looked into Asher's eyes—his beautiful storm-tossed eyes—I saw none of the above. Nothing but concern swimming in their depths. The Joker was taking me seriously.

I forced myself to unclench my fists.

"So . . . at the wedding," Asher added in a hesitant voice, as if he didn't want to push me, "was this the real reason you freaked out?"

I nodded reluctantly, feeling my face burn in embarrassment from the memory. "Which is so stupid, I know," I said. "I mean, I wasn't in any danger whatsoever—and I totally knew it. And yet, I couldn't help it. All I could think about was . . ."

I clamped my mouth shut. I wasn't ready to talk about that part yet. Not with him anyway.

I waited for him to press me, to encourage me to spill the rest of the story. But to my surprise, instead, he pulled me into his arms. Part of me wanted to protest, to jerk away and put distance between us. But at the same time he felt so warm, so good. And so I found myself nudging closer instead, against my better judgment. Cradling my head against his chest, feeling his strong, steady heartbeat against my ear. Allowing him to stroke my hair with a gentle hand, his fingers weaving through the strands, sending chills down to my toes. His other hand remained securely clasped at my waist, keeping me flush against him. I closed my eyes, breathing in his musky, soapy scent.

If this was wrong, I didn't want to be right.

"I feel like a moron," I mumbled after a few moments. "You obviously went to great lengths to plan this whole thing. And I'm sure it must have cost a fortune." I lifted my head. "Maybe you should go inside and see if there are any hot girls in there, hankering for a cruise."

He laughed. "Is that what you think of me, Red?" he asked. "That I'm the type of guy ready to trade out his dates halfway through?"

I blushed. "But this isn't a date," I reminded him. "We're just . . . coworkers."

"Well, I don't switch out my coworkers either, sweetheart. I asked you to dinner. And we're going to have dinner."

I looked up, eyes wide. "But I can't . . . the boat . . ."

"I know," he assured me. "And if you want to go home, I'll take you home now. But I did sort of have another idea . . ."

I cocked my head in question. "What do you mean?"

He rose to his feet, holding out his hand. "Do you trust me?"

I paused, looking down at his hand. It was a loaded question, not that he would know that. I didn't trust anyone. Not after the way I'd grown up. Trust meant making yourself vulnerable. Allowing people to hurt you. As I'd said to Jayden, I'd realized long ago the only person you could truly trust was yourself.

But I wasn't going to get into all that now. And I was admittedly curious about this alternate plan he'd cooked up. So I placed my hand in his, allowing him to pull me to my feet, trying to ignore the sparks of electricity that crackled as our palms connected.

"This way, m'lady," he said grandly.

I followed him around the restaurant, noting with appreciation how he chose to go the way that was further from the sea. As we came around the corner, my eyes caught sparkling Christmas lights decorating a small gazebo. Under the gazebo was a table with a white linen tablecloth, candles, and place settings for two.

Asher turned to me, a questioning look on his face. "What do you think?" he asked. "If you sit here, you can have your back completely to the water. You can pretend you're in Kansas or something. Completely landlocked."

I shook my head, marveling. "When did you set this up?" I started to ask. Then I remembered him whispering to the attendant. I thought he was getting his car. But clearly he had had other plans.

His eyes sparkled. "I figured you didn't want to go into the restaurant. So why not have the restaurant come out to you?"

I smiled at him. "You didn't have to go through all this trouble."

"Please. I love trouble. I live for trouble." He laughed. "Now sit, woman. And let's have this dinner you promised me."

So we did. And a few minutes later three waiters appeared, carrying silver trays of food. They set them down in front of us and pulled off the lids, revealing an absolute feast underneath. Shiny lobsters and thick cuts of steak. Huge baked potatoes, buttery asparagus. I let out a low whistle.

"Think this will do?" Asher asked. "I didn't know what you liked to eat, so I ordered a little bit of everything."

"Uh, yeah. This will more than do." In fact, I wasn't sure I'd ever seen such a feast in my life.

"Excellent. Then my work here is done." He waited for the waiters to fill our water glasses, then held out his in a toast. "To my new producer," he said. "Who has the amazing superpower of getting my ass out of bed at a decent hour."

I giggled, grabbing my own glass. "To my new weather-man," I said. "For showing me the ropes."

"To my producer," Asher added, "for managing to not fall asleep during the aforementioned showing of ropes."

We clinked glasses and drank our water. The cold liquid quenched my parched throat and I let out a long breath. Here in the privacy of the gazebo, away from the churning sea, I was starting to relax, my panic subsiding and my stomach warming.

"Honestly," I said, "I found the whole Weather 101 lesson really interesting," I told him. "I mean, I love the idea that you can take all this information and mash it together and get this bigger picture. Like a big weather puzzle, I guess."

"That's how my dad used to always describe it," Asher agreed. "But when I was a kid, I used to think it was magic. I mean, we could be standing out in a perfectly blue-skied day and he'd open an umbrella. And lo and behold five minutes later the storm would roll in and everyone would be soaked—except for him." He laughed. "He was so good at his job. And he loved it, too. It wasn't just a job for him, you know? It was his passion."

"He sounds like a great guy," I said. "And he must be proud of you, too. Following in his footsteps and all."

Asher didn't reply at first and I watched as a shadow seemed to flicker over his face—just as it had earlier in the day when he'd brought up his dad. But just as I was about to question it, he shook his head and it was gone, as if it had never been there at all.

"So what's your deal with the water, anyway?" he asked, clearly wanting to change the subject. "Were you always afraid of it? Like, since you were a kid?"

I shrugged. "Pretty much."

"Did something happen? Something to scare you away?"

I set my fork down, staring at my plate.

"Sorry," Asher said quickly. "I shouldn't have asked. We don't have to—"

"My brother drowned," I blurted out, before I even really realized I was doing it. "In the ocean. When I was six."

Asher's eyes widened in horror as I knew they would. As everyone's did when they heard the tragic tale. And he didn't even know the half of it. I felt my cheeks heat, waiting for the follow-up questions that were guaranteed to come. The ones that always came and that I could never truthfully answer.

Stupid Piper. Truly stupid.

What was I thinking, telling him this? I could have made up another excuse—any excuse. Like I'd seen *Jaws* too many times at an impressionable age. That jellyfish scared the shit out of me. Salt water made my skin turn green. Something—anything—except the truth.

But it was too late now.

"What happened?" Asher asked cautiously.

"He was playing in the ocean," I said, repeating the story as I'd done a thousand times before—to police officers, EMTs, reporters. "Evidently he got caught up in a riptide or something that dragged him out to sea. He was only four—he couldn't really swim. They"—I swallowed hard—"found his body three days later—washed up on the shore a few miles away."

And it was my fault, I added silently, feeling the familiar lump rise to my throat. *Completely my fault.*

"I'm so sorry, Piper," Asher said, his voice filled with sympathy. He reached across the table, taking my hand in his. I hadn't realized how cold my skin had gotten until I felt his warm palm cover mine. "I can't even imagine."

I gritted my teeth together. "Well, anyway, it was a long time ago," I muttered. It took everything I had not to pull my hand away. To deny myself the comfort he wanted to give me. Comfort I didn't deserve.

I could feel his eyes on me, intense, searching. "I'm sure that's not something that's easy to get over," he said quietly. "No matter how long ago it was. When I almost lost my father . . ." He trailed off. Then he shook his head. "Anyway, the water thing—it makes perfect sense. You shouldn't be embarrassed about it. Most people in your situation would probably feel the same."

I could feel the tears springing in the corners of my eyes

again. I squeezed them shut, trying to will them away. It was killing me how rational he was being about the whole thing. How kind. It was almost too much to bear. If only he knew the whole story. He wouldn't be looking at me like this. With such sympathy in his eyes. He'd be looking at me with disgust.

The revulsion I deserved.

I swallowed hard, pushing back in my chair with a little too much force, causing it to crash to the ground. A waiter appeared immediately, asking if I was all right. He looked disdainfully at the chair, as if it itself was to blame for my actions.

"Are you okay?" Asher asked, rising to his feet. "Is it the ocean? We can go inside . . ."

I glanced over at the yacht club. Even from here I could see the chandeliers, dripping with crystals. The suits. The cocktail dresses. The warm woods and the bright lights. The pretty people.

Asher's people. Asher's world.

Another planet. Another solar system.

"I'm sorry," I said. "I'm just . . . tired. Can we try this another time?"

Or, you know, like, never again?

"Of course." Without hesitation he was at my side, escorting me back to the valet. Behind us, the waiters converged to take the plates away. Asher didn't even acknowledge them. His attention was totally on me. I wondered what it must be like to live in such a world. Where you could waltz through life, never looking behind at the mess you made. At what you left others to clean up.

But that wasn't fair. *I* was Asher's mess. At least for the moment. And he was definitely cleaning up after me. I wondered if he regretted asking me out now. How my little performance tonight would affect our working relationship the next day. *This is exactly why I shouldn't be out here in the first place*, I scolded myself. It only made things more complicated. And I really didn't need complicated right now.

We reached the front of the restaurant and Asher handed

my ticket to the valet. Then he led me back over to the bench we'd sat on earlier. Like a strange déjà vu. Back then I'd been in full-on panic mode. Now, I just felt sad.

"I'm sorry," I said. "I didn't mean to ruin tonight."

Asher shook his head, looking at me with fond eyes. "You didn't ruin anything. I had a great time."

"Liar."

He laughed. "Fine. I would have had a much better time if I thought you were enjoying yourself, too. But that's my fault. I dragged you out here without ever asking if it was a place you wanted to be. And I'm sorry for that. The next time I take you out, I'll let you choose."

I looked up, surprised. Next time? After all I'd put him through, he still wanted a next time? My heart thudded in my chest.

"I'll make you a deal," he declared. "You agree to a do-over tomorrow night. And I will show up to work on time. Maybe even a little early, for extra credit." He winked at me and I couldn't help but laugh.

"That's not even fair," I protested.

His eyes zeroed in on mine. "Who said I played fair?" Then, as if to prove his point, he leaned in, pressing his mouth against my own.

Holy crap.

For a moment I couldn't even react—just sat there like a freaking stone statue as his lips moved against mine, the slight hint of stubble on his chin lightly scraping my face. I could hear my heart hammering in my ears, blood pulsing at my temples as his hand curled into my own, squeezing it gently as his tongue coaxed my mouth open and slipped inside.

Sweet baby Jesus. Talk about unfair.

The kiss was soft. Almost hesitant at first, as if asking my permission before increasing in intensity. Not that my body, at that moment, had any capability left to say no. My toes were curling in my shoes, chills were running up and down my spine, and when he licked the seam of my lower lip, a soft moan escaped my throat. I could feel his mouth stretch into a pleased smile at that.

Permission granted.

His hands dropped to my sides, clamping down on my hips, pulling me closer to him, until I was practically sitting in his lap. Locked secure against him. I didn't try to pull away. I don't know if I could have, even if I'd wanted to.

Feeling suddenly brave, I reached up, digging my fingers into his hair, which turned out to be so much softer than I'd imagined. He groaned in response, clearly seeing my boldness as an invitation to push his mouth harder against mine, the kiss becoming deeper and hungrier and more urgent by the second. I kissed him back, trying to match his intensity, and all the while my stomach spun into a tailspin of crazy and my body melted like Jell-O in the heat. I dropped my hands to his shoulders to steady myself, rejoicing in the feel of corded muscle flexing under the thin fabric of his shirt. In fact, in that moment it was all I could do not to reach down under that shirt and run my hands up his chest. Exploring the hard steel inlaid under soft skin.

I knew that was wrong of course. Hell, I knew all of this was wrong. I shouldn't have been kissing Asher Anderson. My coworker, my boss, the holder of my future. But somehow I couldn't bring myself to pull away. The night had been such a flurry of ups and downs, highs and lows, joys and sorrows. I needed something like this now. Something where I didn't have to think. I could just be. And feel.

And oh God, did he feel good.

"Ahem. Um, your car, ma'am?"

I jerked at the sound of the valet's voice, breaking through the fantasy. I pulled away, my heart thudding in my chest. My whole body vibrating with need. I glanced over at Asher, who was looking just as dazed, blinking a few times before turning to the valet. As if he'd just woken up from a deep sleep.

Or maybe a perfect dream.

I watched as he shook himself, laughing. Then he gave the valet a scolding look. "Might want to work on your timing, buddy," he said dryly. But he handed the guy a big wad of bills anyway. Then, he turned to me, reaching out and taking my hands in his own. His hands were huge, I suddenly realized. Able to swallow mine whole.

"I'll see you tomorrow?" he said.

I nodded, still feeling like I was on some distant cloud. My lips still swollen from the kiss. "Bright and early," I managed to say.

A smile danced on his face. "I assure you, sweetheart. The early bird will have nothing on me."

twelve

ASHER

I watched as Piper pulled out of the yacht club, my heart thudding hard in my chest. I still felt the ghost of her lips on my own. Her hands in my hair. My hands on her hips.

Oh God. That was nice. That was really nice.

And really stupid, too.

Truth was, I hadn't planned on kissing her. I mean, eventually I did. There was no way a girl with lips like that was not going to be kissed at some point. Just that at that moment, I was trying to be a gentleman. The knight in shining armor. Trying to make her feel safe and secure and make her see I wasn't some asshole trying to take advantage of her current vulnerable state.

But then I'd caught her face. Her soul-deep brown eyes. And suddenly all common decency flew out the window. The knight in shining armor replaced by the caveman yet again. And I had kissed her. And I had enjoyed the shit out of that kiss. Before that cock-blocking valet showed up anyway.

But that was for the best, really. It was better to let her go. Let her go home. Live to make out another day. Which was a funny thought coming from me, actually. I mean, let's face it, the majority of my dates ended in a sleepover; sometimes without me even knowing the date in question's last name. Not a fact I was especially proud of, but it had become routine all the same. Wine them, dine them, bed them. Then begin the hunt for new prey.

But Piper was different. For one thing, she was my coworker. She was going to be in my life far beyond a morning after. Not to mention she had already proven a lot more difficult to impress than other girls. Which meant I'd need to take my time with her. Get to know her as a person. Figure out what made her tick. What turned her on.

Like that licking thing I did to her bottom lip. The one that had produced that soft moan of hers that had been like a jolt of lightning straight to my groin. I definitely had to put that one in the old memory bank for future reference.

Licking, yes. Water dates—definitely no.

I groaned, thinking back at my idiocy. What had I been thinking, hiring a yacht for the night? I should have totally realized she had a thing about water after her freak-out at the wedding.

But no, I'd wanted to impress her. To show off. To give her a magical night to remember. To be the Asher Anderson everyone expected me to be.

I sighed. Well, it had been a memorable night all right. But not exactly in the way I had planned. Thank goodness for that last-minute panic save. The clinch move in my playbook with the picnic out back. She'd relaxed out there—at least for a little bit. That was until I had stupidly brought up the whole water thing again. God, I really needed to work on my game. Usually I was so smooth. But she was so different from other girls. I felt unbalanced, awkward. I clearly needed to make some adjustments at halftime.

Still, I reminded myself with a small smile, I had gotten her to kiss me in the end. So it wasn't a total loss. And I'd get to see her tomorrow, too. Bright and early, as she'd said. A time that should have filled me with dismay.

But somehow excited me instead.

Still smiling a little, I headed back into the main building. I had to pay the tab or at least put it on my mother's account and let them know I didn't need the boat tonight after all. I walked inside, heading toward the maître d'. But before I could reach him, a tall, willowy blonde stepped into my path.

Sarah Martin. Awesome.

"Asher!" she cried excitedly, her shining blue eyes fixing on me. "I can't believe you're here! I haven't seen you in ages!"

I shrugged, trying to glance behind her to catch the maître d's eyes. But he was clearly busy with another guest and would be no good for a rescue. "Yeah, I've been busy."

"I bet!" she declared, nodding her head knowingly, her blond locks bouncing prettily against her shoulders. "I've been so busy myself! It's crazy this year. I barely have time to get my nails done." She giggled, presenting me with what looked like perfectly polished fingernails. But what did I know?

"Are you looking for your parents?" she asked. "'Cause they're in the main dining room, hanging out with my dad."

Of course they were. 'Cause heaven forbid I catch a break tonight.

Fuck it. They could put the dinner on my parents' tab. I gave Sarah a smile before turning to leave. "Actually, I was about to—"

"Asher! I didn't know you were going to be here tonight!"

I looked down to see my father, wheeling himself toward me in his wheelchair, a delighted look on his face. So much for a quick exit.

I watched as he approached, my heart squeezing a little as it always did when I saw him in this state. The once tall, proud man, reduced to a shadow of his former self.

The man who had hit him hadn't bothered to stick around. And my father had almost died. He should have died, probably, with all the blood he'd lost. His leg had been shattered. His lung punctured. It had been touch and go for days afterward before he finally managed to fight his way through.

Dad had always been a fighter, after all.

"Hey, Dad," I said, giving him a weak smile. "I didn't know you would be here, either."

He waved a hand. "You know your mother," he said. "She hates eating out anywhere else. She and Sarah's father are in there, blabbing about business again." He made a loud huffing noise. "So as you can imagine I'm basically stuck here until I die of old age."

I laughed. "Poor you," I said. My mother's lengthy "business dinners" were legendary. Legendarily boring, too. "Will she at least let you slip into the cigar room to pass the time?"

My father shook his head, looking mournful. "Sadly, my cigar days are behind me. Gotta keep in good health, don't you know?" He made a gesture to his useless legs and rolled his eyes.

I nodded sadly. Sometimes I got the feeling that my father wished the accident had killed him outright. Allowed him to go out in a blaze of glory, rather than a dwindling flame. Once he'd been so vibrant. So full of life. Now he was a shell of the man he used to be. And it hurt to see him reduced to this.

"Come on, you two," he broke in, gesturing to Sarah and me. "There's room at the table for both of you. And you can assist me in not dying of boredom."

I glanced longingly at the front door. It was the last thing I wanted to do. Just sit there and listen to my mother talk shop with Sarah's father, a prominent businessman who was rumored to be running for mayor of San Diego. He already spent a ton of money advertising his businesses on News 9. Now the idea that he might be adding campaign money to the pile had prompted my mother to do a full-court press. Wine him, dine him, kiss his ass. Get him to agree to give her all his money to promote him on TV.

The worst part was, if I joined her, she'd expect the same from me. She loved the idea of the daughter of News 9's biggest advertiser and potential government official on the arm of News 9's golden son. Sarah and I had been pushed together since right after college when her longtime boy-friend took off overseas, neither of our parents evidently real-izing that arranged marriages were no longer actually a thing in the USA.

Okay, it could have been worse. Sarah was super hot. And she was pretty fun, too. She had tons of energy and was always looking for the next party—and usually knew where to find it. We'd hooked up half a dozen times over the past few years—friends with benefits, I guess you'd say. She might have wanted more from me, but she also knew better than to ask for it. Which I had always appreciated.

I reluctantly allowed my father to escort the two of us over to the window table where Mom and Sarah's dad were talking. Mom looked up and saw me—me and Sarah—and predictably her face lit up like a Christmas tree.

"Asher! My baby!" she crowed, rising from her seat. Sarah's dad stood as well, sticking out his hand. I shook it then duti-fully hugged my mother. She smelled of too much perfume and too much brandy. Guess the after-dinner drinks were being served as a first course this evening. What a surprise.

"How's the meeting of the minds going?" I asked, sitting down at the table like a good son. I considered looking at the menu: I was still pretty starving. But I didn't want to get stuck here longer than I had to. I could pick up something on the way home.

Before my mother could answer, the manager stepped up to our table. He looked down to address me. "Sir, I see the boat you reserved is still in its slip," he said. "Did you decide not to take it out tonight after all? The captain was wondering."

"Ooh! You signed out a boat?" My mother's eyes glittered.

"Yeah," I said. I turned back to the manager. "But actually I'm not going to—"

"You should take Sarah out!" Mom interrupted. She turned to Sarah's father. "I mean, if you don't mind."

"Not at all!" her father exclaimed, after swallowing a large slug of scotch. "We're going to be here a while, after all. And I'm sure poor Sarah is bored out of her skull."

I watched as Sarah opened her mouth to protest, but her father waved her off. "I know, I know, sweetie," he said. "You're a good girl to humor your father. But why don't you and Asher go and have some fun? Leave us to talk boring business. We'll see you in the morning."

Sarah turned to me. "Is that okay with you?" she asked. Her eyes were shiny and her cheeks flushed with excitement. She clearly wanted to go. Of course she did. And normally I would have had no problems taking her. Especially knowing what she'd be willing to do once we got out into open sea. Like I said, she was hot. I liked her a lot.

But damn it, now all I could think of was Piper. And the fact that I had sworn to her I didn't trade out my dates halfway through the night. What would she think if she could see me here now? I imagined disappointment in her wide brown eyes. But not surprise.

Because this was the guy she expected me to be. The guy everyone expected me to be. Even my own mother.

I could feel all the table's eyes on me. Waiting for my answer. My mom's especially, drilling into me with a hard look. *This is a big deal*, those eyes said. *Don't fuck it up.*

If I said no, Sarah would be hurt. Her father would take it as a personal affront. He might even decide to end the business dinner prematurely. Before handing my mother all the advertising money she was after. The money she would pretty much have sold her own soul to acquire.

Or, you know, the soul of her only son.

"What a great idea!" I declared with as much bravado as I could muster. I turned to the manager, flashing him a large grin even as I died a little on the inside. "Tell the captain to get her in gear. We'll be out in a few minutes."

Sarah smiled widely, clapping her hands. "Awesome," she pronounced. Everyone at the table nodded, seeming to agree. My mother shot me an approving look but it only served to chill my insides.

This is the last time, I tried to broadcast silently. *I won't keep doing this for you.*

I rose to my feet, reaching out to take Sarah's hand. She

leaned into me, so close her breast brushed against my arm. A move I was positive was intentional. An intention I once would have appreciated. But tonight . . .

"A night cruise," she whispered, her breath against my ear. "How romantic is that?"

And suddenly, for the first time in my life, I was the one who was dreading the sea.

thirteen

PIPER

I was halfway home when my phone rang. At first I assumed it was my mom: After all, who else would call me at such a late hour? But as I glanced at the caller ID, I realized it was Toby at the Holloway House instead.

Which could only mean trouble.

I slipped the earpiece in my ear to answer. "Hello?"

"Piper," Toby's voice barked from the other end of the line. "Where are you? Can you come in tonight?"

I glanced at my car's clock and cringed. It was almost ten already. Which meant by the time I got home and got to bed, I'd already be hurting when it came to my six AM wakeup call. If I took a shift tonight, I'd be pretty much guaranteed to be dead on my feet come morning. And, of course, I didn't dare sleep in—not after all I'd done to make sure Asher would show up on time. Hell, if I arrived at News 9 even one minute late, he'd never let me hear the end of it.

"Toby, I worked last night, remember?"

"I know," she said, her voice sounding guilty. "And I wouldn't ask if it wasn't an emergency. But Jayden's been crazy tonight. He flipped out on an orderly and broke his nose. A new guy—who threatened to call the cops."

I winced. Jayden was probably only one call away from entering the juvenile detention program as it was. And once he went in, it was doubtful with his attitude that he'd be out anytime soon.

Oh, Jayden. Why do you do this to yourself?

But deep down I knew why. I knew all too well why he acted like he did. He was angry. He was confused. He was alone and scared. Just like I used to be. So he lashed out at those trying to help him—just like I used to do. He didn't trust anyone to treat him right, because no one had ever treated him right before. And the only way to earn that trust was to shower him with love and attention and people who cared. Even when he didn't deserve it.

Just as Toby had once done for me.

I let out a heavy breath. "Okay," I said. There was really only one answer, after all. "I'm on my way."

I kept driving, skipping the exit that led to my cozy apartment. To my warm, soft bed. Instead I kept on the freeway, heading further south, toward Chula Vista. Toward a night of confrontations and likely little sleep.

As I passed the exit to News 9, I wondered if Asher was on his way home now, too. I imagined him parking his car, walking into his house, stripping off his shoes and shirt, then his pants. He'd probably grab a beer and slug it down before heading to bed, dressed only in those boxer briefs of his. Those damn boxer briefs whose memory still made me feel a bit gooey.

As did that earth-shattering kiss I'd just received from the guy who wore them.

I groaned. Oh my God had that been a good kiss. Like Olympic medal–winning good. The way his mouth had clamped down on my own, his tongue invading without invitation. The way his hands had pulled me to him and the way my body went—as if it were made of magnets and he was nothing but iron. This was a guy who knew how to make a girl weak in the knees. A guy who could make a girl forget everything but the way she felt when she was in his arms.

Asher Anderson is the last person you should be thinking of right now, I scolded myself.

But how could I help it? In addition to basically being a real life sex god, Asher had also been so damn sweet. So understanding about my stupid phobia and so quick to change plans to accommodate me. I mean, he had probably spent hundreds of dollars renting that boat for the night. Yet I saw not a flicker of disappointment on his face when I refused to get on board. Sure, I supposed a couple hundred dollars was nothing to him—probably chump change he found in his couch cushions. But still—most guys would have been annoyed at the inconvenience at the very least.

But not Asher. He had taken it all in stride. Simply switched gears—no big deal. For all his reputation of being a playboy who went through women like, well, boxer briefs, he was surprisingly accommodating when the woman in question didn't fall in line right away. He could have easily sent me home. Gone into the club and found easier prey. But he hadn't. He'd stuck with me instead. He'd made the night end magically, despite my initial resistance.

And then there was that kiss. A kiss that hadn't felt like a come-on, like an invitation—or insistence—for more. It had been just what it was. A simple kiss, no strings attached. Even if the valet hadn't interrupted like he had, I knew somehow that Asher wouldn't have taken it further. Wouldn't have put me in the position where I had to turn him away.

I frowned. I needed to stop this—now. It was getting out of hand. So Asher was hot. A great kisser. A perfect gentleman to boot. None of that mattered in the end. Because it didn't change who we were. Two people from different worlds.

It was like my favorite John Hughes movie, *Pretty in Pink.* Sure, Molly Ringwald and Andrew McCarthy got together in the end, but no one who watched the film would bet on them remaining a couple much after prom. They were too different, their upbringings like night and day. She would never be accepted in his upper class circle—and eventually he'd get sick of being ostracized by his friends and family due to his loyalty to her. He'd realize being poor wasn't a cute quirky trait—and that Molly's abandonment issues ran deep. A guy like him would never be able to completely understand a girl like her—even if he desperately wanted to—and all the money in the world couldn't save her from herself.

I tried to imagine bringing Asher home to meet my mother. How horrified he'd be when he saw her broken teeth and scarred arms. About as horrified as I had been, I suppose, at the idea of going into that fancy club with him and enduring people's stares.

Sure, I was a curiosity to him right now. A novelty—different than the usual girls he dated. But if I were to allow myself to succumb to his charms? To let him have his way with me? I knew exactly what would happen. What always happened with people like Asher. The curiosity would be sated. He would get bored. He would walk away. And then our work situation would become beyond awkward. If it continued at all.

I didn't kid myself; they would not fire him if things went south between us. And I couldn't afford to lose my one opportunity. Not at least until I had enough experience under my belt to get a new job at a new station in a similar capacity. Right now, at best, I'd be relegated to production assistant again. At worse, I'd be blackballed from TV forever.

Sorry, Asher. You're hot. But you're not career-ending hot.

I arrived at the Holloway House thirty minutes later. Toby met me at the door, her face flushed with relief. "Thank you for coming," she said. "I'm so sorry to have to ask this of you. I know you must be exhausted."

"I'm fine," I assured her, giving her a hug. "Now where's Jayden?"

"He's in the TV room," she told me. At my raised eyebrows she shrugged. "I know, I know. He should be on restriction for what he pulled. But I needed him to calm down so we didn't have another incident."

I nodded grimly. Then I headed down the hall to the lounge where the kids would come and watch TV. There were a few teens there now, hanging out, watching some surfing competition in New Zealand. Jayden was sprawled out on one of the threadbare couches, his glassy eyes glued to the screen. But I wasn't entirely sure if he was actually seeing it.

I dropped down next to him. "Hang ten, bro," I said, making my best surfer signs with my hands.

He didn't look over at me, just kept his eyes on the screen. I sighed. So it was going to be that type of night, was it? Instead of pushing him, I turned to watch the show myself. It was funny: Even here in the safety of the TV room, I felt a little nervous watching the surfers crest over the waves. When one took a huge fall, I found myself gripping the afghan next to me with white knuckles until he bobbed back to the surface.

Jayden noticed and looked at me like I was crazy. "You okay?" he asked.

I sighed, leaning back on the couch. "Just not a big fan of the ocean."

"Really?" He looked surprised. Then he turned back to the TV. "So I guess you're not a surfer then."

"You couldn't pay me to get on one of those boards."

"Yeah, well, I would pay big money to do it," he told me. "It looks fucking amazing."

I opened my mouth to reprimand him on language, but then decided to let it slide. The light in his eyes as he watched the surfers was an in. I couldn't let it go out before using it to my advantage.

"Where would you surf?" I asked him. "If you could surf anywhere in the world?"

"Hawaii," he pronounced without hesitation, a shy grin spreading across his face. "So I could go, like, check out the volcanoes while I was there. I've always wanted to see a volcano."

"I'd be all over checking out volcanoes," I agreed, "if I could skip the surfing."

Jayden shook his head, laughing. "You're crazy, miss. The volcanoes are like ten thousand times more dangerous than a little wave."

"If you say so."

"Anyway"—he slumped back on the couch, the laughter fading from his face—"that'll never happen. Not while I'm stuck here." He sighed loudly.

I studied him for a moment, my heart squeezing in my chest. I knew that look all too well. That feeling of hopelessness you got from being stuck in a place like this too long. The trapped feeling—like you were in a cage and you'd never fully escape the life you were given to live.

Sure, I could tell him there was life after the Holloway House. That if he worked hard he might escape his past as I had. But I knew all too well that words only went so far. And at the moment the boy didn't look much in the mood for a lecture. He didn't need to be told of some nebulous future. He needed something solid, right here, right now. Some kind of escape from the monotony of group home life. Some kind of treat to show him it paid to keep fighting the good fight.

Suddenly an idea struck me. I glanced back at the TV. Watched the surfer take on a ridiculously huge wave. *Yes, this could totally work.*

I turned back to Jayden. "I've got a proposition for you," I said.

"A propo—what?"

"Sorry," I said. "I mean a deal. I've got a deal for you."

He gave me a skeptical look. "I don't need any more cake."

"This is way better than cake," I assured him. "But first you have to do your part. You need to start behaving and promise not to keep beating up on the poor staff."

"And if I do?"

I smiled. "I may be able to arrange a surf lesson for you."

"What?" Jayden stared at me, wide-eyed. He jumped from his seat. Like literally launched halfway across the room. Then he turned back to me. "A surfing lesson? For real? Like in the ocean for real?"

I nodded. "I can't take you to Hawaii, so you'll have to save the volcanoes for another time. But I do have a . . . friend . . . who surfs. I could ask him if he knows of a good instructor who could take you out one afternoon. But . . . !" I added, holding up a hand to stop him from interrupting. "You have to prove to me that you're capable of handling this kind of freedom first. Which means I want to see one week of perfect behavior. No demerits. No fights. I want to walk in next week and have the staff tell me you're their favorite Holloway House resident."

Okay, that was maybe pushing it. The staff would probably never be endeared to Jayden. But if he could just manage to stay out of their way . . .

"It's a deal, miss," Jayden declared. His eyes were flashing his excitement. "I promise! I'll be the best-behaved kid in all of Holloway House, you'll see. And then I'll get to go surfing!" He turned to the teens watching TV. "I get to go surfing!" he bragged loudly.

"Get out of the way," one of them yelled in return. Jayden wasn't, unfortunately, very popular with the other kids here, either. But he didn't seem to care right now. He was practically bouncing off the ceiling.

"Now," I said, "how about you go up to your room and go to bed? You should have had lights out an hour ago."

"Aw," he started. I gave him a sharp look. He grinned sheepishly. "I mean, oh yay! Bedtime! I love bedtime."

I rolled my eyes. "Now get up there and get your teeth brushed. I'll be up to check on you in ten minutes. And I better find you under the covers with the lights out."

"You will!" he cried, dashing to the door. A moment later I heard his footsteps banging on the stairs. I smiled. *Mission accomplished.*

I rose from the couch and walked out of the TV room. Toby met me in the hall.

"Where's he going?" she asked, gesturing to the stairs.

I gave her an innocent shrug. "To bed," I said, as if it was no big thing.

Toby gave a low whistle. "You just have a way with them, don't you, baby doll?"

"I *was* them," I reminded her. "And I don't know. I think sometimes we all just need something to look forward to, you know?"

She smiled. "You have a good heart, Piper. Don't let anyone tell you otherwise." Then she gave me a curious look. "By the way, I never asked you—how did your first day as a big-time producer go? Was it everything you dreamed of and more?"

I considered this for a moment. Then I nodded my head. "It was different than I expected," I told her. "But I think it's going to be okay."

fourteen

PIPER

Thankfully the rest of the night was quiet. With Jayden subdued, the other residents also seemed to find peace and soon everyone was tucked in their beds and I was able to catch a nap on the cot in the office. When the morning shift supervisor woke me the next day I felt almost well rested.

I took a quick shower there, thankfully finding a change of clothes in my locker. Then I grabbed a large cup of coffee and headed straight for the station.

When I arrived, I ran into Richard in the hall. He stopped me and gave me a thumbs-up, a big grin on his face.

I cocked my head. "What's that for?"

"Your producer magic," he declared. "Seriously, I don't know what you did to him but whatever it is, please keep on doing it."

"What are you . . . ?" I started to say, before realization hit me. "Oh. You mean Asher? Is he here already?"

My heart started thudding a little harder in my chest. Partially from the fact that Asher had kept his promise. Partially from the idea of seeing him again. And, of course, partially from the look of approval on Richard's face.

"Please. He's not only here, but he's dressed appropriately for once," Richard marveled. "He even showed up to our morning meeting and pitched a story idea about riptides being spotted offshore and how parents can better protect their kids from drowning." He shook his head. "I should have promoted you a year ago!"

I gave him a weak smile, my insides twisting into excited knots. *Thank you, Asher.*

"I'm glad it's working out," I said, trying to appear like it was no big deal, even though inside I wanted to break out into a Snoopy dance right there in the hallway. "Let me know if you need anything else."

"Oh, I will," Richard said. "Keep up the good work, kid." And with that, he slapped me on the back and walked away. I watched him go for a moment, feeling giddy with happiness, then turned to head upstairs to the weather center, my steps feeling lighter than air. When I spotted Asher hard at work at the weather computer, my heart pretty much flipped in my chest.

God, he looked good in a suit. I mean don't get me wrong—he looked good in casual surfing clothes as well. And I wasn't even about to bring up those boxer briefs. But even here, now, dressed in a sensible, probably custom-fitted navy suit and tie he looked completely and utterly delicious. His unruly hair had evidently been subjected to some powerful gel, slicked back against his head. And he was completely clean-shaven to boot. Suddenly I felt the nearly irresistible urge to run my fingers across his cheeks, just to see if his skin was as soft and smooth as it appeared.

"Well, well, well," I said, giving him a slow clap as I approached. "You clean up nice."

He looked up at me, flashing me one of his trademark grins, his emerald eyes dancing with merriment. "Boss lady insisted," he teased. Then his eyes dropped to me, lazily roving my body, taking me in. I blushed a little, realizing I probably looked a bit less than completely professional myself.

"Sorry," I said. "I didn't have time to go home last night."
He raised an eyebrow. I laughed.

"Not like that," I protested. "I mean, I ended up having to work. My other job needed me to fill in last minute."

"You worked all night?" he asked, his eyes darkening with concern.

"No. I mean, I got some sleep in the office. Once I got the kids to settle down. It's not a big deal, trust me. I've worked on less sleep than this."

He frowned. "Are they not paying you enough here? You still have to work another job? I could ask them for more money if you needed it."

"No, no!" I shook my head, horrified at the idea of him going and asking for more favors on my behalf. "It's not about the money. I've just been working at this group home for years now. Helping out kids who have no families. It's more of a labor of love than anything else—but I couldn't just leave them high and dry once I got my new job."

Asher nodded slowly, giving me the most thoughtful look. Then he smiled. "That sounds cool," he said. "Just . ... I don't want you to burn out. So let me know if you ever need a day off or whatever. Or maybe a nap? I happen to know the closet at the back of the weather center makes a great napping space."

I laughed. "I'm fine, I promise," I assured him. "In fact, I'm more than fine after running into Richard this morning. He was pretty excited about you showing up to the morning meeting, by the way."

"I'm glad he appreciates it," Asher said. Then his eyes locked on me. "But I didn't do it for him."

I swallowed hard, my stomach flip-flopping all over again.

Coworkers, I scolded myself. *You are supposed to just be coworkers.*

"So!" I said brightly, trying to ignore the heat pooling between my legs. "What's on today's agenda anyway? Richard said something about riptides?"

Asher nodded. "I got an email this morning from one of our

weather spotters. Evidently there have been quite a few riptides spotted over the last week—more than usual for this time of year. I thought we could do some kind of feature piece on that. Give people tips about what to do if they're caught in one. That kind of thing." He paused, then added, "I hope that's not too personal. I mean, given what happened with your brother . . ."

I shook my head. "That's exactly why we *should* do the story," I said. "I can't save him. But if we can save others . . ." I looked up at Asher. "Let's do it."

So we did. Working together to set up the piece's interviews: first, a professor at San Diego State University who could talk about what causes riptides and then a spokesperson for the Coast Guard who was willing to do a safety demonstration on camera, showing people what to do—and what not to do—if caught in a current.

According to him most people sucked out by a riptide just panic and subsequently drown—thinking they can't get back to shore. But if they're able to swim horizontally, they can often move beyond the current and be able to head back once they're free. I was pretty sure I would have ended up in the panic/drown camp if ever in that situation, but maybe others watching would be able to keep their heads now that we'd shown them what to do.

Asher recruited one of the news photographers to do the shoots with him while I stayed back at the station, ordering up some charts and animations from the graphics department and gathering applicable statistics. For example, I learned that rip currents had been credited with killing over fifty people in the last year alone. (Just another reason to stay clear of the sea, thank you very much.)

At first I assumed when Asher returned from shooting the interviews he would start writing the segment himself. But to my surprise he suggested I get started on it while he prepped his forecast. Then, when he was done, he said, he'd look it over and see if it needed any tweaks to better fit his personal style and speech patterns.

In other words—holy crap! My first on-air script!

I sat down at the computer, pretty much equally thrilled and intimidated beyond belief. The idea of me writing a script that would be read on air was a dream come true. The reality, however, was as frightening as a nightmare. After all, top market producers usually spent quite a bit of time in the trenches rewriting AP copy for twenty-second news stories before tackling a full-length feature. And here I was, ready to take on an entire script, my second day on the job.

But what choice did I have? I couldn't exactly go back to Asher and tell him I was chickening out. He'd hired me to help him and he had a lot on his own plate already. The last thing he needed was to be babysitting me on top of his other duties.

He was trusting me to make this happen. I couldn't let him down.

And so I began, first logging all interviews and choosing the best sound bites. Then I started putting together the script itself. At first, the words came slowly, almost painstakingly, with me second-guessing every sentence I put down on the page and doubts assaulting my brain.

What if Asher hated it so much he had to completely rewrite it? Or worse—what if he felt bad for me and read it as is—and Richard freaked out that such garbage had gone on the air? I'd be exposed as a fraud. The girl who didn't deserve the job she'd been given. They'd send me back to production assistant land. Or worse—fire me altogether.

Shit. I looked up at the clock. The second hand was ticking forward, like a metronome of death as the newscast loomed ever closer. I had no more time to stall. I had to get this done. I glanced over at Asher, who was completely absorbed in his computer, as if he'd forgotten I was in the room.

He clearly believed I could do this. It was time I believed in myself.

Grabbing my headphones I shoved them over my ears,

blasting my favorite video game playlist off Spotify. I had always found writing to soundtracks helped me gain focus— the music swelling in my ears, drowning out all other noise. And right now I needed that. Big-time. To get in the zone— to push away all doubts and fears. To get the script down on the page. After all, I could edit a bad script. A blank page on the other hand was completely useless.

Now, as the music blasted in my ears, everything else slid from my focus and soon my fingers were flying over the keyboard, alternating between reporter track and the sound bites between it. I typed and I typed and I forced myself not to look back at what I'd already written. And line by line, a script miraculously began to take shape.

I was doing it. I was really doing it.

Lost in the music and the words, I didn't notice, at first, when Asher came up behind me. Until, that is, he laid a hand on my shoulder—causing me to nearly jump out of my skin. I yanked the headphones off my ears and gave him an accusing look.

"Sorry," he said, a smile twitching at the corner of his mouth. "I did try calling your name a few times first."

I watched as his eyes flickered back to the script. I bit my lower lip. My heart pounded in my chest. Doubts assaulted my brain all over again. Would he like it? What if he didn't like it? What if he thought it was the worst script in the history of scripts?

What if my first on-air script ended up being my last?

"It's still rough," I stammered. "I was going to go back and polish. And if you want to change anything—"

"I don't," he interrupted. "And I don't want you to change anything, either."

I stared up at him, my eyes widening. "You don't want any changes?"

"Nope," he declared. "Print it and I'll find an editor to record my track."

With shaking hands I reached for my mouse, dragging the cursor over to the print icon on the screen. My mind raced, wondering if he was just being kind, not wanting to tell me how much it sucked. But no, he was the one who had to go on the air with it. Put my words in his mouth. All the viewers at home—and probably many right here at News 9—would assume he was the one who wrote the story. So it would be his reputation on the line if it were bad.

So did that mean it was actually good?

I rose to my feet to go grab the script off the printer. But Asher stopped me, putting another hand on my shoulder. "No," he commanded. "You're not an assistant anymore. I can fetch my own script."

I stared at him, speechless. He flashed me a grin, then walked down the stairs and into the newsroom to the master printer. I watched from the balcony as one of the newer production assistants, a girl named Greta who I didn't know too well, giggled and blushed as she tried to grab for the script and dropped it. Asher stopped her from leaning over, then gallantly grabbed the paper himself, giving her a playful little bow in the process. She looked as if she was going to keel over in delight.

My stomach sank a little as I watched their interaction. Here was the Asher everyone knew. The one I needed to keep at arm's length. The flirt. The player. The one who could have any woman—and probably did.

Sure, he might like me now. He might enjoy kissing me, too. But at the end of the day it couldn't go further than that. I was his producer. His coworker.

But not his assistant.

A smile crept to my lips again as he reentered the weather center, waving the script with a silly grin. I turned back to my computer, rereading the script on the screen. The script that I wrote that would soon be read over the airwaves of all of San Diego.

It was good. It was really good.

Maybe I could do this after all.

fifteen

ASHER

"*That's* your car?"

I laughed at Piper's shocked expression as I stopped in front of the old refurbished Volkswagen bus at the back of the News 9 parking lot. I reached into my pockets to pull out my keys then unlocked the passenger side door, pulling it open to allow her to climb inside.

"Sorry, Maserati's in the shop," I teased. "Damn luxury sports cars, always breaking down on you. Unlike Fiona here." I patted her rusty side with affection. "She's dependable as rain."

Truthfully, I didn't own a Maserati. Well, not anymore anyway. My mom had tried to foist one on me as a birthday present after Dad's accident. But I'd crashed it my first weekend down in Baja—where I'd driven without bothering to acquire Mexican insurance—and it had been a complete loss. Which meant, *arrivederci* Italian sports car and *Guten Tag* German hippie bus.

Which was fine by me. My baby was far more practical anyway. Sure, zero to sixty in any amount of seconds was more of a challenge, but she made up for it in other ways. Like being able to carry all my surf gear. And having room to camp out in if I wanted to catch some extra early swells.

Plus, her existence pissed my mother off, which made Fiona even more loveable in my eyes.

"Wow, I can't believe this old thing is still running," Piper marveled as she climbed into the passenger seat.

"Hey! Don't you be going and hurting Fiona's feelings!" I protested. "She's a lady, you know. We don't talk about her age."

Piper laughed. "I'm sorry, Fiona," she cooed, running her hand along the dashboard. "You are looking quite fetching tonight. And may I just say sea foam green is a lovely color on you."

I smirked, closing the door behind her and running around to the other side. I'd insisted on driving tonight—for our dining "do-over"—telling Piper it was silly to take two cars to go to one place. I wondered if she regretted her decision to hitch a ride, now that she'd been introduced to the ride in question. In the past I'd had some dates who had literally refused to "get inside that death trap" and who'd actually seemed offended that I would consider it a form of transportation befitting their rank.

Let's just say those girls didn't usually get second dates.

When I popped into the bus, I found Piper had left her seat to wander to the back and was examining the set-up with interest. I'd had it completely redone when I'd put in Fiona's new motor, adding a little kitchenette and bedroom for the aforementioned overnight surf trips.

"So what do you think?" I asked, and I was surprised to realize I was actually eager to hear her answer.

She turned to me, an amused expression dancing in her eyes. "Every time I think I know you . . ." she said, shaking her head. "You are full of surprises."

"And the ladies love every last one of them," I returned with a smirk. Even though that was definitely untrue. Luckily for me and my track record, however, most were willing to overlook my so-called "quirks" to keep their eyes on the prize.

AKA my wallet.

Piper, on the other hand, despite her earlier joke, now seemed quite enamored with Fiona. Taking her time to check out the kitchen and the bed, making remarks about how cozy and cute it all was. And from the look on her face I could tell this wasn't just her trying to be nice, or trying to get on my good side. She actually thought this was cool. And when she finally did head back to her seat, I caught what looked like a spark of respect in her eyes. As if she approved of this other side of me. As if she actually preferred it.

Which gave me an idea.

"Look," I said, "how adventurous are you feeling tonight?" She laughed. "What do you mean?"

"Well, as you know, I made the reservation at Addison. And we can totally go there if you want to—it's an amazing place and I'm sure you would love it. But . . ." I paused before continuing. "If you were feeling a little more . . . daring . . . I could make another suggestion . . ."

My heart thudded a little as I waited for her reply. Addison was a five diamond–rated restaurant in Rancho Santa Fe and it was nearly impossible to get reservations—especially on short notice. Most girls, I found, would give their right arm to get inside the place. To see and be seen and Instagram the shit out of their meal to impress their friends.

But I'd already determined Piper was not like most girls.

Sure enough, her eyes flashed something mischievous and it sent a small flutter to my stomach. "Tell me more."

I smiled. "It's this little hole-in-the-wall down in National City. Called Miguel's. It's not fancy. But it's got the best homemade tortillas this side of the border."

Piper nodded slowly, as if considering this. "How's their salsa verde?" she asked.

"Out of this world."

"Well then is it even a question?"

I laughed. "Seriously though. It's not fancy. I mean, it's *really* not fancy. You can look it up on Yelp if you want. Just to make sure it's going to be okay."

But Piper made no move to pull out her phone. "It sounds perfect," she declared. "Let's go."

I grinned like a schoolboy at the surety I heard in her voice. And suddenly it was all I could do not to lean over and kiss her—right then and there. "Well, all right then," I said instead, my insides dancing with excitement. "Miguel's it is." I turned the key in the ignition and Fiona grumbled to life. "Okay, girl," I said, patting her dash. "You know where to go."

And with that, we rolled out of the News 9 parking lot and headed south. Toward National City, a destination not usually frequented by tourists. And for good reason, too. Even though it had been somewhat cleaned up since the old days, it was still home to significant drug and gang activities, and violent crimes were commonplace. There wasn't a lot down there to attract visitors, either, and so most people just drove right through or used it as a parking lot on their way to or from Tijuana's bright lights and big clubs.

I myself had discovered Miguel's by accident, after a bad night south of the border a few months after my father's car crash. I'd been angry, drunk, and desperate for a greasy meal to settle my stomach.

And yet I'd gotten so much more than that when I'd stepped through the door. So much more than I had deserved.

Addison—in all its five-diamond glory—couldn't hold a candle to that.

Twenty minutes later, we arrived at the small, ugly strip mall where the restaurant was located. As I pulled into my parking spot, I stole a glance at Piper, searching for that familiar uneasiness I'd seen in so many girls' eyes when I'd taken them here. After all, I'd had plenty of girls pretend to be all excited at the promise of adventure—until they actually got here and saw how adventurous it really was. Then, when they turned up their noses and started making comments—I'd pretend it was all a gag. I'd turn around and take them to Addison or somewhere of that ilk. They would let out breaths of relief and laugh and tell me I was "too much."

And I would silently cross them off my list. Disappointed, once again.

But weirdly Piper didn't seem fazed by the seedy surroundings. Not just fake unfazed—at this point, I could spot a pretender a mile away. But Piper—Piper didn't even seem to register the squalor. If anything she looked more relaxed here than she had at the yacht club. And somehow I didn't think it was just due to the absence of the ocean, either.

"Are you ready for this?" I asked.

"Hell yeah. I'm freaking starving." She jumped out of the car, not a single cautious glance into the dark parking lot—to make sure there weren't muggers or rapists lying in wait—and headed toward the restaurant with a spring in her step.

I followed suit, locking the bus behind me, following her into the restaurant, my heart now beating fast with anticipation. My stomach growled as I stepped inside and my nose caught a whiff of the warm, spicy smells of salsa and fajitas.

I looked around; the place was packed, as was usual for Miguel's. Filled with day workers having just finished their shifts and wanting to grab food before getting back into the endless border line and huge local Mexican families with kids spilling out of each booth talking and laughing loudly.

Piper gave a low whistle. "Wow, this place must be good," she declared. "I wonder if we'll even be able to get a table."

"Oh, we'll get a table," I assured her with a smile. "Trust me. I'm a regular here."

I was proved right a moment later as Miguel's wife, Angelita, approached us with a big smile on her face. "*Mijo!*" she exclaimed. "Where have you been? It's been too long!" She came around the hostess stand to give me a huge hug. I hugged her back, feeling that familiar warmth rise inside of me, that feeling of coming home. Angelita had that effect on people. Which was probably why her restaurant did so well.

"And who is your friend?" she asked, turning to Piper, delight sparkling in her eyes. "She's so pretty! What is she doing with you?"

I snorted. *And here we go again.* Angelita sometimes got a little too excited when I brought girls by for dinner. And when I came solo she usually tried to hook me up with one of her regulars. Which was one of the reasons if I saw my dates turning up their noses outside, I'd turn around before bringing them in. I was nothing if not protective of Angelita and Miguel and their little slice of restaurant heaven. I would never allow anyone to insult them in their own place.

But I was becoming pretty sure I wouldn't have to worry about this with Piper. If anything I should have been more worried that Angelita would call a priest to come by and marry us before dessert.

"Angelita, this is Piper. My new producer at News 9," I introduced. "Piper, this is Angelita. She and her husband own this place. And are single-handedly responsible for fattening me up."

Angelita rolled her eyes, making a dismissive gesture to my stomach. "You call that fat? I'd hate to know what you call my husband."

"Aw, Angelita, you know he's just big-boned."

"Big bones, big belly, big head," she muttered. Then she grinned. "Now let me get you a table."

And with that, she scurried into the restaurant to figure out where to put us. I turned to Piper, giving her an impish look. "Obviously this isn't my first time here."

Piper grinned. "Yeah, I got that."

"This place is worth the trip though," I said. "I've actually tried to get them to move up north. To open a restaurant in a touristy neighborhood, you know? They would do incredible business in La Jolla or Pacific Beach."

"They're not interested?"

I shook my head. "They love it here."

"It looks like their customers love them, too," Piper observed, watching Angelita reach down and hug one of her younger guests, a little girl with straight black hair pulled into two ponytails. "I can see why they'd want to stay."

"And if they do, I'll keep coming back," I asserted.

Angelita returned to the hostess stand. "I have a table for you," she said. "Best in the house for my *mijo* and his pretty lady friend."

She made a gesture for us to follow then walked us to the back of the restaurant, deftly weaving through all the children running around the place and the waiters serving food. We stopped at a large round booth, adorned with a colorful tablecloth. Angelita placed a couple of greasy menus in front of us, telling us she'd return in a moment with some water and chips and salsa.

"So what do you think?" I asked, after allowing Piper to sit down and scan the menu for a minute.

"I think it's awesome," she declared, looking up at me, her eyes shining. "I love discovering these hidden gems." She laughed, then added, "Or maybe not so hidden, judging from the crowd."

"Well, it's not exactly Zagat rated," I said. "But I don't think you're going to be disappointed with your meal."

"I am positive I won't be."

Angelita returned with our waters and we gave our orders, with Piper asking the owner's opinion on various dishes before making up her mind. Angelita, who was always excited to talk food, especially with a new customer, rattled on about this spice and that and the fish market in Rosarito where they imported their daily catches. Finally, Piper made her choice, going for one of the specials, and Angelita headed back to the kitchen to place the order, looking pleased.

I was feeling pretty pleased, too. Angelita, though enthusiastic, was not easy to impress. Most of the girls I brought here had her rolling her eyes. But Piper—Piper had already made a positive impression before the first course. The thought made me weirdly proud.

I held up my water glass. "To our dinner 'do-over'," I toasted. "May it go much better than its poor predecessor."

Piper clinked my glass with her own. "I think it's safe to say it already has."

I grinned. "So you like this place then?"

"I love it. So much energy. So much noise. And," she added with a chuckle, "bonus—no ocean view."

"You might not want to put that in your TripAdvisor

review," I said with a laugh. "But I'm glad I didn't scare you off."

"Please. You made my night. I've been dying for some real Mexican food actually. How did you discover this place anyway?"

I shrugged, feeling suddenly uneasy. Girls always asked me this, usually with a hint of derision in their voices, and I'd end up making up some silly story about throwing darts on a map and going wherever the road took me. But for some reason something inside me didn't want to lie to Piper. Even if the truth was ugly. Maybe because it was.

"It's kind of a long story," I hedged.

Piper glanced around at the crowded restaurant. "I think we have time."

"Right." I squirmed in my seat, now feeling totally uncomfortable. I could feel her watching me, but I couldn't meet her eyes.

"It's okay," she said after a pause. "I didn't mean to pry."

Funny. That was almost the same thing I had said to her the night before at the yacht club, when I had asked her about her fear of the ocean, and she had turned bright red. But in the end, she had confessed it all. About her brother's tragic accident. About her lifelong fear. It couldn't have been easy for her to talk about that, either. But she had done it all the same.

And now it was my turn to share.

"It was a bad night in Tijuana," I said, my voice starting out slow. "Not long after my father's car accident. I'd been drinking all night and had stumbled back across the border, looking for something to settle my stomach. Somehow I found my way here."

I drew in a breath. "The state I was in? I probably should have been shot. Robbed. Left for dead. Instead, Miguel took me to the back room and forced black coffee down my throat. Then he grilled up the most delicious carne asada tacos I'd ever had in my life and made me sit and eat them all. After I had finished, he gave me a blanket and pillow and let me pass out in the back room on an old cot."

I paused for a moment, watching Piper's face. Waiting for a look of disgust, of judgment, of disdain. Yet strangely, I saw none of the above when I looked in her deep brown eyes. Only concern. Compassion. A weird look of understanding. A look that told me I should continue the tale.

"The next morning when I woke up, Miguel had a piping hot breakfast burrito with my name on it," I finished, emboldened by her reaction. "Not to mention a lecture about drinking and driving."

I leaned back in the booth, remembering that morning. It had been a dark time in my life. And Miguel had been my first glimpse of light. I owed him big-time. A debt all the money in the world could not repay.

Piper gave me a rueful smile. "That's pretty amazing," she said. "Most people wouldn't do something like that to help a stranger."

"Especially not a rich drunk gringo like me," I agreed. "Seriously, you may think I'm a big fuckup now, but you should have seen me then. I was on a path to destruction. And no one stepped in to intervene. Not my parents, not my friends. Certainly not the girls I dated. Miguel was the only one with the balls to tell me the truth. That I was an asshole and I needed help."

Piper bit her lower lip. "So . . ." she said carefully, "is that why you don't drink now?"

I looked up, surprised. "How do you know I don't drink?"

She shrugged. "It was just a guess," she said. "You didn't want to drink at the wedding. There were no wineglasses at the table yesterday. And today Angelita didn't ask if you wanted a margarita. Whereas at every other table it's been her first question."

I nodded slowly, feeling flushed at the idea that she'd been paying that much attention. Most people never even noticed my abstaining, too involved in drinking themselves. "Yeah," I said. "I haven't had a drink in two years. And I don't smoke pot anymore, either. These days I like having a clear head. I can get my highs elsewhere. Like out on the ocean, carving a wave. That's when I feel most alive." I stared down at my plate, feeling sheepish. "That probably sounds stupid, right?"

But Piper only shook her head. "No," she said. "I think it's pretty smart, actually. Trust me, I've seen far too many people have their lives ruined by not being able to handle their alcohol or drugs." She sighed loudly. "My own mother for one."

I looked up, surprised. "She's an alcoholic?"

"Among other things."

I stared at her, suddenly remembering what she'd told me at the yacht club about her brother. Had her mother's disease been somehow responsible for his death? Had she not kept a close eye on him because she had passed out drunk or drugged?

The thought sent an uneasy feeling creeping through my stomach. I didn't like to think back about how lucky I'd been that I hadn't hurt anyone that night I'd stumbled in here. That I hadn't killed anyone. Had it not been for Miguel, I would have gotten back in my car. Driven all the way home . . .

"I'm sorry," I said simply, not sure what else to say. "That must have been a tough way to grow up."

Piper turned away, looking uncomfortable, and I wondered if there was more to the story than she was letting on. But I didn't press her—we all had our secrets, after all. And some were definitely best kept hidden.

"So how are you liking your new job?" I asked, deciding to change the subject to something lighter. "Is being my weather producer everything you ever dreamed of and more?"

"Honestly? I'm still kind of freaking out that I had my first real story on the air tonight," she confessed. "I mean, watching the segment, hearing my words come out of your mouth." Her eyes sparkled. "Sure, I know it's every-day reality for you. But to me—it was like freaking magic."

I nodded, my insides warming at the glow I recognized on her face. It was funny: I'd taken my job at the station for granted for so long now it was kind of refreshing to hear her talk about it like this. To see how much it meant to her.

Just as it had once meant so much to me . . .

"Well, I'm glad we were able to make that happen," I declared, holding up my water glass for another toast. "To your first script. And to all those scripts to come. May you always make me look like the rock star that you did tonight."

She laughed and we clinked glasses. When she set hers back down, she looked at me, her eyes thoughtful. "So what's your deal, anyway?" she asked. "I mean, I know you say you're News 9 for life, but did you ever want to be something else?"

I shook my head. "Not that I remember," I said. "I feel like I always knew I would follow in my dad's footsteps and take on the family legacy. Even when I was a kid he used to take me to work and put me on air sometimes. I'd give a lispy little forecast live on TV. Everyone thought it was the cutest thing ever." I made a face to show her what I thought of that.

I expected her to laugh, but instead she looked at me with sympathetic eyes. "That must have been a lot of pressure," she said. "To be told you have to live up to this guy—who's like a legend. And never have a say in any of it?"

I frowned, feeling suddenly uneasy. I tried to shrug it off. "It is what it is, I suppose."

But Piper didn't seem to want to let it go. "What would you do?" she pressed. "If you could do anything at all?"

"What do you mean?"

"I mean if you didn't have this whole legacy thing. If tomorrow News 9 were to just—poof!—disappear. What would you do instead? If you had your choice of anything in the world—besides doing weather on TV?"

Her deep brown eyes seemed to burn into me as she asked the question, and I could feel a blush creep to my hairline. Suddenly I felt vaguely annoyed, here in my favorite place. Annoyed at her, for the unnerving question. Annoyed at myself for not having a decent answer. At least not one I wanted to admit.

And so I squared my shoulders, pasting a cocky grin on my face. "I guess I'd probably surf all day long," I drawled. "Endless summer, baby!"

Her expression flickered and I thought I caught disappointment ghosting her face. The smile fled from my lips, and I immediately felt bad for my stupid answer. She had been asking a serious question and had actually cared enough to want an answer—which was more than I could say for most of the girls I dated. And yet I had, predictably, turned it into a farce.

I really was the Joker, wasn't I?

"Sorry," I muttered, raking a hand through my hair. "I guess I just never thought about it before. In any case, it'll never happen. Not while my mother is alive at least."

She nodded, giving me a look that felt a little too close to pity for my liking. But she didn't press me further and for that I was grateful. Instead she said, "Speaking of surfing, do you know anyone who gives lessons around here?"

I raised an eyebrow. "*You* want to learn how to surf?"

She laughed. "No, thank you," she declared. She paused, then added, "But there is this little boy. He's ten and he lives at the group home where I work. He's had a tough life. And some . . . well, pretty big disappointments lately as well. But he loves surfing. Or at least the idea of surfing—I don't know if he's ever actually done it before."

"Okay . . ."

"Do you know someone who might be willing to give him a quick lesson sometime?" she asked. "I could pay for it, of course. I don't have a ton of money—the Holloway House doesn't have a big budget, but I'm happy to—"

"I'll teach him."

Her eyes widened. "No," she protested. "You're too busy. I just meant if you knew of a surf school nearby that might be able to—"

I held up a hand to stop her. "Piper, I'll do it," I said. "I'll make the time. Just tell me where and when and I'll be there."

"Really?" she asked, her eyes bright with excitement.

"You'd really do that?" She swallowed hard. "I warn you, sometimes he can be difficult . . ."

"So can I, sweetheart," I reminded her with a smirk. "Or haven't you noticed yet?"

She laughed, her black lashes sweeping over her eyes as she looked down at the table, and something hard thudded in my chest. While I loved the idea of helping this boy, the idea of making her happy? That was even better.

"I will give him the best surf lesson he's ever had," I declared. "On one condition."

She looked up. "What's that?"

I gave her a wink. "That you dance with me now."

sixteen

PIPER

That you dance with me now.

Before I could reply, Asher grabbed my hands from across the table, nearly knocking over our water glasses as he dragged me to my feet and toward the small makeshift dance floor in the center of the restaurant. He nodded to the mariachi band and they responded, launching into a fast-paced Spanish tune. Asher pulled me into his arms, locking his hand at the small of my back, then swinging me around in a madcap dance.

I knew he was just being silly—but heat surged through me all the same—and I found myself unable to protest as he led me around the dance floor, his hand scorching my back, his steps never faltering. I was no dancer—not by a long shot—but at that moment I felt as if I were floating. And it was tough not to be infected by his enthusiasm. The grin on his face. The strength and the warmth of his arms. My traitorous skin was practically vibrating with the desire for more than a dance. My traitorous lips begging for a repeat of last night's ill-advised kiss.

"Dancing with the stars, baby," he quipped, then held up

my hand to allow me to twirl. I did, laughing despite myself as I almost fell into another table. He grabbed me just in time, yanking me flush against him. My heart jolted as my breasts pressed against his solid chest, his hands wrapping securely around my waist. I dared to look up into those beautiful storm-tossed eyes of his, promptly losing myself in the dilated pupils.

A weird longing suddenly crept through me. What must it be like to go through life like this? Always moving with such confidence, style, and poise? Never having to worry about tripping up, falling down. Not being able to pull yourself back up. His self-assurance was thrilling—yet completely petrifying at the same time. A man who acted like he had nothing to lose.

Except . . . I thought back to that moment at the table, when I asked him what he wanted to be. I was positive I hadn't imagined the pain in his eyes or the way he deftly turned the question into a joke. Could the fact that he had nothing to lose come from the fact that he had already lost something along the way?

I had always fought tooth and nail to get anywhere in life. But I'd always been able to pick my own path, my own destination. Meanwhile Asher had never had to work for anything. But his journey had been predestined from the start—without anyone asking his opinion.

I wondered, if given the choice, what life I would prefer.

I realized suddenly that he had stopped dancing. We had both stopped dancing. We were both looking at one another. Our faces mere inches apart. Our lips even closer. My heart thudded in my chest. I swallowed hard. Holy crap.

"Um, I think that's our dinner," I stammered, jerking my head to watch a server carry two steaming plates over to our table.

"It can wait," he said. "They always serve it too hot, anyway."

Speaking of *too hot*—he grabbed me again, pulling me back to him. His hands slipped down my arms, dragging me closer. So close I could feel the contours of his chest muscles against my belly. His uneven breaths against my cheek. He reached up, tracing my jawline with a firm, persuasive touch, and it sent a warming shiver straight to my toes.

Suddenly no part of me wanted to pull away. I didn't care a bit about the food getting cold. Or the whole "you shouldn't date coworkers" bullshit, either. I just wanted to dive in and kiss the hell out of this gorgeous man, all common sense be damned. Forget about tomorrow and the day after and the day after that. Hell, my entire future. At that moment, I was ready to say fuck it all and throw everything away, in exchange for just five more minutes of this fantasy.

But that would be stupid. I'd worked too hard, for too long, to put myself at this kind of risk. Yes, Asher was charming. He was hot as hell. And the way he was looking at me now told me he liked me quite a bit. But I knew far too well how fleeting attraction could be. And if I allowed myself to fall for him, I'd fall alone. I'd fall far. And fast. And I might never be able to get up again.

So, against everything inside of me, I took a step back, trying to put distance between myself and this god of a man. It wasn't easy. In fact, it pretty much took all my strength to even put a couple of inches between us. And when he looked down at me with eyes filled with pity it almost did me in.

"Oh, Red," he murmured, taking a step toward me and lowering his head to whisper in my ear. His mouth brushed softly against my earlobe and I practically yelped as the chills ran through me, prickling my skin. "Don't you ever just let yourself go?"

I pulled a breath through my teeth, practically panting with desire. "Not really," I managed to say with a brittle laugh.

Asher slipped a hand under my shirt, skimming my waist. The sudden skin-on-skin contact sent crackles of electricity down to my toes. I jerked, but he only tightened his grip, his eyes locking down on mine as he ran his other hand through my hair, his fingers tangling in each curl.

"Just let go," he whispered huskily, his face inches from mine. "For even a moment. Just let it all go. I promise, there's nothing that can hurt you here."

And suddenly I wanted to do just that. Just for a moment—
to feel what it would be like to live another life. To be someone like Asher, who was so fucking free. What harm could
it do really? We were on a dance floor, in front of people. As
Asher said, nothing could hurt me here.

Staying in control had been a necessity in a life lived in
chaos. Waking up each morning, never knowing if my
mother would be drunk, sober, or worse. Even when I got
to the Holloway House, they tried their best but there was
always an influx of new, troubled kids. Kids who were not
always model citizens. You had to learn to sleep with one
eye open, your valuables tucked under your pillow. *Trust no
one* was the unspoken rule.

But I was not at the Holloway House now. Nor was I with
my mother. I was in the arms of a gorgeous man who was
looking at me with eyes that begged me to trust him—even
for just a moment.

"Okay," I said.

Asher didn't reply, only swept me back into the dance
and this time I let him. Let myself get lost in his beguiling
eyes. His sensuous lips. His firm but gentle touch. His rich,
musky scent. For one precious moment I let myself live
another life. Where I was a fairy-tale princess and he was a
real-life prince.

"God, you're beautiful," he murmured, his breath whispering across my sensitive cheeks. "I have wanted to do this
since the first time I laid eyes on you."

He leaned down, his lips crushing mine, his tongue pushing into my mouth, invading without apology. Then he yanked
me closer to him, so close I could feel his erection, pressing
against my belly, and my whole body burned with fire.

He pushed me against the wall, his hands dropping down
to cup my ass, and heat pooled between my legs as I somehow managed to scissor his thigh. Lost in the spell, I vaguely
realized we were no longer dancing. Just making out in a
crowd of strangers in a random Mexican hole-in-the-wall
in the worst part of town. If you had told me yesterday that
I would be doing this, I would have laughed in your face.

Because I, Piper Strong, did not do this kind of thing. Especially not with my . . .

. . . coworker.

I jerked away, the spell broken as reality crashed over me like a tidal wave. Asher looked down at me, glassy-eyed, still dazed. I shook myself, trying to regain control.

"I . . . think it might be time to eat," I stammered, retreating like a coward to our table. I could feel his eyes burning into me from behind, but I was too chicken to turn around. If I did, I might abandon the idea of eating altogether—as I was now hungry for something not related to food. As I popped back into our booth, I pulled my water glass to my cheek, desperate to cool myself with the condensation from the glass.

A moment later Asher joined me at the table. I set down my glass, waiting for him to say something—anything—to break this weird spell between us. But he said nothing. Only grabbed his fork and dug into his meal, avoiding my eyes. I tried to do the same, even though I wasn't hungry anymore. In fact, if anything I felt a little sick.

What had I been thinking? Oh God, this was exactly what I'd said I didn't want to happen. And yet, it had felt so good. So right. To just let go like that—to allow myself to live in the moment, as if there were no tomorrow.

But tomorrow would come all too soon. And one misstep tonight could ruin it forever.

Forcing myself to concentrate on the food, rather than the suddenly tense vibe between us, I stuck my fork into my chile relleno and stuffed it in my mouth. As the spices hit my tongue, my eyes widened. I could barely manage to withhold a moan of pleasure, the awkwardness of the ill-advised kiss instantly forgotten as my taste buds took over. Man, this was even better than Asher's jalapeño scrambled eggs—and that was saying quite a bit.

"Oh my God," I cried. "This is so freaking good!"

Asher's face relaxed. Then he grinned. "Told you."

I took another bite, my mouth tingling happily. Well, at least if this turned out to be my last supper I'd die with a full belly and a happy palate. There were worse ways to go, I supposed.

"I'm sorry," I said, once I had swallowed another bite. "I didn't mean—"

Asher held out a hand to stop me. "No," he said. "I'm the one who's sorry. I got carried away out there. I shouldn't have, well, you know." He raked a hand through his hair and laughed. "You're just so goddamned sexy when you lose control. I'm only human, you know."

I blushed straight to my hairline. But my insides were dancing. "Yeah," I said, trying to keep my voice casual. "That's the problem with losing control. You end up doing things you don't want to do."

"Oh, don't get me wrong," he replied with an almost feral smile. "I wanted to do that. And a whole lot more." Then he shrugged. "I'm just not sure if you were enjoying it as much as me."

I stared down at my plate of food, my pulse racing. How could I explain this to someone like him? That I did enjoy it. That I enjoyed it far too much, in fact. And that that was the problem.

"Hey!" he cried, reaching out and lifting my chin with his fingers until I was forced to meet his eyes. The teasing look was gone and there was a seriousness there instead that was almost sexier than his smile. "I get it, okay? It's not a big deal. I promise."

I sighed, shaking off his fingers, feeling like an idiot. It wasn't fair. It was so not fair. Why couldn't I have this kind of life? The kind where I was free to make mistakes and do stupid things and hook up with hot guys without worrying about future consequences? Why did I always have to worry about the bigger picture?

"Look, Asher, I—"

But I never got out what I was going to say. Because at that moment, Asher's cell phone chimed, announcing an incoming message. He pulled it from his pocket and his eyes scanned the screen. Then he cursed under his breath.

"Everything okay?" I asked.

He sighed. "Do you mind if we take the rest to go? I need to go meet my mother and give her something."

"Sure," I said, surprised to feel sudden disappointment well in my stomach. After all, hadn't I just wanted to get away from all this only minutes before? And here was the perfect out. "That's fine."

"You could come," he added suddenly.

"Oh. Um." I bit my lower lip. "I wouldn't want to intrude."

"You won't be. In fact, you can help me get away quicker. Otherwise my mom will want me to stay all night." He made a face. Then his eyes locked on me. "Besides, I'm not ready for this night to end. Are you?"

I should have been. But of course I wasn't.

seventeen

PIPER

When Asher said he had to meet his mother, I assumed we'd be going to his parents' house. Or maybe to News 9 even, where she had her office; from what I heard she put in crazy hours there and would often stay quite late into the night. Instead, forty-five minutes later, we pulled into an elegant golf club in Rancho Santa Fe and before I knew it, the valet was opening my door, addressing me as *ma'am*.

And here we went again.

"Maybe I should wait in the car," I stammered, looking around the parking lot at all the BMWs and Mercedes and Cadillacs. Gone was the down-home, warm vibe of Miguel's and suddenly it was the Del Mar Yacht Club part deux. "I'm really not dressed for this place."

"Neither am I," Asher said, tossing the valet his keys. At first I wondered if the man was going to turn up his nose at the very out-of-place Fiona, tarnishing their shiny, sparkling auto zone, but then I caught sight of the fat wad of bills Asher handed him along with his keys. He probably wasn't judging too hard.

That said, he might be the only one. The other guests,

milling about, especially the women, were definitely staring at us. And judging. And giving me the evil eye.

Asher seemed not to notice any of it. He grabbed my hand. "Come on," he said, leveling those green eyes of his directly at me, as if I was the only person there. "The sooner we get in, the sooner we get out."

I nodded, squaring my shoulders and tilting my chin up high. Gathering together all my inner strength to walk past the staring women, as if I owned the place. As if I deserved to be here, at a country club, with Asher Anderson on my arm.

As we entered the lounge, I looked around. The dining room was clearly designed to give off a rich but cozy vibe, with dim lighting tinged with purple and comfy armchairs surrounding a roaring fire. There were couches and candles and plantation shutters opening up to a sparkling deck overlooking what appeared to be a golf course.

"This place is amazing." I couldn't help but marvel.

Asher looked around, as if seeing it for the first time. "It's pretty nice," he agreed. "A little less obnoxious than some of the places my parents frequent." He shrugged. "Anyway, I won't subject you to my mother. Why don't you wait for me at the bar and I'll be back in five minutes?"

My pulse kicked up in alarm, my confidence fleeing the building. It was one thing to be here with him. Quite another to stand by myself, looking so out of place. Still, what could I say? I couldn't very well demand to butt in on his and his mother's private conversation.

"Sure, that's fine," I said. "Take your time."

Or, you know, hurry the hell up.

He reached out, squeezing my hand in his before disappearing into the lounge. I watched him go, cradling the hand in question, trying not to focus on how warm and nice it felt from his touch. My mind flashed back to the make-out session on the dance floor at Miguel's and I shivered a little, wondering where this night would ultimately lead. What was I still doing here? I should have never agreed to come along. We should have parted ways when the parting was good and not have tempted fate further than we already had.

I sidled up to the bar, figuring maybe I'd order a drink while I was waiting. Just a glass of wine to take the edge off. But then I remembered what Asher had told me at the Mexican restaurant. He was two years sober. And while I myself had no issues with alcohol, I knew from my mom's experience it could be tough to abstain while those around you were indulging. So when the bartender came to take my drink order, I asked for a Diet Coke instead.

A four-dollar Diet Coke, I soon learned as she placed my drink and my check in front of me. Holy crap. Maybe it was a good thing I hadn't asked for any alcohol.

I reached into my pocket for my wallet, but to my surprise she waved me off. "You're with Asher, right?" she asked. "I can just put it on his tab."

"That's okay," I said. "I can pay for my own drink."

I'd tried to insist on paying for my meal at Miguel's as well, but Asher wouldn't hear of it. When he wasn't looking I slipped an extra twenty into the billfold as a tip. (Not that he hadn't already left a generous one himself.)

The bartender looked surprised but didn't argue, just scooped up my money and walked away. I took my glass, bringing it to my lips, surveying the scene.

It was then that I realized I was being watched—by a group of young women across the room. They were all dressed like they belonged here, in simple but expensive-looking sheath dresses and smart stiletto heels that probably cost more than I could have gotten for trading in my car. My skin prickled and I pulled out my phone, pretending to check my messages as I prayed Asher would return before they got brave and approached me.

Sadly my prayers went unanswered and soon I found myself surrounded by the group. Each girl looked me up and down in turn, not disguising her curiosity, as if I was some exotic animal she'd discovered at the zoo. I squirmed a little, suddenly feeling like what a gazelle must feel like, surrounded by lions.

It's no big deal, I told myself. *They can't do anything to you. Just keep your cool.*

"Hiiii!" The first girl who had approached greeted me, her voice far too bright and cheery for my liking. "I don't think we've met, have we? I'm Madison Van Voorhees! And this is Tracy and Rian! You came here with Asher, right?"

She stuck out a well-manicured hand. Reluctantly I took it, giving it a hesitant pump. Her palm was ridiculously soft, as if she'd done nothing but moisturize it for the last six months. Maybe she had.

"Um, hi. I'm Piper," I said, trying to keep my voice casual and unaffected. "And yeah, Asher went to go talk to his mother. I'm sure he'll be back in a second." My gaze darted behind them, searching for the man in question, but unfortunately he was nowhere in sight. I wondered if it would be rude to excuse myself and run screaming away before this got any more awkward. But at this point they pretty much had me surrounded and pinned with the bar at my back. Any escape seemed futile.

The girls exchanged glances and giggled. "I haven't seen Asher in for*ever*," the second girl—Tracy—declared. She was beautiful and African-American and had the shiniest black hair I had ever seen, wound up in a tangle of braids.

"Yeah, well, you know he thinks he's too good for this place," added the third girl, Rian, a brunette with a cute pixie cut that I could have never pulled off if I tried.

"He *is* too good for this place, Rian," corrected Madison with a dreamy look on her face. "God, he is too good for *every*where." She turned back to me, her wide blue eyes locking on to my own, giving me a searching look. "Especially in bed. Am I right?"

"Wh-what?" I stammered, staring at her, my face exploding with heat.

She gave me a skeptical look. "Come on. You are sleeping with him, right?"

Oh. My. God.

"You're embarrassing her, Madison," scolded Rian. "And, come on! Is that even a question? I mean, we are talking about Asher Anderson, aren't we? Haven't we all slept with him at least once?"

"Guilty!" Madison chirped, raising a hand. Then she smiled at me. "Guess you're one of the tribe now, hon."

"I'm *not* sleeping with him," I protested, my eyes darting around the room in total panic mode, wondering who might be overhearing this conversation. There could be people from News 9 here even—people who could affect my employment. "We're just coworkers."

Coworkers who make out and go on dates, something inside me nagged. But I pushed it down. They didn't need to know those gory details. It would only give them more ammunition.

"Don't listen to them," Tracy said, putting a hand on my arm. "They're just teasing. Besides, from what I hear he's totally back with Sarah Martin anyway."

Wait, what? I frowned before I could stop myself. *Sarah Martin? Who was Sarah Martin?*

"That's *right*!" Madison agreed. "Oh my God, I totally forgot. He even took her out on the boat last night—how romantic is that? She called me this morning from his place, looking for a ride home. Of course she was completely wrecked from being up all night—*if* you know what I mean."

The girls giggled conspiratorially. I just stood there, the Diet Coke souring in my stomach. What the hell were they talking about? Asher was with *me* the night before. We'd had dinner. We'd kissed under the stars.

And then you went home, that pesky voice reminded me. And left him all by his lonesome.

We are talking about Asher Anderson, aren't we? as Rian had so helpfully pointed out.

"Are you okay?" Madison asked. She gave me a skeptical look. "You're looking awfully pale all of a sudden. Do you want me to go get your . . . *coworker* . . . for you?" She laughed.

"I'm fine," I managed to say. "Excuse me."

I pushed back on my barstool so quickly it almost toppled over. Then I wrestled my way through the gang of girls, feeling their amused eyes watching me as I forced myself to keep my steps calm and casual. My heart was pounding in my chest and my stomach was churning.

He even took her out on the boat last night.

The boat.

The freaking boat.

Oh God.

I stopped, for a moment not sure what to do. Where I should go. My car was back at the station where I'd left it, so I couldn't just leave. But how could I stay—how could I face Asher now, knowing what he'd done?

She called me this morning from his place, looking for a ride home.

We are talking about Asher Anderson, aren't we?

Finally I spotted the sign for the ladies' lounge and I ran to it like a lifesaver. Thankfully no one was inside and so I collapsed into a stall, locking it behind me. I sucked in a huge breath, trying to calm my racing pulse. Trying to scold my aching heart.

This was stupid. Why was I so upset? Asher didn't owe me a thing. We were just coworkers. We weren't even dating. He had every right to take another girl out on the boat. The boat I had refused, I might add, to board in the first place. He had every right to wine her, dine her, bed her—whatever. It was none of my business whatsoever. I had no hold over him. No rights. I didn't even want any. I didn't want him.

Except I did. Somehow, against everything I had tried, I totally did.

Goddamn it.

I squared my shoulders. This was exactly why I needed to stop this in the first place. Why I shouldn't be here at all. It wasn't as if I didn't know Asher's reputation. Everyone knew the games he played. He had seduction down to a science—make the girl feel all special so she'd do whatever he wanted. Then, once satisfied, he'd move on to the next. What made me think I was any different than the rest of them? Because he took me to his favorite restaurant? Big freaking deal. That was probably part of his typical MO. To make the girl think he was different than your average douchey rich guy. That he was *complicated. Sensitive.*

But at the end of the day, it wasn't complicated at all. In fact, it was glaringly simple. I needed him more than he needed me. And I needed to remember that. And keep my head.

But was it too late? Asher could fire me in an instant. For some stupid reason—hell, for no reason at all. If I refused to play his games now, if I rejected his advances from this point forward, would I lose everything I had gained?

I frowned, forcing myself to firm my resolve. It didn't matter. I could lose my job, but I refused to lose my self-respect. I would not let Asher play me anymore. I would not subject myself to his whims or let my heart get carried away.

He might be the Joker. But I was no fool.

I rose to my feet, squaring my jaw. Stepping out of the stall, I headed back into the golf club ready to hold my head up high. I would cross the floor and walk straight out that front door, never looking back. I could take an Uber home. No big deal.

But I never made it that far. Because when I stepped out into the bathroom, I found none other than Asher himself, standing there, leaning against the vanity.

Waiting for me.

eighteen

ASHER

I watched Piper freeze, her eyes wide, totally a deer in head-lights. Not surprising, I suppose. She certainly wouldn't be expecting me to be standing in the ladies' room.

I had just been finishing up talking to my mother when I caught her out of the corner of my eye surrounded by those basic bitches—as Jess had dubbed them one night when I'd dragged her out here—and even from across the room I could guess they were telling tales out of school. The way Piper had stiffened. The way her eyes darted around the room, as if desperate for escape.

I scowled. I should have never brought her here. Never left her alone for a second. Still, even I hadn't realized how quickly the wolves would circle.

"What are you doing in here?" she demanded. Her voice was raw, the words scraping from her throat. As if she was trying desperately not to cry. My heart squeezed in my chest and it was all I could do not to cross the floor, to pull her into my arms and not let her go.

But I had a feeling, from the look on her face, she wouldn't appreciate the gesture.

"Sit," I said instead, motioning to the couch at the far end of the bathroom. The ladies' lounge, I guess you called it, though why anyone would lounge around in a public toilet was beyond me.

She glanced at the door, as if trying to decide whether to make a run for it. Then her shoulders dropped. She walked over to the couch and slumped down. I nodded my approval then turned to the sink, grabbing a towel and wetting it. I handed it to her without a word.

"Seriously?" she said, looking down at it. "You have real towels in the bathroom here? Like made of cloth instead of paper?"

I made a face. "Only the best for the one percent."

The towel thing had actually been my mother's idea. She'd led this huge campaign with the other ladies of the club about how we must all work to save the environment and how using washable towels prevented waste. Which was ridiculous, in my opinion, since the water used to wash them between uses probably added up to more waste than a little recyclable paper. But I'd long ago learned my lesson on trying to criticize my mom's campaigns.

"Are you okay?" I asked, dropping to my knees in front of her, searching her face with my eyes.

She turned away. "I'm fine. I just didn't feel so good. Maybe it was the spicy food."

I plucked the cloth from her hands and dabbed her face with it. This close I could see the hint of tears at the edges of her eyes, and anger rose inside of me.

"Come on, Piper," I said. "You were fine a few minutes ago. What did they say to you?"

"I just want to go home, okay?" she said, her voice pleading now. "We had our fun. But we have to work tomorrow. I would like to be well rested."

"If that's what you want, fine. I will take you home. But not until you tell me what happened."

And not until those girls are sorry for making you cry.

She rose to her feet, crossing the bathroom until she was standing in front of the full-length mirror. "Look, you have every right to live your life the way you want to live it," she said quietly. "I have no say in that. But I also need to do the same." She turned to me, her face a mask of devastation. "And I can't do this. I don't *want* to do this."

"Do what? All we did was have dinner."

"Come on, Asher. Don't play me like one of those stupid girls out there. I'm not an idiot. I know where this is leading. And it's not somewhere I want to go. Not with you anyway."

Her words hit me with the force of a ten-ton truck. I rose to my feet, stalking over to her. When I reached her, I grabbed her by the shoulders, forcing her to face me. "What did they tell you, Piper?" I demanded, my gaze bearing down on her now. "What the hell did they say?"

Her face turned bright red, but to her credit, she didn't look away this time. "They told me about Sarah," she said.

My grip tightened. Fuck.

"Don't blame them. It wasn't their fault. I told them there was nothing between us so I'm sure they thought it was no big deal. And it isn't a big deal, either," she added. "You're a single guy. You can sleep with whomever you want. It's none of my business."

I snapped my teeth together so hard it almost hurt. It was all I could do not to punch the mirror. "I didn't sleep with Sarah," I said.

She practically rolled her eyes at that. Which sent a jolt of pain straight through me. Because of course she would believe them over me. Because that was the kind of guy she thought I was. The kind of guy who would double-down on his dates until he got one to spend the night.

And maybe she wasn't far off. Under normal circumstances.

I closed my eyes then opened them again. "It's true that I took Sarah out on the boat after you went home," I said. "Her father is a very important advertiser to News 9, and he was having dinner with my mother. She asked me to take Sarah and I couldn't say no."

Piper's face twisted. "So, what, you took one for the News 9 team? How . . . sacrificial of you."

I jerked, her words cutting deep. I raked a hand through my hair, trying to find my voice. "Look, I'm not going to lie. Sarah and I have a history. We've been thrown together a lot, thanks to our parents and, well, we've taken advantage of that a few times in the past. But we're not a couple. We've never been a couple. And I swear to God I didn't lay a hand on her last night."

Piper's eyes flashed fire. "Come on," she spit out. "Do you think I'm stupid? She slept at your freaking house."

"She did," I agreed. "But not with me."

"What the hell is that supposed to mean?"

I turned and walked back over to the couch, dropping down onto it, rubbing the back of my neck with my hand.

"Sarah can be a bit of a party girl," I said. "And she got pretty drunk on the boat. So drunk that I was afraid she was going to do something stupid if I let her out of my sight. So I brought her to my place. And I let her sleep in my bed. I waited until I was sure she was okay—that she didn't require medical attention and just needed to sleep it off. Then I crashed on the couch."

"You . . . slept on the couch?"

I shrugged. "I did."

"You didn't sleep with her."

"I didn't. And I'm sorry I didn't tell you any of this. I was, well, pretty embarrassed about the whole thing to tell you the truth."

She closed her eyes. "Oh God. Asher . . ."

I rose from the couch. Crossed the lounge to her. "Look, Piper, I've done some stupid things in my life. Things I am definitely not proud of. And I'm not saying I'm some saint and I'm certainly no knight in shining armor. But I promise you, Piper," I added after a pause, "there was only one girl on my mind last night. *All* of last night. And it wasn't Sarah Martin."

She nodded slowly, looking at me with those eyes of hers. Those big, fucking beautiful, endless eyes that made me want to pull her into my arms and never let her go.

But I had to finish first.

"Those girls out there?" I said, gesturing to the bathroom door. "They're the ones I'm supposed to be with. The ones my mother expects me to be with. But you know what? You're the one I *chose* to be with tonight. The only one I *want* to be with."

I closed my mouth, wondering if I'd said too much. Stripped myself bare, laying everything out in front of her, casting myself upon her mercy. Now all I could do was wait for her answer. Wait for her to—

—kiss me.

Our lips came together, hard and fast. Our tongues delved into each other's mouths, connecting in a wild, feverish dance. Her hands went to my shoulders. My hands went to her waist, dragging her back on the couch.

Still kissing, I positioned her on top of me so she was straddling my thighs, her core up against my growing arousal. I shifted, needing to feel her against me. Soft, solid, real. My fingers dragged down her arms, slipping underneath to stroke the spot just below her bra line. She moaned softly against my mouth and I jerked in response. Clamping my hands down on her hips, grinding her against me. The feel of her thighs, pressing against my own, her hair falling into my face. It was almost too much. And yet at the same time, not nearly enough.

I reached under her shirt, skimming her flat stomach until my fingers found the softness of her breast. I cupped it my hand for a moment, then slid my thumb over her nipple in a slow circle. It hardened to a sharp peak and she moaned again, her fingers digging into my shoulders, so hard I wondered if she'd draw blood. Not that I would have minded if she did. I nipped at her lower lip, reaching my other hand up to tangle in her copper curls. Trying to resist the urge to rip off her shirt, unclasp her bra. Allow her breasts to properly spill into my hands.

"God, Piper," I groaned against her mouth. "You feel so fucking—"

A knock on the door interrupted my words. Shit. Caught up in the moment I'd pretty much forgotten the fact that we were technically in a public bathroom. I'd locked the door behind me when I'd entered, but of course it would be only a matter of time before someone had to use the facilities or powder her nose. We were probably fortunate they'd held out this long.

Then again, they could probably hold out a little longer, right? I grinned wickedly at Piper, daring her to ignore the interruption. She was properly mussed at this point, her hair sticking out in all directions and her shirt halfway undone. Had I actually started unbuttoning her shirt? I hadn't even realized I was doing it in my lust-filled haze.

"Let's just pretend no one's here," I suggested, reaching up to cup her other breast, dragging my fingers across the nipple. She sucked a breath through her teeth and my groin ached in response. God, I needed to get this girl naked, like, yesterday.

But the knock came again, louder this time. More insistent. And Piper pulled away, the spell between us broken. She stumbled off of me, still looking a little stunned, then headed over to the mirror, peering at her reflection with horrified eyes. I watched her for a moment, feeling my erection press painfully against my slacks. Wishing more than anything I could climb off this couch and hoist her onto the counter and take her right then and there.

But that might be pushing it, even for me.

"Is someone in there?" the voice beyond the door demanded, now sounding impatient. I recognized it as Dawn's, the club's night manager.

I rose from my seat. "Just a minute," I growled.

I walked over to Piper, standing behind her in the mirror. For a moment I just looked at her, at how goddamned beautiful she was. Then I reached up, pulling her hair back gently, taking the elastic band from her wrist and sliding it into place. Once I had secured her hair, I walked over and grabbed another towel and handed it to her.

"Take your time," I told her. "They can wait."

She nodded slowly, still seeming dazed. She washed her face, then set the towel in the basket and headed toward the door. I watched as she unlocked it and readied to step back into the club.

"Wait," I said.

She turned to me, questioning. I walked over to her and reached down, taking her hand in mine. I squeezed it hard, giving her a cocky smile. "When we walk out there, I want them all to see you on my arm."

She bit her lower lip, looking as if she wanted to protest, but couldn't. I pushed the door open before she could change her mind. Then we stepped out together, still clasping one another's hands.

I looked around. The entire club had fallen silent, like something out of a movie. Everyone had stopped eating and drinking and talking and instead was staring in our direction. Let's just say the looks at Piper weren't exactly complimentary, either.

My jaw clenched. They were judging her. They were condemning her. They were trying to let her know, in no uncertain terms, that they thought she was trash.

When they were the ones who were truly garbage.

I squeezed Piper's hand, giving her a warning look. She was pale as a ghost, but she kept her head held high. Didn't let those bastards see her sweat. I wanted to kiss her all over again, I was so proud.

"Come on, Red," I said loudly, to ensure everyone in the club could hear. "This place is seriously played out."

I started walking toward the exit, pulling her along with me. My gaze darted around the room, meeting the eyes of anyone who dared to look in our direction. Most were too cowardly, of course, ducking their heads as soon as I glanced their way.

"Asher!"

I froze in my tracks. Except for *her*, of course. Slowly, I turned around.

"Mother," I said coolly.

"What are you doing?" she hissed, looking like a coiled snake, ready to strike. "You're making a scene."

"And here I was trying to make an exit."

She ignored me, turning her attention to Piper, giving her a disdainful once-over. In response, I slid my hand around Piper's waist, pulling her tight against me. Making it clear to my mother where I stood on the matter. Sure, I'd probably have to pay for my act of defiance later, but I was willing to do that, to defend Piper's honor now.

Mom took a step back, holding up her hands. "Well then, don't let me stop you," she said in a tight voice.

I didn't dignify that with a response, instead stepping around her to lead Piper through the front doors and straight to the valet. I handed him my ticket, then realized they'd already brought my bus up. Obviously my departure had been well orchestrated, just like everything else in this place.

I opened the door for Piper and ushered her inside. She stepped in on shaky legs and I closed the door behind her. Normally this was something a valet would do, but they didn't seem awfully eager to serve at the moment. Probably thought even touching my car would give them some disease. I ran around to the other side, jumped in the driver's seat, and revved the engine. Fiona grumbled to life, and soon we were puttering away.

"So that was . . . interesting," I said after we'd cleared the place. Then I forced a grin to my face, hoping to lighten the mood. "Where to next, Red?"

She was silent for a moment. Then, "Please just take me home."

nineteen

PIPER

To his credit, Asher didn't argue. He just put the bus in gear and screeched out of the country club parking lot, leaving a cloud of exhaust behind. It would have been funny if I weren't already so unnerved by what had happened in the bathroom. By the entire night for that matter.

Once again I had allowed myself to lose control. Even after all the promises I'd made to myself about standing strong—walking away. It was like Asher had cast some kind of spell over me. And I was powerless to resist him.

"Look, I am really sorry about that," he said, glancing over at me. "Trust me, I had no idea they would react like that or I never would have brought you." He paused then added, "Though I have to admit, it was pretty satisfying to see all the shocked faces. It's been a while since I've been able to piss them off this badly. And that many—all at once. Might be a personal record. Achievement unlocked."

"Is there *anything* you take seriously?" I snapped before I could help myself. I knew I should just keep my mouth shut. Let him take me home. But I was so raw and on edge and frustrated at this point. I needed someone to lash out at and unfortunately he was the only person around.

What was I doing? All my life I'd played by the rules. Worked hard, kept under the radar, tried not to piss anyone off—in a vain attempt to get somewhere someday. But Asher—he was like this big ball of destruction, crashing through life like a bull in a china shop, not caring at all about the mess he left behind.

Except he does care, a little voice inside me interjected. *He may try to pretend he doesn't, but he clearly does.*

My mind flashed back to his words in the bathroom. How troubled he'd looked when he'd explained how his mother had forced Sarah on him in an effort to win more advertising revenue. As if he were an asset, a commodity to be bought and sold—rather than a member of the family. Her own son.

On the surface Asher's life seemed so easy. So carefree. But I was fast realizing there was so much more to his existence than he liked to admit. A darkness, a lurking shadow behind those happy-go-lucky green eyes.

But he could always walk away, I reminded myself. *If he were willing to cut the purse strings. If he were truly unhappy, he could give up the cash in exchange for freedom.*

I realized we had stopped at a red light. Asher was staring at me, his eyes brimming with concern. "I take you seriously," he said quietly.

My heart squeezed in my chest. At his words, at the expression on his face. Too earnest, too honest to be a lie. To be some long game of seduction. While I still had no idea why he'd focused his attentions on me, I could no longer deny that he had. He liked me. Asher Anderson, the guy everyone wanted. He wanted me.

I squirmed in my seat, heat throbbing between my legs as I thought back to the scene in the bathroom again. The way his mouth had come down on mine. The way his tongue had swirled into my mouth, the way his hands had gripped my hips. My breasts ached at the memory of his touch, the way he circled my nipples with deft fingers, the tips hardening to sharp peaks under his caress.

Looking back now it seemed almost a dream. Me, grinding up against him, praying somehow our clothes would magically disappear and we could connect for real. Thank God someone had chosen that moment to knock on the door. I had been completely without common sense and ready to incur a lifetime of regrets.

But, oh, they would have been delicious regrets.

I shifted, frowning. "This has to stop," I said. "This whole thing—whatever it is. I mean, don't get me wrong," I added quickly, catching his face, "I like you. I like being with you. But I can't keep putting my future on the line."

He frowned. "What are you talking about?"

"Do you really not see it?" I asked, frustration building. It was so obvious. But evidently not to someone like him. "You got me this job. I'm working for you. If we continued this and something were to happen, who would be out on the streets? Some random girl who scored a job she didn't really deserve? Or News 9's golden son?"

He was silent for a moment, and the look on his face told me I'd insulted him. But what else could I say to make him see? The truth hurt, yes. But that didn't make it untrue.

"Wow," he said at last. And I could see his knuckles whitening as he gripped the steering wheel tight in his hands. "You really think I'm an asshole, don't you?"

"No!" I protested. "It's just—"

"You really think I got you this job just so I could sleep with you?" he interrupted in a cold, hard voice. "Like some kind of casting couch or something? Do you actually think I can't get enough girls to sleep with me that I have to fucking pay them?"

My face burned at the fury I heard in his voice. Oh God. This was going completely wrong. "I didn't mean—"

"Is that why you agreed to go out with me last night and tonight?" he asked in a quiet voice. "Because you felt you owed me for the job? That if you refused me I was going to throw you out on the streets?"

I hung my head, feeling tears brim at the corners of my eyes. He sounded so angry. But there was also this hurt threading through his voice that was nearly unbearable for me to hear.

"I don't think it was that calculated," I managed to say in a hoarse voice. "I believe that you actually like me. But, Asher, you must be aware of your reputation. Of using girls and then ditching them to move on to the next. And that's totally your right," I added. "I'm not asking you to change. I'm just asking you to understand how fucking scary that is for someone like me. You have nothing to lose. And I have everything."

He raked a hand through his hair, suddenly looking much older than his twenty-nine years. "Your job is not in my hands, Piper," he said slowly. "I may have suggested you as a producer candidate, but you are a News 9 employee with all the legal rights and privileges that go along with that. If I wanted to fire you, I would have to give just cause, like any other employee. And that cause cannot be because you didn't want to sleep with me."

I swallowed hard, my stomach buzzing. "But—"

He held up a hand. "Look, I'm not a monster, despite what you seem to think. I am completely aware of how hard you worked to get where you are and how much this job means to you. I would never in a million years jeopardize that— even if I did have that power. No matter what ends up happening between the two of us, I can promise you one thing now. It will never affect your job at News 9."

"Even if I tell you I want this to end now?" I asked, my heart pounding in my chest. "Even if I tell you I want nothing more to happen between us?"

He sighed. "Yes. A thousand times yes. It's not what I want, Piper. In fact, it's the last thing I want. I haven't felt this way about a girl in a long time and I want more than anything to see where this could lead. But if you're not ready or willing to go on this journey with me? I'm not going to force you along. We can be coworkers. Maybe friends—if you're okay with that. But that will be where it ends."

I drew in a breath, my stomach twisting in knots. It was exactly what I needed to hear. So why was there suddenly an aching emptiness inside me? At the idea that this could be it. I could just speak the words and it would all be over. All this drama, this frustration. It could end in an instant.

But did I want it to?

All my life I'd gone after what I wanted. Even if it wasn't easy. Even if it took a long time. Even if it seemed an impossible dream—I had chased it and never once looked back.

And now, here was the most impossible dream of all. Bringing Asher Anderson to shore. I wasn't ready to risk my career. But was I ready to risk my heart?

twenty

ASHER

ey! Wake up! Wake up!"
Rough hands grabbed my shoulders, shaking me awake. I groaned, pulling a pillow over my head, trying to swat them away. But the hands only moved lower, setting about to tickle my ribs instead. I rolled over in bed, my eyes catching the alarm clock on the nightstand beside me. Four AM? What the hell?

"Come on, lazy bones! Surf's up!"

Rubbing my eyes, I managed to sit up in bed to find Jess standing over me, a wicked grin on her face. "Finally!" she said. "Did anyone ever tell you that you sleep like the dead? I've been calling you all morning."

"You clearly need a refresher on the definition of morning."

"Yeah, well, *you* clearly need a refresher on the definition of awesome break out on Black's Beach," she shot back. "And thanks to your bestie here, your sorry ass is going to get one. Now get up and get that wet suit on, big boy."

She yanked the covers off my bed, evidently not trusting me not to crawl back under them as soon as she turned her back. As she did, her eyes zeroed in on my boxer briefs. She made a face and laughed. "At least one part of you is up," she said with a snort.

I rolled my eyes, grabbing a pillow and placing it over my privates. "What?" I growled. "It's a common condition amongst us poor males. Or haven't you heard?"

Of course that wasn't exactly why I was rock hard this particular morning, but she didn't need to know that.

I lay back down on my pillow, staring up at the ceiling, my mind flashing back to the dream I'd been having. Of being back at the country club with Piper. Back on that bathroom couch. But this time there was no one knocking the door. And Piper did not seem interested in retreat.

Instead she was under me, completely naked, miles of soft curves and supple flesh. Moaning in pleasure as I trailed kisses down her flat stomach, taking a moment to explore the dip of her navel. She reached down, digging her fingers into my hair, and I grinned, dropping down to nip her inner thigh, my hands gripping her hips, keeping her locked in place. A cry escaped her lips and her nails dug into my scalp so hard I winced in pain. But I didn't stop. If anything her reaction was only an invitation to press further. To start licking and sucking where I really wanted to be licking and sucking. To see if she tasted as good as she looked.

"Asher. Oh, Asher . . ."

Her words were a prayer. Begging me to take her to a place she'd never gone before. My mouth traveled higher, my breath whispering across her core . . .

"Earth to Asher. Did you fall back asleep?"

My eyes popped open and I scowled. Jess was standing above my bed again, now holding my wet suit in her hands. I raked a hand through my hair, reality smacking me across the face. A hard reminder that the real-life Piper did not want me to take her to a place she'd never been before. In fact, she barely wanted to get in the car.

I sighed heavily, remembering our talk the night before. I still couldn't believe she actually thought I'd hired her in order to hook up. Did she really think me that much of a creep? I mean, sure, I wasn't a saint by any stretch of the imagination. But I'd never force a woman into a position like that. That was just disgusting.

Maybe I should have never taken her on as my producer in the first place. Then we wouldn't have this little work conflict we had going on. I could feel free to ravish her anytime I wanted to. And she would not have a leg to stand on.

Despite what she'd said last night, I was still pretty confident I could get her in bed. Her desire for me might have gone against everything she believed in, but that didn't mean it wasn't there. But if she did allow herself to go down that road, I knew she would hate herself in the morning. And I wouldn't be able to bear the look of regret in her eyes.

Besides, I had to admit, I really did like working with her. Having someone else on my team for once, instead of always me against the newsroom. Piper was smart; she was resourceful. She was a hell of a scriptwriter, too. And, best of all, she made it fun. In fact, for the first time in a long time I was actually enjoying going to work. Maybe that was worth the price of celibacy in the end.

I shook my head. It was for the best anyway. After all, a girl like Piper could do a hell of a lot better than a guy like me. She needed someone who would treat her like the goddess she was. Someone she could trust who would never let her down. Someone who could live up to her high expectations. Her work ethic. Her drive.

"Asher!" I realized Jess was waving her hands in front of my face. "Come on. I've got the Jeep running. Grab your shit and let's go!"

I rose to my feet, then paused. "I don't know if I can this morning," I said, hedging.

Jess stopped in her tracks, turning to me, an incredulous look on her face. "I'm sorry? Maybe you didn't hear me. There is a major swell from the storm last night and it's breaking perfectly over at Black's Beach. Everyone who is anyone will be there and we need to get there first if we're going to find a parking spot."

"I know," I said. "But I have work."

"Uh, sure. Eventually. But not right now."

"Seriously, I need to be there on time."

Jess crossed her arms over her chest. "Okay, who are you and what did you do to my best friend?" She punched me lightly in the arm and laughed. "Come on. You know you want to."

I sighed. She was right. I did want to. I really did. After all, there wasn't anything better than catching a perfect wave, on a perfect beach day. Losing myself in the thunder of the sea, tasting the salt on my lips. The warm sun, baking my shoulders. The rest of the world far away.

But then I thought of Piper's face. The disappointment I knew I'd see in her eyes as I walked into the newsroom late again, proving everyone right. Making her look bad.

"I'm sorry," I said. "I made a promise."

"Please. You make promises all the time. It's not like you ever keep them."

I winced; her words were a punch to the gut. Was that what people really thought of me? What Piper saw when she looked at me? Asher Anderson: rich fuckup. Happy-go-lucky loser. A guy who waltzed through life, making and breaking promises without a care. A guy you couldn't count on to follow through.

A guy who didn't deserve a girl like Piper.

"Well, there's always a first time," I declared. "And I guess this is it. But you go on—I don't want you to miss this on my account. You can even use my board if you want."

Her eyes widened greedily. "Really?" she asked. "Your Damien Hurst SAS board?" When I nodded, she gave a low whistle. "Wow. I think I might grow to appreciate this new and improved Asher Anderson."

I snorted. "Just have the board back by the end of the day."

She grinned, her eyes sparkling. "Oh, I *promise*."

After she left I tried to go back to sleep, back to my delicious dreams. But after tossing and turning for twenty minutes I finally gave up, deciding to shower and dress and head to work instead. Three coffees and a massive breakfast burrito later, I was wandering through the newsroom, which was hustling and bustling with people getting ready for the six AM newscast. I yawned, trying to imagine what it would have been like if Piper had gotten this job instead. Would she have been happier in the end? The hours would have sucked, of course. But she wouldn't have had to deal with me.

"Well, well, now there's a sight I didn't expect to see at this hour."

I looked up, stifling a groan as my eyes met none other than my mother herself, standing in the doorway of Richard's office. Her own office was a few flights upstairs, but whenever she wanted to feel "at one" with the station she'd commandeer the news director's space as her own. Something I'm sure Richard wasn't super thrilled with, by any stretch of the imagination. He was a good guy. Fair, honest, just trying to stay under the radar and run his ship. The last thing he needed was interference from the ship's micromanaging owner.

"Hey, Mom," I said, changing course to head in her direction. Because what else could I do? "You're here awfully early yourself."

She shrugged. "The place isn't going to run itself." Then her eyes locked on me. "We need to talk."

She stepped aside, nodding her head to the entrance of Richard's office. I sighed, realizing I had no choice but to step inside. After surveying the room, I chose the chair behind Richard's desk—the power seat—and plopped down onto it, propping my feet up on his desk. It was a small act of defiance, but it did make me feel a little better to watch my mother relegated to the visitor's seat, a crinkle of annoyance creasing her brow.

"What's up, Mom?" I asked innocently, though I had a pretty good idea what she was about to say. My mother was nothing if not predictable.

Mom reached for Richard's desk, prying a newspaper out from under my feet. I watched as she flipped to the society page then handed it over to me. Glancing down I realized it was an article from the Inside Track, the local gossip column that I had been featured in far too many times over the years, thanks to my exploits. And sure enough, once again, my mug was smirking back at me from the page.

Who is the mysterious woman who emerged from the women's bathroom with a certain weatherman on her arm? Is there a new storm brewing in San Diego? Or maybe a heat wave?

I groaned. "Don't they have any real news to cover?" I asked, tossing the paper back on the desk.

My mother scowled. "This is real news, Asher. You caused an absolute scene in front of everyone. Including Sarah's father! Do you know how embarrassing it was for me to have him come up and demand to know what's going on?"

"What business is it of his?"

"Sarah was in tears when her friends texted her a photo of you and that . . . girl."

I groaned. "Mom, Sarah and I are just friends."

"Sarah doesn't seem to think that. And this is beyond embarrassing for her. Her father called me this morning and threatened to pull all his advertising if you don't apologize to her today."

"That's bullshit."

"No. That's reality, Asher. A place you obviously choose not to live. But someone has to pay the bills around here. And I'm not about to lose my key advertiser over some piece of white trash you decided to screw in the bathroom."

I winced. My first inclination was to defend Piper. But I knew it would only make things worse in the end. Instead, I rose to my feet. "I don't need to listen to this."

"I suppose you don't," my mother agreed stiffly. "You can just go about doing whatever it is you do. No big deal." She paused, then added, "I do worry about your little girl-friend though."

My eyes darted back to her. "What's that supposed to mean?"

My mother shrugged innocently. "Oh, nothing, really. I

was just looking at her resume this morning," she said. "I had no idea how young she was when I agreed to let you hire her as your producer. It seems to me we may need someone a little more . . . experienced . . . for this position. We are running a major news station here, Asher. Not a daycare."

My heart jammed. She wouldn't. She couldn't! My mind flashed back to Piper's words in the car the night before.

You have nothing to lose. And I have everything.

If my mother fired her now—because of me. If she lost her job—because of me.

"No." I shook my head, panic rioting through me. "You can't do that."

"I can do whatever I want to," she replied, rising to her feet. Her cold eyes locked on me. "Just like you, sweetheart."

She turned to walk out of the office. I ran around the desk, grabbing her by the shoulder before she could leave.

"Stop," I said.

She turned, raising a perfectly arched eyebrow.

"I'll apologize to Sarah," I said. "Whatever you want. Just . . . leave Piper out of this. She's a good employee. She doesn't deserve to be punished for my mistakes."

A twisted smile cut across my mother's face. "Of course, sweetheart," she said, reaching up to place a cold, dry hand on my cheek. It was all I could do not to recoil at her touch. But I stood there, stock-still, letting her do it.

For Piper. Who deserved so much better than me.

twenty-one

PIPER

The clock on my dash said six thirty AM as I rolled into work the next morning. Two and a half hours before my regularly scheduled shift, but after tossing and turning in bed all night, chasing sleep, I needed a distraction. I figured I could spend the morning studying the computers and charts, practicing what Asher had shown me. Maybe I could even find a story for us to work on that day.

I walked through the newsroom, watching the writers hard at work, banging out copy for the newscast, which was currently on air. I didn't see Anna Jenkins amongst their ranks; maybe she'd called in sick? Or maybe she'd proven unworthy of the job? The thought should have made me feel better, but in reality only made me feel worse. Because the same could easily be said about me.

My mind flashed back to the conversation I'd had with Asher the night before. He'd insisted he had no power over my job but I wasn't stupid. Maybe if I had been an experienced producer in the first place—someone who deserved the job—I could have fought a firing in a court of law. But as of this moment, I didn't have much of a leg to stand on.

They could easily say I wasn't qualified for the job and no one could argue with that.

Which meant I needed to get as qualified as possible. As fast as possible. And to avoid any further entanglements with Asher Anderson.

"There you are. What took you so long?"

My jaw dropped as I entered the weather center, only to find it blazing with lights. Asher looked up from his computer, a welcoming smile on his face. As if he'd been there all morning.

"I've got a great story for us today," he informed me, beckoning me over to his computer. "The scientists are talking about another possible La Niña season and I thought we could interview a couple of them on what that would mean for San Diegans if it happens."

"Um, yeah. Sounds great," I said, a little taken aback. What was he doing here so early? And hard at work, too? Seriously, the guy had gone from complete slacker to total workaholic so fast it was making my head spin.

As was the cologne he was wearing. A dark heady scent that made my toes curl as I leaned over to look at what he was pointing to on the computer. As my hand accidentally brushed his shoulder a quiver surged through my entire body. The air itself seemed almost electrified from his presence.

Ugh. So much for the whole friend-zone thing.

I bit my lower lip, trying desperately to focus on the task at hand. I forced my eyes to scan the article he was reading. "I can call Doctor Dutchman," I suggested, referring to one of the UCSD scientists making the prediction.

"Already done," Asher pronounced. "Well, he wasn't in his office yet," he amended. "But I left him a message. As soon as he calls back we can head out. I've already asked the desk for a photographer."

"Great. Sounds good," I stammered, completely taken aback at this point. What had gotten into him? Why the sudden enthusiasm? Was it all just an act, his way of proving to me that this hadn't merely been a game to get in my pants?

"Well, did you want to go get coffee then?" I added, feeling lame. "While we're waiting?"

He didn't look up from his computer. "Actually I'm going to work on my forecast a little first," he said. "To get ahead since we'll be out doing the interviews later. But you go on."

I nodded lamely, then turned and headed down to the cafeteria, still confused as hell. What had gotten into him?

Maybe he's still trying to impress you? something inside me suggested. My body warmed at the idea before I could shrug it away. Mostly because it was kind of working. Seeing him there, hard at work, completely focused, in the zone—it was pretty sexy to say the least. Hard work had always turned me on—maybe because I'd seen it modeled so little while growing up. I knew from watching TV that other little girls had daddies who worked hard and supported their families and bought Christmas presents for their kids. I never even knew my father. But my mother liked to talk about what a worthless asshole he'd been.

I entered the cafeteria and ordered myself a coffee and bagel. I still couldn't believe what had happened between Asher and me the night before. From the hot and heavy make-out session in the country club bathroom to me practically accusing him of the casting couch thing. What must he have thought of me? Not only that I thought he would do something like that, but that I took the job regardless, believing it to be a possibility. My face flushed at the thought.

The worst part was—I actually did want to sleep with him. Not to keep my job, obviously—I wasn't that insane. But because he was fast becoming the sexiest man I had ever met. There was just something about him that had gotten under my skin. Not just his good looks, his flashing eyes, his cocky smile, his amazing body. Not that those weren't appealing side benefits. But in the end it was more than that. It was the way he had locked the door to the bathroom so no one could walk in and see me all upset and disheveled. The way he'd pulled my hair back into a ponytail before walking with me to face the crowd. Simple gestures, yet they said so much about him as a person. And then there was the protective way he'd wrapped his arm around my waist when facing off with his own mother. As if he would singlehandedly fight an entire army to keep me safe.

Those were not the moves of a player trying to hook up. Those were the moves of a man who actually cared.

Which only made things harder. Because I could deal with an Asher who wanted to seduce me. But an Asher who genuinely cared about me? That was another beast entirely. And I wasn't sure how I was going to resist it long term.

S o would this weekend work for your friend?"
    I looked up from my computer. Lost in writing the La Niña script, I hadn't realized Asher had approached my desk and was now standing above me, looking down at me with questioning eyes. I drew in a breath. God, he looked so freaking good in his suit and tie. It wasn't fair. Spending the day with him, going out on our shoots, had pretty much been torture. Being so close and yet so far. Thank God we had a photographer with us to act as a chaperone or I wasn't sure what would have happened between us.

"What?" I asked, confused. "What friend?"

"Sorry," he said. "The little boy you told me about. The one who wants the surf lesson. Would this weekend work for him?"

"Oh!" I cried, shocked that after all that had happened, he had remembered our conversation from the night before. "Yeah. Sure. If you don't have any other plans."

"None as important as getting a young man on his first board," Asher declared.

My heart fluttered. "Okay. I'll just have to get permission from the housemothers but I think it should be fine as long as I'm chaperoning. What time do you want us and where?"

Asher raised an eyebrow. "You do realize this will take place on a beach, right? We can't exactly surf on dry land."

I blushed. In my excitement to get Jayden his lesson I hadn't really considered myself and my . . . water issues.

But what choice did I have? Toby would never be able to take off to take him herself. And I didn't trust any of the other staff to keep him in line if things didn't go to plan.

"Yeah," I said at last. "I'll be fine—don't worry about me."

"Okay then," he said. "How about seven AM by the Ocean Beach pier?"

"We'll be there."

He walked over to his computer and I turned back to my script. My heart thudded in my chest and the words seemed to swim on the page. *It's really no big deal*, I tried to tell myself. After all, it wasn't as if I was personally signing up for a lesson. All I had to do was stand there for an hour, watching from a safe distance away. No one could drown on dry land.

Besides, what choice did I have? This surf lesson meant the world to Jayden. I wouldn't be able to live with myself knowing I'd let him down, just like everyone else had in his short life. After all, I knew far too well what it felt like. Jayden needed to know he could count on me. That some adults kept their promises.

Still, the next time I wanted to help a kid? I was so going to suggest bowling.

I typed the last line of the script then read it over. Satisfied, I emailed it to Asher for him to take a look. Then I rose from my seat, ready to head over to the graphics department to see if they'd finished the piece's opening animation. But before I could get out the door, my desk phone rang.

"This is Piper," I said, putting the receiver to my ear.

"Hey, Piper, it's the front desk. Are you expecting a visitor?"

I frowned. "Um, no? Is someone there?"

The man's voice lowered. "Well, this woman just showed up. She's acting a little crazy, to tell you the truth. She keeps insisting she's your mother, but I don't know. She looks like she might be homeless. Do you want me to get rid of her?"

Oh, crap. I glanced at my cell phone sitting on my desk, suddenly remembering my mother trying to call me last night in the middle of the whole country club fiasco. By the time I got home it was too late to call her back and I'd forgotten to do so in the morning.

Looks like I was about to pay for that forgetfulness. Big-time.

"Piper? Are you there?"

"Yeah, sorry," I said. "Just . . . keep her there. I'll be right down."

"Everything okay?" Asher asked as I set down the phone.

"Yes. Everything's fine. I just have to . . . I'll be right back," I stammered, trying to quell the panic rising inside of me. This was the last thing I needed. If someone were to see her. To discover she was my mother . . .

I raced downstairs, through the newsroom and down the hall, toward the front entrance, passing the framed posters of all the legendary News 9 employees along the way. One of which, I observed, was Asher's father, Stormy Anderson. Asher definitely resembled his mother more than his father, but I thought I caught a resemblance in the senior Anderson's eyes. I thought back to what Asher had said about his father—about how much pressure it was to live up to such a legend. Maybe he should try *my* life once in a while— where the bar had been set so low by the parental units, it was practically underground.

The hallway ended at a reception area where the security guard sat behind a wall of bulletproof glass. Which, at first glance, might have seemed a little extreme. But we'd had occasions where we'd aired controversial stories and angry people showed up to . . . argue . . . their counterpoints and the guards needed some protection, just in case.

The guard buzzed me out and I pushed through the double doors, stepping into the lobby. My mother, who was pacing the room, turned to find me, her eyes lighting up in recognition.

"See?" she shrieked at the guard. "I told you I had a daughter who worked here!" She turned back to me, her face a mask of indignation. "He tried to turn me away," she accused.

I sighed. "Mom, we talked about this. I'm very busy at work. You can't come here."

"What else am I supposed to do, when you won't answer my calls?"

I raked a hand through my hair. God, why hadn't I just freaking called her back? I should have set an alarm or something. Anything . . . to avoid this kind of scene. I glanced back at the double doors and then at the security guard, who was pretending not to listen, but clearly was. This was going to be all over the newsroom gossip vine tomorrow, I could just tell. Piper and her crazy-sauce mother.

"What do you need, Mom?" I asked. "Can it wait until I'm off work?"

"No it can't wait! And it involves your work. I want to talk to one of the reporters here. The . . . I-Team or whatever they're called. I've had my civil rights violated and I want to report it."

I cringed. Oh God. This was one of my mother's all-time favorites. Her civil rights being violated. Even though nine times out of ten the "violation" was because of something she did or didn't do herself.

I watched as she stalked the room, her steps eating up the distance between walls. Her eyes were wild and unfocused and her lips dry and cracked. She was grinding her jaw muscles back and forth, too: a telltale sign she had been on a bender—or still was.

"What happened?" I asked, trying to channel my inner saint, even as anger roiled within me. *She's your mother*, I scolded myself. *She needs your help.*

"That slumlord at the trailer park," she spit out. "He locked me out of my own house! Without any warning whatsoever. I come home and there's a big fat padlock on my door—with all my stuff inside!"

"Wait!" I interrupted. "You don't live at the trailer park anymore. I got you an apartment!"

She didn't have the decency to blush. "I know, I know. But David needed a place to crash for a couple weeks— while his house was being fumigated. So I let him move into the trailer until the lease ran out."

I closed my eyes, trying to reset my sanity. Goddamned

David. I knew it had to have something to do with him. It always did. Why couldn't the freaking penal system lock him up for good and throw away the key? Every time he got out I had to deal with this shit.

"Okay," I said, trying my best to stay pragmatic, even though I pretty much wanted to strangle her at this point. "So what did the landlord say when you asked him about the lock?"

My mother turned, refusing to meet my eyes. "Some bullshit about back rent," she muttered. "I'm telling you— he's a slumlord. You should do a story on him. I bet I'm not the only person he's ripped off!"

"Back rent? I give you money every month! What have you been using it for?" I started to demand. Then I shook my head. It was a stupid question. I was stupid for having given her the money in the first place. But she'd been doing so well—until David had come back, that was. "How many months behind are you?" I asked.

"I don't know. A couple, I guess," Mom mumbled. Then she looked up at me, eyes fierce. "But I'm not giving that asshole a dime of my money! He violated my civil rights! I want him to pay for that! I want you to put him on TV!"

"Everything okay?"

I whirled around at the sound of the voice, horrified to realize Asher had stepped into the lobby and was now standing behind me. I felt my face turn purple with humiliation. Of all people—I did not want him to see me like this.

"Everything's fine!" I said quickly. "I've got it under control. You can just go back upstairs and finish—"

"*OH MY GOD*! You're Asher Anderson!" my mother broke in. "I watched your father for *years* on the TV. He was the best weatherman ever. I mean, you're no slouch yourself, and you're actually easier on the eyes than your pop, if you know what I mean." She gave a low whistle. "Asher Anderson. Damn. I'm blushing!"

"Mom," I hissed. "Can we talk about this later?"

But she was done with me, all of her meth-fueled attention directed at Asher now. "I need your help, Mr. Anderson.

My civil rights have been violated! I need to put this asshole on TV!"

"She's fine," I said, stepping in between them. "Mom, I will help you. You don't need Asher."

"What happened?" Asher asked my mother.

She repeated the whole story in one long breath. While I stood there, mortified beyond belief. Asher listened patiently.

When she was done he said, "So you have a new place to live. You just need your things back? Is that the issue here?"

"Well." My mother huffed. "I guess that would be a start at least."

"Okay." He glanced at his watch. "Let's go make that happen."

"Wait, what?" I interjected. "No! We are working here!"

"I put the script into edit," Asher argued. "We have time for a quick trip."

"*Thank* you!" my mother said, beaming up at Asher. "It's nice to know *someone* in this building cares." She shot me an affronted look. I rolled my eyes.

Asher turned to me. "Are you coming?" he asked.

"You really don't have to do this," I said.

"Actually I think I do. Do you want to come or wait here?"

"I'll come," I said, not that I wanted to. In fact, it was the last thing I wanted to do. But I'd be damned if I'd allow my mother to be alone with Asher. Who knew what she would say to him?

We took two cars, Asher insisting that I drive my mother's, which was a good idea seeing as I had no idea how she'd even made it this far in the state she was in. Asher followed behind us in Fiona. As I drove, my mother twisted her body around so she could look out the back window. "Asher Anderson!" she exclaimed again. "What a hottie. I sure wouldn't mind a slice of that bacon."

"Please, Mom. He's my boss. Try to restrain yourself."

She turned to me, her wild eyes glittering madly. "I think

he's more than your boss," she teased. "At least he wants to be. Did you see the way he was looking at you back at the station?"

"No, Mom. I was too busy focusing on you humiliating me and putting my job at risk, actually."

"This is why you never get a man," she pointed out, wagging a finger at me. "You're always thinking about work. Guys don't like it when you think about work. They want you to think about sex." She glanced back at Asher's bus again. "You know, I bet you could totally get with him if you wanted to."

"I appreciate the vote of confidence. But I'm good, thank you."

"Are you a lesbian, Piper?"

"*What?*"

"I don't know. I was telling David the other day how you never bring guys home. And he says, maybe you're bringing girls home. I told him if you were, I didn't know about it. But I would be okay with it either way. I'm liberated, you know? I have friends who are gay. If you got married, I'd even come to your wedding."

"Well, that's good to know. But I'm not gay."

She shook her head. "Then, honey, you must be blind if you don't see the benefits to getting a piece of that Asher Anderson ass."

I let out a heavy groan. "Okay, Mom. Point taken. Just . . . please for the love of God don't say anything like that to him, okay?"

"Of course I wouldn't." She giggled. "It'll be our little secret." Then she giggled again, which told me I couldn't count on it. Sigh. This had better go quick.

We pulled into the trailer park a few minutes later, stopping at the first trailer in the lot, a halfway decent double-wide that the manager lived in. I'd met him before; he wasn't a bad guy. Certainly not a slumlord. Which was why I was worried about how much my mother really was behind in rent. For him to lock her trailer on her—it must have been far more than a couple of months. I tried to mentally calculate how much was in my bank account. I was making more now, but I'd put down a hefty security deposit on my mother's new apartment, which had drained my savings.

I stepped out of the car, looking around, my heart sinking at the scene laid out in front of me. I thought back to the country club, the yacht club—all the places Asher had taken me. The places in his world with the beautifully manicured lawns, the sparkling lights. Of course there were sparkling lights here, too. Tacky, blinking Christmas lights, half falling down on the side of one rusty single-wide. I groaned, watching Asher get out of the car, heading toward us. We needed to get this over with—quick.

The manager stepped out of the trailer, meeting us on the front porch. His eyes zeroed in on my mother. "Oh no, Miranda," he said. "I told you not to come back here!"

"You violated my civil rights!" she shot back. "I brought News 9 to investigate!"

He glanced over at Asher, raising an eyebrow. "That's the weatherman, you idiot."

"Yeah, and he's going to shut you down! You and your— conspiracy to rob good people of their personal possessions!"

"How much back rent does she owe?" I asked the manager with a sigh.

He scowled at my mother. "Six months," he said. "I've been more than patient. She kept promising me she was getting some kind of disability check in the mail. But it never came."

"Six months?" I turned to my mother. "Did you even use any of the money I sent you for rent?"

"He's lying. I might have missed a month or two. But not six months! There's no way I missed six months!"

Shit. I started doing the calculations in my head. Six months, four hundred fifty a month . . . Shit.

"What's the total she owes?" Asher asked, stepping in. "Including any late fees you might need to collect . . . for your pain and suffering."

I watched as the man's eyes raked over Asher greedily, as if assessing his worth and how much of it he'd be willing to cough up. "I'd say four thousand ought to do it," he said at last.

"Four thousand?" I blurted out. "But that's—"

"Do you need cash or can you take a check? I'd need to go to the ATM for cash."

"A check's fine," the manager declared. "I can tell a check from *you* won't bounce." He shot my mother a look. "Unlike *some* people."

"Asher, you really don't have to do this," I protested, mortified beyond belief. Here I was, trying to dig my way out of the debt I already owed him for the job, and now he was doubling down.

"It's already done," he said, handing the man a check. "Now how about you go open up the lady's trailer?" He turned to my mother. "I'll call a moving company to come pick up your things. Just write down your new address for me."

"Thank you!" she cried. "Thank you so much! You're a goddamned hero is what you are! It's nice to know *some* people have decency in this world," she added, sneering at the manager. He ignored her, his eyes not leaving the check.

I turned back to Asher, surprised to see he'd put a hand on my mother's arm and was leading her away from me. I watched, confused as he leaned in to talk to her. I could see my mom nodding her head vigorously. Then, he pulled out his phone and put it to his ear. A moment later, he walked back to me.

"There's a room open at Safe Harbor. She's agreed to let me take her. She'll sign herself in voluntarily, so I can't force her to stay. But I think we need to be thankful that she's even willing to try it out."

I stared at him in disbelief. He'd gotten my mother to agree to go to rehab? Just like that—in one conversation? I'd been trying for years to get her into a program, but she'd always refused. Seriously, I knew Asher was persuasive, but this was amazing.

It was also, unfortunately, impossible at the moment.

I swallowed hard. "Asher, that's really great of you. But we can't afford a program like that. Not right now."

"You don't need to. I got it covered."

"No." I shook my head vigorously. "You've already done too much! I can't let you—"

"This isn't about charity, Piper," Asher interrupted. "Your mother's sick. She needs treatment. If she had cancer would you say no to chemotherapy?"

"No, but . . ." I stared at him, helpless and so damn grateful. "Thank you," I said at last. "I don't know what else to say. You're a saint."

"No." He shook his head. "I'm definitely not a saint. Just a guy who once suffered from the same kind of cancer. If I can help your mom . . . well, maybe I'll finally feel even for what Miguel did for me."

He held out his arms and I collapsed into them, sobbing in relief against him. He stroked my hair gently and I could feel his heartbeat against my chest. Strong, steady, just like Asher himself.

At last we pulled away. He looked down at me with affectionate eyes. "Now let's get a move on," he said. "We need to get back to the station and get that piece finalized. My producer's a bit of a slave driver, you know."

I looked up at him. "Yeah, well, I'm pretty sure you're not half the slacker you pretend to be."

twenty-two

ASHER

Piper's mother was good to her word and three days later she was still residing at Safe Harbor. I'd called my buddy there last night to check in on her, and he told me she was actually already through a good portion of her detox, though she still had a long way to go. He told me she'd been in terrible shape when she'd come in and I'd most likely saved her life by getting her in when I had. I considered telling Piper that, but I didn't want to freak her out too badly. She was already suffering so much—as people did when their loved ones engaged in substance abuse—and I didn't want to add insult to injury. I still remembered all the apologies I'd had to make to various friends and family while going through my steps. I probably had a few more to make, come to think of it.

But it was a start. And now Piper's mother had her start. That was something, at least. In fact, it was a lot.

And my charity, it would seem, was becoming a habit, as I arrived at the beach at the crack of dawn that morning, waiting for Piper and her young charge to show up. I'd hit the surf shop yesterday, picking up a six-foot soft board for the boy—one of those foam ones that were incredibly buoyant and easier to catch waves with. It was also, the proprietor informed me, very stable, making it simpler for a novice rider to stand up. If the boy didn't have much experience with the water, the first lesson would be more about boosting confidence than actual skill.

I was actually pretty excited about the whole idea. I'd taught people to surf before—mostly hot girls who seemed more interested in strutting around the beach in tiny bikinis than actually learning any moves. But I'd never taught a kid.

I remembered *being* taught as a kid, however. It had started one Sunday morning with me sneaking out of my parents' beach house while they slept off the rager they'd thrown the night before. I'd walked the shore, soaking in the sun and the salt and the sand, until I came to a beat-up old shack—very out of place amongst the multimillion-dollar mansions lining the rest of the beach. There I found an old man, with more wrinkles than hair, sitting on a stoop waxing his board. He'd looked up at me and smiled. He'd been missing quite a few teeth.

I asked him if he'd teach me how to surf. He made me finish waxing his board instead. Then he told me to come back next week. I did. And I waxed his board again. It was like something out of *Karate Kid*—and it took three Sundays before he'd let me in the water. But once I got in, I never wanted to get out again.

Mr. Chang considered surfing more of a religion than a sport. He told me the ocean was where life had begun on this planet and was mother to us all. He said the act of riding a wave allowed a surfer to become part of the collective unconsciousness of planet Earth.

Even today I believed there was truth to that. Over the years surfing had become more than just a passion to me—at times it had been my salvation. The ocean, my church. A place of refuge when things got bad at home. No one could hurt you out on the water. And it was the only place where I could truly feel free.

Which was partially why Piper's water phobia was so

foreign to me. The idea that the very same ocean that had given me so much—had so cruelly stolen from her. The very same waters that had brought me back to life offered her nothing but darkness and death.

When she'd said she would be coming today, I was surprised, and also impressed. It couldn't have been easy for her to do—to push past her crippling fear for the sake of this boy. But she'd agreed to do it anyway, knowing how much it would mean to him. Just like she'd done with Beth at her wedding, putting her own fears aside as best she could, to be there for her friend.

Which said a lot about the kind of person she was. A person I still wanted to know better. I knew she was still completely embarrassed about the whole thing with her mother, even though I told her a hundred times it didn't matter to me. If anything, it had explained so much about her— puzzle pieces I'd been desperate to find, finally sliding into place. She'd been a child, subjected to the one-two punch of addiction and tragedy. Two forces that could have easily defined the rest of her life and excused any shortcomings. But she hadn't let them defeat her. Instead, she had used them as reasons to keep fighting. Which made her even more amazing in my eyes. And made me want to know even more.

It was funny, really. With most girls, I just cared what was under their clothes. Yet with Piper I wanted to see so much more. I wanted to crawl inside her head to see what made her tick. To peel back her layers—to see who she was underneath, scars and all.

My secret hope was that this beach adventure would benefit her as much as the boy. If she could just stand on the sand, a safe distance from the water, her fear might start to ebb with the tide. Not like I expected her to be carving a wave anytime soon. But even sticking her toe in the water might be a start. Mr. Chang believed that the ocean was the world's greatest healer. Able to cleanse a person from the inside out. Maybe Piper's wounds weren't as mortal as she assumed. Maybe with time and patience they could begin to heal.

And maybe—just maybe—I could help her with that. "Asher!"

Piper's voice jerked me back to the present and I almost choked as I caught sight of her and the boy crossing the sand. Holy crap. What was she wearing? Was a bathing suit like that even legal?

I shook my head, trying to get my mind back on the game. To avoid dragging my gaze up her long legs, taking in the flare of her rounded hips, her trim stomach, the small scraps of fabric barely covering her breasts. Suddenly my mind treated me to a vivid flashback of how soft those breasts had been, cupped in my hands back at the country club, and I let out a frustrated groan. Seriously, how the hell did she expect me to concentrate on a surf lesson with her standing on the shore looking like that? It was cruel and unusual punishment to say the least.

I held up a shaky hand in a wave, trying to calm my libido. "Hey!" I cried. "There you are."

They stopped in front of me and I somehow forced my eyes away from Piper to concentrate on my new pupil. He was Mexican with large dark eyes and a shock of thick black hair. Stocky, on the short side, wearing a faded bathing suit that looked a few sizes too big. While he looked excited, he also looked a little nervous and his eyes held a trace of suspicion. My heart squeezed a little at that. Piper had told me some of his history—about his drug-addicted mother who was always breaking her promises. About how he would probably remain in the group home until he turned eighteen. I could see why she cared so much about him now. He probably reminded her of herself back when she was a child.

I stuck out my hand. He stared down at it, not reaching out to grasp it until Piper nudged him and he grudgingly obeyed.

"Hey, man," I said, giving him a firm shake. "You ready to do this?"

"I guess," he said, staring down at the sand. As if he didn't want to be here. And yet, somehow, at the same time I could tell that he did. He was excited, but he was wary, too. Like he didn't quite believe this was really happening. That it was some kind of trick and if he showed his enthusiasm, he'd be laughed at and told it was just a joke.

I thought back to what I must have looked like to Mr. Chang that first morning on the beach. An overprivileged white boy who didn't appreciate all he'd been given. That was what most people saw when they looked at me, anyway, and I couldn't say it wasn't true. But Mr. Chang had looked beyond my exterior—to the lonely desperate boy beneath. And in the end, it was *that* Asher he'd taught to surf. That Asher he'd brought back to life.

"Great," I said. "We're going to start the lesson on land. And then when you're feeling good about the basics we can head out into the water, okay?" I paused then added, "You can swim, right?" I actually hadn't thought to ask that first.

Thankfully he nodded. I slapped him on the back and grabbed the board I'd gotten him out of the sand, pushing it in his direction. "Here you go. Grab your board and we'll head down to the shoreline."

He took the board from me, holding it awkwardly, as if not sure what to do. Instead of helping him, I grabbed my own board, demonstrating how to properly hold it, then headed down to the beach. I didn't turn around. I didn't wait to see if he was following. If he wanted to do this, he would. If he didn't, well that was okay, too.

But a few moments later he had caught up to me, stepping into place at my side. We walked down the beach, not speaking, as Piper trailed a few yards behind. It took a lot not to ask her if she was okay. But I could tell the kid looked up to her and I didn't want to embarrass her in front of him. Instead, I just shot her a quick look to make sure she wasn't in full-on panic mode. She gave me a weak smile and a thumbs-up. I had to take it.

I turned back to my student, catching him examining his new board with great interest. "This is, like, brand-new," he blurted out, seemingly despite himself.

"It is," I agreed. "Piper said you didn't have your own board so I picked one up for you last night."

His eyes widened into saucers. "This is mine? For keeps?"

"No, Jayden. It's to borrow," Piper interjected.

"Actually . . ." I gave her an impish shrug. "It's for him to keep. I mean, if that's okay with you?"

Jayden turned to her, an expression on his face that I was pretty sure no mere mortal human being would be able to deny.

"Please, miss? Can I keep it? Please?"

She shook her head, laughing. "I guess so," she said, holding her hands up in defeat. "But, Jayden, we need to keep it in the locker room when we get back, okay? Away from the other kids. They might not understand."

"Hell yeah, we're keeping it locked up," Jayden declared, looking offended that she'd even assume otherwise. "I'm not letting any of those fools touch *my* board."

The way he said it, the pride in ownership, made my heart squeeze. It also made me remember all those boards I'd gone through over the years, never truly appreciating any of them. I'd busted them, I'd lost them—what did it matter to me? I could always get a new one.

Even yesterday, I had barely even given it a second thought when I'd bought him this board—it was just easier than going to a rental shop. But looking at the light in his eyes now as he ran a hand along the board made me realize it meant so much more than that.

"Just promise me you'll take good care of it," I said sternly, attempting to channel my former mentor. "A surfer always needs to keep his board clean and properly waxed."

He nodded solemnly and when he looked up, his eyes were shining with newfound respect. "I will," he said. "I promise."

"Excellent. Then let's begin." I tossed my own surfboard down onto the sand and instructed him to do the same. "Go ahead and lie down on the board," I told him once he'd done it. "Try to center yourself so this line . . ." I dragged a finger down the center of the board, where a small stripe had been drawn. "This is the center of your body."

I waited as the kid complied, dropping down to the board and trying to align his body to the stripe as instructed. In the meantime, I glanced over at Piper. She was keeping her distance from the ocean itself, but looked okay overall.

Okay, fine. She looked more than okay. She looked freaking stunning. But that was beside the point, really.

"Go ahead and scoot down a little," I said, turning back to Jayden. "You want your toes always touching the back. The sweet spot, they call it."

I watched as he wriggled his body back. "How's that?"

"Good." I nodded. "Now, imagine you're in the water. You're paddling really hard." I mimicked the paddling in the air and he tried to imitate from down on the sand. "You're catching up with the wave, you're paddling really hard—like a hundred miles an hour. And suddenly the wave catches you." I gave Jayden a questioning look. "What happens next?"

Jayden grinned. "I ride the shit out of that mother."

"Jayden! Language!" Piper scolded. I laughed.

"That's right, my man," I said. "You pop up. And you ride like the wind." I dropped down to my own board to demonstrate. "Put your hands next to your chest. Then push up." I popped up on my board. "Then, you bring your front foot forward and stand up on your back foot."

Jayden nodded, following my lead. He popped up then tried to fix his feet. He wobbled and lost his balance, crashing into the sand.

"Aw, man!" he cried, slamming his fist into the sand. "I can't do it."

"Yes, you can," I assured him, hopping off my own board to help him. "It just takes practice. Trust me, you should have seen how much I sucked when I first got on a board." I grinned. "And now I'm totally elite."

I helped him back on his feet then adjusted him on the board, kicking his feet into proper position. "You want this line to go down the middle of your arches," I explained. Then

I grabbed his hands and stretched them out so they were over the board in both directions.

"You feel that?" I asked.

He nodded grimly. He was concentrating with all his might to stay in position. I studied him for a moment, then nodded my approval.

"Good. Now drop down and pop up again."

He glanced over at me. "Are we ever going in the water?" he asked.

I grinned, remembering my own eagerness when Mr. Chang had first taken me on. The kid was lucky I wasn't making him wax my board for the next month. "Not until I see at least five perfect pops," I told him.

He groaned loudly. Piper shot him another warning look. He rolled his eyes, but got back down onto the board. This time when he popped up, his position was ten times better.

"That's how it's done!" I cried, giving him a fist bump. "Four more times like that and we go surfing!"

twenty-three

And go surfing they did. While I watched from a safe distance on the beach.

At first Jayden was ridiculously bad—he could barely climb onto his board on his belly, never mind stand up and ride a wave. The ocean showed no mercy to the beginner either, crashing over him and knocking him off balance each time he attempted to swim to deeper, calmer water. It was almost like a Three Stooges episode and at times I had to stop myself from laughing.

But Asher never laughed. Not once. Instead, he encouraged Jayden to keep trying, to shake it off and get back on his board. Told him this kind of thing happened to him all the time—even after years of practice. And that it was no big thing.

He had no way of knowing, of course, that this was exactly the right way to talk to Jayden. To treat him like a person, a peer—rather than some charity case. To set expectations high and let him claw his way tooth and nail to meet them. Most people never bothered to give Jayden anything to work for—and so he didn't usually work. But when he truly wanted something, he went after it with all cylinders fired.

And right now he clearly wanted to surf.

There were a few times where I was forced to turn away. Unable to watch as the waves crashed over his head, tossing his little body around in the soup. I tried to tell myself that he was fine, that he was in good hands. That Asher would never let anything happen to him. But my heart beat a little faster every time he fell off his board and in the end I was forced to grab a book from my bag and concentrate on that instead.

After all, what good would stressing out do? It wasn't as if I could charge into the water and save him myself if things went south. And if I told him to come out now, cutting short what was probably the best day of his life because of my insecurities? He'd never talk to me again.

Jayden deserved this. He'd worked hard all week and hadn't scored a single demerit. In fact, Toby had pulled me aside the day before to marvel at his improvement. Whatever I was doing, she said, keep on doing it.

So I tried my best to concentrate on the words on the page and ignore the sounds of the sea. I'm not sure I absorbed a single sentence, but at least I didn't run screaming from the beach. That was something in and of itself. In fact, for me, that was a lot.

Finally, after what seemed like the longest lesson in eternity (but was probably no more than a couple hours) the two boys emerged from the water. Jayden was grinning from ear to ear, running over to me, clutching his precious board. I still couldn't believe Asher had actually shelled out the money to buy someone he didn't even know a brand-new surfboard, and I wondered if he had any comprehension of just how much a gift like this could mean to a child like Jayden—who had almost nothing in the world to call his own.

"Miss!" Jayden cried. "Did you see me out there? Did you see how I rode that last wave? I was up for, like, ten seconds at least."

I rose to my feet. "I saw it all," I assured him, reaching out and hugging him. He was soaking wet but I didn't care. "You were amazing. I was so impressed."

"Why didn't you tell me this kid was a natural?" Asher demanded, rubbing Jayden's head. I winced for a moment—Jayden usually hated being touched like that—but the kid didn't even seem to notice now. "He's like the next Kelly Slater!"

"Aw, I don't know about that," Jayden said, looking a little sheepish. "But maybe someday!" He looked up at Asher and my heart squeezed at the worship I saw in his eyes as his newfound hero gave him a fist bump. Asher had no idea, I realized, just how much this small kindness could mean to a boy like Jayden.

But I did.

"Do you have something to say to Mr. Anderson?" I prompted.

Jayden turned to Asher and grinned. "Can we do it again?"

I laughed. "I meant you should thank him."

"Oh, right." Jayden blushed. "Thank you, sir," he said.

"The name's Asher," Asher corrected. "And thank *you*, Jayden. Anyone who gives me an excuse to go surfing on a beautiful day is all right in my book."

I looked around. It *was* a beautiful day. And I'd been sitting on the beach for over an hour now without running away screaming. In fact, I'd actually enjoyed the feeling of the warm sun on my back. And the sand had felt kind of good between my toes for once in my life. It might not seem like much, but it was more than I'd ever done before. Jayden wasn't the only one, I suddenly realized, who had accomplished something today.

And once again, it was all thanks to Asher here. Forget the Joker. At times the guy was freaking Superman.

The two of us still hadn't fully discussed what he had done for my mother. He'd tried to bring it up a few times, but I had managed to change the subject each time. It was strange—part of me hated the fact that he knew so much about me now. All the skeletons in my closet I'd worked so hard to hide. And yet, another part of me felt weirdly closer to him because of it. The fact that I no longer had to pretend to be someone else—someone in his world—was such a relief in so many ways. He knew now, for better or worse, where I'd come from and it hadn't changed the way he looked at me one bit. I didn't understand how that was possible, but it was definitely true. I could tell every time I dared to look in his eyes.

"So can we do it again?" Jayden asked. He turned to me, his eyes wide and pleading. "Please, miss? I even have my own board now!"

I sighed, reality crashing back to shore. "Jayden, we talked about this. This was a special treat and—"

"Are you free next Saturday?" Asher broke in.

"Yes!" Jayden cried. "I am totally free!" He bounced up and down like a maniac on the beach. "I'm absolutely totally free."

I turned to Asher. "Seriously, don't feel obligated. I told him this was a special one-time thing before we came out."

Asher waved me off. "I don't mind," he assured me. "Like I said, anything for an excuse to get out on the water."

"Okay," I said, wagging my finger at Jayden. "One more Saturday. But that's it." After all, I didn't want to take advantage of Asher's generosity.

Jayden whooped loudly. Then he and Asher exchanged high fives, giving each other conspiratorial looks that told me this had all been planned from the start. I rolled my eyes. "Now get in the van," I scolded my charge. "They're going to kill me if I get you back late for chores."

Jayden nodded and ran back to the van. I watched him for a moment, observing the way he placed his board carefully in the back, as if loading a precious treasure. Which it was, I supposed. The most precious, valuable thing the kid had ever owned.

I turned back to Asher. "I think you just made his life."

Asher grinned. "I think he might have just made mine. I haven't had that much fun in a long time." He watched Jayden get in the car, an affectionate look on his face that made my heart warm.

"Well, thank you," I said, giving him a fond look. "This

kind of thing—it can make a huge difference for a kid like Jayden. Something to look forward to, something to work for. Someone to look up to . . ."

"Me as a role model." Asher smirked. "Who would have thought?"

I laughed. "And a model employee to boot. Hell, soon your friends and family won't be able to recognize you."

His eyes flickered with darkness. "I should be so lucky," he muttered. Then he shook himself, turning to me. "Speaking of unrecognizable . . . Did you realize, my dear, that you just spent two hours on a beach?"

"I know, right?" I shook my head. "Crazy sauce."

His eyes zeroed in on me, the laughter fading, replaced by something serious that made me shiver. "How are you feeling?" he asked.

"Weirdly not too bad," I replied. "Maybe it was because I was busy watching you guys. Or I was far enough away from the water. But I didn't get that panicky feeling in the back of my throat that I normally get. And my heart didn't feel as if it would explode out of my chest."

Asher grinned. "I'll make a beach bum out of you yet!"

"I wouldn't go that far!" I protested. "But thank you. I appreciate everything you've done today. Maybe you are a bit of a superhero after all."

I glanced back at the van, shuffling from foot to foot. It was funny; when I'd first stepped onto the beach I couldn't wait for it all to be over. Now, suddenly, I almost didn't want to leave. "Anyway, Jayden's all loaded up so I should probably be going."

"I'll come with you," Asher said, not missing a beat.

"What? No. You don't need to do that," I stammered, taken aback. "I'm just going to drop him off and then head home."

"Aren't you hungry?"

"Um, sure, but . . ."

"Well then why don't we drop him off and then get lunch?"

My heart thudded in my chest. "I'm not sure that's such a good idea."

"Why not?"

I twisted my hands together. Truth was, I *did* want to have lunch with him. Hell, I wanted to spend all day by his side. And maybe the night, too. But then . . .

"Asher, I thought we were going to . . . you know, just be friends."

He nodded, but a playful grin danced at the corners of his mouth. "We are," he declared. "And, it just so happens I eat lunch with my *friends* all the time." His eyes caught mine. "Don't you?"

And once again Asher Anderson managed to get his way.

twenty-four

ASHER

We drove down to Chula Vista, Jayden chattering like an excited magpie the entire trip, telling Piper all the details of his surfing adventure. I listened as I sat in the passenger seat, pretending to check my phone, a thrill of pride winding through me at his every word. He was so excited. So enthusiastic. So grateful. Just as I had been with Mr. Chang back in the day. It made me feel good, to say the least. Like for once in my sorry life I had done something worthwhile.

Also making me feel good? The way Piper had looked at me back at the beach. The gratitude mixed with respect I saw in her eyes. It was funny; I'd never really put much effort into getting girls to admire me—usually my looks and my wallet took care of all that. But with Piper I found myself constantly vying for those rare looks of approval. That spark that flashed in her eyes when I did something unexpected. Sure, it bothered me a little that her expectations were clearly set very low. But it made me happy to exceed them all the same. And it made me want to try even harder the next time.

We pulled into a parking lot in front of a cluster of gray

buildings surrounding a rusty playground. Piper parked the van and we all jumped out. I stopped for a moment before following them inside, taking in the surroundings. The buildings were clearly old and not well-kept. In fact, some of them looked like they were one storm away from falling down altogether. But at the same time, all the windows were covered with colorful children's drawings. Like flowers growing in the cracks of a pavement.

I watched Jayden follow Piper inside, still chattering away, and tried to imagine what growing up here must be like for a kid like him. No mother or father or family to care for you. No private space to call your own. Piper had made it sound like he had practically nothing in terms of possessions as well. No iPad, no baseball bat, no Xbox. It made me want to jump in the car and head to Best Buy right then and there and buy the crap out of the place.

No wonder the kid acted out at times. I'd go fucking mental growing up in a place like this. Sure, my own upbringing had had its problems, too. But I'd always had a Spanish-shingled roof over my head, an ocean view. Jayden had nothing at all.

Except he had Piper. And now he had me, too.

We stepped inside and an ancient receptionist greeted Piper with a disinterested grunt, barely looking up. Piper ignored her, turning to Jayden and instructing him to go upstairs and get changed.

"Aw!" Jayden protested. "I want to introduce everyone to Mr. Anderson."

Piper began to shake her head, but I held up a hand to stop her. "It's okay," I assured her. "I'd love to meet everyone."

She gave me a doubtful look—like I didn't know what I was suggesting—but she didn't say no and so I followed Jayden into the hall before she could change her mind. He led me into a small common area with a couple of ratty couches and old-fashioned TVs. There were several other kids of various ages hanging out, looking bored and listless. Until they saw me, that was.

"Hey, everyone!" Jayden announced, jumping onto the

arm of a couch to gain a height advantage as he addressed the room. "This is my new friend, Asher. He's teaching me how to surf."

All eyes turned on me. A few widened in recognition. "Hey! I know you!"

"Yeah, you're the weather guy on TV!"

A moment later I was surrounded by a cluster of kids, all talking at once, all grabbing at me, trying to compete for my attention. I laughed, retreating a step backward, but they only charged again, with renewed enthusiasm. I couldn't understand a word any of them were saying as they all tried to ask me questions at once.

Suddenly a whistle pierced the air. The kids retreated, backing up to the wall. I turned to see Piper had entered the room.

"Everyone sit," she commanded. "Give Mr. Anderson some space."

"Miss! That's the guy from the TV!" one of the kids cried.

"He's *my* surf instructor," Jayden butted in, giving him a dirty look.

"No way, dude. He's famous. He ain't teaching your sorry ass to surf."

"He is, too!"

"Guys!" Piper cried. She shot me an embarrassed look. "Is this how we behave when we have guests?"

"No, miss," they recited in unison.

"Now as I was saying, this is Asher Anderson. And you're right. He does the weather for News 9. You've probably all seen him on TV."

The kids broke out into excited murmurs.

"Can I have your autograph?" called out a tall, tough-looking boy with a crucifix tattoo on his arm.

"Now, Ramon, Mr. Anderson doesn't have time to—"

"Sure," I broke in. Then I glanced at Piper. "If that's not against the rules."

She sighed. "No, it's fine," she said. "If you really want to. But don't feel obligated."

"I want to," I assured her, sitting down at a nearby table,

reaching into my messenger bag to pull out a pen. "Now how about you guys line up and I'll sign something for each of you."

It was like herding cats, but eventually they all lined up and I started to sign. Scraps of paper, napkins—the big kid who had asked first—Ramon—wanted his forehead signed. Why not, right? I Sharpied his head with a flourish and he grinned like a loon, prancing around and showing it off to anyone who would look.

As I talked and signed, I could feel Piper watching me from the corner of the room. She looked pleased, but a little stressed as well. Probably worried one of the kids would say something to offend me or act out and make her look bad. But she had nothing to worry about. I'd been doing public appearances like this since I was a little kid with my dad. And he'd been a pro at handling a crowd—even an unruly mob like this.

Finally, when I was finished, I rose to my feet. "Thanks guys," I said. "Keep watching News 9! Maybe Monday I'll give you a shout-out on air. If Miss Piper here says you've been good, that is."

The kids all cheered. Piper laughed, scolding them and telling them to settle. Then she ushered me out of the room and back to the front office. The receptionist raised an eyebrow when we entered. "Sounded pretty exciting in there," she observed. "I guess it's not every day we have a genuine celebrity here at the Holloway House."

"They seem like a good group," I said to dissuade the whole celebrity talk.

The receptionist snorted. "I've heard those kids called a lot of things, but 'good' isn't usually one of them."

From the corner of my eye I caught Piper stiffen. As if offended on the kids' behalf. As much as she grumped at them, I could tell she was also very proud of all of them and didn't appreciate others putting them down.

"Well, I thought they were great," I reaffirmed, on her behalf. "I'm glad I got a chance to meet them." I turned to Piper and held out my arm. "Shall we?"

She took my arm, shooting me a grateful look, and we headed out of the building toward her car. She stopped in front of it, fumbling for her keys. Then she looked back to me.

"Thank you," she said. "You didn't have to do that. But I know it meant a lot to them that you did. They don't have a lot of excitement in their lives. They'll be talking about this for weeks."

I waved her off, as if it were no big deal. But inside I was dancing. That approving look of hers was like a potent drug and I was getting seriously addicted.

"It was fun," I assured her. "After all, I don't often get a chance to use my celebrity for good. I'd almost forgotten how nice it feels."

She smiled at me and got into her car. I followed suit, feeling warm and happy. That look on her face—it was almost as good as seeing her in that bikini.

Almost.

I closed my door then turned to her. "Where do you want to eat?"

"Is Miguel's open for lunch?" she asked, her mouth quirking.

Oh my God, this girl.

I beamed. "Absolutely."

Ten minutes later and we were back at Miguel's, sitting in our favorite booth, ordering lunch. Angelita was off somewhere, but her daughter took our orders with a knowing grin—and I knew her mother would hear about this repeat appearance of the lovely Piper the second she got back to the kitchen to text her.

"So," I said, turning to Piper after we'd placed our orders. "How did you get involved in the Holloway House anyway?"

To my surprise she squirmed in her seat, as if it were an awkward question. "Um," she said, biting her lower lip, "it's a long story actually."

I looked around the crowded restaurant. "Like you said before, I'm guessing we have time."

"True . . ."

She looked down at her hands. I stared at her.

"You used to live there," I realized aloud.

She nodded, a stain of pink coloring her cheeks. "After my brother died," she said, "my mother was . . . indisposed for a while. At first they tried to put me in foster care and I bounced around to a few different houses. But no one wanted me long term." She gave me a rueful smile. "Not that I blame them. I was a real mess back then."

My heart lurched in my chest as another puzzle piece slid into place. God, I couldn't even fathom the idea of Piper—beautiful, smart, driven Piper—being a mess. But of course she would have been. Who wouldn't be, after suffering such a tragedy—the drowning death of her own brother. I wondered if that was when her mother had started using—a vain attempt to try to cope with the loss of a child. Piper wouldn't have had that luxury, of course—that method to dull the pain. So, while the adults in her life proceeded to fall apart, she'd had no choice but to fend for herself.

Of course she had been a mess. It was a true miracle she wasn't still.

"I'm sorry," I said. "That must have been tough. You were so young, too."

"It *was* tough," she agreed after a pause. "In fact, I probably wouldn't be here today—if it wasn't for Toby, the Holloway House's director. She still works there, actually, but I guess she had the day off today. In any case, she took me under her wing when no one else would. She saw something in me, I guess, that no one else had. That I didn't see in myself."

"She sounds like a great person."

Piper nodded. "Toby pushed me to realize my potential. She forced me to work hard in school, get good grades. She insisted even people like me should be allowed to chase their dreams." She shrugged. "I guess that's why I wanted to do something for Jayden today. These kids—they don't have a lot of joys in their lives. If I could be a light to them—like Toby was to me back in the day—even just a small one . . ."

She paused and I watched her squirm in her seat again, my heart squeezing in my chest. It was all I could do not to get up, cross the table, and grab her in my arms and never let her go. I had no idea she'd had it so tough. Accomplished so much. No wonder that silly morning writer job had meant so much to her. She'd spent her whole life fighting to get to where she was, with the odds always stacked against her.

"You are even more incredible than I thought you were," I whispered with genuine awe.

"I don't know about that," she protested. But she looked pleased all the same.

"So why TV?" I asked. "I mean, I look at you wlth those kids—how good you are with them. Why isn't that your full-time gig?"

She gave a sheepish smile. "When I was twelve the city cut funding to the Holloway House," she explained. "Some politician wanted to divert money to further his own political agenda or whatever—I was too young to understand all the details, I just knew they were trying to shut us down. Anyway, there was this reporter who came down to interview us about it all. She was so beautiful, so polished and smart. You know how the kids reacted to seeing you today? That was me back then with her. It was like I was meeting Angelina Jolie or something!"

"Does that make me Brad Pitt?" I asked with a wink.

"Or Billy Bob Thornton . . ."

I grimaced. "Ouch."

"Anyway, she took me aside and interviewed me, asking me all these questions about my life. Questions no one had ever cared enough to ask before. When she had finished, I asked her if she would be able to save the Holloway House. I was scared, you know? It was the only life I'd really ever known."

"What did she say?"

A smile flickered on Piper's lips. "She said that *I* was going to be the one to save it. By going on TV and showing people that this wasn't about politics, it was about people. Children like me.

"The piece aired a week later. And donations started rolling in. Some other politician stepped in, too, and eventually we were able to get our funding back. The whole thing went viral really. Or as viral as you could get before social media. For a few months I was a bit of a celebrity myself."

I stared at her, something clicking at the back of my mind. "Wait a second," I said slowly. "You're her, aren't you? The little girl who could. I totally remember that story!"

Piper blushed. "*Everyone* remembers that story. It ran for months, all over the country. I became the poster child for at-risk kids everywhere. It was a bit embarrassing to tell you the truth."

"Is it wrong to admit my younger self thought you were totally hot?"

She snorted. "I wouldn't expect anything less from *your* younger self." She grinned. "*Anyway*, that was my first glimpse into the power of journalism. How one person—like that reporter—could turn something so hopeless into something with hope. I decided then and there I wanted to do the same thing someday."

"And instead you're stuck doing weather with me."

"I like it actually," she protested with a laugh. "And hey—it's a step in the right direction, right? I'm very grateful you gave me the opportunity."

"Eh." I waved her off. "Someone would have recognized your brilliance eventually. I'm just lucky I got to you first."

She sighed. "Look, Asher, I'm sorry I accused you of only giving me the job to hook up with me. That was stupid and I had no right to say what I did. It's just . . . all my life people have always had agendas, you know? I've never been given something for nothing."

"You weren't in this case either, may I remind you," I said. "Whether you want to admit it or not, you're a great producer. I just saw that before anyone else did, that's all."

We fell silent for a moment, letting the hum of the restaurant soundtrack the scene. But it wasn't an uncomfortable silence this time. In fact, it was almost . . . intimate. Sitting there, lost in our own thoughts, yet still feeling very connected.

My mind wandered back to the afternoon we'd first met. At Beth and Mac's wedding. The conversation we'd had about her wanting to corner Richard about the morning show writing position. I cringed as I remembered the dumb joke I'd made about it being a terrible job. She must have despised me then—this arrogant asshole being so dismissive of something she'd worked so hard for. This stupid rich guy—who had been given everything—and yet appreciated nothing.

Of course I had more to my story, too. But she wouldn't have known that, just as I hadn't known about her.

I looked up. "Remember what you asked me the last time we were here?"

"You mean about what you wanted to be when you grew up?" she asked, her eyes sparkling. "I believe you chose surf bum as your top career choice."

I raked a hand through my hair, feeling my cheeks heat. "Yeah. That sounds about right," I said with a sigh. "To be honest, the question caught me off guard. I was never given that choice growing up, you know? I was always destined to be a meteorologist from birth."

Piper nodded, giving me a sympathetic look.

"In any case, I really loved working with Jayden today. It'd be cool if I could someday do something like that. Even if it was just on the side."

"What do you mean? Like start a surf school?"

"Yeah, but . . . like a surf school for kids who can't afford it. I mean, I'm guessing the Holloway House doesn't have a lot of money for extracurricular activities."

"Uh, no. They barely have enough for clothing and food."

"Right. Well, what if I could supplement that? Start a program that would allow them to take lessons regularly." I shrugged. "I don't know. Maybe it's a stupid idea."

"It's an amazing idea, actually," she said after a pause. "It wouldn't be easy, though. Jayden was very well behaved today. But he's not always so charming. And some of the others can be a real pain to deal with. They're troubled kids."

"Which is why surfing is so perfect. It's healing. It can boost a kid's confidence," I replied. "And like you said, they need something to look forward to—like you did back in the day. Maybe for some of them, surfing could be that thing."

She nodded slowly, considering, but I could see the excitement rise to her cheeks and it made my stomach flip. She liked the idea. She really liked it. A surge of enthusiasm shot through me, and my mind raced with new plans.

It was time for the Joker to get serious.

twenty-five

PIPER

"The most important tip to remember when you're out in the water? Use the buddy system. It may save your life," Asher said as he addressed the camera. "Plus," he added with a wink, "it's usually way more fun."

I snorted at the impromptu line that, of course, hadn't been in the original script I'd written. But it was *so* Asher and I knew the ladies back home would more than appreciate the sentiment. As would the powers-that-be back at the station. Yet another home run from Team Weather.

The last couple weeks had gone by in a blur. Asher and I had been working overtime—literally—putting together the best weather stories—and accurate forecasts—the station had ever seen. Asher was a man on a mission and I was his right-hand girl and together we rocked each day's story like bosses. News 9's ratings were up and its Facebook page was filled with Asher fans, begging for more of their favorite sexy weather guy. Just like they had once upon a time begged for his father.

Off air, things were equally as busy. I was still pulling as many shifts as I could manage at the Holloway House and Asher was working day and night to pull together all the pieces necessary to start his surf school. When he'd first told me the idea, I'd thought he was just dreaming—that nothing would actually come from it. But I'd evidently underestimated the new and improved Asher Anderson.

He'd found a location on the Chula Vista shore, so the school wouldn't be too far from the Holloway House, and bought a bus to transport the kids to and from the school. He contacted various companies he'd worked with in the past to acquire boards and wet suits and all the other gear needed and he hired instructors who had experience working with beginners. Sometimes I worried about the amount of money he was pouring into the operation, but he didn't seem to bat an eye at any of it. And those same eyes shone with excitement every time he spoke of the venture.

It was as if, for the first time in his life, he had something to look forward to. Something to work toward that hadn't been handed to him on a silver platter. And he was rising to the challenge, working his ass off, and loving every minute of it.

Speaking of loving, I was really starting to love my new job, too. Sure, it wasn't investigative producing—my ultimate dream job. But it was interesting and satisfying and I was learning more and more about how weather worked each day. I was becoming an integral part of the station, too, a vital cog in the wheel, rather than the anonymous girl in the trenches I'd once been.

There was only one thing that was holding me back: my lingering fear of the water. As a weather producer in a beach town, there were several occasions where the stories the assignment desk asked us to cover required ride-alongs with the Coast Guard or spending the day on the beach. Of course Asher would always step in and cover those without complaint, but sometimes I knew him leaving the station meant he couldn't spend enough time on his forecast. He never complained about this, of course. But I always felt as if I was letting him down. Letting the entire station down. And I was pretty sure a few fellow employees were starting to notice.

It was frustrating to say the least. After all I'd accomplished, after how hard I'd worked—how could I let some childhood phobia roadblock me in the end? My mom was in rehab, getting help for her addictions. Asher had transformed himself into a new man. Now seemed as good a time as any to face my own demons and conquer them.

I just needed to get Asher on board. Literally, in this case.

"Base to Unit Seven."

Asher dashed to the truck. "Unit Seven. Are we clear?"

"You're clear," Nancy, the producer, chirped on the other end. "Richard said to tell you good job, too."

Asher raised an eyebrow, shooting an amused look in my direction. "Are you sure it was Richard? And he really used the word *good*? Are you sure he knew he was talking about me?"

Nancy laughed. "Actually, I think he really meant your partner in crime. But I'm confident you'll figure out a way to take the credit."

"Nah." Asher waved her off. "You tell him it was all her genius. Piper wrote the script. She did most of the interviews, too. I'm just the hot guy who reads things that smart people put in front of me."

"Sounds about right." Nancy chuckled. "We'll see you back at the station, hot stuff."

Asher hung up the handset and turned to me. "Another day, another job well done," he pronounced. "We make quite a team, Red."

"That we do, Anderson."

"So what are you doing tonight? Besides celebrating that awesome story we rocked, that is."

"Well," I said, "I was thinking of binge watching *Orphan Black*. But I did have another thought . . ."

Asher's eyebrows raised in interest. "Yes . . . ?"

I drew in a breath. *Here goes nothing.*

"Would you take me out on the boat?"

His smile faded. "What?"

I stubbed my toe into the sand. "It's time," I said. "I need to get over this stupid fear I have of the water before it kills my career."

Asher frowned. "It's not a stupid fear. It's perfectly justified after what you went through."

"I went through a lot of things," I interjected. "But I've never let any of them stop me—except this. I'm sick of living in fear. Of not being able to do my job. What if one day you can't go on the water assignment for me and I have to go by myself? What if I can't handle it and make a fool of myself? What if it gets me fired?"

Asher opened his mouth to protest, but I held up my hand. "I'm going to do this," I told him. "One way or another. So you can either take me out on the boat tonight. Or I'll find someone else who will."

"Absolutely not," Asher replied. "If you're going on the water, you're going with me."

twenty-six

I'm not going to lie; I almost bailed on the boat ride at the last minute. What had seemed like a good idea when I mentioned it to Asher earlier had now grown into a completely crazy proposal as the afternoon ticked away. What had I been thinking? What on earth had possessed me to voluntarily subject myself to my worst nightmare?

But in the end I forced myself to stay strong. I reminded myself how embarrassed I'd been at Beth's wedding, freaking out and interrupting the ceremony over some silly wave. And how pathetic I'd felt when I had had to bail on the boat ride Asher had set up our first night together. How, because of my fear, he'd ended up being forced to take Sarah out instead.

And lastly, of course, there was work. It was interfering with my work and I never wanted anything to interfere with that. I had to get over this. One way or another. And if Asher was willing to help, well, so much the better.

I figured a boat ride was a good jumping off point, too—pun certainly not intended. For one thing it would allow me to get used to the water—without actually touching any water. I wouldn't have to swim. Someone experienced could captain the vehicle. All I had to do was sit back and enjoy the ride.

Or, you know, survive it at the very least.

So I handed my keys over to the valet and walked down to the dock at the yacht club, once more with feeling. There I found Asher, standing on the shore, holding a life jacket in his hands. I drew in a breath; he looked so good standing there. Tall, strong, in charge—his silhouette illuminated by an old gas lamppost. The silhouette of a guy who would never let anything happen to someone in his charge.

I bit my lower lip. *I can do this. I can totally do this.*

Asher handed me the life jacket. "You don't have to wear it," he explained. "By law you just have to have it accessible."

I put it on anyway, strapping it to my chest. I wasn't taking any chances. To Asher's credit, he didn't make any jokes.

"Are you ready for this?" he asked instead.

"As I'll ever be."

He slipped a hand into mine and we walked in silence down the dock. Which was absolutely *nothing* like walking a plank, I scolded my frenzied brain. When we reached the boat, he stepped one foot onto it, to help me board. As I took a step, his hand brushed my waist, sending a jolt of heat straight through me—so hot I almost didn't notice the way the boat rocked as I set my weight on it.

And so it began.

As I'd mentioned before, the last few weeks had been great for my career. What I hadn't mentioned was how terrible they'd been for my libido. Asher had been a total gentleman—never once trying to make a move after I'd asked him not to. Unfortunately the more unattainable he became, the more I found I wanted him. In fact, at times, when we were alone in the weather center, it was all I could do not to lock the door and jump his bones. But that would just complicate things further. We were coworkers. We were friends.

We were alone on a romantic boat ride and all he'd had to do was casually touch me and my body was humming. This was going to be a long night.

I had to admit, the boat he'd picked out was pretty sweet.

Smaller than I'd pictured, with white-leather cushions and a fancy big brass steering wheel. There was even a little hatch down below with a small sleeping area—like a cozy little sea cave. A good retreat, I decided, if things got too real above deck. I could crawl inside, shut the door, and pretend I wasn't at sea.

"Are you sure you want to leave the dock?" Asher asked. "We could just have lesson number one right here. Get you used to being on the boat."

"No," I said. "I need to do this for real. I want it to count."

"Okay," he said. "But you let me know when you start feeling nervous. I can stop and turn around at any time."

I nodded, gratitude washing over me at his obvious concern. Over the past few weeks I'd seen such a different side to Asher than most people saw. The layers of his callous, arrogant exterior had begun to peel away and a sweet, gentle man had emerged from beneath. Which was even more enticing, in my opinion, than his handsome outer shell.

I settled into my seat and Asher took the wheel. Soon we were gliding across the bay, leaving the dock behind us and heading out into open sea. At first I tried to focus on the horizon, but as the distance between the boat and dry land stretched out farther and farther, I turned my eyes to Asher instead.

Did I mention he looked good? 'Cause he looked really, really good. Standing at the wheel, straight-backed and broad-shouldered. As confident as I was petrified. The look on his face said this was no big deal—that this was nothing to worry about. I just needed to sit back and enjoy the ride. He would take care of the rest.

He would take care of me.

I forced myself to look back out onto the water. Watch the brilliant sun slip down beneath the horizon, casting golden shimmers on the sea in its wake. Out here, I noted, there were no frothy waves to toss us around, no frightening sounds of the surf crashing against the shore. Just a slight bobbing up and down as the boat navigated the sea's glassy surface and the sound of a few small, almost inaudible splashes as the water licked the sides of the boat. It was almost weirdly peaceful—as long as I didn't look down to see how deep the water went.

Finally, Asher dropped anchor, joining me on the couch. Reaching into a lower hatch, he pulled out a picnic basket draped in white linen.

"The chef at the yacht club makes the most delicious surf and turf," he informed me in an ultra-serious voice. "But I told him we had other plans." In a *ta-da* movement, he yanked off the linen, revealing a basket of peanut butter and jelly sandwiches and a big bag of potato chips.

"I made them myself," he declared, looking all too proud.

I laughed, clapping my hands together. "Perfect!" I pronounced. And it was.

Feeling brave, I slipped out of my life jacket, setting it beside me, and grabbed a sandwich from the basket. It wasn't the prettiest PB&J I'd ever seen, with jelly leaking out the sides, but at that moment, to me, it was better than any five-star meal in the world. Because of the guy who had made it. The guy who had paid attention enough to remember how I'd said eating peanut butter and jelly as a child had always made me feel better.

"How are you doing?" Asher asked, after taking and swallowing a bite of his own.

"I'm okay actually," I said. "I'm trying not to think about how far out we are. Or how deep the waters are."

"I'm proud of you," he replied, his voice taking on a husky tone that almost succeeded in making me forget about the aforementioned deep waters. "I know this can't be easy. What you went through with your brother—I can't even imagine." He paused, his cheek reddening. "Sorry, I shouldn't be bringing that up, should I?"

"It's okay," I assured him. Then I drew in a breath. "But to be honest? I'd rather talk about why you love the sea than the reasons I don't. What makes it so special for you? When did it become such an important part of your life?"

He nodded slowly, clasping his hands together in front of him, staring out into the water. For a moment, he didn't speak and I half wondered if he was going to answer the question. Then, at last, he opened his mouth.

"Most people look at me and see someone who was born with every advantage," he began in a slow voice. "And they wouldn't be wrong, I guess. Growing up, I never worried about having food on the table or clothes to wear or a roof over my head." He raked a hand through his hair. "But that didn't mean my childhood was particularly happy."

He sighed. "It's hard to justify complaining about it—especially to someone like you who had to deal with so much real shit growing up. What is it they joke about? First world problems? But they were still problems for me. At times—big ones."

"Go on," I urged.

"Growing up, my family spent a lot of effort keeping up appearances," he said. "Like any family in the public eye would, I suppose. My father was a household name and everyone expected him to live a certain lifestyle. And my mother—well, she had to always hustle to keep the station in the black. Wine and dine the advertisers, make them feel special. You should have seen the parties they used to throw. Wild swinger bashes at our beach house—with all the who's who in San Diego. You'd be shocked if I started naming names." He made a face. "I guess that's called living the good life. But to be the only kid amongst all that hedonism—it was a bit of a nightmare."

"I can imagine."

"Usually I'd hide up in my room at night, pillow over my head, hands in my ears. Trying to block it all out. But sometimes they weren't content to leave me alone. Sometimes my drunken mother would try to drag me downstairs to put on a show for her guests. Like I was some freaking show pony or trained monkey. And if I refused to perform? Well, let's just say letting the family down came with . . . consequences the next day."

I winced, my mind flashing back to what he'd said about Sarah and the boat ride. About how his mother had practically pimped him out to her favorite advertiser's daughter.

As if he were a prop, an asset to the family business, rather than an actual member of the family. Had she been doing this to Asher his whole life? No wonder he treated everything like a joke—when he himself had never been taken seriously.

"Anyway," Asher continued, "on the bad nights, on the nights when I knew she would come for me, sometimes I'd escape out my window and run down to the shore. Down to the ocean where everything was quiet and peaceful and no one would demand anything from me. I could walk the shoreline all night, imagining I was some brave explorer, discovering a new world. One where no one could hurt me.

"The ocean didn't have expectations of me. It didn't need me to impress its friends. It didn't try to make me into someone I wasn't. Instead, it embraced me, welcomed me, warts and all." He stared out into the calm waters, a contemplative look on his face. "It also gave me a feeling of power, too. I mean, there I was, some scrawny, scared kid who couldn't even say no to his own mother. But out here, on the ocean, I was suddenly a god, able to tame nature itself. Taking on a mighty ocean wave and riding it to shore—reclaiming all the power I'd lost in real life." He gave me a sheepish look. "Okay, that sounds dumb when I say it out loud."

"Actually it doesn't," I assured him. "In fact it sounds amazing."

"I guess that's why I love the idea of doing a surf school for those kids," he said. "They feel as helpless as I did back then—even if it's for a different reason. If I can help them reclaim their power, their sense of self-worth, who knows what they may be able to channel that into someday?"

He turned to me, his face fierce with his ambition, and my heart squeezed at the determination I saw in his eyes. *This* was the Asher no one else saw. The one everyone dismissed before getting to know. This was the Asher who was *worth* getting to know.

The Asher who I was falling for—despite my best efforts.

I leaned forward, my lips crashing into his own with reckless abandon, my tongue plunging into his mouth. No

longer content to hear his words—I needed to taste them.
Devour them whole—despite the fact it was a terrible idea.
In that moment, I needed skin against skin. Flesh against
flesh. I didn't care about the consequences, the future. All
that mattered was Asher—sweet Asher—in my arms.

For a moment, he sat still, as if shocked into stasis by my
unexpected move. But it didn't take him long to recover. And
soon his hands were dropping to the small of my back as he
pulled me to him, my stomach swirling madly as he sat me
on his lap, coaxing my mouth to widen, the kiss to deepen.
My mind spun as I drank in the sweetness of the kiss, the
heat from his hands as they slipped under my shirt and connected with bare skin. Soon I found myself grinding against
him, rejoicing at the feeling of his growing arousal pressed
up against my core.

"God, Piper," he murmured, planting kisses along my
jawline, his hands searing a path from my back to my hips,
locking me in place. "You are seriously going to kill me."

His hands reached up, cupping my breasts, and I moaned
into his ear as his lips trailed kisses down my neck to the
hollow spot in my clavicle. I pressed myself against him
again, trying desperately to satisfy the soul-deep ache burning inside of me. My hands wrapped around his neck.

I knew it was wrong. I knew we shouldn't have been
doing this. But at that moment, for the life of me I couldn't
remember why. All I could focus on was the here. The now.
The man who had his hands up my shirt.

Suddenly, the boat jerked, causing me to lose my balance.
My stomach lurched and I would have fallen if Asher hadn't
tightened his hold on me at the last second. Heart pounding
in my chest, I scrambled to my feet, breaking our embrace,
looking around with horror.

The once glassy sea was now a blender, rocking and
rolling and spitting chunks of foam. My eyes rose to see
angry storm clouds had rolled in, smothering the horizon,
all but blocking out the setting sun. A moment later, I felt
the first drops of rain.

Asher rose to his feet. "Shit," I heard him murmur under his breath. He walked over and scanned the instrument panel while I waited, barely able to breathe.

"What is it?" I demanded. Something about the look on his face told me whatever it was, it was not good news.

"Everything's fine," he assured me, though his tense expression told another story. "It's just a small storm rolling in. A bit faster and harder than I would have liked but it's no big deal."

I swallowed hard, the adrenaline spiking through my veins. I tried to keep my eyes on Asher and not look out over the water. "We should get back to shore then."

Asher was silent for a moment, staring at the instruments.

"Come on!" I cried, stomping over to him. But I had to stop and grab a pole for balance as a wave smacked against the side of the boat. The wind had picked up, too, and I had to reach up to push the hair from my face. "What are you waiting for?"

Asher turned to me, a guilty look on his face. "I'm not sure we'd make it to shore on time. And we don't want to be capsized by the break. We're fine out here. The boat can take a little rocking. We'll just wait it out. Should pass completely through in about a half hour."

I shook my head, fear thrumming through my veins. The ship might be able to take a little rocking, but could I? As if in response, the wind wrested the hair from my grasp, whipping it back in my face. The rain began to fall faster and my eyes stung from the salt.

"Are you okay?" Asher asked, peering at me. "Look, I'm sorry, Piper. I had no idea . . ."

"But you're a weatherman!" I cried angrily, hating this feeling of panic welling up inside of me. It was so stupid. So embarrassing. Yet so, so strong. I stared out into the rain and wind and waves. My mind flashing back to that night. That terrible night.

Where's Michael? Piper, where's your brother?

I stumbled backward, nearly falling over, the panic

gripping me with icy fingers. What had I been thinking? This was the worst idea ever! I'd wanted to lose my fear of the ocean—not double down on it, for God's sake!

Vaguely I could feel Asher's hands on me, pulling me upright. Then, he led me down the stairs, into the little sleeping cabin I'd discovered on boarding, and closed the door behind us.

I sucked in a shaky breath, looking around. Thankfully the door had shut off most of the noise and chaos outside. And it was a relief to no longer be able to see the sea. At the same time, I knew it was still up there, the storm still hammering us from outside, and I could feel the boat rocking angrily in response. And here I was, clinging to Asher, as if he were my only lifeboat. We were both soaking wet at this point and water dripped down onto the little bed.

Finally, I managed to let him go, sinking down onto the bed, working to get my breathing back under control. Trying to ignore the way we were being tossed back and forth like a toddler's toy.

"Do you get seasick?" Asher asked. "Because it may get rough in a few minutes."

"Um, isn't it rough already?" I managed to squeak. I had no idea, of course, if I got seasick, seeing as I'd never been to sea.

He gave me a rueful smile, then grabbed a pillow and offered it to me. I sank down onto it, staring up at the dark ceiling, working the breathing exercises the shrinks had taught me long ago.

It's no big deal. It's just a little storm. Think of it as trial by fire. If you can survive this, you can survive anything.

Asher scooted up beside me, propping his head up with his elbow and hand. With his other hand he reached out, gently pushing up my T-shirt and stroking my bare stomach with careful fingers. And as his thumb lightly dipped into my navel, I stifled a gasp, something other than panic now spiking within me.

"Shhh," he soothed, still stroking. "Everything's okay.

The boat is very seaworthy. We're in no danger, I promise you. We will not capsize. We will not sink. We can stay down here and forget it's even happening."

"Maybe *you* can," I retorted before I could stop myself. But then his fingers drifted a few inches lower and suddenly I was feeling pretty damn forgetful myself. I bit my lower lip, heat surging through me at his touch.

"I can help you forget," he whispered, his lips curling into a small smile, "if you're interested."

I was interested. I was very, very interested. In fact, I was ready to go for full-on amnesia mode if he was willing to take me there.

"I—" I started to say then *eep*ed out loud as, without warning, his hand slid between my legs. Oh God, oh God. What was I supposed to be remembering again?

Asher pushed my knees apart, brushing a thumb along my inner thigh, all the while keeping his eyes locked on my face.

"This feel okay?" he asked in a soft voice.

"Um, yes?" I squeaked. Because in truth it felt far beyond okay. Far beyond ridiculously good if we were going to be technical here.

He grinned. "What about this?" He slid his hand upward, softly brushing against my mound. I almost bit my tongue. "Not . . . bad?"

He laughed huskily, then reached up to unbutton my slacks, sliding them over my hips. I helped him shuck them off until I was bare except for my panties. He caressed me through the thin fabric, taking his time with me, while I did everything I could not to buck against him, desperate to relieve the pressure building inside of me like a wildfire.

Somewhere, deep down, I knew this was a bad idea. Something I should stop, something I would regret tomorrow if I didn't. But right now, at this very second, I didn't want to push his hands away. He felt good. He felt right. And his gentle strokes were making amazing strides in relieving me of my fear. In fact, when Asher pulled aside my panties and slid his fingers into my slick folds, I pretty much forgot I was on a boat altogether.

I was soaking wet—and not from the rain, either. I was grabbing the sides of the mattress with white-knuckled fingers. I was moaning and thrusting my hips against his hand.

But I was no longer shaking in fear.

"Do you like when I touch you?" Asher asked, his green eyes burning into me now. Filled with lust and desire.

"Y-yes," I managed to say, pretty sure I was sweating at this point. "Oh, yes."

He grinned wickedly, then lowered himself down before me, burying his head between my thighs. I almost leapt out of my skin as his velvet, hot tongue slid across my sex.

"Oh God, Piper. You taste as good as you look," he said, sucking my cleft into his mouth, his fingers slipping, one after another, inside of me. His other hand reached up, cupping my breast, toying with the nipple as his fingers slid inside and out in a torturous rhythm. As his mouth sucked and nipped at my sensitive skin. Soon I found myself rocking against him, riding the wave of ecstasy, higher and higher until I crested at the top and practically screamed as the pleasure washed over me.

"Asher . . ." I managed to moan as heat and hormones pulsed through my body like fire. Asher looked up from between my legs, his mouth quirking to a pleased smile.

"Still afraid of the storm?" he asked.

"There's a storm?"

He laughed. "Oh, yes, baby. There's a storm. And it's not even half over. Which means, you're in need of more distraction."

"What about you?" I asked, feeling a little guilty he was there, making me come, and I wasn't doing a thing in return.

"Oh, you're all the distraction I need," he assured me. "You just lie back and let me do the work for once. That's what you wanted, right? For me to step up to the plate?" He grinned wickedly. "You keep making those little sounds and I'm going to become a fucking workaholic."

And with that he slipped between my legs again and I gasped as the sensations rocked over my now all-too-sensitive skin. I had heard of girls having multiple orgasms during sex, but had barely ever been able to achieve even one with any of my previous boyfriends. Mainly because they were more interested in achieving their own.

But Asher didn't seem to care about that as he effortlessly brought me to climax again. I clutched the sheets and bucked against his mouth, scarcely able to believe anyone could feel this good.

"Okay, okay!" I protested, as, a moment later, he started in for round three. "I need a break! There's got to be an OSHA regulation that says no three orgasms in a row."

"Quitter," he teased, but obliged, crawling up beside me and pulling me into his arms. I settled in, breathing in a sigh of contentment as my head rested in the nook between his head and his shoulder. I could feel his lips press against my hair for a moment, before he leaned back and looked up at the ceiling, still stroking my back with his fingers. All the raging hormones from before settled into a sated sleepiness.

"This is nice," I said. And I meant it.

"It is," he agreed. "Maybe the ocean isn't half bad after all?"

I stiffened, his words sending reality in to crash the party. I turned to face the wall, feeling my throat tighten. A moment later the tears slipped from the corners of my eyes. At first, Asher didn't move, as if he knew enough to give me that moment alone. Then he placed a hand at the small of my back, stroking me gently.

"What's wrong, sweetheart?" he asked.

I squeezed my eyes shut, trying to bring things back into focus, then opened them again. "Nothing. I mean . . . I don't know. I just . . . I want to let go of this fear, you know? And you're doing a pretty bang-up job of making that happen. But at the same time it feels like a betrayal, I guess. Like by being this happy and this content I'm somehow betraying Michael's memory."

Asher's hand stilled, but he didn't pull away. "You don't think your brother would want you to move on?"

"I don't know. He was so young. To be honest, I barely remember him." I groaned. "That sounds awful, right?"

"It sounds normal," Asher corrected. "How old were you again when he drowned?"

"Six. He was four."

"Then it's amazing you remember anything at all."

"Yeah, well, my mother does a great job reminding me."

Asher's eyes zeroed in on me. "Why would she do that?"

I turned away. I didn't want to talk about this. I really didn't want to talk about this. But at the same time I knew if I didn't, I was never going to get over this fear. I was going to have to live with it forever, a weight, dragging me down more every day. I didn't know what Asher would think of me if I told him the truth. I didn't know if it would change what was happening between us. But at that moment, I realized, I did need him to know. If we were going to move forward with whatever this was, he had to know the truth.

"Because it was my fault," I blurted before I could chicken out. "I was supposed to be watching him and I let him drown."

I turned, waiting to see the revulsion on his face—the horror in his eyes. The condemnation at the idea that I could just live with myself and move on with my life, knowing I was a murderer. That I had practically murdered my own brother.

And yet, as I studied Asher's face, I saw none of the above. Just . . . confusion . . . if anything. But definitely not disgust.

"I don't understand," he said. "You just told me you were six years old. How could you be expected to watch him?"

"I watched him all the time," I protested. "When my mom would go out or whatever. It wasn't a big deal. I mean, I didn't think it was at the time."

"What happened, Piper? Tell me the whole story."

I sighed. "It was Thanksgiving night. My mom and her boyfriend at the time . . . they had something they needed to do. So they left me and Michael on the beach. Told me to watch him while they were gone."

"They left you alone on the beach?" Asher demanded, looking offended on my behalf. "At night?"

I opened my mouth, ready to spit out the familiar lie. The

one I'd told a thousand times, to prosecutors and defenders and police and juries. But this time, to my surprise, the truth fell from my lips instead.

"They had to rob a house," I said, the words tasting bitter as they left my mouth. "For drug money or whatever. A lot of the beach houses were vacant for the day—with everyone going over to relatives' houses for turkey and stuff."

I could feel my face growing hot at the confession—I'd never told anyone that part before. But Asher knew firsthand about addiction. He'd been through treatment; he had to have met people like my mother. People who had let their disease rob them of their humanity.

"Anyway, I was so tired. My mom had been on a bender the last few days and when she was high she never shut up so it was tough to sleep. Michael was playing on the blanket and he seemed fine. So I closed my eyes, just wanting a few minutes to rest."

Michael! Where's Michael?

Where's your brother? You were supposed to be watching your brother!

"Piper!"

I jerked back to reality, my eyes locking on Asher's, his face inches from my own. I moaned and lay back on the bed, the tears slipping from my eyes again, unchecked.

"You can probably guess the rest," I said dully. "I fell asleep. He wandered into the water. When my mother came back she woke me up, demanding to know where he was. I still remember looking out into those dark, deep waters and realizing he was gone. That I had killed my own brother."

A choke escaped my throat. Asher grabbed me, pulling me close, his arms wrapping around me, crushing me against his chest. I burrowed my head against him, the tears falling like rain now. He stroked my hair and kissed the top of my head over and over until I lost count of the times.

Finally, he pulled away, meeting my eyes with his own. "You were a child," he said, his voice hard and raspy. "You should never have been put in that situation. You can't blame yourself for this, Piper."

I closed my eyes. "I know that in my head," I said. "Of course I do. But there's this gaping hole in my heart and I've never been able to sew it up. Every time I look out into the ocean, the memories come raging back. My mother, waking me up, screaming at me, asking me where Michael was. The three of us searching the water." I cringed. "I still remember how cold the water was that night; like shards of ice stabbing at my legs. But I refused to get out. Not until we found Michael." I hung my head. "Eventually my mother's boyfriend dragged me out and threw me into the van. I waited there, shivering half to death, while they continued to search."

"Didn't they even call the police?"

"From what I understand someone called the cops when they heard my mother's screaming. When they showed up the boyfriend had disappeared and she was completely hysterical—they had to take her to a psych ward for the night."

"What about you?"

I shrugged. "I slipped out of the van after they'd all left and looked for Michael some more. I looked all night—I almost drowned wading through the water in the dark. But I never found him. The next day they picked me up—my mother had sobered up and remembered leaving me in the van. They took me straight to the Holloway House and then stuck me with my first foster family while they investigated. For months I was frantic, not knowing if they'd ever found Michael."

"Did they?"

"I found out later his body washed up on shore three days later. There was no evidence of foul play, of course. But they arrested my mother anyway on child endangerment charges and tried her for second-degree murder. I had to testify in the trial. For months I was coached on my testimony. I told them all my mother had been there, that she had been watching, but my brother had been swept away by a riptide, too quickly for anyone to do anything." I shrugged. "I don't know if anyone believed me. But they did downgrade her sentence to involuntary manslaughter and drug possession.

She went to jail for a few years before she was released for good behavior."

"Did you ever talk to her about it again?"

I scowled. "Are you kidding? She never lets me forget it. She loves to remind me how she went to jail to protect me. For not letting them know who was really responsible for Michael's death."

I could see Asher's hands tighten into fists, knuckles whitening to bone. "Addicts never take responsibility for their actions. But that doesn't make them not responsible," he added. "Piper, what happened to your brother was a terrible tragedy. But it was not—in any way—your fault. You were a child! You should have never been put in that situation!"

"No," I agreed. "But that doesn't change anything now. I can't undo what happened. And I've had to live with it every day of my life." I shrugged slowly. "I guess now you can see why I don't like to lose control," I added. "Because the one time I did, I pretty much lost everything."

"Oh, sweetheart."

Asher grabbed me, crushing me into a fierce hug. Pulling me close, kissing and cuddling me and holding me in his arms. I could feel his heartbeat against my ear, feel his warmth sneaking into my freezing skin. I may have been afraid of the water, but I had never felt as safe and protected as at that moment.

I should have been embarrassed. My face should have been burning in shame. I should have been petrified that he would go tell everyone my darkest secret. And yet, as we sat there, Asher stroking my hair and whispering in my ear, I felt none of the above. Instead, I felt a strange sense of freedom.

I'd told the truth—after all these years—the total truth, no holds barred. And just like that, the truth had lost its power over me. All those years my mother had held it over my head. All that guilt I'd bottled up deep inside. It was as if the truth had been a weight that had been resting on my chest this entire time and now it had been lifted and I could raise my head. Sit up. Stand. Run free.

It was exhilarating. Petrifying, too. But mostly exhilarating. Like a door had been opened and for the first time I could step out into the light.

We lay like that for a while, no longer speaking. But the silence between us was more comforting than awkward. And eventually, Asher lifted his head, listening. Then he turned to me.

"You know, I think the storm may have passed," he remarked.

I stared at him, surprised. In all the distraction I hadn't even registered the fact that the boat was no longer rocking like crazy.

"Do you want to go back?" he asked. "Get the hell off this boat?"

I considered this for a moment, then a smile tugged at my lips. "Maybe we should wait a little longer," I said. "To tell you the truth, I'm feeling pretty comfortable right about now."

He leaned over and kissed me soundly on the mouth. "You and me both, baby."

twenty-seven

ASHER

I woke the next day before the sun, but I had no interest in getting out of bed. Normally on a Saturday morning I'd want to be the first one out there, catching the perfect wave. But not when I'd already caught the perfect girl in my bed.

I glanced down at Piper now, all rumpled and sleeping under a sheet, her red curls splayed out across the pillow. We'd returned here after our boating adventure, under the guise of wanting to talk about the experience, but really I just didn't want her to go home. I'd offered to let her have my bed and for me to take the couch. But she just looked at me with those big brown eyes of hers and said we could share.

I wasn't going to argue with that.

We didn't sleep together. I mean beyond what had happened under the deck of the boat, which still had my entire body humming. But it didn't go beyond that, and once we crawled under the covers all we did was kiss. Which was kind of nice actually. The girls I normally dated were so quick to jump into bed. Almost as quick as I was to jump out of bed the next morning. But kissing Piper and talking to Piper and sharing with Piper—that was something new.

And the intimacy was proving almost more erotic than actually doing the deed.

I wanted to wake her now, to cover her body with more kisses, teasing her into consciousness. But I knew I should let her sleep. She was clearly exhausted—both physically from all the shifts she'd been pulling for her two jobs, and mentally from the ordeal on the boat the night before. I still couldn't believe that we'd gotten stuck out in a storm; I really was a lousy weatherman. But what happened during that storm made me pretty happy that I sucked as badly as I did.

I was so proud of her I could hardly stand it—how she'd faced her fears head-on like she had. Not just in getting on the boat itself, but in opening herself up, trusting me with the story behind the phobia. Even thinking about what she'd gone through filled me with rage—no person should have to live like she had, and half of me wanted to go down to that rehab and smack her mother upside the head. For being so weak, so selfish. For pushing her own guilt onto her daughter because she couldn't bear to live with it herself.

But in the end, I knew it would do no good. The woman was an addict; she had a disease. She had to fight her own demons, just as Piper was now fighting hers. Maybe someday she would reach the point where she could ask Piper for forgiveness. Admit responsibility at last—and free her daughter from the shackles of guilt she didn't deserve to wear. At least she was in the right space to do so this time—the rehab I'd placed her in was one of the best in the country. If anyone could help her, they could.

Speaking of helping, today we planned to head to the Holloway House and tell Piper's boss about the surf school and get permission to enroll the kids. I was excited—but also nervous. I'd never taken on anything so big before. Never tried something that could so easily fail. But with Piper on my side, I felt nearly invincible. She had faced her fears last night. Now it was time for me to man up and do the same.

Piper groaned, rolling over in bed and blinking up at me with sleepy eyes, shuttered by long thick lashes. Most redheads I knew had very sparse, light-colored lashes—so light you could barely see them. But Piper's were thick and curly and long, perfectly framing her large brown eyes. I couldn't get enough of them.

Of her, either.

"Good morning, sleepyhead," I teased, leaning down to kiss her forehead. Her skin was warm on my lips, almost dewy, and suddenly it was all I could do not to grab her and yank her flush against me—until her soft curves melted into my hard frame. I imagined reaching down, cupping that perfect ass of hers, and pulling her leg on top of me before closing the gap between us.

But instead, I remained a gentleman. Or tried to, anyway, until I felt her reaching out, dragging a lazy hand over my morning wood, an impish look on her face. I froze, staring at her.

"You had your turn last night," she reminded me with a sly smile. "Turnabout is fair play, don't you think, Anderson?"

Then, before I could even register the movement, she was under the covers, pulling down my boxer briefs, freeing me from their constraints. I groaned as her fingers wrapped securely around the length of me, her thumb sliding over the tip and toying with the bead of moisture that had formed almost instantly. I lay back, staring up at the ceiling, as she began to stroke me, softly, rhythmically. And when she lowered her mouth to take me inside, I almost had a heart attack on the spot.

Truth was, I'd had plenty of blowjobs in my day. Quickies in the car at the end of a date, mostly, so I could get home and get on with my night. But I'd had very few performed in the early hours of the morning, while I was warm and cozy and still half-asleep. As I lay there now, eyes closed, rejoicing in the feel of her hot mouth sliding up and down my cock, I suddenly understood the appeal of the morning after just a little bit more.

"God, Piper." I twitched and my hands went instinctively to her hair, digging into the soft strands. "You have to stop."

"But I'm only getting started," she teased, pulling off of

me to speak. The sudden absence of her mouth on me was so abrupt and harsh I almost grabbed her head and shoved her back on.

Thankfully I was able to restrain myself from that kind of caveman behavior and instead pulled her into my arms, cuddling her close to me and kissing the top of her head again, then her cheeks. She splayed a hand over my chest and snuggled up against me.

"Didn't you like that?" she asked sleepily.

I groaned. "Sweetheart, you have no idea," I said, still feeling the heat pulsating through my body. "It's just . . . I want to make sure you're really okay with all of this—with us—before we take it any further."

I could feel her heavy sigh against my chest. "Can't we just not think about that right now? Just enjoy this for what it is?"

I stiffened. At her words. At the lines I'd used myself on countless girls in the past, echoing back in my ears. *Why ruin what we have with labels? Why analyze it to death? Let's live in the moment—let's not ruin this night. Tomorrow will take care of itself.*

Even when I would say those words to the others, I'd know deep down I was being a dick. But I had no idea just how much they would hurt when thrown back in my face. By someone I truly cared about.

The one girl I wanted more from. The one girl I did want to think of a future with.

The one girl who had no interest in a future with me.

I slipped out of bed, trying to ignore the crushing weight on my chest. I could feel Piper's eyes on me, worried now, but I ignored them, grabbing my jeans and shucking them over my hips.

"Come back to bed," she begged. "I'm sorry. We can just sleep or whatever."

"You sleep," I said. "I need to get all my papers in order for our pitch to your boss this morning."

"That's not for hours, Asher."

"And I need every minute. I want to make sure this proposal is the best it can be."

She sat up in bed, giving me a pleading look. "You're mad at me," she said. "I'm sorry, Asher. I didn't mean—"

I waved her off. "There's nothing wrong," I assured her. "I'm not mad." I walked over to the bed and kissed her quickly on the head. "Everything is exactly how it was before. I just need to work, that's all."

But that was a lie, I thought as I walked out of the bedroom, closing the door behind me. Something *had* changed between us. Changed inside of me, anyway. Somewhere along the line Piper had gone from a prize to be won to a girl I needed to have.

And I wasn't sure what I'd do about that if she didn't feel the same about me.

We arrived at the Holloway House later that morning, pulling into the lot and parking my bus. As I stepped out of Fiona and grabbed my paperwork from the back, I could feel my heart thrumming a staccato beat. I wasn't sure why I was so nervous. I mean, I was offering something to them, free of charge, not asking for anything in return. If anything, they should have been falling over backwards in gratitude at my generosity.

But all the rational thinking in all the world couldn't calm my rapidly beating heart. Nor did the skeptical look on the face of Piper's boss as I walked through the front door. Piper had spoken highly of Toby on more than one occasion, telling me the woman had basically single-handedly made her into the woman she was today. But I could tell from a quick look that while Toby might be Piper's number one fan, she was holding out judgment on me.

Which was to be expected, I supposed, though it didn't do anything to calm my nerves.

"So what's this all about?" she asked, plopping down behind her desk, crossing her arms over her chest.

Piper gestured for me to sit down as she did the same. "Toby, this is Asher Anderson," she introduced. "The meteorologist I work with at News 9."

Toby gave a small snort in response, giving me a critical once-over. Letting me know in no uncertain terms the TV thing didn't impress her much.

Piper kept talking. "Asher is opening up a surf school for at-risk kids," she explained. "He'll provide all the equipment and the teachers and the busing back and forth. And he's willing to take on any kids from the Holloway House who want lessons for free."

Toby was silent for a moment, pushing her bottom lip out, as if in thought. Then she frowned. "Sounds like a waste of good money," she declared at last.

"Excuse me?" Piper stammered. She was clearly not expecting this.

"These kids need food and clothing—their basic needs met. They don't need to learn how to surf."

Piper's mouth clamped shut. She gave me a helpless look. I leaned forward in my chair. My turn.

"We all need food," I said, keeping my voice even. "But sometimes we need to feed our souls as well."

Toby narrowed her eyes. "They go to church on Sunday."

"I'm not talking about that." I raked a hand through my hair, trying to order my thoughts. "It's just—these kids have been dealt a bad hand, right? They're all struggling to gain control over their lives. Surfing can give them a feeling of accomplishment, of control. They'll take on waves, bend the ocean to their will—break down something that feels, at first, so massive into something totally manageable. It's empowering, to say the least."

Toby turned to look at me—to really look at me this time, her dark eyes drilling into me, as if she could peel back my skin and see my soul beneath.

"Go on," she said in a grudging voice.

"Surfing will give kids something to look forward to. Something they can be proud of. It's physical, too, so it helps with keeping them in shape. And it's mentally challenging as well—you need to observe the waves, analyze where they will crest and break. And above all," I added, a little sheepishly, "it's fun. And don't these kids deserve to have fun sometimes, like everyone else?"

Toby gave a slow nod. "It sounds like an ambitious project," she said. Then she frowned. "What if it fails?"

I cocked my head in question. "Fails?" Of all the questions I'd tried to anticipate, this hadn't been one of them.

Toby folded her hands in front of her. "No offense, Mr. Anderson," she said. "But I've seen your kind in here before. Pitching these grand do-good projects to so-called 'help' my kids. They all sound amazing. So splendid and cool. But ninety percent of them sputter out before they can really begin. And the rest?" Her mouth set in a scowl. "They get bored and move on to the next venture."

"But I wouldn't—"

Toby raised a hand to stop me. "Look, Mr. Anderson, these kids aren't a bucket list item that you can check off and feel good about your privilege. They need people they can depend on. They've had enough adults waltzing in and out of their lives, crushing their little hopes and dreams under their heels. They're only children and yet most of them have already suffered more disappointments than you will in your entire life. And I can't have you coming in here, promising them the world, only to leave them high and dry once you get bored."

I sat there in my seat, dumbfounded. Not sure what to say. I wanted to protest—to tell her that I wasn't like that. That when I committed to something I followed through. But she would never believe me. Mostly because it wasn't true. In fact, up until now I hadn't truly committed to anything in my life except meteorology. And that was only because I hadn't been given a choice.

Anger surged through me. At Toby—for her hesitation to commit to the project. At myself—for being the kind of guy who prompted such hesitation.

I tossed the proposal on her desk, then rose to my feet. "Look it over," I said. "Let Piper know what you think. You have three days to decide before I take the offer to another group home. I'm sure someone will appreciate my charity."

"Asher . . ." I could feel Piper reaching for my arm. I shook her off.

"I'll be outside when you're ready," I told her. And with that, I stormed out of the office, my stomach roiling with nausea.

So this was what people truly thought of me. And maybe they were right to think it. Before Piper had come around I wouldn't have cared, either—I would have probably turned it into a joke. *Look at Asher, such an irresponsible clown.* Hell, I'd worn my Joker status as a badge of honor.

But Piper had changed all of that. She had made me want to be a better person. The kind of person a girl like her could be proud of. The kind of person a girl like her would want on her arm.

"You okay?"

I whirled around to see Piper standing there, watching me. I groaned, leaning up against Fiona, banging my head against her side. "That did not go as I hoped," I muttered.

I could feel her step behind me, wrapping her arms around my waist, leaning into me, her head resting on my back. "I'm sorry," she said. "I had no idea Toby would react that way. I honestly thought she'd be thrilled." She shrugged. "I guess she's just protective of the kids."

"Which is what she should be," I replied. "She's just doing her job. Keeping the fuckups at bay."

"You're not a fuckup, Asher," she said.

"I don't know if most people would agree with you."

"Most people don't know you. Not like I've gotten to know you now. I've seen you work hard these past few weeks. I know how important this is to you. I believe you're in it for the long haul, and it's not just a passing fancy." I could feel her smile against my back. "Trust me, all my life people have been trying to tell me what I can't do. I just use that as an opportunity to prove them wrong."

I turned to her, pulling her into my arms, my heart soaring at the belief I saw radiating from her eyes. The fact that she believed in me. That she was willing to put her own reputation on the line for me.

Oh God. This girl . . .

I couldn't help it. I leaned down and kissed her hard on the mouth. She *eep*ed in surprise then laughed, kissing me back with a hunger that practically took my breath away. For a moment, we just stood there, locked in one another's arms, our mouths pressing against one another. My stomach flip-flopping in my chest like a fish and my heart racing—though not from nerves this time.

I pulled away from the kiss, meeting her eyes with my own. Such beautiful eyes. Filled with such passion and belief. Eyes I wanted to wake up to every morning. Fall asleep with every night.

And suddenly I knew exactly what I needed to say.

"If you really believe in me," I said slowly, "I want you to prove it."

Her brows furrowed. "What do you mean?"

"I mean, this thing between us—whatever it is. I don't want it to be casual. I don't want it to be about hookups and occasional lapses in judgment. I want to commit. I want to be in it for the long haul—just like the surf school."

She turned away and I could see her swallow hard. The flash of doubt in her eyes that sent a chill straight to my heart. "Asher," she said gently. "I don't know . . ."

"Come on, Piper. Give me a chance. I promise you—I will prove you wrong."

"Asher, we talked about this. We're coworkers."

"Fuck News 9. I don't care about them. I care about you."

"I care about you, too," she said, her eyes taking on a pleading look. "But I also care about my career. I'm sorry—I know that makes me sound heartless. But I've worked so hard to get to where I am. I can't just put everything on the line . . . for whatever this might turn out to be."

I rubbed the back of my neck with my hand, frustrated beyond belief. I wanted to be angry with her—for putting her career over me—but how could I be that selfish? Her passion for her career was one of the things I loved most about her. How could I ask her to give that up for me?

"Fine," I said. "Then I will."

"What?"

"You're right. You love your career. And I'd never want to be responsible for putting it in jeopardy. So fine. You work at News 9. And I'll quit."

"But, Asher, you can't!"

"Maybe I can."

"But your mother . . ."

"Will have to deal," I declared. "Come on, Piper. What do you say? Will you take a chance on me? Will you let me prove myself to you?"

For a moment she said nothing and the silence stretched out long and hard between us. I tried not to fidget, not to speak. Wanting to give her a chance to think about it, even though I was desperate for an answer. One thing was for certain—the next thing that came out of her mouth would have the power to change my life forever.

Finally, after what seemed an eternity, she looked up, meeting my eyes with her own. Her expression told me her answer before the words could escape her mouth, and it made my heart soar.

"Oh, Asher," she said with a small smile. "Do you always get your way?"

twenty-eight

We barely made it back to Asher's place and when we did we fell straight onto the bed. Him covering me with kisses. Me digging my hands into his hair. I still didn't know what the hell I was doing. But somehow I knew I had to do it anyway.

Because Asher. Oh, Asher.

All my life I had played it safe. Kept others at arm's length. Knowing in the back of my head that if I never trusted anyone to begin with then no one could let me down. And it had worked. At least to an extent. My mind had kept me safe. But it also kept me from being happy.

Asher was a risk. Yes. But life was filled with risks and if you didn't take any, you would always remain stuck in the same place. I thought back to that moment on the boat. When he pulled me under the deck and kissed away all my fears. I had emerged from that voyage a stronger person, a better person, and Asher had been a big part of that. Now he was asking me to take it one step further. To put all my bets on the table.

I might lose everything.

But I might just win the jackpot.

He pressed his lips against mine, his kiss hungry and urgent as his hand raked up the side of my body. He was trying to be gentle, trying to be slow, but it was sort of killing him, I could tell. And so I reached down between us, where I could feel his arousal, pressing against my belly. I took him in my hand through his pants and wrapped my fingers around him. He jerked, an involuntarily gasp whooshing through his lips. His fingers gripped my arms tight.

I smiled against his mouth. "My turn. And this time I'm not taking no for an answer."

"Don't worry," he managed to say. "I'm not up for launching much of a resistance."

My hands found the waistband of his pants and those damn boxer briefs and I pushed them both down over his thighs. He helped by kicking them off his ankles, stripping himself bare in front of me. I gripped him with one hand, the other resting at his waist. Then I dropped my head down, slipping him into my mouth, taking in his entire length. He groaned and his fingers dug into my hair. A feeling of power surged through me. He was putty in my hands. And I liked that. Asher Anderson, who so many women had tried to tame. But I was the one who had done it.

My mouth slid up and down his shaft, trying to find my rhythm. He was so hard, yet so smooth, his skin like silk sliding in and out of my mouth. When I swirled my tongue along the tip, his whole body stiffened. He grabbed me by the shoulders.

"You gotta stop, sweetheart," he said. "Give a guy a fighting chance at least."

Smiling, I pulled off of him. He grabbed me, flipping me over on the bed, pulling down my pants, and yanking off my shirt until I was just in my bra and panties. Then he deftly relieved me of those as well, until I was lying before him, completely naked. Completely vulnerable.

Yet I didn't feel vulnerable somehow. Not when I could see the adoration in his eyes as his gaze raked over me from head to toe. No, I didn't feel naked at all. I just felt beautiful.

Asher thought I was beautiful, and for once I didn't want to argue the fact.

He reached down, circling my breasts in his hands then lowering himself to take a nipple into his mouth, sucking it into a diamond-hard peak while tracing lazy circles along the outer areola of the other breast. I gasped, gripping the sheet in my hands, squirming against him, desperate to relieve the pressure that was building up inside of me like an inferno. But Asher didn't allow me any relief, dropping his hand to my thigh, preventing me from grinding against him. His tongue flicked at my nipple and I stifled a scream of frustration mixed with joy.

He lowered his head, skimming my stomach with kisses, still stroking my inner thigh. Lower and lower until his mouth reached his hand and he licked and nipped at the sensitive skin. I practically yelped from the sensations coursing through me. God, I wanted this man. Like I'd never wanted anyone—or anything—before.

Without warning, he pulled away, looking up at me with sparkling eyes. "There's still time to play it safe," he teased. "I could get up and walk away."

"Don't you fucking dare."

He laughed, dropping his head back down between my legs. This time abandoning my thighs to slip his tongue between my folds. I held my breath, taking in the sensations of his mouth moving against me, exquisite torture rioting through my entire body.

"I want you inside me," I found myself begging. "Please."

He lifted his head and the sudden break in connection felt like a lost limb. But he was only crawling over to the nightstand to pull out a condom. I watched, practically panting as he ripped it open and carefully put it on. Then he turned back to me.

"I have wanted to do this since the moment I first laid eyes on you," he said. "But I am so glad you made me wait."

He climbed over me, spreading my legs to him, his thighs pressing against my own, opening me up, exposing me totally. Then he grabbed his cock in his hand and positioned it against my core. For a moment, he didn't push in. Just stayed there and I swallowed heavily at the feel of him pressing against my entrance, his hands clamped against my hips, holding me in place. Then, with one fluid movement, he pushed himself inside of me and at last we became one. Flesh against flesh. Man against woman.

"God, you feel even better than I imagined," he groaned against me, dropping down to find my mouth with his own, his tongue prying apart my lips and giving me a deep kiss. I kissed him back, feeling the shock waves of ecstasy pulse through me with every stroke, and my hips began to thrust in response, unable to let him do all the work. Together we found a tempo that worked for both of us, binding our bodies together. Push and pull, but never losing that connection. I wrapped my legs around his back, hooking my ankles together, and he groaned in approval, pushing himself even deeper inside of me. He dropped his head down to my breast, sucking in a nipple, and I squeezed my eyes shut, trying to register all the different sparks of electricity that were dancing through me.

"No," he said suddenly, bringing me back to the present. A hand to my face. I realized he'd stopped thrusting. "Don't close your eyes, Red. Look at me. I want you to look at me when you come."

And so I forced my eyes back open, meeting his own. It was weirdly intimate, just staring into one another's eyes, and for a moment I almost forgot what was taking place lower down. But I couldn't forget for long as the fire burned deep inside of me, building and building until it reached a crescendo. Ecstasy throbbed through me and I pushed against him over and over, riding the wave to shore. Through it all, he kept my gaze, never wavering, always looking, something deep and important in those eyes.

And suddenly I was so fucking glad I'd taken a chance. No matter what happened after today, after this. It was worth it. This was worth it all.

He came a few moments later, collapsing on top of me when he had finished, his breath hard and ragged in my ears. For a moment, we both just lay there, tangled in an embrace, and it felt so damn good to keep the connection a little longer between us. Eventually he slid off of me, discarding the condom before crawling back into bed. I snuggled up against him, my head lodged in the nook between his shoulder and his chest. He reached up, stroking my hair, while his other hand dropped down to cup my ass, keeping me pressed against him.

"It's funny," he said. "Usually after sex I'm ready to bolt for the door. But right now, I can't imagine getting out of bed." He grinned wickedly. "Or letting you get out of bed for that matter. Can we just stay here forever?"

I chuckled against him. "Well, we do have to work tomorrow," I said.

He lifted his head in surprise. "But I'm quitting, remember?"

"No," I said, shaking my head slowly against his chest. "No way. Not that I don't appreciate the offer, but you asked me to trust you, right? If you truly believe we can be coworkers—and a couple, too—well, that's what I think we should do."

"Aw," he said, putting on a teasing pout. "And here I thought I was getting a girlfriend *and* a free pass to go surfing every day."

"Nice try," I said. "But you're not getting off the hook that easily. I expect my boyfriend at work tomorrow and I expect him to be on time."

"That shouldn't be a problem," he replied. "As long as you're here to wake me up."

twenty-nine

ASHER

I'd love to say we showed up to work the next morning completely well rested, but that would be a lie. In fact we'd barely gotten any sleep, too busy exploring each other's bodies while exploring each other's minds. In fact, it felt like only a brief second that we closed our eyes before the sun peeked through my windows, demanding we face the day. I was pretty sure, when I saw Piper's face, I could easily convince her to call in sick. To spend the day in bed with me. But I had promised her our relationship would not interfere with her job, so I resisted leading her into temptation.

Somehow we got up, we got dressed, we grabbed breakfast on the way and then headed into work. Separate cars, but definitely together. I wondered, as we walked through the newsroom, if people could tell something had changed between us. No longer just meteorologist and producer, but something so much more.

Things continued in this vein for the next few weeks. With us working together, going home together, maybe working some more at night. I'd never worked so much in my life—the upcoming launch of the surf school taking up almost all of my free time. But I didn't mind: There was something so satisfying in seeing it come together. Especially the night we gave Toby a tour—and she grudgingly relented into letting her kids participate in the launch. That was pure victory. The school had become this larger-than-life thing that I had built with my bare hands—with sheer force of will. Okay, sure, it had been funded by my family's accounts, but at the end of the day it was still mine. The first thing I could ever truly say that about.

I still didn't love working at News 9. But it was a minor sacrifice to get to spend the day with Piper. Also, it served to keep my mother off my back and ensured she didn't balk at my extracurricular activities.

"So Beth had a good idea today," Piper told me Friday night as we sat on the floor of the surf shop, waxing the new boards.

"Oh, yeah? What's that?"

"What do you think about her doing a feature on the surf school? You know, like an opening day kind of thing? We could invite some of the kids down from the Holloway House and get video of them checking out the school for the first time."

I nodded thoughtfully. "That's a great idea. Maybe the publicity would get us some attention from other local businesses as well. We could always use more donations. And I'm sure my mother would love it. A great PR moment—News 9's golden son, giving back to the community. She loves that kind of shit."

"Not as much as I love *you*," Piper declared, abandoning her board and crawling over to me. She slipped into my lap and curled her hand around my neck. "You know," she said, a teasing look in her eyes, "we haven't officially christened this place yet . . ."

"That's true actually," I agreed, kissing her soundly on the mouth. "Maybe we should . . ." I moved to her jawline. "Get that . . ." Her neck. "Over with—"

Her cell phone broke into song. I groaned.

"Ignore that. Please."

She gave me a rueful look, then pulled the phone from her pocket. Her playful expression faded as her eyes caught the caller ID and she pressed answer.

"Hello? . . . Yes. This is Piper Strong."

I cocked my head in question. She held out a finger to tell me to wait. Her expression was ashen and my heart stirred with worry.

"Okay. Yes. I understand. Thank you for letting me know." She hung up the phone.

"What is it?" I asked.

"My mother," she said in a dull voice. "She checked herself out of Safe Harbor this afternoon."

"But she still had a week left I thought!"

"Exactly."

"Oh, Piper . . ."

I watched as she rose to her feet, wobbling a little on unsteady legs. "I thought she was doing so well . . ." she moaned. "She was so close to finishing . . ."

I leapt to my feet, pulling her into my arms. She laid her head against my chest and I could feel her small sobs ratcheting against me. "Do you know where she would go?"

"Hopefully her new apartment. But a better guess would be David's. He's her boyfriend. And, well, her . . . supplier."

"Let's go get her," I said. "I'll pull Fiona around. You lock up."

"No." To my surprise, she shook her head.

"No?"

She gave me an apologetic look. "I mean, I appreciate you offering. I really do. But this is something I need to do myself. She and I have a lot to discuss, as you know."

I wanted to argue. I didn't want her to leave—to have to face her mother, and maybe this drug dealer guy David, alone. But the look in her eyes told me I needed to let her go.

"Okay," I said, kissing her on each cheek. "I understand. But call me if you need me, okay? Or if you feel unsafe? I'll have my phone on me. I can meet you anywhere. Anytime. Just call."

"I will." She looked up at me, her eyes filled with gratitude mixed with worry and sadness. "I appreciate that. And I'm sorry—I didn't mean to ruin our night."

"We have a thousand nights in front of us," I assured her. "A million nights. Just go and do what you need to do. Make sure your mother's safe. I'll be here when you get back."

We embraced and she pulled away, giving me one last rueful smile before heading out the door. I watched her go, my heart wrenching in my chest, wishing there was something I could do for her. For her mother. But I knew better than anyone that you couldn't help someone who wasn't ready for that help. I just hoped Piper understood that now, as well. I couldn't bear to see the look on her face when her mother disappointed her, all over again.

I settled down to finish the board I was working on, but my mind was no longer on the task and I eventually put it away. Maybe I'd go grab some tacos from the nearby takeout Mexican place for dinner. I could get a few extra, too, in case Piper was able to get back at a reasonable hour. And then maybe we could—

A knock sounded at the door. I frowned. Was it Piper? Had she forgotten something? But no, she had a key. I rose to my feet, brushing myself off. "Just a minute," I said, walking into the front room and peering through the window to see who was on the other side. It took me only a moment to recognize my visitor.

My mother.

Shit. I let out a heavy breath as I watched her, her eyes darting around the really-not-that-seedy neighborhood with great unease. For a moment I considered pretending that I wasn't here, but she called my bluff before I could make it.

"I know you're in there," she called through the door. "I saw that thing you call a car down the street."

Stifling a groan, I pulled the door open and stepped aside, allowing her to enter. "Well, this is a surprise," I declared as she walked in, watching her glance around the room with a pinched nose.

"Oh, I just figured I'd come down to see what all my money was going toward these days," she replied, her eyes roving over the surf posters we'd hung on the walls. Then she turned to me. "How . . . fun!" she pronounced in a voice that made it clear she thought it was anything but. "And . . . so . . . colorful, too!"

"Thank you," I said, not taking the bait. "We've been working hard. Looks like, depending on the insurance and such, we should be ready to open sometime next week."

"How wonderful," she declared. "Just wonderful." She walked over to the counter and ran her hand along the side, before turning back to me. "And what are your plans for the grand opening?"

I shrugged. "Beth suggested News 9 do a feature on it, if that's okay with you."

"Oh, definitely. We'll definitely do that. But we should think bigger, too. This is such a marvelous gift to the community, I'm sure all the stations and the newspapers, too, are going to want to cover the opening."

"You think?" I looked at her warily.

"Oh, definitely!" she declared. "In fact, you should hold a huge press conference on opening day. You can invite all the poor children from that home to come and introduce them to the media. They would eat it up, I'm sure!"

I considered this for a moment. Oddly, considering the source, this actually sounded like a great idea. "It'd take a lot of organizing to get everyone here, though," I reminded her. "And we're stretching things pretty thin between Piper and me already."

"Oh, leave that part to me," my mother said, waving a hand. "Publicity is my specialty."

"Really? You want to help?"

"Of course, sweetheart! Whatever I can do! Why, I want all of San Diego to know about this wonderful new Anderson/Martin philanthropic venture."

Wait, what?

"Um," I said, narrowing my eyes at her, warning bells

going off in my head. "Did you just say Anderson/ Martin? What do the Martins have to do with any of this?"

My mother's smile dipped to a frown. "Come on, Asher. Who do you think paid for all of this?"

Oh God. "I thought . . . we did."

"Well, we did. With money we acquired from Martin Enterprises in exchange for ad time on News 9." She shrugged. "In fact, if it weren't for Sarah and her father's extreme generosity and philanthropic spirit, we absolutely wouldn't have been able to get any of this off the ground." She gave me a saccharine sweet smile.

I stared at her, my stomach roiling with nausea. I couldn't even speak. Suddenly all the puzzle pieces were sliding into place, and it was making a pretty ugly picture. I should have known my mother had something up her sleeve when she'd been so willing to hand over the start-up capital. But I had no idea she would have gone this far.

"Come on, Asher," she said, now giving me a disgusted look. "Where did you think the money came from? A tree?"

"No. But . . ." I didn't know what to say. Half of me wanted to spit in her face. Tell her to take the Martins' money and stuff it up her ass. But how could I? If I did, the school would never be able to open. Which, of course, was what she was counting on when working this clever trap in the first place.

I thought back to Toby's skeptical face. She was betting on me failing. Walking away when things got tough. I couldn't let that happen. I couldn't let her think she was right about me.

It's not a big deal, I tried to tell myself. *So they've put money in. So what? It doesn't affect what you're trying to do here. You're still going to get to help the kids. That's all that matters in the end.*

"Anyway, back to the press conference," she said. "We'll invite all the press from all of San Diego and you and Sarah can answer all their questions about the school."

Oh, no. No, no, no.

"Absolutely not," I declared. "Sarah has nothing to do with this."

"Her family paid for it!" my mother reminded me, her voice rising. "You would not have a school without her!"

I squeezed my hands into fists, anger rioting through me. How stupid I'd been! To not have realized she was playing me from the start. Just like she'd played me my entire life. To her, I was still that trained monkey—and she wanted a show.

"Fine," I said through clenched teeth. "Sarah can stand up with us, too. It'll be the three of us. But I'm not leaving Piper out. This wouldn't even be happening without her— she deserves some credit."

My mother's eyes narrowed. She'd been amused before. Now she was pissed. "Look, Asher. I'm not going to lie. After you caused that scene at the country club, I hired a private investigator to look in on this girl. Did you know her mother has been in and out of jail on drug charges and prostitution for the last twenty years?"

"So what? Piper is not her mother."

"Trash begets trash, Asher, and it's time you learned that. I've overlooked your indiscretions in the past. I understand a young man must sow his wild oats. But you're twenty-nine years old now. The time for play is over. You are my only son and you stand to inherit News 9 someday. It's time you start taking that seriously. And that means not dragging our family's lifework through the mud.

"Without Sarah's family News 9 will not survive. And everything I've worked for will have been for nothing. You need to stop thinking about your dick for once in your life and start thinking of the good of this family."

Fury exploded within me. "Just like you did, right, Mother?" I snarled.

Her hand shot out, connecting with my face before I could even identify the movement. As I reached up to touch my stinging cheek, her steely gray eyes set on me. "I did what I had to do to keep this station on the air," she growled. "Now it's your turn."

I watched as she walked to the door, yanking it open. Before stepping out, she turned back to me, her face twisting into an ugly smile. "I know you'll make the right choice, sweetheart," she said. "After all, you don't want to upset your father, now do you?"

And with that, she strutted out the door, knowing she'd won, yet again.

thirty

PIPER

I made it to my mother's new apartment in record time. But when I banged on the door, as I suspected, there was no answer. So with a heavy heart, I headed to David's house instead.

David lived at the end of a dead-end street, in a small neighborhood with rundown houses, most of them abandoned. I'd only been there once before, years ago, when my mother had gotten herself in a bad way and couldn't figure out how to start her car. I still remembered the smell of the place like it was yesterday, however. A kind of burnt rubber stench permeating the residence. And that wasn't half as disturbing as the people who had been there. People just hanging out, their dead eyes staring listlessly at the television set, which hadn't even been turned on. It was horrifying, to say the least, and at the time I had made a vow to never return.

So much for that.

With trembling hands, I walked up the front steps and reached up to bang on the door. At first, there was no answer. But I caught sight of my mother's car parked in the street and so I banged again.

"Hold your horses, I'll be there in a second."

The door squeaked open a crack. A pair of watery blue eyes peeked out from the other side. "What do you—" David started to say, then stopped. "Oh. It's you." He pulled the door open wide. "She's in the kitchen. Rambling on like a crazy bitch. I need you to get her out of here. She's annoying my customers."

I pushed past him, not dignifying him with a response, making my way to where I remembered the kitchen to be, stepping over piles of trash—some of them possibly people. The stench of burning rubber rose to my nose again—eau du burnt meth chic—and my stomach lurched in disgust.

Oh, Mom. Why? You were doing so well.

I stepped into the kitchen. My mom was sitting there, eating a bowl of cereal. She looked well, surprisingly. She'd gained a few pounds in rehab and her eyes looked less sunken and less shadowed than they'd been.

She looked up, surprised. "What are you doing here?" she asked, her voice laced with suspicion.

"I've come to take you back to Safe Harbor."

She shook her head. "I'm done with that place."

"Mom, you have a week left of treatment."

"Don't need it. I'm already cured."

"Why are you here then?"

She frowned. "I was just visiting David. Am I not allowed to visit friends?"

"Not if those friends are drug dealers, no."

She rose to her feet. "I'm not doing drugs anymore," she shot back indignantly. "I told you—I'm cured!"

"Okay." I forced out a breath. "Then can I give you a ride home? Maybe buy you some groceries?"

Her expression softened. "Thank you, sweetie, but I have my car. Though . . ." She gave me a searching look. "Now that you mention it, I am a little short on cash right now. Maybe you could spare a few bucks for gas? And food, of course. I'll swing by the grocery store on the way home."

I bit my lower lip. Sometimes I wondered if she actually believed the lies she told me herself. That she was truly delusional enough to think if I gave her money she'd spend it on food and gas. I had to hope that was true—that she wasn't purposely trying to scam me each and every time.

"I'm sorry," I said. "I can't give you money. At least not until you complete your rehab. That was the deal."

"I did complete it!" she snapped, her calm façade crumbling away. "And I'm fine! I'm telling you. I mean—look at me! I'm here at David's and I'm eating fucking cereal! Everyone here is high—except me!"

"Yeah, 'cause you don't have any money," I shot back, anger rising inside of me. "I'm not stupid, Mom!"

"No. You're not stupid," she jeered. "You're just a self-righteous bitch! You think you're better than me? With that fancy job and that rich boyfriend of yours? How dare you come here—to *my* world—to tell me how to live *my* life? Especially seeing as you're the one who fucked it all up to begin with."

"Mom . . ."

"I lied for you. I went to prison for you. I spent years locked up so you wouldn't have a black spot on your record. What would your fancy little job or your rich little boyfriend say if they knew the truth about you? That you murdered your own brother!"

I flinched, her words twisting in my gut like knives as panic rose to my throat again. In an instant, my mind flashed back to that night. That terrible night.

Piper! Wake up! Where's your brother?
Where the HELL is your brother?

Then, out of nowhere, Asher's voice broke through the scene.

Addicts never take responsibility for their actions. But that doesn't make them not responsible.

I swallowed hard. I squared my shoulders. I looked my mother in the eyes. "I did not murder Michael," I said.

"You were supposed to be watching him!"

"*You* were supposed to be watching him. You were his mother. But you chose to leave him. You chose your addiction over your own son."

She stared at me, horror clear in her eyes. But I wasn't finished yet.

"Yes, I fell asleep. And I will live with that guilt every day for the rest of my goddamned life. But I was not the adult in that situation. I was not the one who should have been in charge. All my life I've heard you tell me that you lied for me, that you went to prison to protect me. But that's bullshit, Mom. All you wanted to do was protect yourself. Because if you didn't make up that story? I wouldn't have been the one charged with murder. You would."

My mother's face crumbled. She fell back in her chair. Her skin was white as a ghost's and her whole body was shaking.

"Piper . . ." she tried, but I shook my head.

"I'm done letting you guilt me into feeding your disease. I'm done lying to you to make you feel better about yourself. You either go back to rehab and face your demons for real or I am cutting you off forever. Either way—you will never, ever blame me for Michael's death—ever again."

I swallowed hard, going silent, waiting for her answer as my heart thrummed madly in my chest. I tried to tell myself that her response didn't matter—that I had stood up for myself for once in my life—forced her to listen to the truth and that was a step in and of itself. But deep down, I wanted her to hear me—to really hear me. Because until she did—until she accepted what happened in the past—she could never truly move forward. Just as I hadn't been able to—until Asher and that boat set me free.

For a moment, she said nothing, just stared at her hands. Then, finally, she rose to her feet.

"I think I'm . . . ready to go back," she said, her voice cracking on the words. "To Safe Harbor, I mean." She drew in a shaky breath. "Please . . . Piper . . . can you take me back?"

I pulled her into my arms. She sobbed against my chest and tears fell from my own eyes as well. I stroked her hair—which was still so brittle and thin—just as my mother herself. My heart wrenched in my chest. So many years—so many years just wasted. But now, finally, a chance to start again.

"I'll take you back," I said. "I will always take you back."

thirty-one

ASHER

After my mother left, I went surfing. It had been a while since I'd been out on the water, besides that one lesson with Jayden, and I'd almost forgotten how good it felt to paddle out beyond the surf. To sit on my board, feeling the waves gently rock me up and down as I waited for the perfect swell. Out here, one with nature, my problems started to ebb away—at least for now.

I read somewhere online that you can think a thousand thoughts while waiting for a perfect wave and when you paddle toward that wave you can think a few thoughts. But when you finally catch that wave—there's only one thing on your mind.

Joy.

And that was what I was chasing today. Mindless joy. That moment where I could forget everything else and just be happy.

But for some reason, today the waves weren't working the way they once had. Sure, they had no issues in bringing me back to shore. But once I arrived, my problems were still there, still waiting for me where I'd left them. Try as I might I couldn't lose myself. I couldn't shut them out.

I still couldn't believe the trap my mother had constructed—or the way I'd just wandered right in, no questions asked. Now she had me right where she wanted me, and I didn't know what to do about it. I could go along with her scheme, and maybe Piper would understand. But where would it end? How long would I be trapped under her thumb? Once upon a time, I had resigned myself to this life—never seeing an alternative. But now that I'd felt the sunshine of freedom—shining on my face—I couldn't bear to bring myself to step back into the shadows.

As I rode a wave to shore, I observed a lone figure emerge from the parking lot and step out onto the sand. At first I didn't think much of it. But then, my eyes widened in recognition. Was that Piper? What was she doing here, willingly walking out onto a beach?

I took the wave as far as I could, then dragged my board to shore, out of the water and up the beach. She was standing closer to the water's edge than I'd seen her stand in the past and she looked radiantly happy. My heart squeezed in my chest.

This girl. This beautiful freaking girl.

"There you are!" she cried. "I thought I was going to have to send out a search party!"

I blushed, remembering I had told her I would wait for her at the surf school. "Sorry," I said. "I didn't mean to disappear. I just . . . needed some time alone."

Her brow creased. "Do you want me to leave?"

"Absolutely not!" I grabbed her and pulled her toward me. She laughed and jumped away.

"You're soaking wet!" she cried.

"And you love it!" I leapt forward, grabbing her again. She squealed, but I wouldn't let her get away, tackling her to the sand. Then I kissed her soundly on the mouth. "I missed you," I said when I had finished.

"I've only been gone two hours."

"Two very lonely, terrible hours."

She rolled her eyes, then gave me an affectionate look. "I promise, it won't happen again."

"So you look happy," I said. "What happened with your mother? Do I dare hope for good news?"

Her smile widened. She pulled her knees to her chest. I listened as she told me about finding her mother and giving it to her straight for the first time in her life. When she got to the part about her mother returning to rehab, my heart soared. I pulled her to me again, cradling her in my arms. And this time she didn't protest getting wet.

"That's wonderful, Piper," I whispered.

She nodded. "I know, right?" she asked. "I still can't believe it. I finally stood up to her. And she totally responded. It was amazing." She turned to me, her eyes shining. "I think it might really stick this time. She might actually be ready to accept the help she needs."

"I'm so proud of you, sweetheart," I murmured in her ear, my heart feeling very full.

Piper nodded, giving me a happy look before rising to her feet, looking out over the sea. Then, to my surprise, she started walking toward the edge. I watched, breath caught in my throat, as she stopped a few feet from the water, then turned to look back at me.

She held out her hand.

Realizing her meaning, I scrambled to my feet, running over and grabbing her hand, squeezing it tight. Then, together, without saying a word, we walked to the water and stepped in.

Then we took a second step. And a third.

As we took a fourth step, I stole a glance over at Piper. She was shaking a little and her skin was stark white. But she didn't turn around and she didn't stop. Instead, she took a fifth step, then a sixth, until she was up to her waist in water, still wearing her clothes. The waves crashed all around us, splashing us, but she ignored them, turning to me and meeting my eyes with her own as she took my other hand.

Then she kissed me, her hands pulling me closer to her, until our bodies were flush against one another, our mouths fusing together. And in an instant, the ocean was gone, my problems were gone, and it was just her and me—nothing else mattered but the taste of salt on her skin. Our mouths moving against one another, hard and desperate. As if the simple act had the power to chase away a lifetime of demons.

And hell, maybe it did.

The kiss went on for eternity, but even that wasn't long enough for me. When we finally parted, she looked up at me with glassy, dazed eyes. But she didn't make a move to step out of my embrace—or run to the shore. And so I stroked her back, smiling down at her. Soaking wet, maybe a little cold, but oh so happy.

"You are truly amazing," I told her.

She blushed. "I don't know about that."

"Well, I do. And, haven't you heard? Asher Anderson is always right."

I scooped her up into my arms, as if she were a baby, carrying her out of the sea. I laid her down on the towel I'd brought and started to dry her off and warm her up, taking my time with each and every body part.

"I love you," I said.

"I love you, too."

"And I'm proud of you."

She smiled up at me, looking a little sheepish. "I finally got into the water!"

"I'm proud of you for so much more than that."

We lay on the beach for a long while, cradled in each other's arms. Talking a little, but not about anything big or important. It was nice and peaceful and I was so proud of Piper—for pushing past her fear. I thought back to the first day I had seen her on the beach at Beth's wedding. How scared she'd been. Like a little mouse. Now she was a fucking lion.

Unlike . . . say . . . me.

"What's wrong?" Piper asked, clearly feeling me stiffen. She propped herself up on her elbow, cradling her head with her hand, looking at me with worried eyes.

I groaned, falling onto my back, staring up at the sky. I

didn't want to tell her. But how could I keep it a secret? She was going to find out eventually. Better she hear it from me.

"After you left, I had a visitor," I told her. "My mother. She suggested we do this huge press conference to get everyone excited about the surf school."

"Really? But that's great! The more press, the better!"

"Yeah. I mean, that part is great, you're right. It's just . . . there's more."

I drew in a breath and spit out the whole story. She listened carefully, without comment. When I had finished, she nodded.

"So you do it with Sarah. No big deal."

"No." I shook my head. "It *is* a big deal," I argued. "I refuse to let them disrespect you in that way. I mean, there would be no surf school without you. People need to know that."

I squeezed my hands into fists, watching the knuckles whiten over the bone. "I should have never asked her for the money. After all, I know better than anyone it always comes with strings attached."

I rose to my feet, pacing the sand, trying to quell the anger I could feel rising inside of me. I thought back to all the times my mother had manipulated me—used me—for her own personal gain. And I had let her do it all these years. Like a trained monkey. A circus bear.

She may not have been an addict like Piper's mother. But I had enabled her all the same.

"I wish I could be as brave as you," I muttered. "I mean, you stood up to your mother . . ."

"And you can, too," Piper said. She rose to her feet and crossed over to me, pulling my hands into her own. "And you will. Once the school is fully, independently funded, we won't need her anymore. We can write up grants and present them to the city. We'll hold fundraisers. We'll make our school completely self-sufficient. Then you can finally be free."

I groaned. "You make it sound so simple."

"It's not simple," she replied. "But the difficulty would be worth it in the end, don't you think?"

"Yes," I said. "Of course. But . . ." I trailed off. "It's complicated," I said at last.

"You're worried she'll disinherit you," Piper observed. "I get that—I do. Walking away from all that money would be scary. But it might also make you happy. And wouldn't it be better to be happy than rich in the end?"

"Of course it would!" I snapped. "But it's not about the money. Have you seen the way I live my life? I don't give a shit about the money."

She frowned. "Then what's wrong? I mean, if you're not worried about the money . . ."

I stared out onto the water for a moment, not sure if I wanted to answer. But she'd shared everything with me—even the stuff that was hard. The stuff that was humiliating beyond belief. And when she had—it had helped her break free of her own shackles. Maybe it was time for me to do the same. Maybe it was finally time to come clean to someone at last. Someone I could trust with this secret that had been weighing me down for three years.

"You remember when my father had his accident?" I said at last. After she nodded I continued. "Well, he lost a lot of blood. He needed a transfusion and, of course, I wanted to help. So I went to have my blood tested—to see if I was a match."

I paused, the memory of that day flooding my brain. I had been so worried about my father. My childhood hero. If something were to happen to him. If he were to die . . . to leave me all alone . . .

I drew in a breath, turning back to Piper. "Well, I wasn't a match."

"So you . . . couldn't give blood to your father?"

"I don't know. The man in the hospital wasn't my father."

"Wait, what?" She stared at me, incredulous.

I raked a hand through my hair. "My parents both have O negative blood. That means they're universal donors. They could give blood to anyone and would always make a big show of donating when there was some local tragedy or whatever. After all, my mom never turned down the chance for free publicity." I made a face. "But when I got my blood tested, they said I had type A. Which means there's no way I could be biologically related to both of them."

Piper stared at me, her face warring with confusion. "But that's not an exact science, Asher. You can't prove paternity through blood type alone."

"You're right," I said. "Which is why I had a DNA test done to confirm it. Turns out the man I called father my entire life—the one I always looked up to and in whose footsteps I wanted to follow—he isn't any relation to me at all."

"Oh, Asher . . ."

"I went straight to my mother, of course. After arguing with her for a while, she finally admitted to the affair. Not a love affair, mind you," I spit out, the anger coursing through me now as I relived that day. "Hell, I could almost forgive her for that. But she—she slept with one of the advertisers. Some married guy with deep pockets and a lusty eye. She got drunk with him and slept with him so he'd give her money for News 9. It wasn't until a few months later that she realized he'd knocked her up.

"My father was thrilled when he found out she was pregnant. He'd wanted a son forever and they'd been trying for years with no luck." I shrugged. "So she let him believe it was his. Why not, right? Certainly my real father—the fucking bastard with another family—wouldn't want me. And this way my mom had an heir to the family fortune like she'd always wanted."

Piper's face was awash with horror mixed with pity. "I'm so sorry, Asher."

I waved her off: I needed to finish. "Anyway, after she confessed she swore me to secrecy. She reminded me how vulnerable my father was now. How fragile. If he were to find out the truth, that I wasn't his son, it might just kill him."

The sympathy on Piper's face twisted to indignation. "So that's why you let her push you around now? Because you think she'll tell him if you don't do what she says?"

"Yes," I agreed. "Everyone thinks it's because of the money, of course. But I don't give a crap about the money.

In fact, I would love nothing more than to lose all the money. Money has destroyed my mother. My entire family. I would gladly give every penny away if it meant I could be free."

My voice broke and I found I couldn't continue. Piper pulled me into her arms. At first, I just stood there, trying to stanch the rage that radiated through me, too angry to accept her comfort. But she didn't give up, stroking my back, planting small kisses on my chest. And at last I gave in, wrapping my arms around her and attempting to accept the warmth and love she was offering me.

"What was it you said to me?" she murmured. "That we are not our parents? We can't let their mistakes define our lives. I know it's scary—believe me, I've been there myself. But I think you should tell your father the truth."

I shook my head. "No."

"But, Asher—"

"You don't understand! It would kill him!"

"So you'll let it kill *you* instead? Come on, Asher. It's clear this has been tearing you apart for the last three years—I'm sure he can tell something's wrong. Doesn't he deserve to know the truth—however painful it might be?"

"No," I said. "I can't destroy his life. I can't let her hurt him like she's hurt me."

Piper gave me a sorrowful look. "Okay," she said. "I understand. I don't agree—but I understand." She sighed deeply. "And I guess you need to do the press conference with Sarah then."

"Wait, what? No. I won't disrespect you like that."

"It doesn't matter."

"I made a promise to you. *That* matters."

She gave me a loving look that pretty much broke my heart. "What matters is I know you," she said. "I know you love me. I know we did this thing together—you and I. Who cares what the rest of the world thinks? I don't need credit—I need those kids to experience something amazing. And if this is the price we pay to make that happen? To keep them and your father safe? Well, it's pretty damn small in the larger scheme of things."

I nodded slowly, sinking back down onto the sand. Piper dropped down beside me, putting an arm around my back, stroking it softly. I stared out into the sea for a moment, letting out a long sigh.

"I guess you're right," I said dully.

But it didn't feel right. It didn't feel right at all.

thirty-two

PIPER

A re you guys ready? We're on in five minutes."
   I watched from the sidelines as the producer barked
orders to the various people backstage of the press conference while Asher and Toby worked to try to line up the half
dozen excited kids we'd shuttled over from the Holloway
House to stand behind them as they did the dog and pony
show. As could be expected they were all jumping out of
their skins at the chance to be on TV. Not to mention being
part of the surf school in the first place.

   I stole a peek out from behind the curtain to where all the
reporters were waiting. We had a full house, which was kind
of crazy if you thought about it—seeing as this wasn't exactly
a huge news story. But when the man rumored to be running
for mayor of San Diego was sending out the press releases,
people showed up. There were reporters from all the major
news stations and some of the local cable stations, too. Print
journalists and bloggers and magazine editors, all ready to
write about what was being billed as the philanthropic event
of the year.

   I caught Beth's eye at the back of the room where she

stood with her new husband, Mac, who was getting his camera in position, and I waved. I hadn't seen much of her over the past few weeks now that we weren't roommates anymore. Not to mention how busy I'd been. I made a mental note to schedule some John Hughes time before she popped out that kid of hers.

"Miss!"

I felt a tug on my arm and turned to find Jayden had come up behind me. He was practically bouncing up and down in excitement. "Are you ready?" he demanded. "They said five minutes!"

I gave him a rueful smile. "I'm not going to be on TV," I told him. "I'm just here to watch."

He frowned. "But you helped!" he protested. "Mr. Asher said if it weren't for your help there would be no surf school!"

"That was sweet of him to say. But I'm happy to stay on the sidelines, don't you worry."

Jayden didn't look pleased at this, but thankfully didn't continue to argue his point. Because how could I explain to a ten-year-old why I wasn't front and center at this press conference—where I totally deserved to be? Even Asher hadn't understood—he wanted me to at least make a brief appearance to answer questions about the Holloway House. But in the end, I'd refused. The last thing I needed was to piss off his mother and Sarah all over again. It was better to lie low, let someone else have the glory, until we could achieve our own alternative funding. This wasn't about me—this was about those kids standing over there. Those kids for whom hopefully this school would make a difference. After all, if one single kid was able to parlay this experience into a better life? Well, I'd trade all the fame and glory in the world for that.

My eyes roved the backstage, falling on Sarah, who was standing over by her father, checking her hair and makeup in her compact. My stomach soured a little as I looked her over. She was even more beautiful than I had imagined her to be—and I had imagined quite a bit. So delicate, too. So thin she was almost frail. With huge doll-like blue eyes and perfect blond hair. I felt like a bull in a china shop even standing in the same room as her.

But Asher doesn't love her, I reminded myself. *He loves you. He chose you.*

I turned to Asher, watching him position each kid in line, handing the ones in the back row boards to hold during the press conference. He dropped down in front of them, on their own level, saying something I couldn't quite hear. Then he raised his hand and they all let out a loud cheer. I smiled. He was so good with them—just as he'd been with Jayden on the beach. A total natural. And I could tell he was having just as much fun as they were.

Maybe someday he'd be able to do something like this full time. Leave his family and News 9 behind to work a job that really meant something to him. Of course that was going to be impossible—at least until he gained the courage to tell his father the truth. Until then, his mother would always have a hold over him. Be able to control his life.

My hands tightened into fists as I thought back to his confession. To the pain I'd seen in his eyes. I knew his mother was controlling—but I'd had no idea what a monster she truly was. Not only to have done something like that to begin with, but then to hold it over her son's head in order to keep him in line. She may have been successful, she may have climbed the ladder further than I ever dreamed of going. But underneath her glamorous shell, she was no better than my own mother. Living a life carved from lies.

"One minute!" the show producer, Nancy, barked. She turned to Asher. "Are you ready?"

Asher straightened up and shot her a grin. "I was born ready!" he declared, and I could see the swagger in his stance, the cocky smile, the flashing emerald eyes. This was the Asher everyone expected to show up today, the one who could put on a show. And while once I couldn't stand this sort of arrogance—this bravado—now it only served to make me smile. Because I knew what was underneath it. The true Asher he only revealed to people he trusted and loved.

On cue, Sarah took her position next to him, wobbling a little on too-high stilettos. I had to admit, the two of them looked good together, standing side by side. A golden couple with golden hair and golden futures. They looked as if they belonged together. It was hard to believe, watching them now, that for some reason Asher had chosen someone like me instead.

Nancy pointed to her assistant who worked to pull open the curtains, revealing the stage to the press. As cameras flashed, Sarah's father stepped up to the podium to begin to address the room. The crowd erupted into excited murmurs, but he waved his hand to silence them.

"Thank you for coming!" he boomed into the microphone. "You are too kind! I know you have a lot of news to cover—and it's immensely gratifying to see you take time out to report on my little . . . charitable venture instead."

I scowled from the sidelines. *His* venture. As if he had anything to do with it, except writing a check. Asher and I had put in all the sweat equity, all the blood and tears. All so this buffoon could take the credit.

It doesn't matter, I scolded myself. *It's all about the kids.*

I watched as he turned to Asher and Sarah. "But enough about me," he said. "Let's introduce the real stars of the party. My beautiful daughter, Sarah . . . And a man who needs no introduction—News 9 meteorologist, Asher Anderson!"

The crowd clapped politely and Asher and Sarah took center stage.

"Thank you for coming," Asher began.

"Tell us about the surf school!" a reporter from the audience interjected. "Whose idea was it?"

Asher gave a dutiful smile. "As you know, the Anderson family has a long tradition of giving back to the community," he said, as we'd rehearsed. "Now it's my turn to take on the family mantle. And what better way to do that than to combine it with something I love. Surfing!" He grinned. "Anything for an excuse to hit the waves, after all!"

The crowd laughed appreciatively. "What do you hope

to accomplish by teaching at-risk kids to surf?" asked another reporter.

Asher took a look back at the kids behind him. Then he turned to the reporter. "Surfing can do so much for a kid," he said. "It can benefit their physical and mental health. It can empower them, give them something to work toward, look forward to. Help them make healthier choices in all aspects of their lives."

He paused and Sarah stepped in. "Studies show participating in a sport like surfing can lead to advanced educational outcomes, increased social skills, and all sorts of other benefits." She smiled, flashing her perfect white teeth. "Something we in the Martin family have always advocated for our community."

"Sarah, are you a fan of surfing, too?" called out a newspaper reporter in the back.

Sarah giggled. "No," she said, shaking her head. Her perfectly flatironed hair bounced prettily from the gesture. "I'm just a fan of Asher here."

The room erupted in conversation. I could see Asher shoot a look at Sarah, and her cheeks colored in response. She clearly hadn't meant it to come out like that, I realized. But behind her, her father was grinning like a loon. Of course.

"Inquiring minds want to know!" cried a voice from the side. "Are you two a couple?"

Everyone laughed. Except Asher. His face darkened. Shit. *Don't ruin this*, I begged him silently. *Just go with it. For the kids' sake. It doesn't matter what they think.*

"Now, now," Sarah scolded the reporter. "We should try to keep the questions on topic, don't you think?" She gave him a saucy grin. "Let's just say Asher and I are *very* good friends." She wrapped a possessive arm around him and gave him a little hug. I watched as he stiffened like a board.

Uh-oh.

Time seemed to slow down as he jerked from her grasp. He turned, looking offstage, meeting my eyes with his own. I shook my head, trying to tell him, without words, that he shouldn't argue. That I knew his heart. That the rest didn't matter.

But Asher, it seemed, did not feel the same.

"No," he said, turning back to the crowd, which was watching with bated breath. "No. I'm sorry. I won't do this. I can't do this."

The room erupted into conversation, reporters buzzing with excitement. They'd come to cover a simple, boring charity event, and now it was turning into so much more.

"Asher," Sarah tried, looking very concerned. She tugged on his arm, but he pulled it away.

"I'm sorry," he said softly, clearly meaning only to talk to her. But the microphone picked up his voice, echoing it across the room. "I have to set the record straight."

I watched, helpless to stop him as he turned back to the press, squaring his shoulders and lifting his chin. "Sarah and I are not a couple," he said flatly. "We never were. And we never will be. Because I have a girlfriend. A girlfriend who I love very much." He turned to look backstage again, beckoning with his hand. "Piper? Can you come out here for a second?"

"Asher, what are you doing?" I could hear Sarah hiss beside him. But he ignored her, beckoning for me again. Shit.

I had no choice. I took a hesitant step forward.

"There she is!" Asher announced excitedly, crossing the room and sweeping me into his arms. "My beautiful girl-friend. Piper Strong, ladies and gentlemen!"

The cameras started flashing madly. The room erupted in questions.

Asher dragged me back to the podium, then held up his hand to silence them. "Piper, ladies and gentlemen of the press, is the true brains behind this surf school. She was the one who introduced me to these kids. And she helped me build the school from the ground up. Without her, *none* of us would be standing here today."

And with that, he grabbed my hand, made a silly little bow, then yanked me offstage with him, leaving Sarah standing there by herself, her face tomato-red.

"So, uh, thank you for coming?" she stammered, trying to be heard over all the chaos rampaging through the room. "All the information for the school is on our website." And with that, she practically ran offstage.

I turned to Asher. He was grinning from ear to ear. "Oh my God," he cried. "Was that as good for you as it was for me?"

"Asher, that was not good," I protested. "That was so not good. You just embarrassed Sarah—and her father—in front of the entire San Diego press."

"No. I told the truth. She embarrassed herself by pretending we were a couple."

"You think her father's going to see that? You think he's going to keep funding the surf school now?"

Asher set his chin. "Yes," he said. "Don't you see? He has to. Otherwise he'll look like a total asshole—only participating in the charity to get his daughter laid rather than help those poor kids on stage. Now he'll have to keep paying until people lose interest. And by that point we will have applied for all the grants we need to keep going without his help."

"So you tricked him."

He shrugged. "They tricked me first."

"And what about me? Did you ever stop to think about me?"

"Of course I thought about you. Piper, that's the whole reason I did what I did. It wasn't right—them disrespecting you like that."

"No, Asher. *You* are the one who disrespected me. I told you, point-blank, that you should do this with Sarah. That you should not make a scene. But you didn't respect that. You didn't listen to me. You did it anyway 'cause you never see the big picture."

"Piper . . ." His face twisted in anguish.

"You told me if we got together it wouldn't affect my job. Now what's going to happen to me?"

"Nothing. She can't do anything. And if she tried, you could sue."

"I don't want to sue. I just want to do my job. The job I've been trying to prove to people that I deserve. But now?

Now it looks like I'm only here because I'm hooking up with you. Do you think the other stations will hire me now? Do you think they'll even look at my resume?"

His face fell. "Piper, I never meant—"

"Of course not. You never *mean* to do anything. But you do it all the same," I snarled. "I should have never taken this stupid job. I should have just stayed in production assistant land until I was promoted for my skills, not my body."

"Come on," he begged, his expression pleading. "Don't go back to that. You excel at your job. You deserve to have it. Who cares how you got it in the first place?"

"I care," I whispered, rising to my feet, my whole body shaking. "*I* care," I said louder. "And that's something— Asher Anderson—you will never understand."

thirty-three

PIPER

After leaving the surf school, I wasn't sure where to go. I drove around for a while, not wanting to go home to an empty house and be alone with my tormented thoughts. But where else could I go? Not Asher's place, that was for sure. And my mother was still at Safe Harbor. In the end, I decided to head to News 9. I had work to do, after all. I needed to put together a resume reel of my work. Just in case I was soon out of a job.

I didn't have much to put on tape. I had barely been in the weather center for a month. But I had to come up with something. Asher might claim I couldn't be fired, but he didn't live in the real world. Sure, they wouldn't fire me for what he did on stage—not directly, of course. Like Asher said, if they did that I could easily sue. But I wasn't stupid. It wouldn't be hard for them to find some other excuse. Some other reason I wasn't right for the job—for the station. And then it would be, "See you later, Piper. Don't let the door of opportunity hit you on the way out."

And in the end, I could only blame myself. I'd known from the start it was a bad idea. That I was putting everything I'd worked for at risk for some stupid relationship that had no guarantees. Well, at least for me. Asher would never get fired. He would never suffer the consequences of his actions. He could be a total idiot on TV and it was no big deal in the long run.

The worst part was, he didn't even get it. He actually thought he was doing some noble thing, standing up for me. Which proved, once and for all, how little he understood the real world. People like me didn't get to be noble. We didn't get to make stands. We kept our heads down; we worked hard. We appreciated what we accomplished and we didn't care about the fame and glory. As long as we got our paycheck at the end of the week.

But Asher wouldn't understand that. How could he?

I slumped onto my desk, too distraught to even pull up the list of stories I wanted to compile for the tape. Looking around the empty weather center, my heart panged in my chest. The worst part was I still had feelings for Asher. I still loved him—even after he'd blown up my career. It was going to take me a long time to get past this.

But I would. I would rise again. As I had in the past and would in the future. I would refocus and start fresh and this time I wouldn't let my personal weakness for a charming smile screw things up for me. I'd gotten into TV news to make a difference, after all. And I could still make that difference—if I stayed focused this time.

"Piper. Good. There you are."

I looked up, my eyes widening as a lone figure slipped into the weather center. She took a step forward into the light and I almost gasped as I realized who it was.

Asher's mother.

She was dressed as she had been for the press conference—in a smart, probably custom-fitted suit, a string of pearls around her throat. She was beautiful for her age—though rumor had it she'd had a bit of work done—and she was always so polished and poised. But there was also a hardness deep in her eyes. The fierceness of a woman who had taken life by the throat and strangled it to her will.

I sat up in my seat, trying to square my shoulders. If I

was to be fired, I wanted to at least retain some dignity. No matter what, I couldn't let her see me cry.

"We need to talk," she said, sitting down in a nearby chair and peering at me with those piercing gray eyes.

I sighed. "Look, I didn't tell Asher to do that. I actually told him he needed to play nice with Sarah and her father. That I didn't need any credit."

"I know," she said, surprising me. "Or—at least that's what I assumed. You strike me as a very sensible girl, Piper. My son, on the other hand . . ." She shook her head slowly. "He grew up in a very different world. Partially my fault, I'm afraid. He never had the chance to fail at anything. So he never learned how to try."

"No," I blurted out before I could stop myself. Even as mad at Asher as I was, I couldn't let her just dismiss him like that. "He *has* been trying. He created the surf school from nothing. He's been working day and night to make it succeed." I gave her a beseeching look. My job might be over, after all, but I could still fight for the school—for the kids. "Please don't pull his funding because of me. It'll crush those poor kids. They need something like this."

"I'm not a monster, Piper," his mother said sternly. "No matter what my son has implied to you. I'm simply a business-woman, trying to balance a very precarious ecosystem here at News 9. We need advertisers—especially political advertisers—to keep this station afloat. To allow us to do these kinds of good things for unfortunate people. My job is to solicit these advertisers by any means necessary. When I see an opportunity, I take it. But you know all about *that*, don't you, Miss Strong?"

She arched a questioning eyebrow and I could feel my face heat. "I—" I started, but she waved me off.

"You don't have to be embarrassed," she said. "If anything you should be proud of yourself. You saw an opportunity to rise in your career and you grabbed hold of it. I would have done the same thing in your position."

I hung my head. Her approval was almost worse than her criticism.

"My dear girl, don't you see? We're all on the same side here. I'm looking out for my family—and News 9. You're looking out for your career. And . . . your mother, too, right? I understand she's in some kind of rehabilitation program?" She gave me a pointed look and I stiffened. Oh God. She knew about my mother? Did she know Asher was funding my mother, too?

I thought back to what Asher had told me—about how money always came with strings attached. I had no idea, at the time, just how tightly they were all woven together.

Asher's mother gave me a fond look. "You know," she said, "I look at you and I see myself. Someone who's driven, who wants to go the distance. But we both have to accept help once in a while to get the job done. I need help from people like Champ Martin. And you need help from people like me." She paused, catching the look on my face. "Oh, come on. It's not something to be ashamed of. If someone wants to help you, why shouldn't you use that to get what you want?"

She paused and I waited. Clearly this was leading up to something and I wanted to just get it over with. "So what do you want to help me with?" I managed to spit out.

She gave me a smug smile. "Did I mention I like you?" she asked. "Straight to the point. Most people are too fond of bullshitting around first." She nodded. "You are correct. I have a proposal for you, Piper."

"I'm listening . . ."

"When you first interviewed here, you spoke of wanting to be an investigative producer—at least that's what I read in your files. Is this still the case?"

"Y-yes . . ."

"Well, I've heard through the grapevine that the Santa Barbara ABC affiliate is looking to hire an associate producer for their investigative unit. Would that be along the lines of what you're looking for?"

I stared at her, shocked. That was so not what I was expecting her to say. At all.

"I admit it's not the most glamorous job in the world," she added before I could reply. "From what I understand much of it will just be answering phones and emails from people reporting scams and rip-offs." She shrugged. "But it would be a foot in the door—and more along the lines of what you're looking for long term, correct?"

I swallowed hard. I didn't know what to say. It sounded like the perfect job. And yet . . .

"I don't . . . want any more favors," I managed to spit out. After all, that was what had gotten me in trouble in the first place.

"I wasn't offering one," she returned. "I can't give you the job, Piper. I can only give you a recommendation—as I would give any potential employee who was looking to move on. You'd still have to apply and interview and convince them you're the right person for the job." She smiled. "I can open the door, Piper. But you'd still have to walk through it."

I gave her a skeptical look. "And what do you want, in exchange for opening that door?"

Her smile twisted. "Come on, Piper. You take this job and everyone wins. Asher gets to keep his surf school. Those sweet kids get to experience something amazing and your mother gets to stay in rehab. I get to keep my advertisers happy and you . . . well, you get a second chance to prove yourself. A *real* chance this time."

I swallowed hard, my mind racing. "I need to think about it," I said at last, realizing she was waiting for some kind of answer.

She nodded. "Of course," she said. "Think it over. I'm sure once you do, you'll see this is for the best . . . for everyone involved."

thirty-four

ASHER

And to finish up—do we ever, ever go into the water alone?"

"No!"

"What do we do instead?"

"Use the buddy system!"

"All right!" I cried, walking down the line of kids and high-fiving each one of them. "You guys get an A plus today. Tomorrow we're actually going to get in the water!"

The kids broke out into cheers. I grinned. "Okay. Bring it in." I put my fist out. They circled around me, adding theirs to the pile. "On the count of three—go Team Surf! One . . . two . . . three!"

"Go Team Surf!" they cheered, raising their hands.

"All right!" I slapped Ramon on the back. "Now hurry up and put your boards back. The bus driver is going to kill me if I get you back late."

They all moaned, but did as I said, working to put their boards back into the lockers before shuffling out the door and toward the waiting bus. I watched them go, not able to help a small smile on my face. I had to admit, I'd been a little nervous about the first lesson and how my new pupils would respond. But, it turned out, I had no reason to worry. They had listened, they had been engaged, they were raring to go. Tomorrow was going to be epic.

"Hey, Mr. Asher?"

I turned to see Jayden had left the pack on its way to the bus to approach me alone. "Yeah?" I asked with a grin. I had made him my honorary partner—since he'd already gotten a few lessons on his own—and he'd been relishing the role, to say the least.

He looked up at me now, his eyes wide and shining. "Thank you," he said. "For doing this, I mean. We were all talking about how awesome it was last night." He shrugged. "No one's ever done anything like this for us before."

"Yeah, well that's their loss," I told him. "You guys are going to be the best surfers ever. And I'll get to take all the credit." I ruffled his hair. "Now go—get your butt on the bus before you get me in trouble!"

I shooed him out the door, my insides dancing. I watched him climb onto the bus and sit down with his friends. Piper had told me that Jayden had had a tough time making friends at the Holloway House. But now that he'd been instated as my right hand man, he was suddenly quite popular.

"You're really good with them."

I whirled around to see Piper, standing in the back doorway. How long had she been watching? I felt my face heat, and I gave her a shrug. "Thanks," I said. "They're good kids."

"Not to everyone, trust me," she said with a laugh. "You must have the magic touch."

I looked at her, my mood suddenly deflating. "I wish I did," I said sadly.

She sighed, walking over and sitting down on the bench. Leaning over, she scrubbed her face with her hands. "Look," she started. "I'm sorry about what I said at the press conference. I know you thought what you did was for my benefit. And I appreciate that—I really do." She gave me a regretful face. "It's just—another reminder of how complicated things are."

"No," I said. "I'm the one who should be sorry. I know I

should have just kept quiet. But how could I? I love you, Piper. And I wanted everyone to know it. Is that so wrong?"

"No. It's not wrong." She stubbed the floor with her toe. "But it's not realistic, either. Our whole relationship, I mean. When I agreed to do this, it was under the promise of it not affecting my job. But now I see how impossible that is. Nothing we do is in a vacuum. It's going to affect us—and the people we love."

I raked a hand through my hair, frustrated. Mostly because I knew she was right. But what was the alternative? Dating in secret? I couldn't bear to disrespect Piper like that. She wasn't a dirty secret. She was the one thing I'd actually done right in my sorry life.

"I love you, Asher," she continued before I could speak. "But I also live in the real world. This is not just about my job, either—if it was, maybe I'd be willing to take the risk. But too many people are depending on us now. If we keep going down this road, your mother will find a way to close down the surf school. And those kids—the ones who are counting on you—they'll be the ones to pay the price."

I closed my eyes for a moment, trying to reset my sanity. "I can raise the money," I protested. "Get grants, whatever. Like we talked about. Whatever it takes!"

"And what if she targets your father instead?" she asked. "Are you willing to let him pay the price as well?"

I fell silent, my heart wrenching in my chest. I thought of my father. Of my mother making good on her threats and telling him the truth. It would kill him. And any relationship the two of us might have left would be over forever.

"Asher, there's a job opening in Santa Barbara," Piper said quietly. "For an associate producer in the investigative unit. Pretty much the job I've been waiting for my entire life." She paused, then added, "I think I'm going to apply for it."

I stared at her, her words hitting me with the force of a punch to the face. I had expected her to break up with me. But leave altogether? To another city? To another life? Leaving me behind? I swallowed heavily, my whole body feeling like lead. For once in my life, I had absolutely nothing to say.

Except I did have something to say. I had everything to say. A million reasons whirling through my head for why she shouldn't take the job. Why she shouldn't give up on me—on us. That we were worth fighting for. That I would do whatever it took to keep her safe and that I would never stand in the way of her career.

Except I already had. *I* was the reason she felt the need to leave. *I* was the problem. She'd worked so hard, for so many years, to get to where she was. And I hadn't respected that enough. In my effort to protect her, I'd thrown her to the wolves. And now she was forced to pack up and leave because of me.

Part of me wanted to be angry. To yell at her and accuse her of choosing her career over me. But why shouldn't she do that? What did I have to offer that was worth staying for? She'd asked me for one thing—and I hadn't respected her enough to give it to her. Like everything else in my life, I'd turned it into a punch line.

I didn't deserve her. But I did love her. And because of that, I had no choice but to let her go.

"I understand," I said, my heart smashing into a thousand pieces in my chest. "It sounds like a great job. I think you should go for it—if it's what you want."

Her shoulders sagged. She looked so sad, and for a brief moment I thought maybe she'd change her mind. That she'd tell me she was just kidding—that she'd never leave me. That she and I belonged together forever.

But of course I was the Joker, not her.

"It's what I want," she said at last.

And like it or not, I knew I couldn't stand in her way.

thirty-five

ASHER

Piper left immediately after the conversation. After all, what good would it do for her to stick around? Only prolong the inevitable, the torture of the Band-Aid being pulled off slowly. It was better for her to head home, to go apply for her dream job. I'd stood in her way long enough. As she walked out the door I managed to mumble something about giving her a reference if she needed one. Which was ridiculous, but I couldn't think of anything else to say.

After that I found myself alone in the surf school. Alone with all my torturous thoughts and what-ifs that would never come to pass. And soon I felt a familiar hunger begin to grow inside of me, twisting through my stomach like barbed wire.

No. Not a hunger. A thirst. I needed a drink. And I needed one, like, yesterday. So, with an aching heart, I locked up the school and jumped in Fiona and drove down to the one place I knew I couldn't get one.

Miguel's.

I parked the car and stumbled into the restaurant, my head whirling with thoughts I didn't want to think, feelings

I didn't want to feel. When Angelita saw me enter, she started to smile. But her smile quickly faded as she caught the look on my face.

"Miguel!" she barked. "Get your ass out here. Now!"

A moment later, my angel of mercy, a swarthy bearded Mexican with arms sleeved in tattoos, appeared before me, putting an arm around my shoulder and leading me through the restaurant, toward the kitchen. I could feel the other diners' eyes on me—as usual, the place was packed—but I ignored them as best I could, focusing my attention on Miguel. Once we were in the back room, I collapsed onto a nearby chair, scrubbing my face with my hands. My stomach was churning now and I didn't know where to begin. Luckily, unlike his wife, Miguel wasn't a big talker.

"Carne asada?" he barked at me. I nodded, and he went to the grill.

As he cooked, I stared down at the cement floor, the conversation with Piper replaying over and over in my mind. Crazy thoughts swirled through my brain—like maybe she wouldn't get the job and this would all be for nothing. But of course I wanted her to get the job. If it was the job she wanted—I wanted her to have it. Of course I did.

But at the same time, if we were being honest, I wanted her to want me more.

Was that wrong? Selfish? Was I just being a spoiled brat again? *Asher always gets what he wants*—that's what she always said. But now I wanted her. Desperately, irrevocably, more than anything I'd ever wanted—I wanted—needed—Piper in my life.

But that wasn't going to happen. And I needed to come to terms with that. Or I was going to drive myself insane. I needed to be happy for her. She'd been waiting for a job like this her entire life, after all. Who was I to begrudge her that?

Still, it hurt. Goddamn, it hurt. To know she'd looked at both lives—one with me here in San Diego and one with a new job far away. She'd looked at both of them and chosen the job over me. Just as my own mother had done over and over again. Choosing News 9 over her husband. News 9 over her son.

But my father hadn't. He'd turned down all those offers to work at the National Weather Center over the years, choosing to stay with his family. And look where that sacrifice got him. His wife had cheated on him with another man; he'd been reduced to life in a wheelchair. Maybe he should have left us high and dry. Maybe he should have chosen that amazing job.

Maybe Piper should, too. Of course, she already had.

It wasn't as if she hadn't warned me. She'd told me from the very first day how important her career was to her. And I understood it—I loved that about her, actually. The idea that she worked so hard, that she went after what she wanted with such gusto. I loved that. I just wished what she wanted was me.

God, I was a selfish bastard.

I wondered what she'd say if I suggested I go with her. Be like my father and give up my own stuff to follow her. But how could I do that? I had just started the surf school and she'd never forgive me if I walked away from that. Plus, I wouldn't be able to forgive myself—disappointing those kids. They needed me. I needed to be here.

Miguel handed me a paper plate of steaming hot tacos. I blew on them to cool them, then took a bite. The spicy meat kicked at my taste buds and I felt a little better. Something about carne asada, the meal I'd had on my first night at Miguel's, always helped me quell the urge to dive into the bottom of a bottle. It put things back into perspective.

Okay, so I was now eating my troubles instead of drinking them, but at least I'd be able to drive home. And still look at myself in the mirror the next day.

Miguel sat down in the chair across from me, leaning forward and propping his elbows on his knees. "So," he said, "what happened?"

"Ah, you know." I tried to snort. "Girl problems. What else is new?"

I tried to say it with as much bravado as I could muster. Just as the old Asher would do. The one who liked to pretend he didn't care about anything.

But Miguel only narrowed his eyes, looking at me with disbelief. He had never bought into my bullshit—not from the very first night I had walked through his front door. Why would I expect him to buy it now?

"What happened?" he repeated.

And so I told him. About Piper. About how I'd tried to defend her honor and how it had blown up in my face. About the new job she was applying for and how soon I would lose her forever.

"I was willing to give up everything," I said. "But it wasn't enough."

At last I fell silent, staring down at my hands, feeling the frustration well inside of me all over again. I could feel Miguel's eyes on me, regarding me thoughtfully. Then, at last, he opened his mouth.

"So you want her to stay."

"Of course I do!"

"Have you given her a reason to?"

I looked up. "What?"

Miguel met my eyes with his own. "Sounds to me like she has a very good reason to leave," he said. "Maybe it's time to give her a reason to stay."

"But how do I do that?" I demanded. "Without sounding completely selfish?"

Miguel shrugged. "You give up everything. Like you said. Don't talk about doing it. Just do it. Take the risk."

I stared at him, my heart pounding in my chest as I digested his words. *Don't talk about doing it. Just do it. Take the risk.*

Lightning struck me—square in the face. Of course. It made perfect sense. Time and time again Piper had forced herself to face her fears. She'd conquered her water phobia, she'd stood up to her mother, she'd risked her career to be with me. And what had I done in return? Nothing. Absolutely nothing. I'd winged the whole relationship—just like I'd done with everything else in my life, never looking at the big picture.

Of course she didn't believe me. I'd done nothing to inspire belief. Of course she wanted to leave. I'd done nothing to inspire her to stay. Sure, I'd said all the right words. But to a girl like Piper, words were meaningless. People had made promises to her her entire life—only to break them. Why wouldn't I be the same? I needed to show her I was serious— that she could count on me.

I needed to take a risk, as she had.

I needed to prove she was wrong.

thirty-six

ASHER

My hands were shaking as I walked through the front door of my family's La Jolla mansion, my feet echoing on the marble floors. I didn't get three steps in before the housekeeper met me at the door. She looked down at my muddy feet and frowned.

"Your mother's at the station," she told me.

"I was actually looking for my father."

She raised an eyebrow, looking surprised. But then she shrugged and pointed in the direction of his study before going back to her dusting. For a moment I just stood there, feeling frozen in place. Then, I kicked off my shoes, sucked in a breath, and headed into the room.

"Asher! This is a surprise," my father boomed as he turned his wheelchair to face me. I stood in the doorway, my whole body trembling, as he wheeled himself over and reached out to clasp my hand. "My son," he said with a smile.

It was almost too much, and I half wanted to run out the door and never come back. Instead, I forced myself to return the greeting.

"Hey, Dad," I said, trying to swallow down the huge lump that had formed in my throat. "How's it going?"

Looking down at him now, at his dark brown eyes, his cleft chin, his strong nose, it was hard to believe anyone could think we were related. But people only saw what they wanted to see, I supposed. After all, I'd lived my entire life and never doubted it once.

I let go of his hand, retreating over to a nearby leather armchair, collapsing down onto it. I could feel his eyes on me, watching me steadily. "I take it this is not a social call," he observed in a wry voice. "But then, you don't do those anymore, do you?"

I winced at the jab. Before his accident we had been so close. I'd come over to the house and we'd spend hours together, talking about everything and anything. When I had a problem, he'd been the first number on my phone. Back then I would have done anything for my father. And I was pretty sure he felt the same way about me. Still did, most likely. Though maybe not after this conversation.

"Dad, I have to tell you something," I said slowly, feeling a weight fall upon my chest, so heavy it made it difficult to breathe. Much like the weight I'd felt when I'd first opened the DNA test and learned the truth. I'd been on my way to see him in the hospital. He was bored to death, he'd told me, and my mother was driving him crazy. He needed a distraction from his number one son. I'd even considered sneaking him in some of his favorite brandy.

But that was before I'd read the test results. Before I'd learned the truth. Once I saw them in black and white—unmistakable—there was no way I could bring myself to visit. And so, like a coward, I'd turned the car around. I'd driven straight to Mexico as fast as my Maserati could take me—with little regard to anyone else on the road. Once there, I'd consumed my weight in tequila and later woken in some dark alley, my wallet nowhere to be found. I'd had to beg the border officials to let me back into the US. Lucky for me, they'd recognized me from the television.

As Stormy Anderson's son.

I could feel my father's eyes on me now. Intense and questioning. "What is it?" he asked, concern clear in his voice. "Is everything okay, Asher? Is it your mother? I heard her rampaging about something or other this morning. Something about a press conference gone wild?"

I rubbed the back of my neck with my hand, his concern seeping into my skin like poison. "Oh, that," I said. "She's just trying to make the advertisers happy as usual."

My father snorted. "That woman is a machine," he declared. "She never quits. That's why she's been able to do so well over the years. News 9 owes her a lot. We all do, I guess."

"No!" I shot back with more venom than I'd meant to. My father raised his eyebrows.

"Okay, what's wrong?" he demanded, wheeling himself over to me. With effort he climbed out of his chair and onto the couch. I watched as his whole body trembled from the movement and sweat beaded on his forehead. I scowled. It wasn't fair. He'd already suffered so much. And now I was going to hurt him all over again.

Doesn't he deserve to know the truth—however painful it might be?

I thought back to how horrible I'd been to him since his accident. Pulling away, cutting myself off. Because I'd been a coward. Because I didn't know how to hide the truth when he looked into my eyes. It had been terrible for me—to cut him off like that. But how much worse had it been for him? To have your own son turn from you in your greatest moment of need—without any explanation as to why.

"Come on," he said, taking my hands in his own and squeezing them tight. "Talk to me. Whatever it is—it's going to be okay."

"I'm not sure that's true in this case."

"Trust me. Nothing you say will change the way I feel about you, son."

I jerked my hands away. "Even if . . . I'm not your son?"

"What?"

My father's face paled. My heart beat madly in my chest.

I felt as if I was going to throw up. Silence stretched out between us, long and suffering, as I opened my mouth and closed it again. I knew I had to continue—to finish what I'd started. It was out there now—and there was no taking it back. But the look on his face . . . Oh God. What had I done?

"I had a DNA test," I managed to say, the words scraping from my throat. "After your accident. I went to Mom. She admitted it all. She had an affair. She's been lying to you all these years. Playing us both like fools."

My dad nodded slowly; I couldn't read the expression on his face. I sat there, my stomach churning, waiting for him to say something—anything.

"So you've known this for three years," he said at last in a gravelly voice. "Why didn't you come to me sooner?"

"I couldn't!" I protested. "You were in the hospital. You were so weak. It would have killed you!"

"No." He shook his head. "It wouldn't have."

"But—"

"It wouldn't have," he repeated. "Because I already knew."

My head jerked up. "What?"

"I've known since before you were born."

"But . . ." I stared at him, incredulous. "But Mom said . . ."

He shrugged. "She doesn't know that I know."

"I don't understand!"

He gave me a sorrowful look. "Your mother and I tried to have children for years, Asher, when we were first married. But it never happened. We'd pretty much given up on the idea and our marriage was in shambles when suddenly she became pregnant out of the blue. I was suspicious, so I went to the doctor to get tested. He told me I was shooting blanks. There was no way I could father a child."

"But . . ." Horror churned through me. "Why didn't you confront her? How could you just stay with her knowing she cheated on you?"

He blushed, staring down at his hands. "Because I loved being a meteorologist," he said simply. "It was all I ever wanted in life. And she knew that—and used it against me anytime she could. If we had a fight, if I threatened to

leave—she made it clear I would lose everything if I did."
He stared down at his hands. "It sounds pitiful now, as I say
it out loud. But back then I was so emotionally bankrupt. I
figured it was worth it to stay silent and keep my career."

I shook my head, squeezing my hands into fists. I thought
back to all the times my mother had done the same to me.
Threatening me, threatening people I cared about. Emotional
blackmail to get her own way. I had no idea it had been going
on so long—with my poor father, too. And that by trying to
protect him—I had only prolonged his suffering.

"At first I figured I would just let her raise you," he continued. "That we could coexist in the house but stay clear
of one another." He snorted. "But you weren't content with
that and soon you were crashing through my weather center,
this little person, bursting with questions about clouds and
rain and the stars. You were so innocent and trusting. So
fascinated by everything I would show you." He gave me
an affectionate smile. "And so, slowly, you became my son.
In every sense of the word. And I've never thought of you
otherwise since." He shook his head. "It's funny—how the
very thing I thought would kill me—ended up bringing me
back to life."

Tears sprung to my eyes. I swallowed hard, past the lump
in my throat. Even as the words came from his mouth, they
felt too good to be true. The fact that he'd known. He'd
known all along and it hadn't even mattered. I wasn't his
son—but I was. I absolutely was.

"Oh, Asher," he said, gazing at me with sad eyes. "I wish
you had come to me when you first found out. The fact that
you've been living with this . . . secret . . . all this time . . ."

I hung my head. "I was afraid to tell you. Mom kept
saying it would kill you if you knew. Just another way to
keep me in line, I guess."

His expression darkened. Something angry flickered in
his eyes. "It's funny—I've kept silent all these years to protect you. I didn't want you to have to suffer like I had. But
you were suffering—all along. And I couldn't protect you."

"Don't blame yourself," I scolded him. "You didn't do

anything wrong. She did. She's the one who's been playing us both all these years." I scowled. "I don't know about you, but I'm through playing her games."

My father shook his head. "Trust me—she'll never let you quit."

"She's not going to have a choice."

My father looked up at me and I saw something sparking in his eyes. Something I hadn't seen in a long time. And it made my heart soar.

"I take it you have a plan?" he asked.

"Oh, I have a plan," I agreed. "But I'm going to need your help."

thirty-seven

PIPER

I left work that afternoon, not knowing where I was going. It was funny—for so many weeks now, I'd always had a destination. Asher's house, the surf school. Now I felt so directionless. I didn't want to go home to an empty apartment. Beth was busy with Mac and Ashley. I actually had a day off from the Holloway House for once.

Finally, I made the decision to head to Safe Harbor to visit my mother. I hadn't been there since dropping her back off after her premature check-out, the doctors suggesting she needed to get back in a routine. But the psychiatrist treating her had emailed earlier that week and told me she would be up for visitors if I had some free time. So I parked my car and walked inside, greeting the nurse on duty. She smiled and buzzed me in and an orderly escorted me into the lounge, telling me to wait there.

A few minutes later, my mother stepped into the room. I rose to greet her, looking her over from head to toe. I had to admit, she looked good. She'd gained weight and her skin, while still scarred, didn't appear to have any fresh blemishes.

Her eyes looked brighter, too. And when they fell on me, they lit up in excitement.

"Piper!" she cried. "This is a surprise!"

I gave her a rueful smile. "Sorry I didn't come sooner."

She shrugged. "As long as you're here now. And bonus—you've saved me from afternoon circle time." She gave a laugh. "Actually I like afternoon circle time," she added in a hushed voice. "Just don't tell my doctors. Wouldn't want to ruin my rep."

"Your secret is safe with me."

I sat back down on the couch and she joined me, gazing at me with affectionate eyes. It'd been so long since I'd seen any emotion in those eyes—besides desperation and hunger—it made my heart squeeze. And for a moment, I indulged in a small amount of hope. Maybe this time things would stick. Maybe this time she really had a chance to get better.

"It's good you came," she said. "I've actually been wanting to talk to you. In our sessions we've been talking a lot about making amends. And taking responsibility for all we've done to the people we love while under the influence." She shook a little, as if remembering. "When I think back to all I put you through . . . for so many years . . ."

I gave her a sympathetic look. "You were sick. You had a disease."

"Maybe. But you were the one who suffered. All these years, me blaming you for Michael's death. I was so consumed with trying to get rid of the guilt I felt—I pushed it off any way I could. But you, my sweet girl, were never to blame. I knew that deep down. It was all me." She hung her head.

I nodded slowly as she spoke the words I'd been waiting to hear my entire life. Yet strangely, they didn't hold the weight I thought they would. Not that I wasn't thrilled she was asking for forgiveness at last. But, I realized, what I'd really needed to do all these years was to forgive myself.

And I had. Somehow, on that boat, I had.

"Michael's death will be something we both live with forever," I told her, remembering Asher's words. "But at the same time, I think he'd want us to move forward with our lives, don't you think?"

She nodded slowly, tears slipping down her cheeks. "Oh, Piper," she said. "I feel like I've wasted my entire life."

"No," I corrected her in a firm voice. "Your story is far from finished and now you're starting a whole new chapter. You're here, you're sober. You're getting the help you need."

"I am," she agreed. "In fact, I feel stronger every day. And it's all thanks to that weatherman of yours."

I stiffened. "Yes. Asher has been very generous, paying for your treatment."

"Actually I was talking about him getting me here in the first place. He didn't even know me—and yet he cared enough to try to help. Not just with money—that would have been easy for him, I'm sure. But he took the time to take me aside and tell me I needed help."

I looked at her, curious despite myself. "What did he say to you?" I asked. I had always wondered that. How he'd convinced her to sign herself in.

She smiled. "He told me I was hurting you and that he wasn't going to let that happen. He said no one was going to hurt you anymore. Not on his watch."

My eyes widened, my heart panging in my chest. "He really said that?"

"Oh yes," my mother agreed. "And he wouldn't listen to any of my arguments. He told me he'd been there, done that, spewed the same bullshit. He was so charming about it all though." She laughed. "Even as he was yelling at me. And before I knew it I found myself agreeing to go."

I nodded, feeling my eyes misting. At the time I'd been so concerned with Asher paying for my mother's treatment, I'd basically taken for granted the fact that he'd convinced her to get treatment in the first place—something I, her daughter, had never been able to do. It would have been so easy for him to turn his back on her. Throw money at the temporary problem—treating the symptoms, not the disease. After all, he didn't know her. He didn't owe her anything.

But he'd helped her all the same. Because that's who Asher

was. A guy who genuinely wanted to help people. He'd helped my mother with rehab. He'd helped those kids. He'd helped . . . me. In so many ways. Sometimes he was stupid about it—not looking before he leaped. But his heart—no one could ever believe his heart wasn't in the right place.

"Anyway, he's checked in on me a few times since," my mother continued. "Even snuck me in some of my favorite chocolates. He told me about this halfway house program that he found, too. A place to go after this where I can live with other people who are fighting the same addictions. They'll get me a job and I can make my own money for once—instead of depending on you. It'll be like a fresh start." She looked at me, her eyes wet with tears. "I never thought I'd have the chance for a fresh start. But thanks to that boy of yours . . ." She smiled.

I swallowed hard, past the lump that had formed in my throat. "He's not my boy," I managed to say. "We broke up."

"What? Why? You guys were perfect together!"

"No, Mom. We weren't perfect. We were completely not perfect."

Her eyes narrowed at me. "Do you love him?"

"Yes, but . . ."

"Does he love you?"

"Yes. I mean he says he does. But you don't understand. It's too hard."

"Recovering from meth addiction is hard," my mother shot back. "Allowing yourself to be with someone who loves you and wants to care for you shouldn't be." She sighed. "The fact that it is . . . well, I blame myself."

I scrunched up my face. "What do you mean?"

"Growing up, I never gave you a reason to trust anyone, Piper. I never showed you how to accept love that didn't come with strings. I let my disease rob you of the childhood you should have had—the love you deserved. And now you're paying the price." Her voice broke. "You can't trust Asher's love, because you've never seen a love that worked. You've only seen love tear people apart. Not bring them together."

"Yeah, well, this is just another example of that. If I stay with Asher, I'll lose everything I've worked for in my career."

My mother gave me a sad look. "You're such a fighter, Piper. Unlike me—who has always given up too easily. All your life, you've worked overtime trying to prove to anyone who would notice that you are good enough. Smart enough. Hard-working enough. But sometimes I wonder who you're really trying to convince in the end. Other people? Or yourself?"

I flinched a little. "I'm not going to apologize for wanting to be successful."

"No one expects you to. Least of all Asher. God, you should hear the way he talks about you. It's like you hung the moon." She shook her head. "Trust me, there's no one who doubts your dedication. Your drive. And I am positive wherever you end up careerwise, it'll be at the top of your field." She met my eyes with her own. "But I'm worried in the end, it won't make you happy."

I shifted in my seat. "Yeah, well, maybe happiness is overrated," I muttered.

"No, baby girl. Take it from someone who has thrown away chances to be happy most of her life. There isn't anything in the world more important. Except maybe love." She gave me a pointed look. "And now, here you are, with the opportunity to have both. I just hope you won't decide to throw them away."

thirty-eight

ASHER

What are you doing here, Asher? You're not on the schedule tonight," Nancy said as I walked into the newsroom.

"I'm filling in for Frank," I explained. "He has a bit of a cold."

In truth, the only thing Frank, our eleven PM weatherman, was suffering from was stuffed wallet syndrome, which I'd inflicted on him earlier that day. But she didn't need to know that.

"And Mr. Anderson!" she exclaimed, catching my father wheeling in behind me. "This is a rare treat! It's nice to have you back!"

My dad grinned. "It's nice to be back, actually," he said. "I've been away far too long."

"Come on, Dad," I said. "Let's get up to the weather center. We've got work to do. Oh, and Nancy? Can you keep my dad's presence on the down low? He doesn't want a lot of attention tonight."

Another lie, this one more blatant. But thankfully Nancy only nodded her head and turned back to the police scanners she was monitoring. Dad and I headed up the elevator to the weather center and I locked the door behind us.

Once inside, I looked around. It had been a torturous day, working side by side with Piper. Neither one of us had talked much. I'd tried to find out if she'd actually gotten the new job, but she shut me down pretty quick. I would have been angry at that had I not caught the hurt in her eyes as she snapped at me. Miguel had been right. She was suffering, too. She was giving up everything—not just for her career—but for me.

Now it was my turn to show her I could do the same. Without a safety net this time.

"Are you sure you want to do this?" my father asked, wheeling over to the Doppler radar, which was always his favorite weather tool. "Once we do, there's no going back. She's going to disinherit you, no doubt. And you'll never work in this town again. She'll make sure of that."

"I *will* work in this town," I corrected. "We both will. But for once we'll be doing what we want to do."

"True that," my father quipped. His eyes shone. "And it's going to be great." He raised his hand and I slapped it in a high five. Then I shook my head and leaned down to give him a hug instead. The first real hug I'd given him since I'd learned the truth. I had to admit it felt good. While there might be another man out there who could claim to be my sperm donor, this was my dad. One hundred percent.

"Okay," I said, pulling away from the hug. "Are you ready to write this forecast?"

"Oh, I'm ready," he said. "Trust me, San Diego has never seen a storm roll in like this."

thirty-nine

PIPER

Well, we'll need to have a meeting to talk it over, but I have to tell you, you sound great," the investigative producer for News 5 Santa Barbara said over the phone. "And Cathy Anderson has said such wonderful things about you. I have a good feeling about this being a match."

"Thank you!" I said. "I'm really excited about the opportunity. Thank you for considering me."

We said good-bye and I hung up the phone, mixed feelings swirling in my stomach. I was thrilled the phone interview had gone so well. But at the same time, I was freaking out. Everything was happening so quickly. If they hired me, I'd have to move almost immediately—they needed someone right away. Which should have been exactly what I wanted. This was, after all, a dream job come true—and a quick escape from what I was trying to leave behind. So why was I feeling so apprehensive about the whole thing?

My mother's words rolled through my head again, as they had been doing all day. *I'm worried it won't make you happy. I'm worried it won't make you happy.*

"Happiness is overrated," I muttered again, though I wasn't sure who I was trying to convince this time.

I stepped out of Toby's office, where I'd holed up to do the interview. She was waiting out in the hallway, giving me a suspicious look when I emerged. Typical Toby; she always had a knack for knowing when I was upset.

"What's wrong, baby girl?" she asked, putting an arm around my shoulder and leading me back into her office. She sat me down in a chair and closed the door behind me. "Did the interview go badly?"

"No." I shook my head. "I think it went great. I think they're going to offer me the job."

"That's wonderful!" Toby cried, clapping her hands together. "Oh, honey, I'm so proud of you." She paused, then added, "Though truth be told I expected you to look a little happier at the moment all your dreams came true."

I sighed, closing my eyes for a moment, then opening them. "I know," I said. "I thought I would be, too. It's just . . . I'm scared I guess. San Diego is the only home I've ever known. I have friends here. My mom is here. She's doing well now, but I worry about being away from her. What if she backslides and I'm not there to help her?"

"Then she'll be forced to stand on her own two feet," Toby said firmly. "In fact, it'll probably be good for her to have some distance from you. It'll force her to grow up, not always having her daughter around to bail her out."

I nodded slowly. "That's what the therapist said, too," I admitted. "But then there's you guys! Are you going to be okay without me? Do you have enough hands to do the work?"

"We'll be fine," Toby said. "We'll soldier on like we always do. Actually I was talking to a great girl today who just moved here from Boston. She has a degree in child psychiatry from Harvard, but she's sick of writing Ritalin prescriptions for rich brats who don't really need them. She wants to do something more meaningful, and I think we may be it."

"Wow. That's . . . great," I said, feeling a huge lump form

in my throat. I knew I should be happy I wouldn't be leaving them high and dry. But at the same time, it kind of stung how easily I was able to be replaced.

"And," Toby added, "may I remind you, Santa Barbara is not exactly Mars. You can take the Surfliner down on weekends anytime you miss us. Easy as pie."

"You have an answer for everything, don't you?"

"Sure I do," she said. "*If* any of that was actually bothering you. But I think you have something else on your mind. Or should I say some*one*?"

I hung my head. "That obvious, huh?"

She gave me a sympathetic look. "I've known you a long time, honey. And I've never seen you so conflicted."

I nodded slowly. She was right. A few months ago, getting this job would have been an ultimate dream come true. And yet now, somehow, it didn't give me the joy I'd expected to feel. The satisfaction, the accomplishment. The achievement unlocked. Instead, I just felt . . . kind of empty. Like I was giving up more than I was getting in return. The old me, I knew, would think this was ridiculous. But I had changed over the past month. And now I wasn't so sure.

If I took this job, it would be a step in the right direction. To all my career goals coming to fruition. But then I looked at someone like Asher's mother—on the top of the News 9 food chain. Did I really want to end up like her?

You have no choice, I scolded myself. *This is not just about the job. It's about keeping the surf school open. It's about Asher's father. Your mother's treatment.*

In the end, I had no choice. I had to go. Whether it made me happy or not. I might as well force myself to be excited about the opportunity. Because at this moment I had very little else.

"I made a promise long ago," I declared. "I was going into TV news to make a difference. I can't just abandon that now."

Toby surprised me with a laugh. I gave her a sharp look. "What?"

"Come on, Piper, you don't need a fancy TV job to make

a difference. You make a difference every day you walk this planet. When you take care of these kids. When you help your mother recover from addiction. Hell, you single-handedly turned that crazy surf bum Asher into a one-man charity machine." Her eyes sparkled.

"Oh, so now you're singing Asher's praises?" I demanded. "You didn't even want the surf school."

"Yeah, well, I think we're all allowed to change our minds once in a while," she said, giving me a pointed look. "Not to mention our priorities. If it's for the greater good."

I groaned, scrubbing my face with my hands. "You are seriously not making this easy for me."

"Good. Big decisions like this should be hard."

"Miss, miss!" Jayden burst into the room, his eyes wide and excited. I looked up questioningly.

"Yes, Jayden?"

"It's Mr. Asher! He's on TV!"

I glanced at my watch. "No, he couldn't be," I said. "Maybe you just saw a commercial for him."

"No!" Jayden shook his head. "He's going to be live with a special forecast in five minutes." He paused, then added, "With some old guy in a wheelchair."

Confused, I rose to my feet. I could feel Toby giving me a questioning look, but I ignored her, walking out into the hallway and down toward the lounge. Jayden scampered behind me. Sure enough, News 9 was on the air, in the middle of the eleven o'clock broadcast. But what would Asher be doing as a part of it? He'd already worked all day. Surely they wouldn't have made him work a double. And if he had been called in, why wouldn't he have mentioned it to me?

Because you're leaving him, a voice nagged inside my head. *He owes you nothing now.*

The station went to commercial, but not before the anchors teased the upcoming forecast. "From meteorologist Asher Anderson and a special guest." I frowned. Okay, this was really strange. Asher working a double was weird enough. But why would his father be there?

I dropped down onto the couch, still watching the TV.

Jayden, seeing his work was done, wandered off into another room. Soon the commercials were ending and a moment later we were back on air. The anchors smiled into the camera.

"And now it's time for the News 9 weather update with meteorologist Asher Anderson. And tonight, we have a special treat, don't we, Asher?"

"That we do!" Asher replied as the camera cut to the weather center where he stood beside his father. My heart squeezed a little as the camera focused on his face. God, I missed him already. And I hadn't even left yet.

"Most of you will recognize my father here, the great Stormy Anderson," Asher continued. "The best meteorologist San Diego has ever had." He smiled down at his father. Then turned back to the camera. "My father and I have a special announcement to make tonight. But first—I know you want to hear the weather report." He smiled. "Dad? Will you do the honors?"

I watched, still confused, my heart pattering in my chest as Stormy went through the forecast. I couldn't really focus on it, though. I was too busy wondering what on earth the special announcement could be.

"Great," Asher pronounced once his father had finished. "Now for some good news—and bad news. The bad news is"—he looked directly in the camera—"tonight is my last night at News 9. I've enjoyed working here, but it's time to move on." He gave a sly smile. "I hope you don't all miss me too much."

"I'm sure they'll survive," his father said, rolling his eyes. "Why don't you get to the good news?"

"Okay, okay. And it's great news, actually. Especially for those of you who have missed seeing my father on TV. As of this morning, he and I have started a brand-new venture. A web show called Storm and Ash." He grinned. "A place where all you weather lovers out there can geek out over the craziest weather stories across the globe. And get your forecasts right from your computer. From my dad," he added. "So you know they'll be accurate."

"And best of all," his father piped in, "we'll be giving

fifty percent of the site's proceeds to programs that help at-risk kids. Starting with the amazing surf school my son has founded right here in San Diego."

Oh my God. I stared at the screen, my jaw practically on the floor. Were they for real? Then, as if he'd heard me, Asher stared directly into the camera, his smile fading, replaced by an ultra-serious look.

"There's a girl out there—who I care about very much—who once took a big risk for me. And, well, I figure now it's my turn to take one for her. Piper—if you're out there—this is all for you. Because nothing matters more than you. And I'm going to prove that to you if I—"

The feed cut. The station rolled commercial. Ironically it was a commercial for Champ Martin's mayoral candidacy. But I couldn't hear what was being said on TV. Not with Asher's words still echoing in my ears. Asher taking a risk. Asher giving up everything.

For me.

For *ME*.

Tears started rolling down my cheeks unchecked; I didn't bother to swipe them away. If only I had been DVRing the broadcast so I could rewind and listen to his words again—to make sure he'd really said all I'd heard him say. That he'd really walked away from his career, his fortune—everything. For me.

"For me," I whispered.

"Actually I did it for me," a voice behind me corrected. "I did warn you I'm a selfish bastard, right?"

I whirled around, my eyes widening as they fell on Asher's face. Confused, I glanced back at the TV and then at him.

"How did you . . . ?"

He grinned. "Taped the forecast in advance," he confessed. "Don't tell my producer. She hates that."

I sank down onto the couch, my whole body trembling. A million thoughts whirled through my head.

"I know what you're thinking, and you don't have to worry," he said, sitting down beside me. "The surf school is safe. My father has some money squirrelled away from the insurance settlement after his accident. He's going to loan it to me until our new website is contributing enough money to keep it going." He gave me a grim smile. "After that, my days of playing with someone else's money are over. If my mother does decide to keep me in the will, which I sincerely doubt at this point, I'll allocate every penny of it to go to Holloway House and the surf school. I don't want a dime."

I stared at him. "You'd really give up millions of dollars?"

His eyes were tender as he looked back at me. "It's already done, sweetheart." He smiled. "As well as my job. My beach house. I did keep Fiona, though. I figure my mother owes me something. And I like the idea of that something being something she despises."

I didn't know what to say. I just shook my head in disbelief, my heart flooding with emotion. "So your dad . . . ?"

"Knows everything. Actually he already knew. Turns out I haven't been the only one my mother's been manipulating all these years. But you know what? That's over now. *She's* over, as far as my dad and I are concerned."

My heart soared at the happiness I saw on his face. "Oh, Asher . . ."

"Look," he added, "I don't expect this to change anything. You should still take that Santa Barbara job—it sounds like a great career move and I would never want to hold you back. But . . . maybe we could do the long-distance thing for a bit? I could come up on weekends to visit you?"

I didn't know what to say.

Asher gave me a searching look. "I know it won't be easy," he said. "But I also know it would be worth it. And while I would never want you to sacrifice your career dreams in any way for me, if there's any way for you to fit us both in? Then I am prepared to move heaven and earth to make that possible for you."

"Asher . . ."

He held up a hand. "For the first time in my life I don't have a safety net, Piper. But I also don't have any more strings. Soon I won't owe anyone anything. I won't be living the life someone else wants me to live. I'll be living for me. For . . . us . . . if you'll have me."

The tears fell from my eyes like rain. My throat choked. I looked at Asher. At his beautiful, sincere emerald eyes, shining down on me with such pleading it took my breath away. He'd given up everything for me. And he wasn't asking me to give up anything for him in return. I could have my dream job—and my dream guy. I could have a happily ever after like those in the storybooks. All I had to do was let it happen. Allow myself to choose happiness.

"Oh, Asher," I said, my voice choking. "One day I promise you, you will not get your way."

His eyes locked on me. "I'm okay with that," he said. "As long as today is not that day."

epilogue

PIPER

W hat a day!" I cried as I kicked off my shoes and walked down to where my boys were hanging out, waxing their boards on the beach. "I swear the executive producer is trying to kill us with last-minute changes. I had to revise three scripts two minutes before they went on air."

"And you loved every minute of it," Asher reminded me, looking up from his board. "Don't even pretend you didn't."

I laughed and dropped down onto the sand, giving him a kiss on the lips. Then I turned and gave Jayden a hug. "Yeah, yeah," I said, rolling my eyes. "You think you know me so well."

"So any news on that morning producer leaving?" Asher asked, raising an eyebrow.

"Rumor has it she's gone at the end of the month. Of course I let everyone know I was up for the job."

"That terrible, terrible job," Asher teased, winking at me. "I'm never going to see my fiancée again."

"You never see me now—with how busy you are with

the school and the website. Maybe this way I'll actually get to come out and hang with you guys during the day."

"I'd be down with that," Asher agreed. "Maybe someday we'll even get you on a board."

"Yeah, right." Jayden snorted, giving Asher a knowing look. "And pigs will fly."

I shoved him playfully onto the sand. "Whatever. You talk to me when you stop being freaked out by creepy clowns."

The boys laughed and went back to waxing their boards and I leaned back, sticking my toes in the sand. I'd started to like the feeling of sand between my toes, the warm sun on my back. In the last six months I'd been out on the beach more than I had been in the last twenty years. But somehow I'd become okay with that.

I was pretty much okay with everything these days. In fact, I dare say I was happy.

I hadn't taken the Santa Barbara job. They had tried their best to tempt me, offering a more than generous salary and vacation policy, but in the end I knew it wouldn't make me happy. I had a life here, in San Diego. I had friends, I had family, and I had a boyfriend I loved. Asher would have moved to Santa Barbara had I asked, I was sure. But he had a life here, too. He had his surf school. He had his father—who he had a whole new relationship with, now that the truth was out between them.

And while this pissed off Asher's mother more than anything else—she couldn't do much about it, once Stormy had filed for divorce. Seeing Asher take that step had inspired him to change his life, too, it seemed. And these days all his effort was going into the website venture, which was becoming very successful indeed. In fact, he'd gotten nibbles from Weather.com looking to acquire it someday—hopefully for a boatload of cash.

It was unfortunate that Asher's mother never had a similar change of heart. She continued running News 9 with an iron fist and had managed to keep Mr. Martin's advertising money in her pocket as he declared his candidacy for mayor. From what I'd heard they even gave Sarah a job at News

9—as some kind of entertainment reporter. But I didn't tune in to see for myself.

I was too busy working for the enemy—as a news writer for the CW station in town. It was a demotion from my previous position, but I was more than okay with starting my climb up the news ladder over again. Because this time, I had gotten the job on my own.

To save money—since we were both now pretty broke—Asher and I had moved in together. To an unfashionable apartment far from the beach—but much closer to the Holloway House, where I still worked, and his surf school. It was small and a little cramped, but it had an extra bedroom. Perfect for an extra person.

A small, enthusiastic extra person.

Yes, Jayden was now our foster child. The plan was to hopefully adopt him one day once we got married and had enough money saved. In the meantime, we'd already become quite the little family. Away from the Holloway House, Jayden became a whole new kid—blossoming with all the love and attention he got. Sure, he screwed up from time to time and wasn't always a model citizen. You couldn't undo years of neglect in a few short months—I knew that firsthand. But he tried hard. And he was fun to have around. He brought light to both our lives.

And that was how life felt these days. Filled with light. And happiness. Even though we'd both given something up to come together, we never felt as if we were lacking a thing. Because we had each other. And we still had our dreams. And now we had both the freedom to pursue them—and the support to make them a reality. And if I did start to get a little crazy—and start obsessing about work too much? Well, let's just say Asher had a *very* convincing way to bring me back to shore.

"I'm going out," Jayden announced. "I can see you two need alone time." He snorted to tell us exactly what he thought of *that*.

Asher ruffled his hair. "A couple more years, kid, and you'll get it. Don't you worry."

"No, thank you! I'll stick to surfing!" Jayden laughed, grabbing his board and dragging it down the beach.

"I'd be okay with him sticking with surfing," I observed with a smile. "Keep him out of trouble."

"But trouble is so much fun!" Asher teased, rolling over and clucking me under the chin. His green eyes met mine and he waggled his eyebrows at me. "Don't you think so, Miss Strong?"

"I suppose it's okay once in a while," I said with a small smile. "As long as it doesn't interfere with work."

"Oh, don't worry. I'm going to make you work. Very, very hard."

Asher leaned in to kiss me. I closed my eyes, ready to feel his breath on my face, his mouth against my own. But before our lips met, a splash of cold water surprised me and I practically jumped out of my skin.

"Easy, Red," Asher said, his mouth quirking.

I laughed. "Not easy," I corrected. "Never easy."

His eyes locked on to mine. "But worth it."

"Definitely worth it."

Turn the page for a preview of the next
Exclusive Romance from Mari Madison

At First Light

Coming soon from Berkley Sensation

SARAH MARTIN

In a perfect world, once you broke up with someone, you would no longer be required to see them on a daily basis. You could move your stuff out of their apartment, block them on Facebook, pick a different Starbucks so you don't end up waiting in line together for your Triple Venti Skinny Vanilla Lattes (you) and Grande Java Chip Frappuccinos—yes, I'm *that* confident in my masculinity and metabolism—(him).

Sure, once in a while you might find yourself at the same wedding (no one ever scores the perfect friendship split in these sorts of things) but no bride in her right mind would sit the two of you at the same table. And hey, if you got drunk enough you wouldn't care if they did.

In a perfect world, once you broke up with someone, they slipped away from your life like rain down a gutter—exactly where they belonged—and you never had to deal with them again.

Unless, that was, that *someone* happened to have a job on network TV.

"I'm Troy Young, reporting live from Afghanistan . . ."

It was enough to turn a girl to Netflix. Every time I turned on my television and flipped the channel, Troy Young, ex-boyfriend extraordinaire and former love of my life, re-entered my living room once more with feeling. Usually looking annoyingly hot in the process with his clipped, sandy brown hair and piercing eyes that were so blue they caused my TV settings to look oversaturated. Add in a deep, baritone voice that made even the driest of politics sound absurdly sexy and you could start to see why the guy was responsible for launching a thousand fan girl Tumblrs.

And don't even get me started on his wardrobe. As always, Troy seemed to be allergic to the traditional shirt and tie motif of most respectable reporters, choosing instead to wear completely inappropriate button-down shirts that emphasized his broad shoulders and smooth, tanned chest, paired with dark-rinse jeans that hung low on his narrow hips. Emphasizing, well, other things.

Forget Netflix. It was enough to drive a girl to drink. And I'm not talking triple venti skinny vanilla lattes, either.

And yes, I am completely aware I had the power to change the channel. Skip the news, go on a reality TV show binge or start a House Hunters marathon. Or hell, even turn off the TV entirely and go to the beach or something. One single click of a button and Troy Young could be blasted into oblivion, banished from my living room forever.

But sometimes, for some reason, that seemed the hardest thing to do—even if it was the smartest. And instead I found myself stupidly lingering on the broadcast, finger hovering over the remote as I tried to will myself to keep up with some Kardashians instead of Kuwait. In fact, on really bad days, I sometimes surrendered to my patheticism entirely, curling up in my recliner, closing my eyes, and letting that sweet honeyed voice of his roll over me like a wave. Remembering how husky it would get when he used to lean in and whisper naughty things in my ear. (Oh Tumblr fan girls, you have *no* idea!)

I squirmed in my seat. It had been five long years since he'd taken the job overseas and yet sometimes it still felt like yesterday. And while I could turn off the TV, turning off the memories had proven a lot more difficult. Memories of those large strong hands of his, touching me in all the right places. His warm body moving over mine. The way those piercing blue eyes would lock on to me—making me feel, for one brief moment, that I was the center of the universe. *His* universe.

Of course that had not actually been the case. I hadn't been the center of his universe at all. Turned out, I wasn't even a distant star. And now *he* remained the sun—his brilliance and passion and confidence radiating from halfway across the world. While I had been reduced to a black hole of misery, perfect for sucking in solar systems of hurt. (Or pints of Ben and Jerry's, as the case might be.)

"Oh my God. Sarah, are you even kidding me right now?"

I looked up, my face reddening as my neighbor Stephanie walked into my beach cottage, without bothering to knock, catching me in the shameful act of spying on my ex on TV. I cringed. I was so busted. Stephanie shook her head in disapproval, as I could have predicted she would.

"Seriously, if you looked up glutton for punishment, I'm positive the Wiki would have your picture." She pushed a glass of champagne into my hand, still holding the open bottle in her own. "Now, down the hatch, girl," she commanded. "And stay focused. We've got major celebrating to take care of tonight and I refuse to accept anything less than full-blown, party-pony-level enthusiasm from my bestie."

I straightened up in my seat and did what I was told, tipping back the glass and swallowing down the sparkling wine in one long gulp. A moment later, my stomach warmed, already feeling a little better as I prepared to party-pony up as best I could.

We were celebrating Stephanie's triumphant return to News 9 tonight and I didn't need to rain on her parade. It had taken her over a year to get back in the game after being wrongfully accused of sabotaging another reporter's career and she'd been slaving away as a waitress ever since.

But now she was back—like a heart attack (her words)— and we were about to head to Rain, one of our favorite nightclubs, to mark the occasion—Tinder apps locked and loaded and ready to go.

I had to admit, the two of us looked pretty swipe-rightable, too. Stephanie, stunning in her short, sequined dress and stiletto heels. Me, in my cute cropped top and red maxi skirt ensemble, a color Stephanie had insisted brought out my blue eyes and long blond hair. No doubt we'd at least be attracting a few of the society photographers tonight, if not any hot men. Which, to be honest, would be fine by me. I didn't really need a hookup. It was just . . . something I did sometimes, to pass the time. And it pissed off my dad, too, as an added bonus. Somehow he had it in his head that twenty-six was a ripe old age to settle down and start popping out grandbabies. Future voters of America and all that.

For a while my dad had really pinned his hopes on this guy Asher who used to do the weather for News 9, where I now worked as an entertainment reporter. Asher was fun. He was super hot, too. And for a brief moment I actually had entertained the idea of getting serious with him. After all, on paper it was a match made in society heaven. Asher's mother was the owner of News 9. And my dad was the new mayor of San Diego—and one of News 9's biggest advertisers.

But Asher wasn't in love with me. He was in love with his producer. Some girl from the wrong side of the proverbial tracks who was completely wrong for him—yet somehow completely right. Which I understood—truly. After all, hadn't that been the way with Troy and me, back when we were in college? My dad had hated Troy and his outspoken left-wing ideals and save-the-world causes. At one point I think he was convinced Troy would turn me into a socialist. Which wouldn't have worked well for his Right Wing Campaign O' Hate and Misogyny™ he'd been preparing to unleash on the world. (Troy's description at the time, which had made me laugh for days.)

My eyes drifted back to the TV. Troy's story had ended and he was back on camera, wrapping things up. I watched, my stomach squirming a little, as it always did when I saw him this close up. It was this weird juxtaposition of him appearing so near—while being halfway across the world.

I scowled. What was I doing? I was more than a glutton for punishment—I was a complete masochist. And all over a guy who didn't deserve a second of my thoughts, especially after how he left me. On that day five years ago—the day that should have been our greatest victory—turned into my own personal nightmare. Changing my life forever.

But what did Troy care about that? He hadn't even cared enough to show up.

Feeling a lump in my throat, I reached for the remote again, this time ready to zap him out of my life for good. But just as I was about to hit the off button, something caught my eye at the back of the screen. I squinted; was someone coming up behind him? Some kind of man, dressed in black?

I scooted to the edge of my seat, the hairs standing up on my arms, though I wasn't exactly sure why. It was probably nothing, after all, just a random guy, out for a stroll . . .

. . . with something that looked a lot like a gun in his hand.

"Stephanie," I called out. She had gone over to the kitchen to open a new bottle of champagne. "Do you see that?" I asked as she poked her head back in the living room. I pointed at the screen.

"Sarah . . ." She started to lecture, then stopped. Her eyes widened. "Wait. Is that—"

"Troy!" A voice off-screen suddenly broke through the broadcast, sounding tense and worried. His cameraman? His producer? "Troy—I think we need to—"

The sound of gunshots burst through my speakers, cutting him off, popping through the air in quick, sharp bursts. I watched, heart in my throat, as Troy jumped back, his face stark white as he seemed to realize the danger he was in for the first time. Before he could do anything, the man behind him leapt into action, grabbing him and shoving a black hood over his head.

"Oh my God!" I cried.

I watched, paralyzed with shock, as Troy tried to wrestle free and for one brief second I thought he might escape. But then, the man placed a gun up against his temple and yelled something unintelligible at him. Troy stopped moving, his shoulders slumping.

"Troy . . ." I gasped. "Oh my God, Troy!"

I wanted to crawl into the TV. To rescue him myself, against all odds. Instead, I could only sit there, helpless and horrified, watching the scene unfold. Stephanie stood behind me, her hand squeezing down on my shoulder so hard it would have hurt had I not been completely numb.

The man turned to the camera. He was wearing a mask, but it didn't hide the ugly smirk on his face.

"We have your journalist, America," he spit out in a halting accent. "Tomorrow morning, unless you comply with our demands, he will be beheaded."

Oh my God. Oh my God.

I rose to my feet, my knees buckling out from under me. Stephanie grabbed me, holding me close, tears falling down her face.

But I couldn't cry. I could only stare blankly at the screen as the feed cut back to the newsroom. Back to where the anchors were sitting behind their desk, their faces mirroring the fear and horror on my own.

For a moment, no one said anything. And the silence stretched out, sharp as razor wire. Then, finally, after what seemed an eternity, the female anchor opened her mouth to speak.

"We're not sure what just happened," she said in a shaky voice. "We have lost contact with the crew. We will continue to update you as we learn more about this . . . situation."

Her voice broke. The station cut to commercial. A small cry escaped my lips and I staggered, black spots swimming before my eyes. Stephanie caught me before I collapsed, pulling me back down to the couch and holding me close.

"He'll be okay," she whispered in my ear. "I know it looks bad, but . . . You know Troy." She attempted a smile that didn't quite reach her eyes. "He can get out of anything."

It was true. Or it had been true, at least, once upon a time. Troy was a master of escaping tight situations—that was part of the reason he was so good at his job.

But this time . . . This time . . .

I swallowed hard. Suddenly the one man I'd wanted so desperately to exorcise from my life, was now the one man I wanted to see again—more than anyone in the world.

The one man I wasn't sure that I would.

Now Available From

MARI MADISON

Just This Night

An Exclusive Romance

Betrayed and abandoned by his wife and left to raise their young daughter on his own, TV news photographer Jake "Mac" MacDonald has moved to San Diego for a fresh start. He's sworn off women forever and devoted his life to his little girl. But when his brother-in-law drags him out to a night club, drawn to the cute blonde who asks him n make an exception...for just one night.

hat news reporter Elizabeth White had ght Mac home. A quick cure to help her end. But things get awkward when her urns out to be her newest colleague. Now traction behind them and find a way to en someone starts sabotaging Beth's ca- s the only one she can trust. And maybe the makings of an exclusive after all.

] delightful debut."
—*Publishers Weekly*

marimadison.com
ok.com/LoveAlwaysBooks
penguin.com

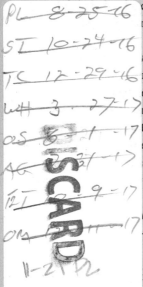